MURDER NEW YORK STYLE

An Anthology by 21 Authors of
Greater New York

*For Carol —
Enjoy! M. E. Kemp,
p. 319*

L & L Dreamspell
Spring, Texas

Interior Design by L & L Dreamspell
Cover Design by Rebecca A. Kandel
Sketches by Kat

This is a work of fiction, and is produced from the authors' imaginations. People, places and things mentioned in this anthology are used in a fictional manner.

ISBN: 978-1-60318-032-0

Visit us on the web at www.lldreamspell.com

Published by L & L Dreamspell
Printed in the United States of America

The contributors of this book heartily thank:

Michael Mallory, who gave infallible, unstinting step-by-step guidance on how to create and publish a "chapter" anthology;

Janice Greer, who made anonymous judging possible by lugging stories from and to the post office, and keeping the secret list of authors' names;

G. Miki Hayden, who polished our stories to a perfect shine with the light and skillful touch of a Master;

Bob Stein, who volunteered his practical and professional wisdom;

Laura Kramarsky for doing the many tasks of readying the manuscript; and

Peggy Ehrhart for her diligent and meticulous copyediting.

CONTENTS

MANHATTAN: AROUND PARK AND FIFTH

MANHATTAN: UPTOWN AND DOWNTOWN

THE BRONX

MANHATTAN:
AROUND PARK AND FIFTH

PICK UP DRY CLEANING, COMMIT THE PERFECT MURDER
by Cynthia Baxter

When it came to efficiency, nobody beat Elizabeth Alcott.

As she neatened the pile of papers she'd been rereading before her ten-thirty meeting, a smug smile played at her lips—which were precisely lined with a MAC Mahogany Lip Pencil and shaded with Night Rose Longwear Lustre Lipcolor. Then she placed her notes inside the manila folder labeled with the client's name, Oatie-O's Breakfast Bars.

The trick, Elizabeth thought with satisfaction, was being organized.

Indeed, she prided herself on the fact that being organized was what had gotten her where she was today: Executive Vice President of Strategic Marketing for Dobbins, Dorfman, Ellsworth, and Tate, widely considered the hottest ad agency on Madison Avenue. And she'd only recently turned thirty-nine.

Thirty-nine, she thought, her perfectly colored mouth turning down slightly. An ugly number if she'd ever heard one.

Not that she felt the same kind of pressure that other, less successful women might feel. She'd never been one to buy into the hype about marriage and babies and all that happily ever after rubbish. Her feeling was that if it happened to come her way, she wouldn't exactly run in the opposite direction. In fact, she would embrace it.

But falling in love wasn't something you could add to your "to do" list, jotting it down after "pick up dry cleaning" and "call grocery delivery service."

Love. Now there was a four-letter word, Elizabeth thought, glancing at the framed photograph on her desk. Actually, just keeping it at hand was misleading. Sure, Steven looked the part, the man who would be the perfect mate for a rising star at Dobbins, Dorfman. Straight, sandy blond hair that had a tendency to fall into his eyes, bringing the word "boyish" to mind. Clear, sparkling blue eyes that looked as if their color was enhanced with tinted lenses but were actually completely natural. A square jaw framing a warm smile that revealed two perfect rows of teeth. The man simply exuded charm.

Pictures may say a thousand words, Elizabeth thought irritably, but that didn't necessarily mean those words were accurate.

When her secretary buzzed her, Elizabeth assumed Becky was reminding her it was almost time for her ten-thirty meeting. As if she needed reminding.

Almost as a reflex, she pulled her Filofax forward and checked the page headed with the day's date. Sure enough, in her neat handwriting, next to the 10:30 slot, she had printed the words, "Meeting re: Oatie-O's."

She was the organization queen, she thought proudly.

When Becky buzzed again, Elizabeth answered with her usual professionalism.

"Yes, Becky," she said crisply, looking ahead in her Filofax and noticing that Friday was her secretary's birthday. She took out her "to do" list, printed at the top of each page with "From the Desk of Elizabeth Alcott." In her usual careful handwriting, she jotted down, "Order flowers for Becky," right under "Renew gym membership" and "Manolos to shoemaker for resoling."

"Ms. Alcott? You have a visitor."

Elizabeth frowned. "I think you're confused, Becky. I have a meeting at ten-thirty. I'm not expecting anyone."

"This isn't something that's scheduled. It's—"

"Becky, you know I don't see anyone who hasn't called in advance and made an appointment. Please tell whoever it is to set something up."

"You don't understand." For the first time, Elizabeth noticed the frantic edge to Becky's voice. "The person who wants to talk to you is a police detective from the NYPD. I saw his badge and everything."

Elizabeth's heartbeat immediately escalated. *Don't panic,* she told herself. *You have everything under control. If anyone is a master at seeing to every single detail and leaving absolutely nothing out, it's you.*

"A police detective?" she returned evenly. "Why on earth would someone from the police department want to speak with me?"

"He wouldn't say," Becky replied, her voice squeaking just a bit.

Elizabeth took a deep breath, struggling to remember what she'd learned the one time she'd ventured into a yoga class at the 92nd Street Y. By the end, she'd decided yoga wasn't for her. It was all about relaxing and balance, without being the least bit results-oriented.

"Of course," she finally said. "Send him in."

Breathe in, breathe out, Elizabeth instructed herself. With deliberate movements, she closed her Filofax and reached into her right-hand drawer where she stashed her personal items. She pulled out a tube of Crabtree & Evelyn Lavender Hand Therapy Cream, squeezed out a dab, and began rubbing her hands together, working the balm into her skin.

When the police detective walked through the door, she was sitting at her desk, looking completely calm, channeling whatever nervousness she felt into keeping her hands moving. Another little trick she'd learned while climbing the corporate ladder. Never fidget. Always look as if you're doing something productive.

"Ms. Alcott? I'm Detective Kelly." He reached into his pocket, presumably to take out his credentials, but Elizabeth held up one of her overly moist hands.

"No need, Detective," she said with a smile. "I'm sure my

secretary already checked your credentials. Becky is the best."

"Fine. Mind if I sit?"

"Of course not. Please make yourself at home." She studied the police detective, noting the little things that most other people, those who weren't as thorough and detail oriented as she was, were likely to miss. The brown smudge on his shirt, a sign that he had spilled some of his breakfast coffee, perhaps because he'd been drinking it in his car. The frayed shoelace on his left shoe, which told her good grooming wasn't his highest priority. The scar on his otherwise handsome face that made him look seasoned.

"I have a feeling you know why I'm here," he began.

Elizabeth frowned. "Actually, I don't. I just assumed you were soliciting contributions for some extremely worthwhile fundraiser for the police. Am I wrong?"

Detective Kelly didn't react. Instead, he reached into his jacket pocket again. This time, he pulled out a photograph and tossed it on her desk.

"I assume you know this man?"

"Yes, I do. That's Steven Barlow." She hesitated before adding, "He and I have been seeing each other."

"'Seeing each other?' As in dating?"

"I suppose so, yes. Not that the relationship was going anywhere. Anywhere serious, I mean."

"Really? Why not?"

Elizabeth gave a little shrug, one she hoped communicated how little she cared. "Steven is one of those divorced men in their early forties who're still recovering from bad marriages and, as a result, have no interest in settling down. So he and I enjoy each other's company with the understanding that the relationship isn't headed toward anything permanent."

"And how do you feel about that, Ms. Alcott?"

"It's fine with me," she answered quickly. "If you're implying that I'm one of those women who's desperate to get married, Detective Kelly, let me assure you that you're barking up the wrong tree. The fact of the matter is that I'm perfectly happy with my life just the way it is."

"I see. And exactly how would you characterize this life of yours?"

"My life is precisely the way I want it," Elizabeth replied with a smile. "I suppose you could say I'm one of those people who likes to be in control." She gestured with both hands, indicating her large, airy corner office complete with a couch, a coffee table, and huge windows that afforded a spectacular view of the Manhattan skyline. "It's how I got where I am today."

Detective Kelly leaned forward in his chair. Elizabeth resisted the impulse to recoil." I bet I know a few things about you, just by being a pretty good judge of character," he said. "In fact, I'd say that while you manage to stay in control most of the time, you're like most people in that every once in a while, something happens that sends you careening out of control."

Elizabeth sat up indignantly. "Detective Kelly, just ask anyone who knows me. Never in my life have I thrown a temper tantrum—or even raised my voice, for that matter. Being in control is simply too important to me. I'm meticulous about writing down all my appointments in my Filofax. I methodically enter the name and number of everyone I meet in my BlackBerry. I keep an ongoing 'to do' list to make sure I never forget to carry out an errand." Sitting up a little straighter, Elizabeth added, "If ever anyone was organized, anyone had mastered the art of being in control, it's me."

"I don't doubt that," the detective said evenly. "And I can see that, in most contexts, your personality quirk has served you well."

"I'd hardly call it a 'personality quirk,'" Elizabeth shot back, for the first time letting her irritation show. "It's a conscious decision made back when I started out. You see, Detective, I never intended to end up like the women I saw as I was growing up—those small town ladies with big hair and even bigger disappointments. I wanted to be somebody. I wanted to be the type of person who could have anything she wanted, whatever that might be. I was never the smartest girl in school, and when I got myself to the big city and started working, I was never the one who came up with the most brilliant ideas. So I knew I'd have to find another way to get ahead. And it worked. Thanks to my determination, I have a Park Avenue apartment and a Mercedes, and I'm about to close on a weekend house in the Catskills."

"Unfortunately, you have no one to share it all with."

"I don't need anyone to share it with." When Elizabeth realized how defensive she sounded, she forced herself to smile. "I'm completely happy with who I am."

"Right," the detective said dryly. "That super-organized woman who can accomplish whatever she wants simply by making a 'to do' list every day."

Elizabeth could feel the anger rising in her chest. "There's no need to refer to my exceptional organizational skills with such disdain."

"I don't mean any disrespect, ma'am. I'm just trying to understand who you are."

He reached into his pocket once more. And when Elizabeth saw what he pulled out this time, she could feel all the blood draining out of her face.

"Does this look familiar?" Detective Kelly asked, holding it up for her to see but not putting it close enough for her grab.

It looked familiar, all right, even though it was housed in a clear Ziploc bag and marked "Evidence." It was a page out of her "to do" pad, the one that had "From the Desk of Elizabeth Alcott" printed on top of every page.

She gasped. "Oh, my God! Where did you find that?"

"Under Steven Barlow's body, when we discovered him lying on the kitchen floor of his apartment late last night, stabbed to death. And that was after one of his neighbors called 911 having heard an argument, followed by yelling and a loud thump."

Elizabeth opened her mouth to speak. To defend herself, or at least to come up with some explanation that would make all this go away. But no words came out.

"Let me read it to you," Detective Kelly said coldly. "From the Desk of Elizabeth Alcott. Tuesday, February 18. Pick up dry cleaning. Buy butcher knife. Hardware store for rubber gloves, paper towels, plastic garbage bags, cleaning fluid. Renew *New York Times* subscription."

He paused, staring at her for a few seconds before pronouncing, "Elizabeth Alcott, you are under arrest for the murder of Steven Barlow. You have a right to—"

Just then, a woman rounded the corner. "This is Officer Landauer," Detective Kelly explained. "She'll be accompanying us to the police station. It's standard procedure whenever a woman is arrested." He took out a pair of handcuffs and clamped her wrists together behind her back. Elizabeth was so dazed she couldn't even focus on her rights as he recited them to her, just like in the movies.

"But he deserved it!" she cried as Officer Landauer led her toward the door. She sensed she was making a mistake by saying anything at all, but something inside her had snapped, making it impossible for her to keep from doing so. "He said from Day One he was looking for a life partner! He told me I possessed all the qualities he'd hoped for in a wife! So when he suddenly decided he wanted to quit his job on Wall Street and move to Colorado to find himself—*alone*—he should have expected consequences!"

She noticed Detective Kelly and Officer Landauer exchanging glances. "Come on, now," Officer Landauer said in a surprisingly gentle voice. "Let's get you down to the station."

"Wait!" Elizabeth cried. "Can I bring something with me?"

"What?" Officer Landauer asked suspiciously.

"My Filofax. It's over there on my desk."

Detective Kelly's eyebrows shot up. "You want to take that?"

"Of course," Elizabeth returned haughtily. "No doubt there are going to be meetings with lawyers, depositions, maybe even a trial. I'm going to have a lot to do, and being organized is so essential."

Name Tagging
by Randy Kandel

It was a wet September Wednesday when Gatewill Murpill turned up his coat collar, tightened his back muscles against the East River wind, and pondered why his parents had ever left Jamaica to "better themselves," as they called it. He held a wet Starbucks paper cup under his umbrella and grimaced at the over-roasted, over-sugared, chocolate-dosed coffee. He was longing for the sweet aroma of the fresh picked Jamaican mountain beans, although his family had been too poor to taste them then. He shook his head, remembering, but only briefly and carefully, so that the coffee wouldn't splash as he jogged up the front steps of the Metropolitan Museum of Art, two at a time.

Now that he was the chief of security for the Met, he was meticulous in his pacing—brisk enough to look assertive and eager, but not so fast that he seemed to be late, or chasing after a crisis. With so much wealth and financial value "trapped," as he called it, under electronically secured, video-monitored, thick glass, nothing ought to disturb the atmosphere of material and intellectual security, especially on the eve of a major international exhibition like "Name Tagging: Ownership of Art Among the Classic Maya."

Stepping out of the private elevator onto the fourth floor of the Michael C. Rockefeller wing of the museum and walking toward the exhibit, Murpill flipped open his Blackberry and noticed that the time was 8:47 a.m. "The security is perfect," he intended to tell Dr. Sarah Gregg, director of the MesoAmerican and Caribbean Department. Suddenly, a muted thud and then the crackle and crash of old pottery echoed in the corridor.

"Someone needs caffeine," Murpill thought and tossed his Starbucks cup into a nearby wastebasket in order to look ready for anyone coming out of the makeshift lounge and lunchroom that the curators laughingly called Las Ruinas. Instead, the three curators of the department—Gregg, Dr. Golden Silver, and even chunky Dr. Winniker Grass—emerged from an office in the other direction, shaking their heads with worried faces. Using proper protocol, Murpill greeted the director.

Gregg answered softly, "We're just checking on things. All the plates and cups in Las Ruinas are paper. They're stamped with pictures of the Met's mascot, William, the turquoise hippopotamus. Every piece of pottery and ceramic on this floor, along with the gold and silver jewelry, is at least fourteen hundred years old and belongs to the Name Tagging exhibit. We're afraid that an artifact must have shattered." Sarah, with her sensible shoes, straight skirt, straight sweater, and straight hair, blushed as though Murpill had caught her with just a wet bath towel on. "You see, only the curators use Las Ruinas and we have no ordinary pottery in Las Ruinas or on this floor. One of the curators must have been playing dangerously with an artifact."

Murpill thought that he would have used the word "expensively," rather than "dangerously." Even so, he shuddered for a moment before remembering that part of his job in emergencies was to stay calm and help others stay calm. He threw his right arm over the shoulder of round-faced, nearsighted Dr. Winniker Grass, the ceramics specialist, who was keening, "Every piece, every piece invaluable. Every piece a baby Rosetta Stone," as though he were a grieving mother.

"We know, Winniker," said the metals specialist, Dr. Golden Silver, who looked like his name, tan, muscular, and turning silver in his fifties. Silver turned to Murpill, continuing his lecture. "All the pieces here are covered with glyphs, many not yet understood. Each is a clue to deciphering the Maya writing system.

Even if gold doesn't break, I can understand professional loss. Grave robbers take gold and silver ahead of potsherds, stealing names and dates of artists and owners. Intellectual value, Winniker. Not the kind you get at Tiffany's. Right, Chief?"

Murpill nodded and swallowed his ironic thoughts about the value of dead men's words. He registered the bickering among the curators—and the fact that Dr. Sarah Gregg had seen him registering the bickering and had blushed as if she had no towel on at all. Still, Gregg took the lead as they approached Las Ruinas, and she barged through the partially open door.

Murpill followed her and heard her gasp, "Oh God!" when she saw Dr. Marvin Schwartz, the Maya exhibit consulting director lying, probably lifeless, on the marble tiled floor. "Lila, his fiancee, is already on the plane from London!"

The wedding that had set the whole museum abuzz was scheduled for tomorrow afternoon. In prior circumstances, Murpill had been inclined to smirk about the May-December marriage between Lila, the voluptuous thirty-eight-year-old assistant curator of the Victorian and Edwardian Department, and the renowned, seventy-nine-year-old New York University professor emeritus of archeology and epigraphy.

Now, here he lay on his left side, his arms stretched in front of him, cradling what was left of a ceramic goblet. Just below his left knee was a light trickle of blood and a small bruise, like the kind children get when they bump into things while playing. His head lay in a puddle of blood. The professor's yarmulke was askew, disclosing wispy strands of white hair above his bald spot.

Expecting to see an old broken cup and suddenly finding a broken elderly man as well made Murpill dizzy. He knew he had to cover that up or he'd be a laughing stock. In the split instant he leaned against the wall to steady himself, the curators were all over Schwartz, and Murpill watched them intently.

"It looks as if Marvin tripped on the corner of the saweddown steel workbench that passes for our coffee table." Gregg said. She dropped to her knees next to him, put on her round trifocals, announced she was "no stranger to archeological disaster sites," and attempted to take his pulse.

"Where are Marvin's glasses? He never goes anywhere without them," Silver said, looking around at the floor. "That's what comes from a life of squinting at old gold and ancient handwriting. Blind as a bat, like me, before I got my laser surgery."

Grass made a clumsy attempt at mouth-to-mouth resuscitation, then raised his head. His voice quivered. "He's dead. That lethal hazard of a bench should have been replaced long ago with a substandard antique table from the Met's storehouse. Maybe he had a heart attack and fell on it."

Hearing the word "dead" re-energized Murpill. He applied what he knew of determining vital signs, then repeated, "He's dead," in his graceful British Caribbean lilt.

"I know, it looks like an accident. But sudden death is always suspicious. If you call in his doctor, you get media leaks. If you notify the police, they alert the medical examiner and you get scandal. They'll want an autopsy. His family are Orthodox Jews. They won't want it. More bad publicity."

Gregg nodded strenuously at everything Murpill said. "Of course do the internal investigation first. We need to be discreet. Use the museum's labs, if they're needed. Competition is fierce, so they work under strict confidentiality. No information leaves the Met, unless the public relations director signs off on it."

She gave her assistant curators a no-nonsense look and sighed. "We've broken artifacts and will be embroiled in insurance rigmarole. The board of directors will blame us for the heightened costs. Add to that, bad luck shadowing an internationally publicized event, and death. Pull together team, please. It's stormy weather."

Murpill had almost stopped listening to Gregg. "A smoke screen, her attempt to regain control," he thought. He bent down to examine the broken ceramic goblet that was more palatable to his forensic tastes than blood. It had been forgotten by the others, in the face of Schwartz's sudden death. Immediately, Murpill's focus was drawn to a disgusting ooze coming from the goblet Schwartz still held in his hand. "What's that slimy brown froth?" he asked.

"Chocolate." Gregg nodded definitively.

Once more, Murpill started to feel queasy. He felt even sicker when he saw the two assistant curators smile and wink at each other, evidently enjoying some practical prank on the macho security guy. He wanted to puke. "Chocolate? That gloppy mess! Who would drink that? It looks like a mixture of old blood and fresh dung! And it smells like bitter baking chocolate, chilies, oregano, garlic, onions, and almonds, all rolled into one."

"Yup! And honey too," Golden Silver threw in.

"The Maya elite cherished the stuff. They drank it at religious rituals, ceremonies, and celebrations like weddings. Some believe that it was used as an aphrodisiac," Gregg said in her no-nonsense way.

"No wonder that civilization died."

"It didn't die."

"Anyway, that gook couldn't have been stuck in the goblet for a thousand years for Dr. Schwartz to drink."

"No, we made it for him as a wedding present," said Gregg. Murpill stared in disbelief. "Well, not exactly a wedding present." Gregg blushed.

Grass took over. "Well, more like maybe a bachelor party present."

Murpill swallowed hard. He held two thumbs up, in appreciation of Lila, and to take the attention away from his sickness. It wouldn't have looked professional to throw up on the corpse.

"Forty-one years makes a difference between newlyweds. We thought he might need a little help the Mayan way, you know," added Grass.

Murpill nodded, gulped, and felt a bit better.

Gregg stopped blushing and took up the story line of the previous twenty-four hours. "Yesterday evening, after the museum had closed, Dr. Grass, Dr. Silver, Dr. Schwartz, and I were taking a slow 'last rehearsal' sort of walk through the exhibit. Dr. Schwartz was particularly studying one of the goblets lent to us by the Guatemalan National Museum. He was fascinated, really. He came back to look at it several times. He said he thought he knew the artist/scribe who had made it, but he hadn't seen this piece before."

Murpill was incredulous. "Really? He knew the artist?"

"Not personally, of course. But every one of these goblets has writing on it. Something that we call the primary standard sequence, or PSS. Among other things, it has a name glyph of the artist and a name glyph for the artist's patron, the person who owned the goblet. It's like a signature. Seeing the signatures on different pieces tells epigraphers like Dr. Schwartz a great deal about ancient Maya society and history. Anyway, you know the sarcasm that goes on in this department?"

Murpill nodded.

Gregg continued, "Dr. Silver asked Dr. Schwartz if the goblet reminded him of a kiddush cup—a cup used in Jewish rituals—like the one he got for his Bar Mitzvah, when he was thirteen. To my surprise, Dr. Schwartz looked Dr. Silver right in the eye, and with a twinkle, he said, 'No, it reminds me of a wedding draught.'"

"At that," said Gregg, "Silver and Grass started teasing Schwartz about giving him a Mayan style chocolate aphrodisiac. Dr. Schwartz grinned, so I got on board as well."

Grass chimed in. "I agreed to buy the chocolate, honey, chilies and stuff at Whole Foods. I thought a Mayan ritual should be pesticide free."

Gregg nodded. "When I got in this morning, it was all there on the desk in my office."

"Yeah." Silver sort of snorted. "Sarah and I mashed the mush. Blended it actually. Sarah keeps a little blender in her office to make fresh fruit juices for lunch when she's dieting. Then we gave it to Schwartz, in one of those waxy paper hippo cups, as soon as he came in. We thought we'd let him microwave it himself."

Gregg glared at Silver. Murpill thought that was because Gregg believed Silver was talking too much, but he wasn't sure whether it was about the paper hippo cups, or the dieting.

He put a stony cop face on for them, and it got stonier as he listened, in part because he was trying to fend off the nauseous idea of taking the Mayan aphrodisiac before breakfast.

Murpill turned to Grass, "Where were you when they made the brew?"

Grass started talking a bit overconfidently, in Murpill's view, like a good student who's been waiting in studied casualness for the teacher to ask him a difficult question. Grass told Murpill that he had gone to open the exhibition case and remove the goblet that Dr. Schwartz was so interested in.

"I really liked Marvin Schwartz. He's done fantastic work on the Maya decoding, and he puts up—or did put up—with all of our kidding. We've worked together, and we both know ceramics. He's taught me a lot about the different styles of Maya scribes from different sites. I wanted to give him something *really* special this morning, the real experience a classic Mayan prince would have had with the chocolate. I called him into my office and I coaxed him into taking the goblet to Las Ruinas, and drinking the chocolate from it. It was just my childish exuberance. And, oh my God, cradling that goblet lost him his life."

"Okay," said Murpill, "I'll get the lab to pick up some of the breakage and the brew. Now, Drs. Gregg and Silver..." He turned to them, emphasizing their titles with a slightly sarcastic overtone. "You understand I'll have to question you both, separately."

Sarah Gregg volunteered first and strode briskly down the corridor, her no-nonsense shoes producing loud echoes. Murpill could feel her gently pushing his upper back to emphasize that it was *she,* not he, who was in a hurry to get to the bottom of this sad business.

Once in her office, she sat down behind her ornately carved desk. To Murpill, it looked like a piece she had commissioned from some African carver, who she'd probably paid a pittance.

Murpill sat down in front of her, at ease and alert, and stretched his long legs out so that they seemed to be merely inadvertently resting on the carved lions at the base of the desk.

He put his hands behind his neck, signaling comfort but not intimacy. "How long had you known Dr. Schwartz, Dr. Gregg?"

"More years than I'd like to tell." Gregg blushed slightly, making her look younger than she actually must be. "He was my advisor for my Master's degree in archeology at NYU." She casually pointed towards the packed bookcase on her left.

Murpill turned his head toward where a slim volume with a leather binding in the distinctive deep violet of NYU stood next to a fatter one announcing itself as a Ph.D. dissertation in museum studies from Covington U. Next to those stood a long row of books and museum catalogs with "Gregg" on the binding.

"You must have known him very well, then?"

"Yes, intimately. He showed me how to do things properly and set me on my career path." Gregg blushed again. Her eyes shone with tears. She looked nostalgic.

"I can see this is hard for you." Murpill nodded, and took his hands away from his neck, suggesting his readiness to leave soon. "Does Dr. Silver feel the same way?"

"He barely knew Dr. Schwartz." Gregg bit her lower lip for an instant. "I don't think he could have had any feelings about him at all." She bit her lip again and blinked. Tears sparkled under her eyelashes. "Except, well, except, Golden Silver and Lila were an item for a while. They lived together for a few years a long time ago. I never knew which of the two broke it off. But Golden walked around in a daze for months after that. It was as if he didn't know who he was anymore."

Murpill left Gregg, tears running down her cheeks, her right hand clenched in a fist, and her left drumming on her great, carved desk. He knocked on Dr. Silver's office next door, turned the doorknob, and entered without waiting for a reply. Inside, he found Dr. Silver moving at high speed on his Nordic Track.

"Don't mind if I keep going while you talk to me, do you? Got to keep fit, you know. Keeps the blood pressure from going sky high, when things like this morning happen."

Murpill just shrugged sympathetically, as though his security work had the great benefit of keeping him fit without the use of contraptions. He gave Silver a man-to-man look and said, "Dr. Gregg tells me you and Lila, Dr. Schwartz's fiancée, were a live-together couple for a long time. Says you were devastated when you broke up."

"Not devastated. Disoriented." Murpill could feel Silver's own man-to-man stare, as Silver meticulously wiped sweat from his muscular neck and cruised Murpill's body from head to toe to emphasize what he was going to say. "Lila and I broke up because I realized I was gay."

"Not jealous, then?"

"Not at all. Lila understood it before I did, and helped me through it. And I'm forever grateful to her. I love Lila as if I were her big brother. Sarah Gregg doesn't know because, well, you know her. Can you imagine talking about sexual matters to her?"

Murpill gave a soft chuckle. "Nothing against Dr. Schwartz then?"

"Nothing at all. Except he is—*was*—a stickler for veracity. Wouldn't let me write a description that said 'circa 800 A.D.' for a piece of jewelry if the inscription said '801.' Made Sarah's life miserable when she was a student. He found two paragraphs of quotations in her Master's thesis without any quotation marks and told her he wouldn't let her go on for her Ph.D. at NYU. It became a kind of public secret, because she's so bright and diligent everyone knew something was wrong. That's why she switched to museum studies. How many people have ever heard of Covington University? She's lucky she's a striver, or she wouldn't be where she is."

Murpill said, "Thank you," and, taking his passkey out of his pocket, let himself out through the MesoAmerican and Caribbean Department's little workshop, which abutted the department offices. There, artifacts were sometimes examined, cleaned, or repaired. He gave a cursory glance, came out the other side, and stepped into Las Ruinas for a bit of quiet. He pressed some numbers on his Blackberry, and asked Grass, Gregg, and Silver not to leave the museum all morning in case they were needed. He told them he would be ordering-in lunch for the four of them, and he would meet them at 1:00 p.m., for a little wake and debriefing.

True to his word, an hour after noon, Murpill stood in front of the curators, looking both stern and smirky, having lightly covered Schwartz's corpse with a sheet. He stared at Gregg and Silver.

"For all I've never been at NYU, I can Google the Internet and find an ancient recipe. And Mayan ritual chocolate contains bitter chocolate, honey, and chilies, like Winniker Grass bought. No garlic, no bitter almonds. Almonds come from the Middle East. Mayan ritual chocolate doesn't smell like garlic. Arsenic does. And Mayan ritual chocolate doesn't smell like bitter almonds. Cyanide does. Right?" he asked rhetorically.

"Right," said Gregg and Silver, nodding their heads. Murpill thought they might be merely shaking, in unison, involuntarily now.

"Of course, you have to say that, on pain of bald-faced lying, especially in front of Dr. Schwartz, the stickler for truth, because you both know the scents." Murpill could almost feel the heat rising from Gregg's blushing face. He watched Silver peek at her from the corner of his eye.

"I know you know the smell of arsenic and cyanide, Dr. Gregg, because they're used for cleaning metals. And both are in your workshop. I know that because I saw them there. That's what you learned to do in graduate school, didn't you? And I know that, because I have a Master's degree in forensic science from John Jay College of Criminal Justice. If you smell it, you test for it. That's a no brainer in my line of work."

Murpill looked from Gregg to Silver. Each looked guilty, but each also looked startled. Silver gave Gregg a raised-eyebrows quizzical look, and Gregg gave Silver a "how dare you" kind of glare. That confused Murpill. Even arrogant as they were, they couldn't be that surprised that he had a Master's degree. He started to talk them up, trying to figure out who was the perp.

"Dr. Gregg, Dr. Silver told me how Dr. Schwartz crippled your career. And Dr. Silver, you said you love Lila like a big brother. I have little sisters, Dr. Silver. I wouldn't want one of them to marry a man forty years older than her, and actually tottering on the edge of the grave. You both had motive and opportunity. One of you squawks, or I'll consider you partners."

Gregg and Silver continued staring at each other curiously. For people in a puzzle-solving sort of profession, they seemed awfully slow. Then Murpill suddenly got it. Neither of them would have used both arsenic *and* cyanide. They both spoiled the brew, but separately. One added the arsenic, and the other added the cyanide. Neither had known about the other's action.

"They both did it to him! I can't believe it!" Grass, who had been standing silently, shouted out.

Just then Murpill's Blackberry rang out a bit of Bob Marley's "Trench Town." "I'm glad you're here. We're all hungry." Murpill grinned widely. "It's not over yet," he said to the curators.

He slipped some string that looked like heavy transparent fishing line out of his pocket. Then he walked over to Grass, tied the string around Grass's index finger, and told him that the string was to remember to keep the culprits where they were.

Murpill returned six minutes later with three brown bags. One had four large burritos. One had two regular Cokes, a Jamaican ginger beer, and a Dr. Brown's cream soda—all in cans. One held something unknown. Murpill handed out the food and drinks, and then said casually "I found something else in those shards that I think is latex."

Murpill thought Grass reacted as if he'd been hit by a paint ball.

"What's that from?" asked Silver.

"Is it lethal if eaten?" asked Gregg, who suddenly stopped

picking at some peeling paint on the wall next to her.

"Before I tell you," said Murpill, "I want you to know that I've looked at Dr. Schwartz's saliva. It looks as if his lips never touched that chocolate. Probably the poisons never got ingested. He fell and died before he took a sip. An autopsy would probably never find either substance. No one need ever know. It might be a good idea to discreetly postpone all the lab tests indefinitely. But I'll tell you the conditions for that after I explain about the latex."

He continued. "Latex is used in modern white slip for ceramics. It's a synthetic. That means it's modern. The goblet is a forgery."

"Thank heaven, there's no loss then! I mean no loss of ancient artifacts, of course," Grass said when the others stared at him.

Murpill walked over, grabbed Grass's left pointer finger with the fishing line tied around it, and pulled it into the air. "Come on. You can't possibly be surprised. I gave you the fishing line to remember what happened. I found two of them, strung across the room, tied end to end to the filing cabinets, one at ankle level and one at around knee level, right in front of the steel table. You wanted Dr. Schwartz to trip over them. I just cut a little bit of the fishing line. It's still there."

Murpill turned Grass around in a circle, took him under the arm, and half walked, half dragged him to the place where the fishing line was tied. "You see, you can barely see that fishing line, even with your glasses. And your eyesight is much better than Schwartz's was."

Murpill made Grass touch the place where the line was tied and then look up. Some kind of rock sat on top of the file. "Probably the department intended to use that rock as a mock stele or some such. You see that's a trip line. If he hadn't smashed his head on the steel table, which was your first hope, in struggling to get up, he would have tripped the line, and the rock would have fallen on him and on the forged goblet as well. You didn't want him to be able to see," he told Grass as he pulled Dr. Schwartz's eyeglasses out of the third brown bag. "I found them using a skeleton key, in a locked drawer of your desk."

Grass squawked, "Why would I want to play such a practical joke on an old man? How would I know that the goblet was a forgery?"

"Because," Murpill began, as he slid the goblet slowly out of the brown bag, "the real one was in your drawer, the drawer with Dr. Schwartz's glasses in it."

Murpill saw Grass move to knee him in the genitals and grab for Murpill's pepper spray. But Murpill thought faster, anticipating that Grass would hesitate when he realized the genuine goblet might break. In that split second, Murpill handcuffed him.

"Why would I want to hurt someone who loves these Maya artifacts as much as I do? It must be Gregg and Silver who set me up like this. I don't understand," Grass whined.

"I think you do," Murpill said quietly. "You told us all why this morning. Last evening, when the four of you were walking through the exhibit, Dr. Schwartz kept coming back to one particular goblet. Studying it. Studying it again. You knew that goblet was a forgery. You knew that you had removed the original. You had become so obsessed with it, you were willing to steal it, hide it, even take it home. Dr. Schwartz was fascinated with it as well. I myself saw him look at it many times during the installation of the exhibit. When he kept coming back, you sensed he saw something fishy, that the goblet had been replaced.

"You could have returned the original to the exhibit last night, and Dr. Schwartz would have thought that he had just been paranoid. But love, or avarice, or obsession stopped you. You wanted to give Dr. Schwartz a test, to see if he really noticed the difference, before you even thought of returning the goblet. So you took the forgery out of the exhibit case this morning, put it in on your desk, and watched as Dr. Schwartz scrutinized the goblet. He revealed nothing verbally. As you coaxed him, he pretended to be coaxed, looking at it up close and lovingly. When he took off his glasses to squint at some particular glyph, you hid them.

"You knew when Dr. Schwartz agreed to drink his aphrodisiac from that goblet at Las Ruinas, especially walking down the corridor without his glasses, that Dr. Schwartz knew it was a forgery, and that it was your doing. He never would have endangered the original goblet. You knew, like everyone who knew him, that Dr. Schwartz was a stickler for veracity, and sooner or later he would blow the whistle on you. So Dr. Schwartz, and the goblet, had to be gotten rid of. And this plan got rid of both of them."

"You can't prove that," said Grass.

"I think I can. You see, you left the roll of fishing line in the same locked drawer, Dr. Grass. But you're right that I'm the one critical living witness who ties it all together." Murpill smiled first at Dr. Gregg, then Dr. Silver, and then Dr. Grass.

He said, "Dr. Gregg, in accordance with your suggestion, I have done things discreetly in this matter. I have spoken with Dr. Schwartz's family physician. In consideration of the delicacies about autopsies of Orthodox Jews, he has consented to come here within the hour to determine the cause of death. If he's satisfied, as he undoubtedly will be, that Dr. Schwartz died of cardiac failure after an accidental fall, news of this morning's events need go no further. And more important, in consideration of the MesoAmerican and Caribbean Department's new permanent partnership with my two brothers, Farewell Murpill, in Belize, and Goodwill Murpill, in London—both antiquities dealers very interested in Maya artifacts—I will act discreetly forevermore."

Gregg, Grass, and Silver, looking sheepish, grateful, and guilty all at once, shook hands with Murpill, and gazed into one another's fearful eyes.

Only Silver asked one last question "If Dr. Schwartz knew the goblet was a fraud, why did he try to cradle it so lovingly as he fell?"

"Don't you see," said Gregg, "He knew if the goblet broke, it would be put aside for a while, so that bad luck and insurance issues wouldn't dog the exhibition. By then, Grass might have disappeared some of the telltale shards, or concocted an alibi or story that exonerated him. Schwartz wanted the evidence to be preserved. He loved total veracity as much as Maya epigraphy. Even maybe as much as his own life."

Mister Right
by Ronnie Klaskin

Sara feels nauseated. She walks to the phone, careful to avoid Amy's body lying in a pool of blood on the floor. A chef's knife lies right next to the dead woman. Sara dials 911. Then she sits down to wait.

Sara had met Amy in the relaxation room at the spa in Nolita, which stood for North of Little Italy, and was becoming a very trendy area, filled with crowded restaurants and expensive boutiques. Both she and Amy went for a massage there every Saturday morning, Sara's one big extravagance. After a few times of seeing one another, they began to talk, and one day Amy asked if Sara would like to join her for lunch at a restaurant in Chinatown

Sara loved Chinese food, and it was one type of food in New York that wouldn't strain her budget, so she agreed to go. They had dim sum and the bill for both of them came to under twenty dollars.

They enjoyed each other's company and decided to add a post-massage Chinese lunch to their weekly ritual.

Amy was a small, thin woman of twenty-five. Six years younger than Sara, she wore her blonde, frosted hair in a ponytail. She wasn't exactly pretty, but her sharp-featured face was animated, and she had a ready smile.

Sara was tall, nearly six feet tall, and had always felt gawky growing up. She'd reached her full height at thirteen and was shy around boys. While people told her she was pretty, with her dark brown curls and bright blue eyes, she never really believed them.

"I wish I had a boyfriend," she confessed one day over an egg roll and a dish of twice cooked pork.

"Were you ever married?" Amy asked.

Sara shook her head. "I was engaged once. In college. But he left me for someone else."

"I was married once," Amy said. "For three years, between nineteen and twenty-two. But he hit me."

Sara flinched. She would never tolerate a man who hit her.

"I've got a nice boyfriend now," Amy said. "We may be getting married soon. Or he may just move in with me. I'd like to get a bigger place. I only have a studio, kind of on the edge of East Harlem and it's a bit small for two people. How big is your apartment?"

"Five rooms. Two bedrooms, a dining room, a big living room, and a smallish kitchen. But I don't cook that much."

"Where is it?" Amy asked.

"On Park Avenue in the Eighties."

"Oh, God, it must cost a fortune."

"Well, it's not cheap," Sara said. Which was a lie. By New York standards, it was quite inexpensive, only seven hundred dollars a month, since it was rent controlled. When Sara came to New York after college, she'd moved in there with her grandmother. It was all she could afford if she wanted to live in Manhattan. When her grandmother died, Sara inherited the tenancy of the apartment.

Sara liked to pretend to be more affluent than she was. Somehow it gave her a feeling of security, so she bought expensive clothes from thrift shops and accessorized them with her grandmother's jewelry, which was mostly antique and probably worth a lot of money.

She worked as a secretary, but she enjoyed telling people she was the assistant to the president of a large, multi-million dollar corporation.

"How did you meet your boyfriend?" Sara asked. Meeting new men was always so hard.

"Oh, I made a list of my requirements and put them out into the universe. After that it was easy. He simply appeared one day."

"He simply appeared?"

"On the check-out line in the supermarket. His wagon was filled with vegetables and fruits and dried beans. Vegetarian was one of the items on my list. And so was handsome. He's very handsome."

"I don't know if looks are that important," Sara said.

"Oh, yes." Amy lifted her chopsticks full of tofu and broccoli. "You must consider looks. My friend Karen made her list of what she wanted in Mr. Right. She wanted a doctor who was clever and funny and very rich. She wanted him to be a sharp dresser and own horses. Why horses, I don't know, although I think she actually may prefer them to men."

"Lots of young girls like horses," Sara said.

"She wasn't, like, that young," Amy told her. "Well anyway, she said looks or age didn't matter, so she refused to put them on her list. Then at the racetrack she met this cardiologist who also had a string of racehorses. But he was really ugly. Only five-two. with buck teeth and these really thick glasses."

"But she fell in love with him anyway?" Sara said.

"Are you kidding? She found him utterly repulsive. She tore up her list after that and went to the Bahamas for a holiday. There she met a retired obstetrician who was forty years older than she was and owned a small farm in Vermont. He had a horse that was nearly as old as he was. He wasn't bad looking if you don't mind old and bald. He died of a heart attack a year and a half after they got hitched. Now she lives with that ancient horse up in the sticks."

"You think these lists really work?" Sara asked.

"Sure they do, but you got to put down everything you want. Everything."

"Then what do you do?"

"You put it out into the universe. You give a copy to another person to read. And she signs it. And then you put it up some-place, like on your refrigerator, where you can see it every day."

"And then?" Sara asked.

"And then you'll meet him."

"Maybe I'll try it," Sara said.

"Do it this week, and bring me the copy next Saturday," Amy said. "I'll sign it for you. Make two copies, one for me and one for you."

While Sara waits for the police to arrive she makes a second phone call. Her hand trembles as she calls her next-door neighbor, George. She dials his cellphone number, since she doesn't have his office number. Luckily he answers. He's at his office today and not at court.

George is a criminal attorney. Sara's concerned that the police might suspect her of the murder.

When Sara returned home from that lunch with Amy, she went right to her computer and got to work on her list. She typed: *smart, good sense of humor, kind, loves animals—particularly dogs.*

Tiny Nap, her Yorkshire terrier looked at her and whimpered.

"You'll always come first with me, Tiny Nap," Sara said. "Maybe he should have a dog for you to play with." She added, *owns a dog—a small one. Preferably a male.* Tiny Nap did not particularly care for female dogs.

Sara thought about Amy's boyfriend being a vegetarian. She added: *He eats meat.* Then: *He likes movies and theater and museums and dining out. And travel.* Sara always wanted to travel to Europe, particularly Italy and France, but she hated the thought of going alone. She typed: *He listens to me when I talk to him, and tells me he loves me and is always on time. He's good in bed.*

And he's not gay.

He's healthy, has a good job, is rich and likes to spend money, and leaves a good tip. Sara had worked as waitress through college. Now she always tipped at least twenty percent, more for good service.

She decided she had better add things about looks. And age. *He is between thirty-five and forty-five, over six feet tall, has all his hair and good teeth. He is considered good looking but not too handsome.* Sara didn't trust men who were too handsome.

She saved the list in a file headed *Mr. Right.* She made two copies, one for herself and one for Amy. She fed Tiny Nap her dinner and took her out for a walk.

George tells Sara not to say anything to the police till he arrives, but he gets there a few minutes before the police. When the police finish taking Sara's statement and finally let her go home, George asks her out for a drink. "You need to relax a bit," George says.

George has always seemed to like Sara. He isn't really her type. He's shorter than she is, only five nine and a bit chubby. But he's always friendly and once offered to walk Tiny Nap for her when she had the flu. He doesn't have a dog of his own, but seems to have adopted Tiny Nap as his honorary pet.

"I have to walk Tiny Nap first," Sara says.

"I'll go with you," George replies. "You shouldn't be alone right now."

As they leave the murder scene, an old woman with sparse gray hair and missing teeth comes out of the apartment next door. "Why are the police here?" she asks.

"You'll have to ask them," George says.

"All these comings and goings," the old woman says. "All day, comings and goings."

The following week Sara gave Amy a copy of the list. Amy signed it while they waited for their soup. She returned one copy to Sara and kept the other one. You're going to meet him really soon," Amy said. " This really works. Mark my word."

Sara orders two beers. "I'd like a third," she says. "I'm not really hungry."

"You should eat something. It will be better for you if you do," George says.

They both order hamburgers, medium rare, with all the trimmings, bacon, onions, cheese, French fries.

Sara has more of an appetite than she thought she would. While they eat she tells George all about Amy and Mr. Right.

Sara met Mr. Right in mid-November. She was walking Tiny Nap on Madison Avenue, right outside of Central Park. It was a windy Sunday afternoon and she thought Tiny Nap might blow away; she was so small, only four pounds of fluff.

Suddenly Sara saw a nice-looking man walking a little white fur ball, not quite Tiny Nap's size.

As the dogs sniffed each other, Sara asked, "What kind of dog is that?"

"A Maltese," the man said.

"What's his name?" Sara asked.

"Falcon," the man said.

Sara laughed. "A dog his size should be named Sparrow."

The man grinned. His teeth were sparking white. He was quite good looking, almost handsome. "I read a lot of mysteries," he said.

Sara smiled. She wasn't sure what he was talking about, but she liked him. He was about six-four with styled brown hair streaked with gray at the temples. "This is Tiny Nap," she said. "When she was a puppy, she liked to sleep a lot."

"So now we know our dogs' names. But not each other's. Mine is Brandon. What's yours?"

An hour later they sat in a restaurant drinking Merlot and eating filet mignon. Brandon told her he worked with computers. The bill came to sixty-eight dollars, including tax. Brandon left a twenty dollar tip.

When he walked her to her building, he kissed her gently on the forehead. They made another date for the following night.

For the next couple of months they saw each other three or four times a week. Brandon brought a toothbrush, a razor, deodorant, and some clean underwear to Sara's apartment. He and Falcon often spent the night. Brandon was very good in bed.

Tiny Nap was spayed and Falcon was altered. They were more interested in chew toys than in each other but managed to get along without any fights.

For Christmas Sara bought Brandon a Movado watch. It was more than she could afford, but she managed to get it on sale, twenty-five percent off. She bought Tiny Nap and Falcon matching teal-and-gold dog sweaters with their names embroidered in navy blue on the back.

Brandon gave Sara a ring with emeralds flanking a one-carat diamond. "It was my mother's engagement ring," he said. Tears formed in his eye. "I wish my parents were alive to meet you. I know they would love you as much as I do."

He asked Sara to marry him. He said that they would go to Paris on their honeymoon.

Sara said, "Yes," with no hesitation.

Sara could hardly wait to tell Amy. "It worked. The list worked. I didn't think it would," she said over curried lamb. They had switched to one of the inexpensive Indian restaurants on Sixth Street in the East Village, for a change.

"It doesn't matter whether you believe in it or not." Amy picked at her spinach with whey. "It still works. The universe has faith in you even if you don't have faith in it."

"Maybe the four of us could get together one day," Sara said. "Go out for dinner."

"Oh," Amy said. "Well, I don't know. I'll have to ask him. He's, like, busy an awful lot."

Sara doesn't sleep that well. She dreams of being thrown in jail. She'd look awful in those striped dresses. She worries about what will happen to Tiny Nap. She thinks about Brandon. He's away for a few days, and she doesn't even know where to reach him.

At eight-thirty in the morning, her doorbell rings. It's George. "I've come to take you to breakfast."

It's beginning to snow. Sara puts Tiny Nap's new sweater on her. "I have to take Tiny Nap out to poop first. Tiny Nap hates the snow," she says. "When they put salt on the ground to melt the snow, it burns her paws. She refuses to wear little dog boots."

"I'll walk with the two of you," George says. They go outside. The snow is rather light and isn't sticking to the ground. "That's a cute sweater," George says.

"I had them made especially for the dogs. Matching sweaters with their names on them. Custom made."

"Dogs?" George asks.

"Yes, Falcon. A tiny Maltese. He belongs to my fiancé."

"Oh, your fiancé. I didn't know you had a fiancé." George sounds disappointed.

Tiny Nap does what she has to and drags Sara back into the apartment.

Then George and Sara go to the coffee shop for breakfast.

Over pancakes with bacon and sausages, George says, "Tell me why you were at Amy's apartment."

"Brandon is out of town. He left early yesterday morning. He has a very good opportunity to set up a computer consulting firm. If it works out, it'll be wonderful for him."

"Why wouldn't it work out?" George asks.

"Well." Sara pours more syrup onto her pancakes. "He has to invest a bit up front. One hundred and fifty thousand dollars. He went to his uncle to see if he would back him."

"His uncle?" George says.

"Yes. It's a kind of long story. Brandon's parents were killed in a plane accident while he was in college. This uncle was the executor of their quite sizeable estate. When Brandon turned twenty-five, the estate was supposed to revert to him. But it turned out that his uncle had embezzled most of the assets."

"So what did Brandon do?" George asks.

"At the time, nothing. He didn't realize he had any recourse. But recently he found evidence of some of his uncle's wrongdoing that he can use to apply pressure on him. He's going to tell his uncle that he won't bring him up on charges if he gives Brandon one hundred and fifty thousand dollars. Even though his uncle stole a lot more than that."

"How old is this Brandon?" George asks.

"Forty-two."

"Ever hear of the statute of limitations?" George asks.

"No, what's that?"

"Never mind," George says. "What if his uncle says no?"

"Then he'll have to raise the money somewhere else."

"And I bet he asked you to help."

"Well, yes." Sara pours sugar into her coffee. She adds milk George drinks his black. "And?"

"I don't have one hundred and fifty thousand dollars. I don't even have five thousand dollars," Sara says.

"Does Brandon know that your apartment is rent controlled?"

"No. I never told him. But what difference does that make?"

"I bet he thinks you're rich," George says.

"Me, rich? That's silly."

"You wear very expensive jewelry," George says.

Sara's hand shakes. A bit of coffee splatters into her saucer. "He said I should sell some of it. The diamond earrings and the sapphire bracelet."

"And?"

"I said I'd think about it," Sara says.

"What does this have to do with your being at the apartment and finding the body?" George asks.

"I said I would watch Falcon while he was gone. But Brandon said no, he was taking Falcon with him, that his uncle loved dogs. Maybe that would help."

"Then what happened?"

"Oh. Well, I was walking to the fish store yesterday morning, a couple of hours after Brandon left, and I saw Falcon. I knew it was him because of the sweater. It matches the one I bought Tiny Nap, but it's smaller and says 'Falcon.' Amy was walking him. She didn't see me."

"So Amy was a friend of Brandon's?"

"I had no idea they even knew each other. I couldn't figure out what she was doing with Falcon. Besides, Brandon said he was taking the dog to his uncle's."

"Tell me about Amy."

Sara tells George about Amy and how she went about finding Mr. Right. She tells him how Amy had her make the list asking for exactly what she wanted, and that Amy had kept a copy. She tells him how then Brandon turned up and was exactly what she'd said she wanted.

"What did you do when you saw Amy with Falcon? Did you talk to her?"

"No. I didn't want her to see me. It could have been awkward."

"So what did you do then?" George asks.

"I followed them home. I wrapped my scarf around my mouth. Amy didn't notice me."

"I was surprised at the kind of building she lived in. I didn't expect a six-story tenement for some reason. Not even an elevator building.

"I was going to follow her in and confront her, but I got scared. I didn't know what to say. So I went back to the fish market, finished my shopping, and went home.

"But it was bothering me. It was really bothering me. So in the afternoon I went out again and walked back to her building."

"And then?"

"I opened her front door and looked up her apartment number. Then a man came out of the building. When he opened the door, I walked right in. I never bothered to buzz her.

"I went up the two flights of stairs to Amy's third-floor apartment. That old lady, the one who said everyone was coming and going, was standing in the hall watching me.

"The door was ajar. I pushed it open and went in. There Amy was, lying in a pool of blood." Sara buries her face in her hands and begins to sob.

George reaches across the table and puts his hand on hers. He squeezes it. "It's going to be all right," he says.

"They're going to arrest me. I just know they are," Sara tells him.

"Don't you worry," George says.

"I can't help it." Sara's voice quivers.

"Where was Falcon when you found Amy's body?" George asks.

"Oh, God. I forgot all about Falcon till this minute. He wasn't there,"

"Let's go back to her apartment," George suggests.

George rings the old woman's buzzer. He tells Sara he remembered the number of her apartment, 3B. He always notices details. The woman's name is Esther Goldenberg.

Esther Goldenberg's voice comes through the intercom. She asks who they are.

"We were here yesterday. We left before the police did," George tells her.

She buzzes them into the building.

They climb the two flights of stairs.

Esther Goldenberg stands out in the hall to greet them.

"I remember you," she says.

"Yesterday you said there were a lot of comings and goings," George reminds her.

"Just like Grand Central Station. First, in the morning, Amy's boyfriend brings a dog. I never liked Brandon. He's too good-looking. You can never trust the good-looking ones. He's always here. A couple of nights a week, sleeping over," Esther Goldenberg says.

Sara makes a little, whimpering noise.

"What time was it that he brought the dog?" George asks.

"Maybe six, seven o'clock. I get up early all the time. I can't sleep late any more. Not since I got old. I'm eighty-two. I looked out in the hall because the dog was barking. A nasty little thing. Hardly worth calling a dog."

"A Maltese," Sara says. Her voice is shaking.

"Then a little while later, he leaves without the dog. He shouldn't have done that. Dogs are not allowed in this building," Esther Goldenberg says. "Around lunch time Amy goes out and walks the dog. It's wearing a cute little sweater. While she's gone Brandon comes over. He uses his key to get in. Of course, she isn't there."

"Of course," George says.

"Then she comes back with the dog and goes into the apartment. She doesn't even close the door when he starts yelling at her."

"Could you make out anything they said?" George asked.

"Just something about, 'I thought you said she was rich.' Then it was time for my program and I went back in my apartment and turned on the TV loud, because I'm a little hard of hearing.

"Then he goes out again and slams the door. It was during a commercial and I turn the sound on the commercials low. I look out to see what's going on. This time he has the dog with him. A few minutes later you come." She points at Sara.

"Later you come." She points at George. "Then the police come. Then you go."

Sara pretends enthusiasm when Brandon calls. "You're back early."

"I didn't go. My uncle and I talked on the phone. He said he wouldn't give me anything. He said I had no proof that would stand up in court."

"I'm sorry," Sara says.

"Can I come over?" Brandon asks. "I need to talk to you."

"Sure, but give me an hour. I'm not dressed."

When she hangs up, Sara calls George. "Could you take Tiny Nap for a few hours? Brandon is coming over."

"Sure," George says. "I'll walk her for you, if you like."

"Thanks," Sara says.

"Are you sure you'll be safe? I don't like your being alone with him."

"I'm sure I'll be okay." Sara thinks that George's worries are unfounded.

Sara opens the door. Brandon struts in. He carelessly leaves the door open behind him. Sara thinks of closing it, but figures it might be easier to leave it ajar for George to return Tiny Nap after their walk. She doesn't trust Brandon.

Brandon paces up and down. "I need the money now or the business deal is going to fall apart."

"I don't have any money." Sara wears her grandmother's diamond earrings and her sapphire bracelet.

"Sell your jewelry."

Sara takes the engagement ring off her finger and hands it to Brandon. "Here, sell this."

"It was my mother's," Brandon said. "I can't sell my mother's ring."

"My jewelry was my grandmother's. I'm not going to sell it either. Why don't you just ask Amy for the money?"

"Amy?"

"Your girlfriend. The one who told you about me. The one who set me up."

"I don't know what you're talking about."

"Amy told me all about you," Sara says. "How you've pulled this con on a number of women. Got engaged, had them give you money, and then disappeared."

"Amy told you that?"

"And the engagement ring is a fake. It's not a real diamond. You have around a dozen of them, so you can leave them with your fiancées, when you skip out.

"She told me how she got me to write exactly what I wanted in a man. And I gave her a copy of the list. After she showed it to you, you created yourself as the person I wanted you to be. You even borrowed your neighbor's dog. She told me you don't really like dogs.

"You asked me to marry you. You knew I'd say yes because I was vulnerable. Like all of the others. When I trusted you, you would ask me for money. Since I was wealthy, living on Park Avenue in a two-bedroom apartment, I'd be glad to simply hand it over.

"Like the women before me."

"Look, I need the cash, and now," Brandon says. "Either give me your jewelry or I'll take it." He makes a move toward Sara. He looks menacing.

"You can't have it," Sara says. She backs into the kitchen.

Brandon grabs Sara's shoulders. He shakes her. He reaches for her earrings.

Sara backs against the counter. "Amy's dead. She was murdered."

"Dead?"

"You were seen coming out of her apartment."

"I didn't kill her." Brandon's hands fall to his side. "I'd never do anything to hurt Amy."

"I know you didn't," Sara says. She reaches behind her for the serrated bread knife. "I killed Amy."

George walks into the apartment through the door that Sara had neglected to lock.

Two police officers walk in behind George, who has called them in to arrest Brandon for Amy's murder.

Tiny Nap follows. She barks and barks.

Sara doesn't notice them. She's too intent on plunging the knife into Brandon.

Over and over and over again.

Tiny Nap barks and barks. She nips at Brandon's ankles. The police draw their guns. "Stop or I'll shoot," one of them says.

Sara drops the knife.

George doesn't represent Sara on either count. After all, he's a witness to Brandon's murder. Instead he arranges for her to have another good defense attorney. Though it's doubtful that this one can get her off.

Tiny Nap moves in with George for the duration of the trial. George promises that he'll keep Tiny Nap if Sara is found guilty.

This is fine as far as Tiny Nap is concerned. She knows that George is her Mr. Right.

MANHATTAN:
UPTOWN AND DOWNTOWN

DEATH WILL CLEAN YOUR CLOSET
by Elizabeth Zelvin

On the Saturday morning when I finally got around to cleaning my apartment, I found a ton of mouse droppings, seven enormous water bugs, and a body. The body lay crumpled like a Raggedy Ann in the back of the walk-in closet. That closet was the jewel in my rent-controlled crown. It made me the envy of all my friends with one-year leases in the overpriced shoeboxes that had replaced most of the old-law tenements and crumbling brownstones on the Upper East Side. The white working-class neighborhood of Yorkville had fallen prey to developers who put in high-rises with Sheetrock walls as thin as a corned beef on rye in a greasy spoon.

She lay sprawled on top of a pile of black plastic garbage bags filled with old clothes that I planned to donate to the thrift shop on the corner and write off on my taxes. Some day. Probably in my next life.

The closet was deep. In the front row hung stuff I actually wore. When I brushed my pants and such aside with the mop, I'd bumped up against something weirder and more solid than the sexy nighties and assorted female garments left by my ex-wife and a bunch of girlfriends I didn't know any more. I reached for the closet light, a bare bulb on one of those cheap little chains that tend to break off in your hand when you tug on them. This one didn't, but the bulb was dead. And so was she, according to the flashlight.

When you've spent your most sexually active years having

alcoholic blackouts, it is literally possible not to recognize someone you've been intimate with. This can happen as soon as the morning after. On the other hand, I hadn't had a drink in ninety days. For three months I'd been clean and sober and celibate except for a fling with my ex-wife, which didn't count, and a one-night stand that had ended badly.

The girl in my closet had a silk tie knotted around her neck. In the dim light, her face looked blue to me. She didn't look like more than mid-twenties, with spiky, short dark hair, a row of sparkly ear studs, a little silver star in one pierced nostril, and a rose tattoo on her breast just above the line of her black tank top. She wore faded jeans cropped above the ankle with designer holes in them. Her feet were bare. The toenails of the right foot had been painted a glittery silver. It looked as if death had intervened before she got to the left. I had never seen her before in my life.

In AA they keep telling us you can't do it alone. The "it" they mostly mean is staying sober one day at a time. But they also say to practice the principles in all your affairs. The corpse in my closet was my affair, whether I liked it or not. So I called my best friend, Jimmy.

"Bruce. Hey, dude, what's up?"

Caller ID still freaks me out. I'd gotten behind in my technology while keeping up with my drinking. Jimmy, on the other hand, who's a computer genius, is high tech all the way. In the background, I could hear the sounds of battle. I recognized the rebel yell and the hoarse bark of black powder rifles. That made it either the History Channel or Jimmy's interactive Civil War reenactment website. Probably both. Jimmy multitasks.

"I was cleaning my apartment this morning," I began.

"See? I told you that if you got sober, miracles would happen."

"Wait, let me tell this! I burrowed all the way to the back of my closet."

"And did you find Narnia?" Jimmy's girlfriend, Barbara, listens on the extension. She's unbearably perky in the mornings.

"Nope. I found a body. A *dead* body."

The receiver emitted a stunned silence. Then Barbara found her tongue, which never remains lost for long.

"Who is it?"

"I have no idea."

"You're telling me you've been back in that apartment ever since you got out of detox and you never *noticed*?" Barbara screeched. "A *body*?"

"You know it takes a while after detox for all your faculties to come back," I whined.

"Withdrawal is not a synonym for brain dead," Barbara snapped. She's a counselor, and she has no tolerance for alcoholic griping unless she's paid to listen to it.

"Didn't we look in that closet back when we cleaned out the freezer and all that?" Jimmy asked. He'd helped me dispose of some tempting controlled substances.

"The memory is fuzzy, but I think we checked. We didn't burrow."

"There would have been a smell," Jimmy pointed out.

"I did notice a faint stink," I confessed, "but you know my bedroom window looks out on the back of that Italian seafood restaurant on Third Avenue. I didn't think anything of it."

"How long?" Barbara demanded. "When did you first notice the smell? How could someone have gotten in? Where did it come from? Who else has your keys? What about the fire escape? And when? And why?"

"Whoa, there, Torquemada." Becoming a counselor had refined the inquisitorial techniques Barbara was born with. "Let me think."

My brain didn't want to work. I forced it.

"She couldn't have been there that long. She's not stiff, but she's not decaying either." That I would have noticed.

"She?" they both piped up. Guess which one of them added, "Anyone we know?"

"No!" I said emphatically. "And yes, I'm sure."

"You'll have to call the police." Jimmy always does the right thing. It comes from his fifteen plus years in recovery. Integrity. It's one of the things that always scared the pants off of me about sobriety.

"I can't." For once, I could identify the feeling: panic. I had not enjoyed my prior dealings with the police.

"You've got choices," Barbara offered. It's one of those 12-step slogans that seem so Mickey Mouse until you actually try to live by them.

"Yeah, well, that's no help unless one of them is quietly closing the door and pretending I never found her."

"One day at a time, fella. One moment at a time." Either the slogans or Jimmy's soothing voice worked. I began to come back from where part of me hovered on the ceiling looking down and the other part clutched the phone and jibbered. "First things first."

"What *is* first?" Barbara asked.

"How about you start by going back and taking another look at the body," Jimmy suggested. "The police are going to ask a lot of questions."

"Even more than me," Barbara added cheerfully. As she'll inform you, whether you asked or not, self-honesty is one of her character assets.

"You'll stay on the line?"

"We're right here."

I put down the receiver. Jimmy never tires of telling me I need to get rid of my old black AT&T clunker. I do have a cellphone, but I don't have enough recovery to keep it charged reliably.

I marched back to the closet where the door remained open. My clothes hung where I'd left them, pushed to either side. The lighter women's things fluttered slightly in the breeze from the half-open window. The black garbage bags still lay piled haphazardly on the floor. The dust bunnies I hadn't gotten to stirred gently, as if restless. The body was gone.

I stood there with my jaw at half mast. The faint strains of a

Puccini aria floated in from the Italian restaurant. The morning cleanup crew and prep chefs were all opera buffs. As if inspired, a blue jay's creaky voice broke into, "Thief! thief!" from the backyard of one of the neighboring brownstones. Somewhere in the building, a door slammed.

I marched back to the phone.

"She's not there any more."

"Hmmm." Living with Barbara, Jimmy's learned to speak a little therapist.

"Bruce," Barbara inquired sweetly, "is it possible that what you've been smelling *is* the garbage from the Italian seafood restaurant?"

"Maybe she was playing possum," Jimmy said. I knew for a fact that Jimmy had never *seen* a possum. He grew up in Yorkville just like me, and neither of us had ventured south of 79th Street until Jimmy's sixteenth birthday. But he loved the Discovery Channel.

"She looked dead to me."

Jimmy had a point, though. A live person hiding in my closet would make a lot less noise sneaking away than someone dragging a body. It still didn't explain what she had been doing in there. Or how she got in. Or who she was.

"How sure are you that you didn't recognize her?"

That one I could answer. "Very."

"Have you slept with any strange women lately?" Barbara is addicted to minding everybody's business, especially Jimmy's and mine. "Inquiring minds want to know," she added, reading my thoughts with ease.

"No!" I didn't have to fake indignation. "Not since detox. Except for the two you know about."

"Before you got sober, then. Did you give anybody a key?"

"I might have," I admitted. I'd been drinking heavily the last month or two before I'd stopped, though I hadn't woken up with anyone I didn't know during that time. But I might have taken one or more to bed. Post-feminist women get up and go home in the middle of the night just like men. If that's what'd happened, I couldn't recall.

"Do you remember your last party?" Jimmy asked. I did recall he'd stopped by for an hour or so. Once the keg arrived, he'd taken off for an AA meeting.

"Only the first two hours, maybe."

A lot of people, not all of whom I knew, had crammed into my apartment that night. It was a couple of days before the Christmas Eve of the final binge and blackout that had landed me in detox. So anybody might have known the layout. They could have stolen a key. I always lost them, so I tended to keep copies lying around.

"Bruce," said Barbara. "Is your window open?"

"Which one?" I hadn't given up cigarettes, but without the booze to complement them, I no longer took as much pleasure in being half asphyxiated by my own smoke.

"The one leading onto the fire escape."

Duh. That window faced the closet door. I rushed back over there and looked down into the yard. But if she'd gotten out that way, she was long gone.

Relieved as I felt not having to call the police and deal with it, I had lost my desire to clean the closet. I shoved the mop and vacuum cleaner back in there and shut the door without looking. Then I tried to forget the whole thing.

It would have been easier if Barbara hadn't called me at least three times a day with fresh ideas. Could the woman have been retrieving something she'd hidden in the closet? Or stealing something? Had I ever kept dope in there? Did I really think she was dead? What were my mental associations when I saw her? Could she have mummified? Did King Tut cross my mind? My landlord kept the heat way up and loved to pass along the fuel costs to the tenants. So my apartment was dry, but not that dry. Nor was Barbara's well of questions. Was I *sure* I'd never seen this girl? In the neighborhood? At an AA meeting? By the time she finished quizzing me, I could barely remember what I'd actually seen. To the best of my recollection, the girl had looked dead. But in that case, how the hell had she gotten out of the closet?

In the meantime, I went about my business. Did enough office temp work to pay the rent. Met Jimmy twice for dinner and an AA meeting. Met my sponsor at a few more meetings. Kept meaning to raise my hand and share, but never did. Took their flak about it. Lied about developing a relationship with my Higher Power. I barely had a relationship with myself. I wasn't used to being asked if I had prayed or meditated today. So I'd grunt and squirm and hope they'd think I meant: well, sort of.

As I walked around the neighborhood, I kept an eye out for the girl with the star in her nose. She couldn't have gotten far without shoes. Maybe she lived nearby.

Instead, I ran into a lot of people I knew. Jacky Doyle, a cop I'd been to kindergarten with. Buddy Russo, the pizza guy, who Jimmy and I had hung out with drinking Colt 45s in Carl Schurz Park over by the East River in our scruffy teens. Cindy Gomez, the first girl I'd ever almost slept with. She chickened out at the last minute. Just as well, or I wouldn't have been able to look her in the face when we collided in the freezer aisle at Gristede's. She was pushing two grubby kids who barely fit in the shopping cart and buying TV dinners. I was blamelessly selecting fish sticks and wondering if it would be any fun to go fishing off Sheepshead Bay in Brooklyn without a six-pack.

Then I met up with a number of people I almost knew, like my next door neighbor, a guy I thought of as Clark Kent. Maybe it was the horn-rimmed glasses. Or that he would have been a lot less nondescript in a red cape and tights. We often found ourselves sticking our keys in the lock at the same moment. Once I ran into him as I tossed a load of household garbage in the Dumpster at the construction site a few doors down the street, which you're not supposed to do. He was doing the same. We nodded and said *Hi*, the way you do. Just a couple of urban outlaws. He was into heavy metal and liked to cook with garlic, and that was all I knew about him. That's New York for you. A city of strangers.

Except when it's a village where everybody you grew up with either still hangs at the bar on the corner or turns up in the same church basement saying the Serenity Prayer.

It's kind of like Avalon. Or is it Brigadoon? The old Yorkville occupies the same geographical space as the spiffy new Upper East Side, but they're two separate worlds. In my building, for example, the old white working-class families or their kids have the rent-controlled apartments. Old Mrs. Mooney across the hall, whose son Kevin had been killed in Vietnam, would wave and call out, "Feet first!" every time she saw me. She meant that's how they'd have to get her out of her apartment. On the next floor up were the Nagy twins, whose family had come from Hungary in 1956. Jimmy and I had played a memorable game of strip poker with the Nagy girls when we were all twelve. Ilona, the one who still lived there, was a lawyer now. Marta was a chiropractor up in Larchmont. She had a house, along with a husband and kids. But I bet she'd move back to Yorkville in a flash if her sister ever wanted to give the place up. Once an apartment got vacated, decontrolled, and renovated, it went over to the other side—the poor young roommates paying high-priced rents.

I looked for the missing woman at meetings too. I saw plenty of girls with spiky dark hair and silver-studded noses. Many recovering women had tattoos. There was a story for every tattoo, many of which I'd already heard. If I stayed sober and kept coming back, I'd probably hear them all. I tried not to look down anybody's cleavage, since thirteenth stepping, or hitting on fellow AAs, is rightly frowned upon. But I did keep an eye out for that little rose.

On the street among the yuppies and the childhood friends, I ran into half-a-dozen people for whom the three months I'd spent acquiring my sobriety one painful day at a time had passed in a flash, like Rip Van Winkle's twenty years.

"Hey, man, great party!" they said.

I still couldn't figure out how the girl had gotten into the closet. If she'd been in my apartment before, the party remained the most likely occasion. So I asked.

"This may sound dumb—" or "Things got kind of wild that night—"

Whichever way I put it, I felt like a jerk. But I persevered.

"Did you happen to see a girl, not too tall, spiky hair?" My fingers sketched a rooster's comb above my head. "Pierced all along the ear?" I ran my thumb down my own left lobe. "Little silver star right here?" I tapped the side of my nose.

"Hoo hoo," the first one chortled. "Lost your Cinderella? Gotta get that glass slipper out and hit the bars, man, maybe you'll find her there."

"Punk chick, huh," said the second. "Real standout in this part of town—maybe she was reverse slumming up from Alphabet City."

"Nope," said the third, "but I met a real hottie from New Jersey, one a them H towns the other side a the bridge. Practically broke the mattress. Didn't come up for air till Christmas. Hey, that was some party. Ya gonna have another soon?"

Assholes.

Seven days later, one day at a time, another Saturday. Damned if I'd spend this one cleaning. Apart from my reluctance to go anywhere near the closet, the dust had hardly settled yet from last time. I roamed restlessly around the neighborhood. March was almost over, but it wasn't quite spring. Wind nipped at the puny trees, just coming into bud along the side streets in the 80s and pounced on crumpled fast food wrappers plus flapping sheets of newspaper beside the curbs. I spent more than an hour in Carl Schurz Park, just leaning over the railing staring at the East River, where wicked currents eddied between Ward's Island to the north and Roosevelt Island stretching down past the 59th Street Bridge.

Late in the afternoon the wind died and the sun came out. I hadn't slept well the night before. Getting unconscious every night without passing out still presented a challenge. In AA, they say that everything you ever did drunk you have to do sober. So

I did something I'd never done sober before. I stretched out on a bench and went to sleep.

I didn't really think I'd doze off. I doubt I slept for more than twenty minutes. But it was long enough for me to dream. I was walking through a thick white mist toward Avalon. Or was it Brigadoon? I knew I had to get there, and I would, if I only went far enough. But the mist went on and on. I thought about giving up. I almost did. Then Jimmy's voice said, "You didn't pass the lamp post." And I woke up.

"You didn't pass the lamp post." What the hell was that about? Where was there a lamp post? Hey, wait a minute. Avalon…Briga-doon…Narnia! You got to Narnia through the back of the ward-robe, which was just Britspeak for a closet. If you didn't pass the lamp post, it meant you hadn't gone sufficiently far.

I leaped up off the bench fast enough to traumatize the nearest pigeons and went tear-assing through the streets toward home. My fingers shook as I stuffed my key into the lock. The hall was empty, but Clark Kent next door had the heavy metal on. I could hear the thumping of the megabass. I finally got the door open, slammed it closed behind me, and double-locked it. Then I made a beeline for the closet.

I pushed impatiently through the first row and the second. In the dark, the clothes on their hangers pressed close around me like trees in the nastier kind of fairy tale forest. Yep, there was a third row. I could make out the dresses and coats from the forties and fifties that my mom hadn't bothered to take with her when she'd moved out to Long Island. They smelled stuffy and old-fashioned. I guess the actual fragrance was from mothballs. I even found a few of my father's suits that my mom had never gotten around to giving away or throwing out. I thrust them all aside to left and right.

Beyond all that I finally found a door. I'd had no idea that it existed, though I'd lived in this apartment my whole life. York-ville old-timers such as I had accumulated a lifetime's worth of junk and treasures we hadn't seen in decades and never looked for, because we didn't remember we had them. But Upper East Side yuppies moved into empty spaces.

I groped for a knob or lock. When I found it, the whole thing came off in my hand. I took a startled step back and almost tripped. The screws that had held it rolled around under my feet. When I stepped on them, they fled like mice. From beyond the door, I heard the thump of heavy metal. It was a wild night in Narnia. And I smelled garlic.

An hour later, Jacky Doyle and another cop came knocking on my neighbor's door.

LA BRUJA DEL BARRIO
by R.M. Peluso

Latin station WNYL was broadcasting a battle of the divas. "Phone in your choice for the queen of Salsa! *Quien será la reina? La Lupe or Celia Cruz? Llamanos!*" Detective Belinda Torres, too busy at her bookkeeping to vote, turned down the radio and picked up her cane. Damn buzzer! The sign on the door of her private investigations agency read, "Closed/*Cerrado*." Not even 8:30 a.m. Never too early for some illiterate though.

"Who? *Quien?*" Torres shouted over the intercom. It took her several moments to register the name of the crackpot who ran the Pleasant Avenue botanica, right around the corner. Just what Torres needed—a sorceress at the door, and it wasn't even happy hour. Not that the PI celebrated happy hour anymore. Against doctor's orders. Hmmp! Doctor didn't run *his* office on 116th Street.

Torres had never met the La Bruja del Barrio, the so-called white witch of Spanish Harlem, and wouldn't be caught dead in a botanica. Everyone knew what was in *those* places: statues of saints, incense and candles, herbs and potions to treat every disease and condition, real or imaginary. Torres always hurried by the botanica as fast as her lame leg would carry her. The patrons were largely Puerto Ricans of the older generation, or newly landed Dominicans—people without medical insurance, or superstitious idiots. Not hard-nosed, retired Nuyorican police detectives, like Torres.

The PI hobbled from the back office to the storefront of her basement agency to get a look at this bruja. Once Torres pushed the door buzzer, the bruja rushed in along with the aroma of freshly baked sweet rolls from the recently opened Mexican panadería, a few doors down.

"You be the detective?" the bruja said. A half-smoked cigar smoldered at her side.

"Don't be tokin' on that thing in my office!" Torres waved her free hand to disperse the smoke. "Yeah, I'm Torre-th-s-s. My a-s-sistant hasn't come in yet. And I don't talk too cleaw—clear, s-so—"

"Yeah, yeah, you had a stroke. Heard all about it. I got a cure for that."

I just bet you do, thought Torres. "What can I do for you, Miss, uh, Sister—"

How do you address a witch?

"Gladis Fuentes. 'Gladis' be okay."

The voice was dusky, her appearance more African than Spanish or Taino. La Bruja's head supported a tower of cornrows bound in a bright yellow, muslin half-turban matching an ankle-length skirt. She eyed the walls papered with posters of Puerto Rico, the battered sofa and coffee table, and repeatedly lifted her cigar to her lips, up-tempo, like a 1950's mambo bandleader conducting smog. "My daughter, Lydia, she disappear."

"You call the police?" Torres swatted the smoke again.

"She be twenty-two. Gotta wait two days to report her missing. I be afraid if I do, it be too late."

"Any idea where she's gone?"

"A *santero malo* took her."

"The who? An evil S-santaría priest? Mayme you bettew leave. I'm not pokin' my nose into any black magic. Give me plain ol' cwooks, embezzlers, cheatin' s-spouses. Only people living in th-three dimensions, okay?"

"Somebody gotta help me. Maybe they kill her."

Torres shifted her weight against her cane. She recalled Ramirez, the bodega owner across the street, said this Fuentes woman had cured his Aunt Magdi of her rheumatism. When he'd offered Torres one of Fuentes's business cards, the detective had waved it away. Then she'd also found the enterprising bruja's cards in the Ethiopian restaurant, and in Patel's video store. Patel had confided that while he didn't believe in La Bruja's brand of healing, he'd accepted Fuentes's cards as a neighborly gesture. "But she returns every week to add more," he'd said, and pointed to stack that was spilling over much of the counter. Torres scooped up all the cards and dumped them in the trash. Poor man had been too intimidated to liberate his own countertop.

"Why don't ya put one of your th-s-spells on the santero," Torres said now to La Bruja.

"I be tryin', but maybe they kill my Lydia 'fore my magic can work."

"Uh-huh." Torres took a deep breath, weighing her impulse to kick the air-polluting bruja out of the office against the fact that Fuentes's herbal remedies did occasionally help her clients. La Bruja didn't charge much, either—a modest fee for the herbs. Considering all the bad things that went down in El Barrio, Fuentes seemed relatively benign.

"Got a ph-photo of your daughter?"

Fuentes loosened the mouth of the purse looped around her waistband and handed a picture to Torres.

"Beautipool girl."

"*Gracias a los santos*! My only child, Lydia, a model."

A model? Hadn't Torres been reading in *El Diario* that a few models had gone missing?

She beckoned Fuentes to follow her to the back office, a converted storage closet crammed with one dilapidated desk, a corroded filing cabinet, and a couple of dented metal folding chairs. Torres pointed to an ashtray, "Park the c-cigar, and have a s-seat." She grabbed the newspaper off the chair.

"You take my case?"

"You got the minimum thou—thou—uh—*mil* to cover my fee?"

"No problem. My Lydia make good money."

Torres found the newspaper article on the three missing models. Two foreign girls: one Scandinavian, one Czech—and one from Montana.

"You sure a s-santero took her?"

"*Mi hija* had a *problema con drugas.* The santero tell her he cure it. I say to her, 'Take my herbs, go to rehab. This santero no good. *Malo.*' But he convince her somehow."

Torres rose. "I don't know if I'm the wight—r-right person to help you."

"*Espera,*" said Fuentes. She picked up her cigar and handed it to Torres.

"Flick the ash into the tray."

"Huh?"

"*En el cenicero. Por favor.*"

"Screwball," Torres muttered to herself, tapping the cigar against the rim of the metal bowl.

Fuentes picked up the ashtray, shook it, then gave it a gentle blow. "Ah-ha! The ash say you the right person. Okay? You find her?"

Torres wondered why the woman didn't consult the damn ashes to locate the daughter. "Let me get back to you."

An hour later, Lamont Green, Torres's assistant, arrived to work the phone for the speech-impaired PI. Torres had hired him to be her voice and do some of her footwork. He was a big kid, seventeen, and already six foot three inches of muscle hard as the granite under the East Harlem streets. He wore a do-rag on his head, jeans drooping off his butt, looking like the gangsta rappers he strove to emulate. The boy's passion was writing rap songs. But he was also a covert techno-nerd who attended an elite public prep school, and linguistically agile enough to switch from hip-hop to standard English faster than the Lexington Avenue Express could fly through a local subway station.

Lamont placed his hand over the phone and turned to Torres. "Yo, Boricua, now we're gonna get the low-down on the eye-candy."

"The wha-?"

"The eyegasms. The models. Got the detective in charge on the line. Hello? Lieutenant Benson? Lamont Green calling on behalf of Detective Belinda Torres. I'm going to put us on conference call so she can join our conversation."

"Torres! That you? How ya been?"

"Hey, Matt! Go 'head, aks him, Lamot —Lamon-nt."

"Detective Torres is working a missing person's case."

"Oh, yeah? I heard she…you opened your own agency? How's it going?"

"Okay," said Torres, though she had closed only a few easy cases in the six months the agency had been open. If it hadn't been for her checks from the NYPD, she'd have shut up shop.

"The missing person's a 'round-the-way Betty…I mean, a young lady from the neighborhood. Name: Lydia Martín-Fuentes, age twenty-two, dark skin Latina." Lamont thumbed the girl's photo, then sighed, and set it down. "Bo-ri-cua mo-re-na," he sang softly, beating a rhythm on the edge of the desk, "dark ma-ma from—"

"Latina? You tellin'me another model's gone missing? I got no information on any Latina. Hello?"

"The mom ain't inform on her first born; the requisite forty-eight ain't terminate. Bah-da-be—bah—"

"Don't rap to Benson, Lamot!" Torres couldn't tolerate unprofessional conduct, even in a teenager, and she couldn't stand hip-hop. She'd been raised on Salsa. As a teen, she had fallen in love with Javier dancing to the *clave* of timbales and congas. Give her melodic vocals and choral responses. Give her rich orchestration infused with jazz. Hip-hop! Hmmp! Moreover, Lamont wanted to compose songs about their investigations, and, as she'd explained to him numerous times, that was a violation of client confidentiality.

"Okay! Okay! Uh—Detective Torres wants to know if there's a common denominator here. The mom said the girl's been nabbed by a santero."

"What's that? Voodoo?"

"Other side of Hispanola, man. Talkin' Santaría gone nasty. Santero's supposedly treating her for a drug problem," Lamont said.

"Feeding her problem, more like it," said Benson.

"Like you say. But what about these other women?"

"We know the Swedish girl snorted snow. Don't know much about the other two. Haven't located anyone who knows them, except the modeling agencies. And there's this salon that does their hair."

"Mind gibing me their nun-numbers?"

Midday at the Caribbean Salon and Day Spa, wealthy patrons and their image transformers revved up on iced frappaccinos and pulsed to the audio of the latest Paris runway videos in the former Vandervoort Mansion on Central Park South. Lamont Green gave a low whistle at the babes on the screen. "Bootylicious!" he muttered, and clapped his hand against his leg, as he half-skipped to the reception desk and flashed a photo of the bruja's daughter. "Excuse me. This here's my sister. She's a model. Comes here to get her hair done. Ya know her?"

"She doesn't look familiar. But Shamani might know her—she works with lots of models."

"Which one's Shamani?"

The receptionist pointed to a shapely, thirty-something hair stylist, molded into lavender leather pants and a silver lycra tee-shirt. "That one over there, but she's with Mrs. Uldrige now."

"I'll just sit over there and wait, if it's okay."

The Park Avenue matron who must be Mrs. Uldrige gave Lamont what seemed a particularly unsmiling smile when he slid into the chair of the unoccupied workstation next to her. The matron tapped her nails on the armrest of her chair, a half-beat behind the music, then whirled around to face her hair stylist. Shamani Bustier grasped the last strand of her client's hair with a square of aluminum foil, slathered on a fetid goop, folded over the foil, and stood it up on end with all the other silver pieces, leaving the woman's head wearing a halo of metal. Lamont wrinkled up his nose, defending himself from the chemical assault.

Shamani glared at him. "Can I help you with something?"

"I need to consult with you, professionally. I can wait 'til you're finished."

The hair stylist nodded. "As I was saying, Millicent, you were smart not to wait until depression set in. I've seen it so many times before. The wife of an older husband, who stresses himself into an early grave, leaving her alone, unprepared to be single again. This change in your appearance will work wonders, dear, believe me. A little blond chasing away the drab—it's just what you need to get on with your life."

"You make it sound so simple, Shamani." Millicent Uldrige glanced up at Lamont, who was studying his dreadlocks in the mirror. "I'm not that young, you know," she whispered. "I'll need more than a new hair color. Frankly, I've been thinking of something more radical."

Shamani snapped to attention. "You mean, a face lift? Liposuction? Darling, that's a wonderful idea. Why, you'll look like a teenager! Have you decided on your surgeon yet?"

"You must know someone, Shamani. You style all those glamorous models for the magazines."

"I can give you a name, if you like. The most exclusive surgeon happens to be in New York right now. Have you ever heard of Dr. Beatrice Rivera?"

"Rivera? I don't think so."

"Why she's the best!"

"You think I can get an appointment?"

"If *I* refer you, of course!"

Shamani wound the timer that would tick off the minutes

until Millicent's hair turned to spun gold. "There. Now you sit over in that chair for thirty minutes—say, why don't you let Andrea do a manicure and pedicure meanwhile? So relaxing. I can schedule you a massage upstairs with Antonio after we wash out the hair. And Margarite can do a make-over with our new line of cosmetics after I style you. You need a new palate, darling. Your colors are *tired*." Shamani glanced up. "Talk about coincidences: You see the redhead at the reception desk?"

Millicent leaned forward to get a look at the six-foot, mini-skirted eye-riveter. Lamont's eyes were not far behind.

"Now how old would you say she is?"

"I wouldn't think a day over twenty-two, twenty-three."

"She's fifty-six."

"U-h-h-fifty-six? That-that's impossible."

"Nothing that you yourself can't achieve! Trust me. You look far younger than she did before her surgery."

Fifty-six! Sumpin' bogus here, thought Lamont.

"Tell ya what," said Shamani, "let me call Dr. Rivera's office for you and set up an appointment." The stylist picked up the telephone on her workstation and punched in a number. "Cherí, this is Shamani Bustier. I have a client who'd like a consultation with Dr. Rivera. No new clients this season? But this is a very special client of mine. I'm sure the doctor will be happy to...you can? For me? Tomorrow at six p.m.?" Millicent nodded. "Tomorrow's okay." The stylist hung up, pulled a business card out of her smock and handed it to Millicent Uldrige.

"Isn't that address the same as the salon's?" said Millicent.

"Yes, but they're on the third floor. Use the side entrance."

Belinda Torres's car was a pile of scrap that spent more time in the shop than out on the street. But she managed to turn over the engine and drive to the address given her by Gladis Fuentes.

"I tell you sumpin' ain't on the up and up at that salon!" said Lamont, who sat next to her on the passenger side. "And that pigeon Shamani—her mouf say she don't know Lydia, but when she look at the photo, her eyes say she a liar. Why don't we surveil this doctor's office? I tell you, there's some kind of skeelo goin' down there."

"It doth-does s-sound like they're s-setting up this-s Uldw-rige."

Torres parked the car diagonally across from a botanica on Fort Washington Avenue, out of which the santero supposedly conducted his business. This store was nothing like Gladis Fuentes's open, sun-filled shop. Instead, black drapes prevented any view of the interior. But people kept coming and going, and Lamont snapped their photos.

Finally, an old man emerged and locked the door behind him.

"Got the third eye that be our santero," Lamont said.

"Third eye?"

"Intuition, Boricua."

"And th-s-stop callin' me Boricua! How'd you like it if I called you Africa?" Boricua! The name the original Taino Indians had used for the island of Puerto Rico before even the Spanish arrived.

Lamont shrugged.

"Hmm. He s-s-seems to match the description." Torres watched the old man wend his way down the street, waited a few moments, then started the car. She shuddered at the boom-thud-boom of the engine.

"I'm gonna give that mechanic of yours a talkin' to in the alley," Lamont said. "This can o'spam-on-wheels'll blow our cover. Why don't ya get a new one?"

Torres smiled as she kept her eyes on the road. It had taken years for her car to acquire all the damage that discouraged theft. She could park the wreck anywhere without worry.

A few blocks away, the santero entered an apartment building.

Over the next several hours, Lamont worked his way through

slices of pizza, bags of plantain chips, chocolate cup cakes, cans of soda. Still, the old man failed to exit the building.

"Gotta be the santero's crib."

Torres nodded.

Back at the agency, Torres had Lamont call bunko about the salon, but they had no information on Shamani Bustier or Dr. Rivera. Then Torres reported the addresses of the botanica and apartment building to Detective Benson.

"I'll check 'em out. Owe ya one, Torres," Benson said, "We sure miss you at the PD. Too bad they stuck you with that desk-job after the…uh…"

"The throke? S-stroke?"

"Yeah. We were shocked, you being so young and all."

She had only been thirty-seven. But she'd pushed herself hard to get ahead— obsessed with clearing Javier of a wrongful conviction for murder— and had run up her blood pressure with years of overtime and sleepless nights. Only since the stroke had she renounced a diet of caffeine, alcohol, and tobacco. "Young. Yeah. Young and th-s-stupid." She regretted ignoring the blood pressure, but not freeing Javier, the only man she'd ever loved, from Sing Sing.

"You don't get to be the youngest officer to earn a shield in the last fifteen years being stupid, Torres. You take care now… and keep me informed."

Lamont grinned at his boss. "Youngest officer to—"

She silenced him with a flip of her hand.

Lamont turned away, downloaded the digital camera into the computer, and printed out the pictures.

At closing time, Torres double parked across from the salon. Lamont attempted to match faces to photos, but came up with nothing. Torres shrugged, keyed the ignition, cringed as it startled pedestrians, then eased the car around the corner to wait for Millicent Uldrige to show up for her appointment.

No Millicent, but... "Yo! Isn't that one of the Bettys we snapped at the botanica this morning?" Lamont shuffled through the photos. "Yo. There she is."

"There she goth. After her!"

"And there be Millicent now."

Lamont leapt out of the car and dashed into the building while Torres watched him through the double glass doors. Torres emerged slowly from the car and made her way into the building. Once there, she scanned the office directory. *Third Floor. Dr. B. Rivera, Cosmetic Surgery.* Rivera's was the one suite on that floor.

Lamont cracked the door of the stairwell and peered out, just as Torres stepped from the elevator into the physician's reception area. Torres gestured for her assistant to remain where he was.

"May I help you?" The receptionist had turned her attention on the PI.

Torres' appearance was obviously inconsistent with the upscale patients expected here. "I'm with Mrs. Uldrige," Torres whispered.

Torres nodded to Millicent Uldrige as she took a seat across from her.

A moment later, the heavy walnut door leading to the inner office opened. A blonde with the curves of a Victoria's Secret model pushed her way through and strode to the exit.

"Oh, to look like that!" said Millicent to Torres. "I can't understand how the doctor could possibly achieve such results for me. I'm petite. I can understand tightening, lifting—sure. But how can surgery elongate my legs and neck?"

Torres smiled and shook her head.

The receptionist approached Millicent. "You may go in now. This way."

Lamont had found his way, meanwhile, to the service entrance of the medical suite, and he entered in time to see the woman in the photo, now dressed in white, meet Millicent at the other side of the walnut door. "Mrs. Uldrige? I'm Dr. Rivera's assistant, Mrs. De Santo. Follow me, please," the woman said in a monotone.

De Santo appeared oddly aloof, her expression flat, eyes rolled up almost entirely under their lids. Moreover, she didn't even glance in Lamont's direction.

Heavy dose of downers, thought Lamont.

He picked up a chart, examining it purposefully while he walked along the corridor following De Santo, who led Millicent past a suite of examining rooms reeking of antiseptic.

The assistant opened the door that read "Dr. B. Rivera."

"Come in!" said a woman standing before an ex-ray illuminator. Millicent entered and shut the door.

Damn! Lamont waited for De Santo to leave, then scooted into the room next to the doctor's. He figured he'd only be able to listen, but was able to pop the door open a sliver and peer into Rivera's office.

"Please, have a seat," said the doctor to Millicent. "Won't you tell me what brings you here?"

On the wall behind the surgeon's desk hung photocopies of her board certification and diplomas.

"Shamani, from the salon, said you can make me look like a model from top to bottom. Is that true?"

"It is possible, but…quite expensive. I don't recommend the procedure for most patients."

"How much money are we talking about?" Millicent kneaded her handbag.

"For a woman with a career that warrants the expense, or for a wealthy patient who has a few hundred thousand dollars to throw around, we can accomplish amazing results. Are you in either of those categories, Mrs. Uldrige?" Beatriz Rivera folded her hands on the desk and waited.

"Perhaps I am," Millicent said, drawing her purse closer.

"Then, there's only one way to get the results you desire. Fortunately, I have pioneered in this procedure. The recovery time is far less than conventional cosmetic surgery. And there are no scars. At least none that will be visible."

"No scars? Really? How do you do that? Liposuction? Skin grafts?"

Dr. Rivera's steepled fingertips fluttered against each other till she checked herself. "We will not be doing either, Mrs. Uldrige. There are no incisions."

"No incisions?" Millicent gasped. "What do you call this procedure?"

"It's a TBT."

"Is that some sort of acronym?"

"It stands for Total Body Transplant."

"A total—"

"Believe me, it is the future of cosmetic surgery."

"Oh, I believe you. But how is it accomplished?"

"Through the use of donors, Mrs. Uldrige."

"Donors? You mean like transplanted organs? Aren't there problems with rejection?"

"We're not transplanting individual organs, so we have no problem with rejection."

"Then how? I don't understand. I mean, what is transplanted?"

"Like I said, Mrs.Uldrige, it's a *total* body transplant." The doctor rose from her seat and rotated her computer monitor toward Millicent. "Have you ever wondered what happens to models, young, beautiful women who die before their time?"

Millicent shook her head to indicate she had never wondered that.

"Well, I've made it my business to convince the families of such young women to donate to my program so the beauty of their daughters may live on."

"What a magnanimous gesture—to donate beauty!"

"Isn't it?" Dr. Rivera switched on her computer. "Let me show you the images of unfortunate young women who came to New

York with the most fervent hope of making it big in the modeling business, only to become caught up in the drug culture and subsequently overdose. Tragic cases cut down before their time." Dr. Rivera bore an appropriate expression of grief as she shook her head. "Look at these lovely faces that live again as my transplanted patients. Perhaps you will find an image that you can take for your own."

Dr. Rivera pulled full length and three-angled shots onto the screen, along with the women's heights, weights, and measurements.

"Exquisite, aren't they?" The doctor said, flashing through a half dozen such sets of images.

Millicent nodded.

The doctor scrolled to another half dozen faces.

"Wait!" said Millicent. "That's the redhead I saw down in the salon."

"Oh, yes. You can see by the slash through her photo that her image has been assigned. Very successful transplant. Most gratifying results."

"Hmm. That's odd. Her expression seems different—something about the eyes."

"Remember these girls were drug users."

"Doctor, I just had a frightening thought. If these girls were addicts, wouldn't the recipient of the donation become addicted too?"

"An excellent question. I assure you, I've taken great pains to avoid passing on the addiction.

"Mrs. Uldrige, I'm going to send you for a pre-op blood screening, a psychological battery, an EKG, an EEG, an ESP, and a full length CAT scan. Mrs. De Santo will meet you out at the reception desk, give you pre-op instructions and set up your appointments. Nothing to worry about. You simply give us fifty thousand dollars at the time of your physical, and pay the balance the day of your TBT. Your complete satisfaction is guaranteed, of course."

"That seems reasonable. Frankly, I can't wait to get started."

"Then, let's search my file of donors until you find the image of your dreams, Mrs. Uldrige. Surely there's a face and body here you'd like to wear for the next half of your life. Oh! Here's a lovely blonde. A Scandinavian. Now, wouldn't you just kill to look like her?"

"Ph-photocopies?" said Torres, once they left the building. "That's not right."

"*That* ain't right? That doctor say she gonna transplant Uldrige's whole friggin' body!"

"I heard De S-santo s-schedule a ph-physical for tomorrow and tell Uldrige she'd pick her up in a limouth-limousine the following evening. That's unusual."

"Not when they gonna vic her of a few hundred big ones, it ain't!"

Two days later, Torres parked outside the medical office. De Santo emerged, a hearse limousine pulled up, and De Santo got in.

"What the —" said Lamont, "ain't that a—"

"Hears-se? Yeah."

"Look like there's—"

"Yeah, that's a coffin all wight—right." Torres nosed her car into the traffic lane a few cars behind the limo.

The hearse sped to the corner of Lexington and 73rd and screeched to a halt outside a florist shop.

Millicent Uldrige stepped out of the shop, carrying a briefcase and a bouquet of flowers out to the curb. She looked down her nose at the hearse.

The limo driver rolled down the window, motioned Millicent closer, then spoke to her. She nodded and showed him the briefcase.

The driver stepped out, walked to the passenger side, and opened the door. Millicent slid in next to De Santo, gave a quick glance at the coffin, then jerked forward, hand over her mouth. The limo lurched into the traffic lane and whisked its cargo northward.

Torres shadowed the limo—up the FDR Drive, over the Tri-Borough Bridge to the Major Deegan, north through a large park, past a golf course.

"Where the hell we at? Canada?"

"North Bronx. Van Cortland Park."

The limousine crossed a roadway, bounced up a driveway and passed through a large, gated arch.

Torres extinguished her lights and followed a quarter mile through a tree-lined drive.

"Oh, man! Peep that! Neo-classical architecture. Domes. Columns. Outrageous! What the— Where we at?"

"They're mausore-mausoleums. This is Woodlawn Cemetery."

The limousine crawled a steep incline, then stopped in front of a cluster of structures fit to inter royalty. From the bottom of the hill, Torres could only see the tops of the monuments. She dared drive no closer, parked, and signaled Lamont out of the car. They hunched down and rushed up the sloping lawn, keeping the trees and mausoleums between themselves and the passengers of the limousine.

The others now stood beside the limo. When the driver out held his hand for the briefcase, Millicent shook her head and pointed to the coffin.

The driver opened the back of the limousine, pulled out a dolly, and slid out the coffin. He had a hefty build, but still he needed Millicent and De Santo to help steady the box down. He pushed up the coffin lid. Millicent looked in, grimaced, nodded, then forked over the briefcase. The driver placed the case on the hood of the car, opened it, removed a packet of cash and did a rough count.

"That case's full of cheese—fresh from the bank!" Lamont said. "What she doin'—buyin' her own casket in case the procedure turn ugly?"

"Sh-sh!" Torres whispered. "Either she's buying a body or there's about to be an irregal burial. Maybe bof."

"Irregal. You mus' mean illegal. Cause it be regal 'nuf in this boneyard for Tutankhamen."

"Sh-sh!"

The driver shut the briefcase and placed it inside the car. Then he eased the coffin across the grass toward a group of graves.

"Man, this is whack!" said Lamont.

"Sh-sh!"

"I can't see nothin' now."

Torres had no doubt they were witnessing several crimes. She removed her cellphone from her pocket and notified Benson.

When she clicked off, she grabbed Lamont's arm and scurried forward, in the direction of the odd group ahead. Behind the grand stairway of a two-story mausoleum, she took up a position, then peered over the steps.

The limo driver escorted Millicent to a cluster of graves where De Santo was setting up candles on the headstones. She lighted the candles and the sticks of incense; their pungent odor swept downwind.

"Phew! Stinks like a chemistry experiment gone nightmare."

"Sh-sh!"

The doctor's assistant closed her eyes, started chanting, swaying.

"What she singin' in that weird voice? What lingo is that? Look! Her eyes rolled up in her head. Hey! She possessed!"

The driver opened the coffin, and Millicent placed the flowers inside. The driver removed a vial from his jacket, thrust it at Millicent. She obediently drank the liquid.

De Santo broke out writhing and leaping in a convulsive dance. Millicent shrank back, trembling. She stared at the heavens, glanced down at her hands, jumped to the right, to the left.

"He musta' slipped her somethin'. Look like she hallucina-tin'."

Torres nodded.

Millicent stared above the coffin, her arms floating out in front of her as if she levitated. "Beautiful! Beautiful!" Millicent said, as she tracked some invisible trajectory, pulling her hands to her chest. "Yes! Here I am."

De Santo chanted on.

The driver poked Millicent. She started to join in, struggled to sing, hesitantly groping to repeat the foreign words.

Millicent whipped herself into a frenzy, then collapsed. She grabbed her throat, curled up, clutching her stomach. She slipped into unconsciousness. Or sleep—Torres couldn't tell.

Sirens began to wail through Van Cortland Park. The driver and De Santo abandoned Millicent and started for the limo.

Torres stepped out, drew her gun. "S-stop! I'll sh-shoot!"

The driver and De Santo dodged behind a couple of trees. The PI couldn't get a clear shot, so she fired a warning into the air.

"I can get'em!" said Lamont.

"S-stay put."

The driver and Mrs. De Santo threaded their way behind headstones and monuments. Finally, they dashed to the safety of the limo.

The car sped off.

Torres made for the coffin. Approaching it, she held her hand up to Lamont to stop him there. She walked the last few steps on her own, popped the lid, stared into the pine box, and shook her head.

Detective Benson ran toward them, gun drawn, tilted sky-ward.

"They just drove off in the limo," Lamont yelled.

Benson pulled his walkie-talkie from his belt.

"Lady, you all w-right?" Torres said to Millicent. "Hep her up, Lamot."

"We found the other girls in the basement of the botanica, like you told us," said Benson.

Before Torres could reply, Millicent Uldrige sat up, stretched, and yawned. "Who are you? Goodness, I feel wonderful! I feel young. And beautiful. Am I beautiful? Have I already had my TBT? Why are you holding that gun?"

Torres glanced at Benson, shook her head. Benson reholstered his firearm.

"Where am I? I can't recall having my surgery. I can't remember anything but a dream…so odd…must have been the anesthesia…something about a garden…or…" Millicent glanced about her. "A graveyard?" she gasped. "Where's a mirror?"

"Just a minute. What's your name, lady?" said Benson.

"I-I'm Millicent Uldrige. At least I think I am, but I'm not really sure."

"Not sure, huh?"

"I-I'm a patient of Dr. Rivera. Where's my doctor? And… who are you, handsome?" Millicent winked at Benson.

Benson flinched.

"Uh—Lieutenant Benson. NYPD."

"Where's Dr. Rivera, sweetheart?" Millicent winked at him again.

Torres raised an eyebrow at Benson.

"Where are you from, lady? What kind'a accent is that, Swedish?"

"Accent?"

"I have to ask you to come down to the police station. Please get up."

"Go with you? Whatever for?"

"For questioning in connection with the deaths of at least one young woman, the one in that box over there, and the kidnapping of several others."

"Murder? There must be some mistake. I'm here for a medical procedure."

"Medical procedure? This is a cemetery, lady."

The woman glanced down and seemed surprised as she felt along the petite frame of her body. She studied her slack-skinned, translucent hands, ran her fingers over her sagging jowl line. "Wh-where's a mirror?"

Benson's walkie-talkie sputtered, "Yeah, Benson. Okay. Okay. Over."

"Something's terribly wrong," Millicent said. "Where's Dr. Rivera?"

"Your accomplices were just picked up on the Grand Central Parkway. Probably on their way to the airport. Now I warn you…anything you say may be used against you…you have the right to an attorney—"

"An attorney? Accomplices? What are you talking about? What are you charging me with?"

"Conspiracy."

"Conspiracy against what—nature?"

"Conspiracy to commit murder," Benson said, then cuffed her. "Come along."

Belinda Torres took a long whiff as she approached her agency. Chocolate and cinnamon, caramelized sugar, and eggy dough straight from the oven. The morning aromas rising from the Mexican bakery were overtaking the cuchifrito deep-fry of the once solidly Puerto Rican barrio. *La gente*, like earlier generations of immigrants, were moving on to the suburbs, buying homes in the outer boroughs, or retiring to Puerto Rico, like Torres' parents.

But Torres had no intention of leaving 116th Street. She'd been born and raised here. She had fallen in love with Javier here, had listened to him practice montunos on his piano here, then lost him here. Torres paused to listen to salsa pouring from the music store down the street. Their music. This was still her Barrio.

Lamont had called the PI agency her ghetto fantasy, just like hip-hop was his. Torres had invested everything she had in her part of the revival that was now sweeping away urban decay from the Hudson to the East River. She had invested everything she had once in freeing Javier. Even if she were the last Puerto Rican on 116th Street, she'd stay. Javier was out now, back in El Barrio. And Torres dreamed of reaping the results of all her labors

"Yo! Boricua!"

Torres glanced up to see Lamont striding toward her.

"Figured I'd come help you settle accounts with Fuentes. And I want you to hear my latest rap. Heh! Heh!"

Torres rolled her eyes, but not so he'd see. She turned the key in the padlock and let her assistant slide open the gate. Then opened the front door and led the way toward her office. Midway there, the buzzer sounded. Torres turned to see Gladis Fuentes and pressed the button to admit her.

Fuentes was still dragging on her infernal cigar, but she was beaming. She threw her arms around Torres and gave her a kiss on each check.

"Thanks to you both for bringing my Lydia home."

"I'm glad Benthon followed up our lead."

"You see, she was with the santero, just like I say. He try to steal their souls for the rich ladies."

"Get out, Gladis, that's whack. S'nothin to do with souls. They just be killin' and scammin. Had to shut'em up, had to show bodies to the TBT recipients. Nothin' supernatural about that."

"They cleaw-cleared Uldrige," Torres said.

"And Benson turned the stylist from the salon. She recruited models right off the runways for the De Santo woman, who turned out to be the santero's ol' lady. Bunch a boosters, on the real."

Fuentes shrugged. She opened her purse and removed a folded check. "Five hundred for the balance on the thousand, like you say. Oh, I almost forget." She pulled out a plastic sandwich bag stuffed with dried plants and handed it to Belinda. "I bring you a cure for the speech and the leg, Detective."

"Thanks," Torres said.

"Gotta go take my Lydia up to Connecticut. To rehab. The

police give her a deal if she testify."

"Good luck, Gladis," Torres said.

The bruja waved her cigar, then mounted the stairs to the street.

Once her client was out of sight, Torres tossed the bag of herbs in the wastebasket.

"What's the matter? Don't you think the bruja can cure you? Heh! Heh!"

"Not what I've got. I've plateaued, thas' what the doctors said. Bes-st they can do now is keep me from having another lousy s-s-stroke, and—"

" 'Nuff, Boricua. Catch my new rap. Ya think it's jump, maybe I perform it next Saturday."

Lamont bounced in place, chopped at the air with his hands.

Rich lady say, "Doc, give my booty a lift,

"But all she liftin' is some diva's stiff,

"Got an flunkie in the boneyard with rolled up peepers,

"And a driver boostin' green ones from their true believers,

"A bruja tell the PI, her daughter ghost,

"A santero nab her and she —"

"Lamot! You can't s-say nothing about the bruja."

"Oops."

"You can't sing that. The client's business is —"

"Yeah, I know. Confidential."

I LOVE ALANA
by Marianna Heusler

I love Alana, she's my life, she's my girl. And I'd do anything for her.

You see, I've fallen on hard times, and let me tell you, it can happen to anyone. I lived in a rent-controlled apartment across the street from Tompkins Square Park. I used to watch them bums in their raggedy clothes, sleeping outside, drinking themselves sick, and think what lazy losers they were. Because I had a real job, working delivery in a pizza parlor on Avenue B. I didn't make much, but it was enough to keep a roof over my head and to buy some decent food for me and Alana. I even had a small colored television, and I managed to hook it up to cable from the guy next door. The best time of the day was when I'd come home at night, and Alana and me would snuggle up and watch them late night movies where justice always won out in the end.

But the landlord wasn't giving us what we needed in terms of heat, and there was them constant blackouts and all sorts of fire hazards. The tenants made a lot of noise so what does the city do? They condemned the building. Then before you know it, the building came tumbling down and a fancy new condo rose up in its place. A bunch of young yuppies moved in, and Alphabet City became the trend with all them fancy restaurants and late-night clubs.

But not for me and Alana. Because now we got no place to live.

Then the pizza parlor burnt down. I always suspected that

the owners did it themselves for the insurance money because a small Italian restaurant opened up down the street. You know the kind of place I mean. Smaller than a kitchen closet with tables squished together and a few chairs outside on the concrete so them yuppies can watch dogs pee and buses spit out smoke as they drink their red wine and dip their stale bread into a bowl of slimy oil. But the restaurant's serving pizza, thin crusted with chicken and shrimp and pineapple on top and if you're lucky, you get a shred of cheese and a teaspoon of canned tomato sauce. Anyway, the customers are loving it and dishing out big bucks, and everyone is smiling.

But not me. Because I got no job.

I kept telling myself that if I could just make it through the long hot summer, by the time the leaves started to turn I would think of something to keep Alana and me safe.

It's the dead of winter and I'm still thinking.

"You stay right here," I told Alana. "I'm going to bring back something to eat. I think that there's that free coffee and sandwich van up the street on Avenue A."

She didn't answer, just looked at me with those sad brown eyes. I knew she felt tired and sick of living on the streets. But I also knew she had faith in me.

"Where you going Pee Wee?" Georgie asked as he sat up suddenly. I noticed that his color was real bad, kind of gray, and his hands were chalk white. He had an odor too, like someone who was about to check out permanently.

"I gotta find something to eat for me and Alana." Georgie sank down again, disinterested. I shook him. "Will you watch her? Make sure no one bothers her?"

He nodded but didn't even open his eyes. It wouldn't matter if he did, he was nearly blind. Something about a detached retina that never got fixed. And the other eye was infected, real bad. But I knew that he wouldn't let anything happen to Alana.

If anyone tried to bother her, he'd scream out. And just the sight of him would be enough to scare anyone away.

If Georgie didn't freeze to death in the meantime.

"Hey, Pee Wee," Georgie whispered. "Will you see if you can bring me back a little something?"

Something wasn't coffee or a baloney sandwich. What Georgie wanted was a sip of something hard and strong.

"I'll see what I can do," I promised.

"I know you will." Georgie's voice was nothing but a rasp. "Because we look out for each other, right? And we don't want no bad karma."

"No bad karma for us," I said, like I gave a shit.

God, my bones ached and my stomach growled. I was so hungry I felt like fainting, but I walked through the cold hard snow, ignoring the hole in my shoe. I kept telling myself that I had to make it—I had to go on, if nothing else then to keep Alana alive because she depended on me. And the strange thing was I really believed that something was going to break for me soon. The two of us, me and Alana, we'd have all we needed, which was just a little food and some hot drinks, and a nice warm room with cable TV.

Was that asking too much? As long as we could stay together we'd be happy.

So that's what I was thinking as I looked for the long-gone van, as I searched through the trash cans, rifling through dog poop and dirty napkins, frozen newspapers and empty soda cans thrown away by those snotty Catholic school students.

But my search was all for nothing.

I used to beg, but I don't do that no more. It's not worth the effort. All them people in their nice warm wool coats and their dangling scarves, carrying messenger bags and looking important as they hurry off to their gray offices, they don't even glance my way. Maybe because I look so bad or maybe because I smell so awful they can't bear standing near me while they fish around for change.

Or maybe they want men like me out of their neighborhood so the price of real estate can keep on soaring.

But I couldn't go back to Alana without bringing her nothing. She wouldn't be mad, she never is. It's just that look of despair in her eyes—a look I couldn't bear. And just when I was about to give up hope—I saw it, in the corner. I went over to make sure that my eyes weren't playing tricks on me because it was so cold my vision was fogging up, but there it was: a half-bottle of scotch. It wasn't the best scotch. I knew that some wino probably drunk from it, got sick, and just tossed it. And he'd be back if he could remember where he'd put it. He'd be back looking for that bottle, but the bottle wasn't going to be there anymore because I grabbed it first.

I took it for Georgie, and for a moment I gotta tell you I thought about just leaving it there, because I didn't think it was a good idea to get smashed in the freezing cold.

Then I saw something else. A prescription vial full of pills. The label was torn off but I thought the pills had probably expired. I took one out of the container and looked at the capsule real good. I was betting they was sleeping pills.

You could never tell when they might come in handy.

I stuffed the vial in my pocket, thinking maybe somewhere along the line I could trade them in for food.

I trudged back to the park and passed the men huddled on the blankets, half dead from frostbite and hunger, all lined up like patients in a ward. Only no soft beds and comforting nurses were there on call. Most of the alkies didn't seem to even feel much anymore, which I guess is a good thing.

And then I saw this guy cutting through the park with a real nice suit and a spiffy overcoat, walking like he don't have a care in the world. For the moment a jolt of fury swept right through me. What made him so lucky? And me and Alana, barely scraping by.

The guy who said life wasn't fair, boy was he smart.

I found my way back to Georgie. Alana was by his side, still asleep. Georgie looked real excited. I never seen him so excited.

"A man came by," he said. "He gave me money. A lot of money." Georgie fished into the pocket of his ripped, stiff jeans and took out a bunch of ten-dollar bills.

I shook my head. "Ten dollars ain't a lot of money."

"Ten dollars?" he coughed. "What you talking about, Pee Wee? This here is one *hundred* dollars."

I shook my head. "Your eyesight is real bad, Georgie. That's only ten dollars. Besides, why would a stranger give you a hundred dollars? Don't make no sense."

"Oh no!" Georgie showed more spirit than I had ever seen from him. "The guy told me he was giving me a hundred dollars! He told me he was coming back too, coming back for me and you."

"Yeah, right, Georgie. He's coming back. But in the meantime, he done a good deed, giving you that ten dollars."

"Pee-Wee, I may not see so good, but ain't nothing wrong with my hearing. This money, it's all mine." He flashed a toothless grin and then he stuck the money into his jacket bottom, right on top of the knife he kept for protection.

"I got something for you, Georgie." I showed him the half full bottle of scotch. His eyes lit up. "You give me one of those bills and it's yours."

He laughed. His spit actually landed near my mouth. "See, Pee-Wee, I'll give you one bill. Just one bill, cause we're friends and I want to save the rest for a rainy day."

What the hell was wrong with him? Didn't he realize that it was already raining?

"I wanna be a good person," he said breathlessly, "cause I believe what you do, it come back to you—know what I mean? This bill here ain't for the booze cause you and I both know it ain't worth more than a couple of bucks."

"Sure, Georgie, whatever you say."

I turned my back and quickly I emptied the bottle of pills into the bottle of scotch. They didn't dissolve so good but Georgie didn't see so good, so it was all right.

Alana woke up, just then. Her eyes were bloodshot but wide like some kind of scared animal. I knew what she was thinking while she watched me. But Alana didn't understand what you had to do to survive, not when she always had me to take care of her.

Didn't she know that I was doing this for her?

I motioned her to be quiet. She turned around looking like she might barf then and there.

Georgie took a big gulp from the bottle and thanked me again for bringing it to him. "You're a good soul, Pee-Wee, cause you brought this back for me even before you knew I had any money."

"Yeah, I'm a good soul all right."

And then I waited.

It didn't take long, maybe a half an hour or so. And I was getting real restless because it seemed to me that as Georgie grew quieter and more still, so did Alana. When I thought that Georgie was out cold, I put my hand in his pocket and grabbed the wad of bills, real sneaky like, because the men who surrounded me might be homeless, but some of them still had morals and wouldn't appreciate my stealing from a corpse.

"Come on." I grabbed Alana by her torn jacket.

"I don't know if I want to go with you after what you done, Pee-Wee."

"Don't talk crazy. He was about to croak anyway. I just hurried him along."

She rose. She was breathing hard and her cheeks were red, like she had a fever or something.

As I stumbled from the gate, one of the boys asked me if Georgie had seen his brother.

"His brother?" I questioned.

"Yeah, he was looking for Georgie, gonna give him some money."

Georgie probably didn't even recognize his brother, I thought.

"He told me that he was gonna come back for Georgie and I heard Georgie say he wasn't going nowhere without his two best friends. So don't go far. I think this guy got a basement apartment or something. Where is Alana anyway?"

I whipped around. Alana wasn't anywhere in sight. She had taken off on me. But I knew I could find her.

At least I had one hundred bucks to my name. And, just like I said, I never was a lucky guy.

Or maybe Georgie was right and it's all karma.

THE KNOCK-OFF
by Chelle Martin

I settled into the seat beside my best friend, Sheri, as the train rolled out of the South Amboy station heading toward Manhattan. The gentle rocking motion, along with the crisp air of a February morning, set the perfect stage for a girls' day out shopping in the Big Apple.

Once the conductor punched our tickets, we dived into conversation about what bargains we hoped to find. Sheri had been making regular trips to Chinatown with her sister and had become a steady customer of a man she knew as Chang. She'd been pleading with him to get her a faux Kate Spade bag, one of the hottest imitations around in the latest design. Myself, I didn't see the point in knock-offs. Granted, they might not cost a thousand dollars, but for a darned good one, you could still pay several hundred. Why not just go with a great bag by a less costly designer?

An hour later, we arrived at Penn Station and hailed a cab on 34th Street. Our driver, not surprisingly, looked to be from some Middle Eastern country and spoke with a thick accent. He drove like an Indy race car driver, weaving artfully from right to left for position, beating the traffic lights when he could.

We passed Union Square and the outskirts of Greenwich Village, went through Little Italy, and wound up on Canal Street, where we paid our fare and exited.

"It's down this way," Sheri said, as she led me past numerous shops and restaurants. The smell of Chinese condiments filled the air. "We can stop to eat on the way back. I want to buy the bag before Chang gets a better offer."

"I thought he was holding it for you."

"He said he'd have one, maybe two, this weekend. He didn't say he'd hold one for me."

"Oh." And here I thought this was the point of our trip.

Chang's shop was tucked between an Oriental herbal medicine store and a Chinese food market. A little chime sounded as we entered. Inside, several customers chatted away in Chinese, while a few Caucasian women passed handbags back and forth, pointing out the not-so-finer points of the knock-off industry.

"See this?" one said. "The logo doesn't line up. This bag isn't worth thirty dollars, let alone three hundred."

I could see her point. I mean, hey, the first thing anyone notices about a bag is if the pattern lines up. A bad stitching job is liable to make one the talk of the office.

"Debbie, over here," Sheri called. She had managed to pull Chang aside. Or someone I assumed to be Chang. The man smiled and disappeared into the back of the store, returning a moment later with a small leather bag in a shade of pale blue.

"Oh, yes, this is it. Kate Spade's new spring design. Isn't it great, Debbie?" Sheri started posing with the bag on her arm in front of a floor length mirror.

I had to admit, the bag was attractive, but I'd never fit all my essentials in it. My bag, when loaded to capacity, could be called a lethal weapon.

As Sheri fished out her credit card, I noticed two Chinese men entering the shop. One Chinese shopper poked another, and soon the ladies dropped their merchandise and scooted past the men at the door. An uneasy feeling jolted my stomach.

Chang addressed the men, pointing toward the door and rattling something off in his native tongue. They approached the counter anyway, one grabbing a handle on the Kate Spade bag with Sheri reluctant to let go of the other.

"Hey, I ordered this bag," she said in that loud, slow way that one does when unsure if someone speaks English. This, I presume, she thought would make her dilemma understood. Then we could all laugh at the big misunderstanding, shake hands, and world peace would reign. But it was not to be.

The second man drew a gun, reached over the counter, and grabbed Chang by the collar. Just then the door bell chimed behind us, throwing a wrench into the scenario. Three young kids barreled into the store with two women behind them, one talking on her cellphone. All were oblivious to the events at hand.

In an instant, Chang grabbed for the gun as the purse holder simultaneously grabbed for Chang. Sheri pulled the bag away as if it were the greater half of a wishbone and ran for the door with me in pursuit. A loud bang erupted, and from the corner of my eye I saw the women and kids hit the floor.

A handsome man in jeans and sunglasses approached the store as we burst out the door. "Wait!" he yelled and reached inside his blazer.

We nearly bowled him over in our scramble to get away.

Shots rang behind us.

We fled down Canal Street, our Nikes speeding us north onto Lafayette as if our very lives depended on it. Which, and I'd rather not think about it, they probably did.

"Over there!" I pointed to a Holiday Inn.

We didn't slow down until we entered the lobby. I feared looking back in the direction we came from, but when we did, neither of us saw anyone in pursuit.

My side ached, and excitement pulsated through my body. I sank into a chair to catch my breath, while Sheri did the same.

"What's with the bag?" I asked.

"I don't know. I don't speak Chinese," she said through panting breaths that would do a Lamaze couch proud. "Do you think they killed Chang?"

I shrugged. "Why would someone knock someone off over a knock-off?"

Sheri smirked. "Is that like a woodchuck chucking wood?"

"Smart ass. Maybe you should just chuck the bag."

"No!"

"You didn't pay for it."

"I meant to. I was looking for my credit card, remember? I'll just go back and pay Chang on the next visit."

"Well, until you do, that bag is stolen property."

"I got scared. I ran out with it. It was an honest mistake."

Sheri shrieked, and I turned to see the two Chinese gunmen scurrying along the avenue, their heads turning in all directions.

We scrambled behind some palm plants near the lobby window and peered through the leaves.

"Do you think they saw us?" Sheri asked.

One stopped to light a cigarette. The other pulled out his cellphone and punched a number.

"Do you think there's a back door?" I asked.

"No, there isn't," came a male voice behind us. "But if you ladies would like to make a reservation…"

Neither of us moved. "No, we're good, thanks," I said.

"Then I'll have to ask you to leave. We don't allow loitering."

"I lost my contact lens," Sheri said, swiping the floor with her hand. "Ugh, when was the last time you dry mopped?"

"Out," the hotelier said. "Now."

We were backed into a corner, so to speak. And like two dancers in sync, we rose slowly, daring glances out the window. The Chinese men had their backs to us, still engaged in smoking and phoning.

Sheri slung her own purse over her shoulder and clutched the Kate Spade under her arm as we slinked to the door, slowly cracked it open, and slithered out. A group of teenage girls bobbed down the street, and we duck-walked into the safety of their herd.

Our false sense of security quickly vanished when one of the men shouted in Chinese. We took off at a run, winding up in Little Italy, and headed for Broadway, where we frantically tried to hail a cab. The driver waved to us in the familiar sign language of the city, a clear indication he had no intention of stopping for two lunatic women.

"Should we take the subway back?" I asked.

"Do you think we can make it there?"

Across the street, we spied the two men and then a Lincoln Town Car stopping alongside them. Two additional Chinese searchers emerged, and the car drove away. The group spread out. Damn. Now we were outnumbered.

"Look!" Sheri said.

A cab slowed to a stop in a taxi stand near a restaurant. Horns blared and brakes squealed as we hazardously darted across the street. Sheri climbed in and I had one leg in the car when a vehicle stopped in traffic and tossed out a little black dog. We both gasped. I'm sure the dog did, too.

"Driver wait," I said, running to the pup who sat frozen in place amid oversize SUV tires. I scooped the frightened creature into my arms.

Chinese shouting again. Crap. Two men, the original pursuers, were gaining on me fast.

I jumped into the taxi and ordered the cabbie to get in gear. We got about a block and a half before we hit a red light.

Our driver must have sensed our duress because I'd seen him looking in the rearview mirror when he picked us up. For good reason. He clicked the door locks seconds before the two men tried the handles and pounded on the windows.

The two stood at the passenger-side door, each waving a gun and rambling on, pointing in the back at Sheri and the purse. One rattled the handle yet again.

Our driver reached beneath his seat and pulled out his own weapon. He pointed it at the men, and a loud crack sent us ducking for cover. A hole appeared in the passenger window. The Chinese men had dropped to the ground. The light changed, and we sped off, our driver taking a side street and weaving up onto the sidewalk to avoid the traffic.

"Where to, ladies?" he asked, as if nothing had happened.

Sheri and I looked at one another, but neither of us spoke. Where could we go? The police station was probably our best bet, but…

I looked at my sweaty hands, which had turned black. "Since when do dogs discolor?" I asked.

"What?"

I rubbed my hands along the dog and they grew blacker still. A small patch of dirty white appeared on the dog. "This dog isn't black. She's white," I said.

The driver had heard me. "You know, a dog was stolen from Westminster yesterday. A poodle."

"Oh, that's right. The dog show is this week," I said. I loved the Westminster show and watched it on television every year. "I didn't hear anything about a stolen dog."

"It just hit the papers this morning."

This dog's coat was cut in a choppy fashion, not a show cut, but the pup did resemble a poodle.

"Lady, I think you got yourself a hot dog there," the driver said.

Oh, boy.

"I think we'd better get to a police station," I said to Sheri.

"Yeah, maybe you should drop off the dog."

"And the bag, too," I said.

"I'm paying for the bag."

I rolled my eyes. "The bag is evidence."

Our driver was forced to stop at the next light since a delivery truck blocked any hope of detouring onto the sidewalk. When the light turned green, a black Lincoln turned the corner and fell in behind us. Sheri groaned. "What's with these guys?"

"There's a police station on West 10th Street. You want to head over there?" the cabbie asked.

We'd been in the car for what seemed like forever and had only made it as far as the Village. I fumbled in my handbag for a twenty-dollar bill so I could pay the driver in case we had to jump ship and make a run for it. In addition to Sheri accidentally stealing a designer bag and me in possession of an allegedly hot show dog, I didn't want to add theft of services to our growing laundry list of crimes.

The driver swore and snapped me out of my daydream of living in stripes for the next ten years. Orange detour signs and flagmen showed up ahead. A one-way street prevented our escape.

I looked behind us. Two men alighted from the Lincoln and straightened their jackets.

"I'll cover your backs, ladies. You make a run for it." Our driver stepped from the cab and whistled for the attention of a construction worker.

Sheri slid out the door and I followed. We speed-walked in the direction of the construction workers, hoping to take cover if necessary.

We'd barely reached the sidewalk when shots sounded.

I saw our cabbie crouched in a shooting stance, and one of the Chinamen hit the ground. Sheri and I gasped when our driver took a hit in the arm and fell over. The gunman turned his attention on us, and we had nowhere left to run.

Sheri and I clutched each other, eyes closed, the Kate Spade bag and the poodle sandwiched between the two of us. I heard someone yell, "Freeze!"—then an exchange of gunfire.

When the popping noises ceased, I ventured a look at the same time Sheri did. Standing over us was the handsome guy we'd run into, almost literally, outside Chang's shop. Only now he clutched a gun in one hand and a badge in the other. So, that was what he'd been reaching for back in Chinatown.

All of a sudden, Sheri started to cry. "Here, take it," she said, surrendering the pale blue bag to the handsome man. "I guarded it with my life. There isn't a scratch on it." She held her arms out waiting to be cuffed.

"Are you okay?" he asked us as he holstered his gun.

Several uniformed officers stormed the area. Where had they come from? And how had they found us?

Sheri and I sipped hot coffee at Federal Plaza, while Special Investigator Jim Finley, the handsome stranger, provided information. It turned out that the DEA had fitted Sheri's designer bag with a tracking device in the handle. The bag was one of many that an undercover investigator had sold to a store run by a Mr. Ping Cheo. One of Ping's employees had then stolen a few of the bags, unaware of Ping's involvement in drug trafficking and the samples that Ping had sewn into the bags' linings. The employee was questioned when the distributors came to pick up the bags and discovered the shortage.

By then, a third party had already sold the bags to Chang, and that's what had brought Ping's hit men to Chang's store. They thought Chang was trying to cut in on their drug business.

"Okay," I interrupted. "You were able to find us because the bag had a tracking device. How were the hit men able to follow us?"

"Cellphones. You weren't moving very fast. One spotted you and called the others with your location and the direction you were headed in.

"Chang had no way of knowing he was putting his customers or himself in danger," Finley said.

Sheri asked, "Is he…?"

Finley nodded. "I'm sorry."

"He was such a nice man," Sheri lamented.

The dog, Champion Wellesley's Pampered Princess, had indeed been the kidnapped poodle. Her owner, Mrs. Violet Dunbar, came to the agency building to claim her, and I expected the woman to be in shock upon seeing the shape her dog was in. Instead, she cried tears of joy and relief when CiCi, the dog's day-to-day name, jumped from my arms into hers. Violet, a true dog lover, was oblivious of the black soot rubbing off on her white Gucci suit.

I refused her offer of a reward, but told her to look me up if CiCi had puppies one day.

Then, as we got up to leave, Sheri asked Finley, "Now that you've caught the drug ring, can I keep the Kate Spade bag?"

"I'm afraid not, Mrs…"

"Miss, it's miss," she corrected him. I'd seen that glazed look on her face before. At the exact moment she'd laid eyes on the Kate Spade bag. Poor man. Of course, Sheri had been in love before. But who knows? Maybe, unlike the knock-off bag, this could be the real thing.

THE BRONX

Strike Zone
by Terrie Farley Moran

Edgar Allan Poe killed him.

That's not what they wrote in the *Journal-American* or any of the other New York dailies, of course. Those newspapers got carried away with gang violence and how maybe it was the Fordham Baldies did the deed. The papers called the Baldies the most dangerous gang the Bronx had ever spawned. But Edgar Allan Poe was the one who killed him. I know. I was there.

Most of the girls I'd played boxball and jumped rope with a summer or two before were spending the summer of 1961 watching the neighborhood boys play softball on a dusty field that took up the whole south end of St. James Park. In the early part of that summer, the girls had clustered in the shade of a big oak tree on our own grassy scrap of the park. We would braid plastic key chains and experiment with Flame Glo and Tangee lipsticks borrowed from older sisters or stolen from Woolworth's, while arguing over which put blonder sun streaks in our hair, lemon juice or peroxide. We giggled about Bobby Vee and Frankie Avalon and tried all the latest dance steps from American Bandstand. Someone always had a transistor radio, a small plastic box, blasting out tinny rock and roll.

By August, the music still sounded tinny but everything else had changed. One by one, each girl claimed her own space on the benches facing the ball field, and stretched out her tan, freshly shaven legs clad in short shorts. The fortunate ones sat ramrod straight to show how nicely they'd "filled out" as our mothers would say. Girls who were best friends in July now sat on separate benches because of a shared crush on some skinny sixteen-year-old boy with a pack of Luckies stuck in the rolled-up sleeve of his tee shirt. We stopped being a crowd of girls and became a bunch of Sputniks revolving around the boys.

Long before Labor Day, I left St. James Park behind and moved my outdoor afternoons to Poe Park, a block or two away. There, I wandered around, looking for my spot, a place to hang out, maybe even a new crowd of girls.

The benches were filled with grown-ups who lived in the five- and six-story apartment buildings towering around the park. The women would knit or crochet, gossiping away the afternoon. Old men sat in groups of four or five and played cards or checkers at small stone tables.

In the open area circling the bandstand, a chubby blond man in a crisp white uniform leaned against a pushcart, his bulk almost hiding the ice cream pop logo. He flirted with young mothers who bought small cups of vanilla for their toddlers.

Closer to the Kingsbridge Road underpass, an old man, his khakis and navy tee shirt covered with a long white apron, sat on the last bench next to the subway stairwell. He tossed salted pretzels with a long-handled fork and spread candied peanuts over the hot coals burning in his shiny metal cart. Sugar water from the peanuts dripped onto the coals, and the sweet sizzle made the whole corner smell like a cotton candy machine at the parish bazaar.

What made Poe Park different from the other neighborhood parks was the cottage—Edgar Allan Poe's little white home with the dark green trim. It sat in the northwest corner of the park and was pretty much ignored by everyone.

About my second or third day hanging out, I saw a girl, older than me, maybe a woman, come out of the cottage. She sat on a bench, opened a red pack of Pall Mall cigarettes, popped one in her mouth, and struck a match. All in one motion, she blew out the match and crossed her legs. I walked over and sat beside her.

"What's in the house?" I wondered aloud.

She just sat and smoked. The hand without a cigarette worried itself along the pleats of her soft pink and powder-blue skirt. Finally, uncrossing her legs, she dropped her cigarette and ground the butt with the heel of her penny loafer. She raised her shoulders and moved her face to within a few inches of mine. Her pageboy hairdo slued toward me.

"You live around here." Sort of a statement, sort of a question.

I nodded.

"And you've never been inside?"

I shook my head.

"Let's go then. I show people around the cottage a few hours a week. I'm majoring in American lit at Fordham."

Her name was Eloise and she came from some small town in Massachusetts.

We stepped into the cottage. Kitchen. Sitting room. Bedroom. Eloise pointed to a dark wooden rocking chair and told me Poe had sat there, day after day, mourning his young wife who'd died in the cottage back in 1847.

She asked me to sign a visitors' book and gave me a pamphlet about the life of Edgar Allan Poe. I shoved it in my pocket. Eloise smiled. "Sure, biography can be boring, but not Poe's. You should read it. You should read this, too."

She handed me a leaflet with a poem, "The Bells," printed on one side and a picture of the cottage on the other, and invited me to come back anytime. I figured I'd stop to see her again, if only for something to do.

I sat on a bench with the pamphlet and read about iron bells and silver bells, golden bells, and so on. I read it again. Until that moment, the bell Sister rang to call us to class, the clang of a fire truck rolling by, the peal of church bells on Sunday morning all sounded the same. But they weren't the same. They would never be the same for me again.

The next afternoon I went to the library and found a slim book of poems that included a few written by Edgar Allan Poe. I checked the book onto my hardly used library card and ran over to the park. I wanted to show Eloise, but the cottage gate was locked. I sat on a bench and began to read.

That became my summer. Once or twice a week, I scouted the library for anything written by Poe. Nearly every afternoon I would find a spot under a tree, lean against the trunk, and read some haunting or romantic poem. Sometimes I would see Eloise and we would talk about whatever poem I was reading. Within weeks, I began to read Poe's stories. I liked the mysteries, but it was *The Tell-Tale Heart* that got me hooked. Imagine killing someone and hearing the constant beating of the victim's heart forever more. In the story, that heartbeat drives the killer to confess. I got chills when he cried, "I admit the deed!"

When school reopened, I would rush home to do my chores. Then, book in hand, I'd fly down the stairs from our third-floor walk-up, across the top of the Kingsbridge Road underpass, and into the park.

I had my own tinny radio, a beige and green boxy thing. I would carry it with me whenever there was a Yankee game. I wasn't interested in the softball games those other girls sat around watching in St. James Park, and I wasn't interested in the boys who played them. The only boys who interested me in 1961 were the M&M boys. Mickey Mantle and Roger Maris, the stars of the New York Yankees. Truth be told, Mantle was kind of old but that Roger Maris, now he was cute, and at fifteen, I was just old enough to notice.

The Yankees were having a great year then. Bats hot, gloves like magnets. This was the year one of the M&Ms would break Babe Ruth's record of sixty home runs in one season. For months, Mantle and Maris were neck and neck. All summer, if the Yankees were playing, you could walk down any street in the Bronx and hear the game blaring from a hundred television sets. Bars sold "Yankee Specials" during game time: beer and hotdogs with a side of peanuts. By the time I started hanging out in Poe Park, Clancy's Corner Tavern was offering a beer on the house to everyone whenever Mantle or Maris hit a home run.

Then Mickey Mantle hurt his hip. Like a racehorse that loses steam on the final turn, he just s-l-o-w-e-d down. By September it was only Roger against the Babe. And, as it turned out, me against Joey Naclerio.

My mother sent me to the butcher one day, telling me to buy ground chuck for meat loaf. I took the long way through Poe Park. Walking to my right but looking to my left, checking if the cottage gate was unlocked, I bumped into someone. "I'm sorry" was out of my mouth before I turned to see if I had crashed into some old person. That always required more than a simple "I'm sorry."

Joey Naclerio stood deliberately blocking my path. He lived on the second floor of my building with his sister Anna and their parents. On warm days, when the apartment doors were open, I would creep up to the second-floor landing and peek between the banister rails hoping his apartment door was closed. Too often it wasn't. Joey would be leaning against the doorjamb, dressed in a muscleman tee tucked into dungarees, his garrison belt pulled tight. I would slide around the corner facing him, my back touching the cast iron banister post. As soon as the heel of my foot hit the first step to the next landing, I'd turn and run to the third floor. Even with all the doors open and the mothers bustling around in their kitchens, I didn't want to be alone with Joey Naclerio in the hallway. Not even for a second.

As I raced to the safety of my home, he would say something in a soft, oily voice that sounded dirty, although his words were innocent enough. "Not for nothing, why waste your time reading stupid books?" or "Hey, Bookworm, next time you're going to the library, call for me." Lately, he was taking shots at the Yankees.

"Bookworm, that Maris is such a stiff. He's never gonna tie the Babe." And, "There ain't been a real baseball team in New York since the Giants left the Polo Grounds."

Now here he was, blocking my path. He grabbed my arm. "Where you goin', Bookworm?"

I pulled away. "None of your business." I stepped to my right and tried to pass, but he blocked me again.

"Hey, if you're going to the library, I could walk you."

I gave him a shove. "Get away. I'm going to the store for my mother. She's waiting for me, so she can make supper."

"Did your ma tell you I pulled her grocery cart up the stairs the other day? Anything for Bookworm's ma." He stepped aside and sat on the iron railing, winding his feet around the second rung, and motioned me to come closer. I turned and headed toward the butcher. Joey called after me, "Bookworm, what's your hurry?"

As September shifted toward October, the apartment doors stayed closed, and I didn't meet Joey in the hallway or on the street, but I was always on the lookout. One afternoon, I was coming home from the library, listening to the Yankee game on my transistor. I sat on the fence in front of Poe Cottage so that Edgar could bring Roger luck. My stomach felt tight all through Tony Kubek's at-bat. Then Roger Maris stepped to the plate. He was within a couple of runs of tying Babe Ruth's record. I held my breath, waiting for the pitch, the swing, and Mel Allan's "Going, going, gone!"

Someone crept up behind me and smacked the radio out of my hand. Another hand swooped down and caught it just before it hit the ground. I slid off the fence, grabbing at the radio. And looked right into the eyes of Joey Naclerio. He hid the radio behind his back and spoke over my shoulder to Benny Isaacson. "Can you believe Bookworm spends all her time reading this Poe guy and cheering the Yankees? We play our balls off over at St.

James but she don't come to watch no more."

Mel Allan was muffled behind Joey's back. I reached up, smacked Joey's arm and demanded my radio. He slammed the book I was holding. It wobbled and Benny snatched it. I stamped my foot.

"Give me my book and my radio or I'll tell your mothers." A childish threat left over from some time around fifth grade.

"Tell our mothers? What a' you? A baby?" His eyes swept from my knees to my shoulders and down again. "Hmmm. Some baby. Benny, let's see the book." Benny passed *The Letters of Edgar Allan Poe* over my head to Joey.

"Bookworm. Bookworm." Joey shook his head at me. "Bad enough you read his stories and poems. Can't a guy have any privacy? You gotta read his letters, too?

"Just because this old house is on our turf, don't mean you gotta be reading everything about the guy." He waved the book in my face. I reached and almost had it but Joey took a step back and threw the book over my head to Benny. Unless I wanted to be "monkey in the middle" until their arms fell off, there was no point jumping for it.

"What a ya think, Benny? What a ya think about a girl who reads Poe and roots for Maris?"

Benny walked around from behind me and handed Joey the book. He draped one hand on Joey's shoulder, rubbed the other across his own rust-colored flattop, and offered me an insolent grin. "You'd do a lot better with me and Joey 'stead a mooning over those two guys. One's dead. The other's old."

Joey gyrated his hips like Elvis Presley. "We could show you some real boss action." He poked an elbow in Benny's side while they slobbered like dogs eyeing a porterhouse steak.

I was doing my best to hold back tears when Nana Ellison came along, dragging her shopping cart from the Bohack on Jerome Avenue. She had a small hunch in her back, and pulling the cart seemed painful for her. She was ancient, with leathery skin and arthritic knuckles on deeply freckled hands. Nana lived on the first floor of our building, and was always ready to hand out cookies and lemonade. She stopped when she saw us.

"Nice. Out in the sunshine. Nice. Joey, what book you got there?"

"It's mine." I reached out both hands. Joey surrendered the book and the radio. I shut off the ball game and showed the book to Nana Ellison. "See, it's Poe's letters. I bet he wrote some of 'em when he lived right here."

Nana glanced at the cottage and nodded. "Nice. Good book to read."

"That's what I told her." Joey threw me a smirk. "Can me and Benny help you with the groceries?"

We all walked home together, Joey pulling Nana's cart. She put her arm around me and leaned heavily on my shoulders while telling us how lucky we were to have the house of a world-famous writer in our neighborhood. And, by the way, did we know that Jack Dempsey, the world famous boxer, used to live on the other side of 198th Street?

At Nana's front door, Joey and Benny dragged the shopping cart into her kitchen and hung around waiting for cookies and a tip.

I quickly said my good-byes and walked up the stairs. I was just past the second floor when I stopped and turned to look at the door of apartment 2D. Joey's door. I put my book and radio on the fourth step and picked up an imaginary baseball bat. It was a long, sleek Hillerich and Bradsby. I pictured Joey opening his door, coming into the hallway, walking toward me. In my hands I had Roger Maris's bat, and I swung it at Joey Naclerio's head. Home run! Joey crumpled and sprawled on the dingy white tile, blood puddling around his head and spattering the door of apartment 2C. That's all it took to get rid of Joey Naclerio. This was my fantasy, not some horror story written by Poe, so murdering Joey didn't touch my conscience or cause me one bit of regret.

I picked up my book and my radio and climbed the last flight of stairs.

And so my days went—school, chores, reading Edgar Allan Poe, rooting for Roger Maris, and avoiding Joey Naclerio.

On the last Tuesday night in September, my family gathered around the television set. The season was close to over, with only a few games left. Roger Maris had fifty-nine home runs. He needed just one more to tie Babe Ruth's record. In the first inning we were jumping and squealing the instant Roger's bat hit the ball. My brother threw his fielder's glove up in the air. My father banged on the arm of his chair yelling, "Go! Go! Go!"

It was only a single.

The Yankee at-bat in the second inning wasn't important to me; Maris wasn't up. But he was number three in the lineup in the bottom of the third. The lead batter was Billy Gardner, an infielder the Yankees had picked up from the Twins a few months earlier. As soon as Gardner stepped into the batter's box, my father and brother started yelling. "Close your strike zone. Close it! Crouch a little more."

My mother asked what they were shouting about. My father posed my brother in a batter's stance with his strike zone, armpits to knees, small as he could make it and still have good balance for a power swing. Sure enough, Gardner struck out.

The next batter was Tony Kubek, a shortstop who, just this summer, had made his third trip to the All Stars. Within a swing or two, Kubek popped to center. Out.

There must have been twenty thousand fans in Yankee Stadium that night and every one of them went wild when Roger Maris stepped from the dugout. Then, silence. No one so much as cracked open a peanut shell. Maris swung. He connected. Whump! Roger Maris tied Babe Ruth's record for sixty home runs in one season. That record was as old as my mother, and she was born in 1927.

The next day my mother sent me to the hardware store for

mousetraps. Most days the owner, Mr. Scagnelli, would ask about the family, especially Grandma Emma, who he'd known in the old country. This time all he said was, "So, you think Roger Maris'll do it?"

On my way home I met Nana Ellison in our courtyard. She sat in a beach chair taking some sun.

"Feels good on my arthritis. I was going to Poe Park, but my knees are so bad. This is better. Nice." She patted the silver arm of her chair. "Did you hear what happened last night? Not nice. Somebody, must be kids, threw rocks at Poe Cottage. I ask you, who would do that? It's the pride of the neighborhood, that cottage. Who would throw rocks? Break windows?"

I knew who. If it wasn't Joey and Benny, it was Joey and somebody. Too bad my daydream wasn't real. I wished I had beat Joey to death with Roger Maris's bat.

I went to the library late on Saturday, just before closing at eight p.m., to pick up a book I'd reserved.

On my way home, I walked through Poe Park, entering near the bandstand and crossing the large open space around it. On summer nights, musicians dragged their instruments up a makeshift ramp and into the bandstand. They played lots of music left over from the forties and fifties. Not much rock and roll. Still, it was free and the whole neighborhood turned out to dance. Next summer I'd be sixteen, old enough to go to the dances. I wondered if a nice boy, a boy with good manners, would ask me to dance.

I followed the pathway to the front gate of Poe Cottage, where I saw a small sheet of plywood tacked over the lower pane of a side window. There was a new announcement on the bulletin board. I could read well enough by the street light dappling through the thinning leaves of an old tree. A lecture—Poe's Influence on the Modern Mystery—next Saturday at the Bronx Historical Society up on Bainbridge Avenue. I started home, wondering idly if my mother would let me travel that far by myself.

I walked out of the park and crossed to the top of the Kingsbridge Road underpass. Joey Naclerio was sitting on the guard wall there, a cigarette dangling from his lips. He took a pull on the smoke and jumped off the wall. "Hey, Bookworm, walk you home?"

Two younger kids on wide wooden scooters came tearing directly at me. I sidestepped. Joey took that as a yes and reached for my hand. I yanked it away. The scooter kids flew past us and disappeared into the park. I stepped back, but Joey moved with me.

"Why would I walk with anyone who threw rocks at Poe Cottage?" I waggled my finger at him. "Do you think I don't know what you did?"

He grabbed my finger and pulled me closer. As I jerked away, he put one arm around my waist. I pushed at him with both hands, dropping the library book that was tucked under my arm. Joey picked it up.

"Let's just see what this is. Oh, Bookworm, I should a known. *The Complete Works of Edgar Allan Poe.* This fat book looks about a hun'red years old. Don't tell me you're gonna read all this crap. Look at the print. It's tiny." He pulled himself back up on the wall and held the book high over his head.

"Give it here," I fumed. "Be careful. That's a library book. Don't wreck it." Those words sealed my fate and Joey's too. He leaned out and held the book over the drop to Kingsbridge Road. It must have been ninety feet or more to the tunnel entrance below. I reached for the book and my right hip pressed against his leg.

"Uh, huh, Bookworm, keep rubbing up against me like that and you'll get your book back." I jumped as if I'd leaned into burning coals.

Joey laughed. He threw his cigarette butt down to the underpass and watched it fade from view. "Man, that sure is a long way down. Half the pages of this old book'll be flying around like snowflakes way before the book hits the ground. Come're. Lean against me again."

I stood mute. Joey grabbed my arm with his free hand, "Come on, or…" He stretched the arm holding the book just a little further over the drop. I moved in and let my hip brush the side of his leg.

"Move over. Stand in front of me."

I slid a few inches to my right and he pulled me into him. His knees were firmly against my stomach and his shins pressed along my thighs. He hooked his ankles around my knees. "That's a good girl." His voice went all husky. "What else would you do for this book?"

I knew I'd lost, but I tried again. Tears streaming down my face, I begged, "Joey, just give me the book."

"You want your book, you let me cop a feel."

I tried to step back, but his ankles were firmly locked behind my knees. I looked around. The street was deserted.

"Come on. What's the big deal? You let me touch you. I give you the book."

Crying harder now, I gave an almost imperceptible nod. He continued to dangle the book above the underpass with his right hand and reached under my sweater with his left. I arched back.

"Put the book on the wall and you can touch them both, but only 'till I count to ten."

"Make it twenty and count slow."

"One…two…"

His hands moved under my sweater and started pulling at my bra.

I reached behind and unhooked it. He sighed, closed his eyes, and began to circle my breasts with his fingers while pressing his palms against them. When I felt his ankles relax, I picked up the book and whacked him in the head with all my strength and all eight hundred pages of Edgar Allan Poe. He lost his balance and he swayed. His hands were no longer under my sweater, but instead of grabbing the wall, he reached for my face, pulling me in for a disgusting kiss. I slid one hand across his crotch. He was as hard as the rocks he had thrown at Poe Cottage.

That was it? He tormented me so he could feel like that?

"No more," I whispered.

His slimy tongue grazed my lips.

"No more being afraid."

I bit his tongue.

His head jerked back. His eyes flew open.

"No more being afraid to climb the staircase." Now I was shouting.

I spit in his face.

His lips tightened and went white. He grabbed my shoulders with both hands. I could feel his fury, but it was no match for my own.

At the top of my lungs, I screamed.

"No more being afraid to climb the staircase to my own house."

I shoved *The Complete Works of Edgar Allan Poe* into the middle of Joey Naclerio's strike zone, every ounce of my body weight pushing the book. Pushing him. He fell back, rolled off the wall, and spun down to the underpass. I hugged Poe to my chest and ran so fast that I was on the other side of the street before Joey screamed. Horns blared. Brakes squealed. A sickening thud.

I might hear that scream and that thud in my head for weeks or months or even years, but I knew I would never hear Joey Naclerio's tell-tale heart.

I ran home, but I walked slowly up the stairs.

The next day the *Journal-American* carried the story of Joey Naclerio's death with the Fordham Baldies angle. That same afternoon, in the very last game of the season, Roger Maris hit his sixty-first home run shattering Babe Ruth's record and took a victory trot around the bases to a standing ovation from thousands of adoring fans. Roger Maris slammed into the history books even as Joey Naclerio faded into yesterday's news.

A VOICE TO REMEMBER
by Margaret Mendel

Arlene no longer lives in our apartment building, as of this morning. And you wouldn't exactly say she moved out. Our nemesis of so many years went feet first and in a body bag.

During the time I watched the medical examiner shove the gurney laden with Arlene's body into his waiting vehicle, I didn't hear even a single neighbor say something nice about her. No one in the building seemed surprised that anything like this could have happened to her, either. She'd lived in our building for nearly a decade, and in that time she'd developed quite a reputation. She wasn't unfriendly or hard to get to know—quite the contrary—everyone had gotten to know her all too well, and I don't think anyone was sorry to be rid of her.

Our building in the Bronx, dinky by New York standards, is a narrow, four-story walk-up with two apartments on each floor. My apartment shared a wall with Arlene's kitchen, and I heard everything that went on in there.

I've lived in this apartment for over forty-five years. My husband, George, may he rest in peace, and I moved into the building when we were first married. We raised our son, George Jr., in this apartment, and we never had trouble with any of the other tenants until Arlene and her husband, Butch, moved next door.

Every evening, it never failed, as soon as Butch walked in the door, Arlene and he would start their bickering and fighting. Some nights, their disagreements would escalate to such a level that none of the tenants in the apartment house could keep their minds on the TV. If my windows were open, the two of them sounded as if they were in the same room with me. I'd slam the windowpane shut and I could still hear Arlene carrying on.

Arlene did the majority of the shouting, and she not only screamed at Butch, she hollered at her children, too. She worked late several nights a week, and when she came home in the evening, she'd shout at her son and daughter the same way she yelled at their father. Poor kids, they never did anything right.

We complained to the super about the noise, but if he spoke to Arlene and Butch about it, they didn't reform.

Arlene called her husband every name in the book, and we'd have to listen to her ugly swearing. Some nights she'd even throw things at him. I telephoned 911 on them once, but that didn't change anything, either.

On some evenings, and I suspect those were the nights when Arlene came home especially late from work, our apartment building would be as quiet as a church. That's the way it used to be, before Arlene and Butch moved in. Back then in the evening we could relax, hear ourselves think, and eat our dinner in peace. But with them in the building we'd first be lulled into a false sense of calm. Then she'd come home and shatter the silence with her irrational ranting.

Butch never said much, and I rarely heard him raise his voice to his wife. On the other hand, Arlene, a skinny, short woman with snakelike muscles that crawled up her bones, could make more noise than any woman I'd ever heard. She frightened me. I never spoke to her when I saw her on the street or in the hallway of our building; I wanted nothing to do with her. But George had talked to Butch a couple of times. He said that the man seemed like an okay kind of guy, and for the life of him he couldn't figure out why Butch stayed married to such a snarling woman.

After George passed away last year, Butch came by with a bakery cake and gave his condolences. He said the cake was from his family. Arlene never showed her face at my door—but you'd have thought that she'd have cut out the hollering during my mourning. No, and she just kept on spewing out her curses. Georgie, my son, said that I should call 911 on them every night. Maybe I should have, but I didn't.

At long last, this unpleasant repetitive family performance came to a climax two months ago when Arlene sent her husband packing. That finale to the marriage didn't surprise anyone. They'd been fighting for years, but the drama leading up to his moving out, that was pretty bad. She'd begun to scream and holler at Butch even more than usual, using profanity quite unlike the language used by the other ladies who lived in our building. I would have never said anything like this to George, no matter how angry I was at him.

The night I heard Arlene scream at Butch to get out was a beautiful evening, so I had my windows open. George and I used to sit by the window on nights like these and just enjoy the freshness of the air. I loved those evenings George and I had spent together. But on this particular night I sat in the living room watching one of my favorite TV programs when I heard Butch pleading, "Please. Let me stay."

Arlene shouted, "No!" I believe that at one point I heard him sobbing, too.

The next day I caught a glimpse of Butch leaving the house with a single suitcase. Later, I saw him come back for a few other items.

One of our tenants, Marcie, had grown up in a housing project with Arlene. Marcie said Arlene had been the leader of a wild band of girls back then, and Marcie told stories about how our noisy neighbor beat up everyone.

I could see Arlene as an angry adolescent, slapping the head of a little boy, grabbing the neck of his coat, and knocking him to the ground where her gang could pummel him even more. And I could see her kicking and punching a bigger boy, too.

Marcie had attempted to rationalize Arlene's behavior by telling us that Arlene's father had been an alcoholic. "I know for a fact," Marcie said, "he beat on his wife and Arlene and her sisters something fierce.

I didn't care about Arlene's troubled childhood, and after George passed away all I wanted was peace and quiet.

One night, after Butch had moved out, I heard Arlene shout at her daughter, the oldest, who attended high school, "If you don't like the way I run the house, go live with your father. Life would be better without having to clean up after you, anyway." A week or so later, I realized I wasn't seeing the daughter around anymore.

That left Arlene alone with the son, a whiny, very thin, nervous kid about ten years old. Like his father, this son never hollered back at Arlene. However, the boy had inherited his mother's vocal ability and could project his voice out into the building as if he'd gotten hold of a megaphone. We heard his pathetic whining as his mother berated him and called him every name in the book simply because he hadn't finished his schoolwork by the time she arrived home.

Not too long after that, while I folded my clean clothing in the laundry room, I happened to overhear the woman from 1W talking to the woman from 3R.

"My cousin's a bum," the woman who lived in 1W said, "a real good-for-nothing drifter who can't hold down a job. But he's a handsome devil, and can always find some women to support him. Well..." the neighbor continued, and now she spoke in a softer conspiratorial tone, casting quick looks in my direction. "He helped Arlene fix a flat tire one day and the next thing you know, Butch is kicked out into the street and my cousin has moved in."

So that's who the guy was. I'd seen Arlene hanging out with a big, handsome man in the last couple of months, but I hadn't known he was related to someone in our building. All I really cared about was that, except for shouting at her son, the all-night fighting between Arlene and Butch had stopped.

However, the quiet hadn't lasted very long.

As I eavesdropped on my neighbors' conversation in the

laundry room, the pieces all began to fall into place. One morning, some time after Butch had moved out of the house, I'd heard Arlene shouting, "You hurt me, used me, and played with my emotions."

Oh, my, and then did she fling some fancy profanity at whoever she'd been raking over the coals. I suspected now that I'd overheard the breakup of Arlene and this neighbor's cousin. From what I could hear, the new man in Arlene's life had turned out to be a bedroom hopper, and he'd been pressing the sheets with another woman down the block.

By comparison, after the ruckus with this neighbor's cousin, who moved away, life in our apartment building became pretty quiet. Arlene continued to give it to her whiny son, but those dressing downs were nothing like the hollering she'd done at the men in her life.

Then this morning, long before the sun came up, a nasty-sounding row broke out, and I was awakened out of a peaceful sleep. Something crashed against the wall. Arlene called out many of her choice curses, and her voice echoed through the halls of the building as if someone had turned on a loud-speaker system. I got out of bed, wondering if we'd ever have peace as long as Arlene lived among us.

I put on my bathrobe and, just when I began to look for the super's telephone number, the sound of gunfire cracked throughout the building. I heard a terrible scream, and a chill scraped down my back as if the devil himself had paid me a visit. I knew then that something horrible had happened to Arlene. I grabbed the phone and called 911.

Within minutes of the gunshot, police cars pulled up to our building, their sirens and the flashing of their lights breaking the calm of the early morning hour. The one thing about a small building is that it certainly doesn't take long for everyone to come out into the hallway. As the officers rushed up the stairs, the tenants had all crowded along the banisters, dumbly wondering what they would see.

Terrible, terrible, terrible. That's all I can say. I'll never forget it as long as I live.

When the officers arrived on my floor, I pointed them to Arlene's apartment.

They knocked on the door, called to anyone who might be in there, and pulled out their guns. Then they opened the door, and from where I stood in the hallway, I could see the silhouette of a man sitting on the recliner in front of the television. When the door was opened, the man switched on the floor lamp beside the chair and turned his head to the entranceway. From the look on his face, I half expected him to say, "Yes? Can I help you?"

But, then, Butch looked down at his wife sprawled on the floor beside him, her white satin nightgown soaked in the dull crimson of her own blood. The officers stepped into the apartment and closed the door.

So, now Arlene is gone. She never did like her apartment anyway. She complained that she didn't have enough light for her plants, that the rooms were too small, and that the kitchen was far too old-fashioned for her taste.

She'd given her neighbors plenty to talk about, and now she no longer remained among us.

Years ago, George and I had talked about telling Arlene that everyone in the building could hear what she said during her arguments. I wondered if knowing we all were listening would have mattered to her. Would she have changed her ways? I doubt it; I'm sure she already knew. She just didn't care.

The neighbors from upstairs and from the downstairs apartments had all gathered on my landing. "What happen? What happened? What happened?" they all chattered on. I said nothing. The image of Arlene on the floor crowded my senses.

I went into my place and closed the door, then opened the window. The sun was just coming up. A garbage truck stood outside our building, the gears of the lifting device making a grinding noise as the men threw large bags of trash into the gaping, waiting, compacting unit.

Screeching brakes from a nearby collision sounded up the street. Teenagers hollered back and forth to each other as they made their way to the high school located several blocks away.

These were the noises of morning on my block. But today certain sounds wouldn't be heard. I wouldn't hear Arlene screaming at her son that he'd be late for school if he didn't get his ass in motion. Arlene wouldn't bang her son's textbooks down on the table and shout that he'd better get his schoolwork done before she arrived home from work tonight.

I stood at my open window for a while. Several tenants had gathered outside our building, one still in her bathrobe and slippers. The sun brought more and more light into the day, as I observed the police taking Butch away, his hands cuffed together behind his back. His removal seemed such a frighteningly silent act.

I fixed myself a cup of tea and sat in the living room watching a shadow creep across the floor before the sun moved behind the building on the other side of the street, a noontime ritual.

I heard people coming and going next door and voices calling back and forth. I suspected detectives conducting their investigation made the sounds.

I remembered one evening Arlene had made such a racket that I knocked on the wall. Someone had banged back abruptly, making far more noise than the paltry rapping of my knuckles. I never tried that tactic again.

My cup of tea cooled. The sounds outside my window jumbled together and no longer made sense. I heard someone slam shut the door to Arlene's apartment, but inside my living room there was nothing to hear. I was alone.

Oh, God, I was all too alone.

BROOKLYN

OUT IN THE COLD
by Meredith Cole

"Open up," Mrs. Zablonsky shouted, pounding hard on Lydia McKenzie's door. "There's a body in the backyard!" Lydia opened one eye to check her clock. Only 8:27. She wished her neighbor could manage to have her crises after ten a.m. on a Saturday. But one thing Lydia knew for certain: Mrs. Zablonsky was not going to give up anytime soon.

Lydia grabbed a red silk kimono, slipped on a pair of black embroidered bedroom slippers, and opened her apartment door with a yawn. "Do you know what time it is?"

Mrs. Zablonsky ignored the question, crossing her arms in front of her "I ♥NY" shirt. Sweatpants and bunny slippers completed her outfit. "You sleep with ear plugs or something?"

"Now that's an idea." Lydia never liked the feel of them, but in her neighborhood they were certainly a temptation. They say New York is the city that never sleeps, but across the river from Manhattan, in Williamsburg Brooklyn where Lydia lived, some residents attempted to sleep while others blasted their music, drove their motorcycles with a roar, and circled overhead in their helicopters. The neighborhood was sleepier and slower than Manhattan, but quiet it certainly was not.

"There's a body out there, I'm telling you."

Lydia's interest, despite her fatigue, was piqued. "You called the police?"

Mrs. Zablonsky shook her head. Lydia knew her neighbor had a distrust of institutions in general, but the police in particular.

"I thought you might know what to do, seeing as you're a private eye and all."

Lydia was not actually a private detective. She was an art photographer who specialized in shooting recreated crime scenes in a film noir style. Her photography didn't pay the bills, however, and she had taken a job as an administrative assistant to the D'Angelo brothers, who were private detectives.

"Show me where it is."

Mrs. Zablonsky led Lydia to the kitchen window, and together they peered through the bars down into the courtyard below.

The backyard was full of garbage, broken bikes, and abandoned car parts, but Lydia obediently squinted in the direction Mrs. Zablonsky pointed. "It looks like a pile of rags to me. Are you sure someone didn't drop clothes off the line?"

"It's a body plain as day," Mrs. Zablonsky said indignantly. "I'm not blind."

Lydia wasn't sure how well Mrs. Zablonsky could see, but she thought it would be impolite to disagree. "I guess we'd better go down and take a look."

The temperature last night had been in the single digits so Lydia wasn't overly thrilled to leave her warm apartment. She retired to her bedroom and put on long johns, suede pants, a shirt, a wool sweater, a down coat, and warm furry boots before she even would put a toe outside. Although her living room had become a large walk-in closet to house her vintage clothes obsession, today she was interested only in staying warm.

She met Mrs. Zablonsky on the landing and they grimly walked down the stairs together to the basement, the only access to the courtyard. The cellar felt colder and damper than the hall, and Lydia began to regret not putting on more layers. They walked past the super's empty beer bottle collection and a large number of broken radiators and appliances, and opened the door to the courtyard.

The air outside was so cold it stung Lydia's face and made her insides go numb. She took a deep breath. A big mistake: Her lungs instantly felt frozen solid. Lydia put down her head and hurried across the courtyard to the place Mrs. Zablonsky had indicated. At first the body did look like a pile of rags, but then Lydia spotted the arm sticking out. Pale with dirty broken fingernails, the hand looked as if all the blood had been sucked from the flesh. She knew without a doubt he was dead and that she shouldn't touch him, but she was unable to resist lifting up a corner of his sheepskin coat to look at him. His face, hauntingly familiar, showed peaceful acceptance. After years of being homeless, Old Bill had gone gently into that good night.

Mrs. Zablonsky watched in horror as Lydia replaced the coat carefully over Old Bill's face. "Old Bill! What should we do?"

"Now we call the police," Lydia told her and whipped out her cellphone to do just that. She suspected that the local cops would treat it as another ho-hum case of a homeless man sleeping off drink or drugs in the cold who had succumbed to the elements, so she resolved to stick around and make sure Old Bill was treated with dignity and respect. In the hustle and bustle of New York, Old Bill had always taken the time to greet everyone cheerily, not because he wanted a handout, but because he sincerely wanted everyone to be happy. Lydia had encountered and spoken with him more than she did her own friends, and yet she didn't know much about where he'd come from or how he'd come to be homeless.

After Lydia hung up the phone with the dispatcher, she looked around with curiosity. The courtyard was completely fenced in, and she'd thought it was only accessible through their basement. "How do you think he got in here?"

Mrs. Zablonsky shrugged. "There's a hole in the fence there," she pointed out. "I told the super about it, but he ignored me."

Lydia walked over and inspected the jagged hole in the fence. It looked just big enough for a man to slip through. "Did you hear anything last night?" Perhaps to make up for her poor eyesight, Mrs. Zablonsky's hearing was uncommonly sharp. She was always complaining about the neighbors being noisy.

"I heard someone banging around about midnight, but I thought it was a stray. I got up and made sure the bars on my window were locked and went back to sleep."

Old Bill must have come in around midnight, but why would he have chosen to sleep in the courtyard? Maybe he thought he could find a way into the cellar. Lydia thought it made no sense, though. The last she knew, Old Bill always had a place to sleep at Dave's Coffee Shop. He did odd jobs for Dave, and slept in the back as an unofficial security guard. She wondered if the two had some sort of fight that forced Bill out on one of the coldest nights of the year.

"You bought a lottery ticket lately you forgot about?"

"Me? Not that I remember."

"They're still waiting for someone to claim a hundred million." Frankie D'Angelo, one-half of D'Angelo Private Investigations, was doing what he did every morning—reading the paper, and devouring his mother's pastries. Lydia was at her desk trying to ignore her boss and get some work done.

Frankie suddenly whistled and dropped his chair down from its tilted position. "What do you know? Old Bill died Friday night."

Curious to see how the paper had written it up, Lydia looked over his shoulder at the headline, which predictably read: "Homeless Man Freezes to Death." She sat back down, not feeling like volunteering that she had been the one to find Old Bill. After seeing her crime scene photographs, the D'Angelos already thought she was morbid enough.

"I'm taking an early lunch." Lydia got up and grabbed her black wool cape and giant Russian fur hat off the coat rack. They were two of those rare pieces of clothing that are both practical and glamorous, and they not only kept her warm but they made her feel like Anna Karenina.

Frankie waved to her absently, absorbed by the sports page.

If his brother, Leo, had been there, he would have looked pointedly at the clock, but he was out on a case. And Lydia wanted to find out if Dave knew anything about Old Bill.

In warmer weather than today, Lydia got around Williamsburg on an old black Schwinn. She hated rubbing against the rest of humanity on the subway, and her limited budget didn't allow for taxis. In the winter, she was forced underground a lot, but she also ended up doing a lot of walking. Her neighborhood was rapidly changing, and so there was always something new to see on her walks. It was evolving from a Puerto Rican, Hasidic, Polish, Sicilian neighborhood with a few artists thrown into the mix, to one that was dominated by the affluent young people with large trust funds who wanted to live somewhere cool. Unfortunately, the new stores and residents made the cost of living in the neighborhood more expensive.

After a brisk walk under the elevated highway eyesore called the BQE, short for the Brooklyn Queens Expressway, Lydia arrived at Dave's Coffee Shop on Bedford Avenue. Located on Williamsburg's main drag, Dave's was a convenient spot for commuters to pop in for a cup of coffee on their way to the train. Dave's was an older business that had made the transition in catering to the newer residents by updating the menu from plain coffee to cappuccinos, while offering soymilk, vegan muffins, and smoothies. Dave's still retained its original pink and green interior, though, and had yellowing photographs of its clientele lining the walls. This was the kind of place where the wait staff never forgot a face or an order.

Dave spotted Lydia and immediately began to make her a cappuccino. Lydia wouldn't dream of ordering anything else there, especially since he was so proud of remembering what she liked. When he brought it to the counter, she could see that he looked tired and worried.

"I'm so sorry about Old Bill," she said.

Dave took her money and began to count out her change. "I don't understand it. He slept in the back of the store usually. He only had to ask."

"I wanted you to know that I was the one who found him. He looked as if he just lay down and fell asleep."

Dave nodded. "I'm glad someone who knew him found him. He wasn't like most of the homeless guys. He didn't drink or do drugs, and he was always a gentleman. He just didn't like to be tied down." Dave patted a can on the counter. "We're taking up a collection for his funeral on Saturday. He's going to have a service up at the church. You should come."

Lydia stuffed a five in Old Bill's jar, and a dollar in Dave's tip glass and retreated, feeling virtuous but definitely poorer. When she opened the door, however, she nearly ran into a homeless man with a long tangled gray beard standing right outside. His dirty tennis shoes had lost their laces, and his brown pants and black coat were both far too big for him.

"Spare some change?" he sang to Lydia shaking his cup. He always sang everything.

"Sorry, I just gave it all to Old Bill's funeral."

The man shook his head. "They say it was an accident, but I know he was murdered."

Lydia stopped, curious. "What do you mean?"

"They did him in for the money, you'll see. Zack's on McGuiness, they'll tell you all about it." The man sang with a strange glint in his eye.

Lydia had to shake herself back to reality. He could be right about murder, although Lydia had seen no evidence of that, but he clearly had a few screws loose. Old Bill'd had no money for anyone to steal. Still, she was bothered by the way the homeless man had died.

She decided it was time to pay a visit to her friend, homicide detective Daniel Romero. The 90th Precinct was in a white brick building on Union Avenue, and was a place Lydia would never have dreamed of visiting until she'd made the acquaintance of the detective. She and Romero had a strange friendship. She'd helped him with some cases, and he had helped her out of some sticky situations. There was also a weird attraction going on between them that they'd mostly done a good job ignoring.

Romero was in, and he looked only slightly annoyed to see her waiting on one of the scarred wooden benches downstairs. Today, he wore a knit cotton shirt and chinos. If he hadn't been so good looking, he would have looked like a total dork. "What's the problem now?"

"Does there have to be a problem?" Lydia asked innocently.

"Most people don't come to the police station to tell us what a good job we're doing," he told her.

Deciding it was no use pretending this was a social visit, Lydia launched into her story on the way upstairs to his desk in the homicide bullpen. Only a few detectives occupied the small cubicles that stuffed the room. Perhaps this week was a slow one for murder. "Did you know Old Bill?"

"Sure. I always saw him in front of Dave's."

"I found his body."

"I'm sorry to hear that. He was in an empty lot?"

"He was in the backyard of my apartment building." Lydia shuddered again to think about Bill slowly freezing to death while she slept under a down comforter. "Are you investigating whether he was murdered?"

Romero studied her for a moment with his expressionless brown eyes. He was really good at not giving anything away, while, annoyingly, every nuance of Lydia's expression could be read by anyone. "You mean did someone force him to sleep outside and freeze to death?"

Her theory sounded preposterous when he said it that way. "Did he have any drugs in his system?"

"I don't know. His death was ruled accidental."

Lydia played with her purse strap for a moment. "Would it be possible for you to find out?"

Romero sat back in his chair with his hands behind his head.

"And if I do, will you promise not to rush into something you can't handle?"

She didn't know why she bothered with the guy. He was completely impossible. "I only thought, in the interest of truth and justice, that you might possibly want to know what really happened to him."

"Truth and justice, huh? I'll have to use that one at the next department meeting." Lydia escaped with only part of her dignity left intact. She was probably crazy to take the words of an insane homeless man to heart. She should let the bearded man's accusations go and say goodbye to Old Bill, letting him rest in peace.

Old Bill's service was held in a big brick Catholic Church in Greenpoint. Greenpoint had been a Polish community since its inception, and it continued to be a place where a recent immigrant could get by without any English at all. The waterfront was still industrial, but farther in were tree-lined streets with single-family houses and apartment buildings. Two commercial roads cut through the neighborhood containing every store you could need, from chains to local markets to ninety-nine-cent shops to electronics stores and clothing shops. Lydia took the bus up to the church, shivering every time the doors opened. She had dug up a black and gold checked kilt, a black velvet blazer, a pair of knee-high riding boots, and some furry black tights, but she was still freezing.

Old Bill had touched many people in many different communities, and Lydia was glad to see that at least a hundred had come to acknowledge him. Some artists were there to pay their respects, along with some of their Italian and Polish neighbors. A group of guys who looked as if they'd cleaned up at the shelter for the occasion shuffled in at the back. Just before the service started, Romero slipped into the pew next to Lydia. She knew he was taking her request seriously, so she rewarded him with a big smile. He simply raised an eyebrow in response.

The priest looked as if he had just graduated from the seminary. He still had a little baby fat around his cheeks, and he didn't look as though he had to shave yet. But it was obvious from his sermon that he had known Old Bill well.

"William Kolchek was a man who embraced life. He believed that every man and woman was holy and that every day brought a chance to do good. He was much beloved by all. Over five hundred dollars was collected from the community for his funeral in just twenty-four hours. We want to thank everyone for their generosity, and thank David Marchese and William's friend, Silas Lawson, for collecting the donations."

Lydia turned to look where the priest was pointing. Dave stood up and waved cheerfully, and Silas, a large man in a back pew, raised himself up about an inch and quickly sat back down. Silas had squeezed into a brown blazer made for a much smaller man, and he hunched over, hiding his weathered face from the crowd. Lydia recognized him from the neighborhood, but had never known his name. When Silas picked up beer bottles, he always pushed a large shopping cart with a Snoopy dog strapped to the front.

Lydia gratefully gulped in the fresh winter air when she stepped outside with Romero by her side. The church had been stuffy and hot, and way too close to death.

"I checked with the lab," Romero muttered near her ear. "Old Bill had a blood alcohol level of .25."

Lydia turned triumphantly to the detective. "But he didn't drink. He was an alcoholic when he was young, and he said he would never touch it again. If someone forced him to drink, wouldn't that be murder?"

"You mean if someone poured it down his throat? He didn't die of alcohol poisoning."

"No, but if the effects of alcohol suspended his good judgment, wouldn't that be a crime?"

Romero shook his head. "I think you're reaching. There's no case."

Maybe he was right, but she wanted to be sure. Old Bill had been a nice man, and it wouldn't hurt her to follow up on her one remaining lead. The crazy homeless guy had mentioned a place called Zack's on McGuiness. He'd said they knew something about Old Bill's death. McGuiness Boulevard wasn't too far away from the church, so she decided to say goodbye to Romero and stroll over to look for Zack's.

McGuiness was a busy four-lane thoroughfare connecting Brooklyn to Queens, and trucks and cars whizzed by her continuously. The wind had picked up and it found a way to sneak past every one of her layers and chill her all the way through. The sky also looked heavy and gray with the promise of snow. Not a good omen for her stroll.

When she didn't immediately see Zack's, Lydia stopped to ask a passer-by. The first person she asked shrugged, perhaps unable to speak English, but the next person, an elderly lady pushing a shopping cart, told her to continue four blocks south. The distance turned out to be closer to six blocks, but Lydia at last found what she was looking for: a tiny convenience store with a yellow awning.

Inside, a fat man wearing a Hawaiian shirt sat behind the counter, glued to Al Jazeera on TV. A few guys huddled around a small table in the back playing dominoes. Lydia walked casually through the store, pretending to look for a box of unexpired crackers but really keeping her ears open. The shelves contained a strange mix of Puerto Rican, Polish, and Arab food. She was about to emerge from the aisle and make up a question when the tinkling door indicated someone else had entered the store.

"Get out, you scum. I don't want your money here!" the proprietor yelled at the newcomer. Lydia's first instinct was to duck behind something, but curiosity drove her out of the stacks to take a peek. Puzzled, she watched as Silas Lawson shook his fist at the man behind the counter.

"They should send you all back where you came from. I got every right to spend an honest dollar like anyone!"

The proprietor turned an alarming shade of purple. "Get out! Get out, or I'll call the cops on you!"

Silas muttered a curse under his breath, glared at Lydia for witnessing his humiliation, and slammed the door with a resounding crash and tinkle of bells. Lydia wondered if she should follow Silas. She wanted to ask him about his friendship with the deceased, but she also wanted to know whether the owner of the store had known Old Bill.

Lydia walked up to the counter and put down a can of tomatoes she didn't need. "Excuse me, but is it all right if I buy something?"

"Sure, sure," the proprietor said with a wave of his hand.

Lydia put down two dollars on the counter. It was all she had left in her wallet. She gestured to the door. "What's wrong with him?"

The proprietor turned his fierce glare onto Lydia and slammed her change on the counter. He turned his back to her and began to rearrange the five-cent candies. Lydia slowly picked up the fifteen cents he'd slapped down for her. She supposed that the proprietor was either reluctant to get involved or had an irrational dislike of Silas. If she waited for him to give her an opening, she was going to be waiting all day. "I wondered if Old Bill was a customer of yours."

The owner shrugged. "Yes, he came in almost every night. Why?"

"I wondered if you could tell me what Bill bought here the night he died. He was in here, right?"

"Yes, yes. The usual stuff. I don't know."

"What did he usually get?"

The owner sniffed. "What everyone gets here. A pack of cigarettes. A candy bar. A cup of coffee. A lottery ticket. A bag of chips. I don't remember exactly."

Lydia nodded. The owner wasn't going to be any help. The store couldn't sell liquor, so she couldn't see how this was anything other than a dead end.

Lydia tried to get on with life during the next day or two. She went shopping. She went to hear her best friend, Georgia Rae, sing in a punk band. She took a few photographs, but the cold weather kept her low, and her thoughts often wandered back to Old Bill's last night. She couldn't believe he'd been so careless, or that he'd been suicidal. As a Catholic, for him, committing suicide would have meant going to hell. And she couldn't believe that he would have turned down a warm place to sleep at Dave's in favor of her back yard on such a cold night. Lydia had to have missed something.

Dodging out of work at lunchtime, she bent her head down against the cold and hurried along Bedford Avenue to get something to eat. The sidewalk was still icy, and so she had to keep her eyes on the ground to make sure she didn't slip. She almost walked right past the crazy homeless man standing on the corner and singing, "Can you spare some change?"

Lydia dug deep in her coat pocket to come up with a quarter and a nickel. She dropped it in his cup. It wouldn't get him a hotel, and it didn't do much to assuage her conscience. He smiled and nodded at her though. She was glad to see that he'd found a pair of black pants that fit a little better than his last outfit and had been given some cheerful red high-tops. She hurried on until she found herself in front of Dave's. The smell of coffee oozed out through the plate glass windows, and the thought of a nice steaming cup led her inside.

Dave nodded when he saw her come in and got busy making her cappuccino. "That was a nice service, huh?"

"I think Bill would have liked it."

"Me too." Dave handed her the cappuccino and Lydia paid for it, but lingered at the counter. Dave had known Bill well, and Lydia wondered whether he could answer any of her questions about his death.

"I was wondering what you knew about Silas Lawson."

Dave shrugged. "They were friends for years. Bill always looked out for him."

Lydia supposed that friendship was one of the few comforts that the homeless had, deprived of so many material things. "I was wondering whether Bill had relapsed on the drinking."

"No way. That man had a few vices, but drinking wasn't one of them. He lost his family, his job, and his home when he was an alcoholic, and he had sworn he would never go down that slippery slope again."

"What kind of vices?"

"Oh, you know, chocolate and lottery tickets. That kind of thing. He played the same numbers every week, and he swore that he was going to win one day."

Lydia was intrigued. "Do you know what the numbers were?"

Dave shook his head. "He never would say in case someone else decided to play them instead."

No one had mentioned previously that Old Bill had loved to play the lottery.

Lydia left Dave's in a daze, clutching her drink. She was beginning to suspect something bizarre had happened, and she needed to gather evidence before she did anything foolish. She walked down Bedford Avenue, popping into two of the nearby liquor stores. Luckily, the second one remembered a man stopping in on Friday night with a bag of coins to buy Jack Daniel's. The description they gave her of the man was detailed enough to be recognizable, and confirmed her suspicions.

Romero turned out to be hard to convince. If Silas had left an inebriated Old Bill to die in the cold, he could not be convicted of a murder. But the detective was unwilling to let her go and confront a possibly violent and insane homeless man on her own. Lydia and Romero got into his car and set out to find Silas. Without an intimate knowledge of his habits, finding him was a bit difficult. They drove up and down Bedford, Driggs, and Wythe with no luck. At last, they spotted the shopping cart with his Snoopy, parked under the elevated train near the Marcy J-line entrance. Silas was making his usual rounds through the

Dumpsters looking for bottles.

Romero pulled the car into a bus zone and got out. No meter maid would dare to give a cop a ticket for parking wherever he pleased, but Lydia was always a little annoyed to see him take advantage of that fact.

"Silas Lawson? Can we speak with you for a moment?"

Silas raised his head suspiciously from the Dumpster and stared at Romero. "I wasn't doing nothing. Just making sure the bottles get recycled, that's all."

Romero must have exuded some scent that proclaimed him to be a cop. Lydia decided she'd better intervene if they were going to get Silas to trust them and talk. "We just want to ask you about William Kolchek."

Silas came forward warily holding a couple of empty bottles. He placed them carefully in his shopping cart. "You found out what happened to him?"

Romero shook his head. "He was a good friend of yours?"

Silas nodded and swallowed hard. "Everyone always wondered why we were friends. He was always looking on the bright side, and I was never like that. But with us, it was like we never even had to talk. We just looked out for each other."

"Then why did you take his winning lottery ticket?" Lydia kept her voice calm and gentle, as if she were dealing with an easily frightened animal. Silas froze and stared at her. "I visited Zack's again and they confirmed that Bill had played the same numbers for years. They knew the winning ticket belonged to him, and although they can't prove anything, they suspect you stole it.

"Bedford Liquors remembers you coming in to buy liquor on Friday night. You got Bill drunk, took his lottery ticket, and left him to die out in the cold, didn't you?"

"It was going to be a party," Silas muttered. "He'd been saying for years that his lucky numbers were going to win, and they finally had. I bought the booze and met him outside. He told me he was going to give all the money to the shelter to help homeless guys. It didn't seem fair. I was his best friend. We'd always shared and shared alike. So I started to wonder what it would be like if I had some of that money."

Tears ran down Silas' face. "I made him drink some, and when he started drinking he couldn't stop. He passed out, and I couldn't wake him. I walked away to get help, but then I wondered what would happen if he died. No one would know who'd bought the lottery ticket. I'd be rich. And I thought about what it would be like to have anything I wanted."

Silas took out a dirty kerchief and blew his nose. "All my life I had nothing and I was treated like nothing. I just wanted to see what it would be like to be somebody for a change. But I never cashed it. I just couldn't."

Lydia watched him with a mixture of pity and horror. He appeared to be doing a good job punishing himself for what he had done. But still Old Bill had been a person and hadn't deserved to die like that.

Suddenly Silas took off and began to run up the steps to the Manhattan-bound elevated train. Without thinking, Lydia took off after him. Ignoring Romero's calls for them to stop, Lydia tried to catch up with Silas, but her furry boots weren't exactly made for sprinting, and the old man was remarkably spry.

As she reached the top of the stairs, she caught a glimpse of Silas leaping over the turnstile as if he were a teenage track star. Then she heard a train approaching the station and the man in the booth yelling at Silas to pay his fare. Romero caught up with Lydia at the top of the stairs and seized her by her arm.

"What the hell are you doing?"

"Following him." Lydia shook off his hand and fumbled in her purse for her Metrocard. Romero rolled his eyes, flashed his badge at the booth, and opened up the emergency door. As they got out onto the platform, she spotted Silas pushing and darting his way between the people standing there. Beneath the slats of the tracks, Lydia could see the traffic on the street below as she and Romero tried to move through the crowd after Silas. He was now twenty feet in front of them and not as careful as they were about avoiding people and not bumping into strollers.

The train curved like a serpent around the bend, and its head-lights gleamed like a pair of eyes. The driver honked in warning as he approached the station. Maybe he spotted the anger and confusion of the passengers on the platform.

Suddenly, the brakes shrieked as Silas left the end of the plat-form and leapt in front of the train, silhouetted for a moment against the lights, before dropping from view. At the last second, Lydia shut her eyes. Then she wished she'd thought to cover her ears as well, because the sickening thump she heard would haunt her for a long, long time to come.

The wind had picked up again. A minute later, the driver of the train staggered out onto the platform, his face gray and shocked. Cops and EMTs flooded the platform, and the passen-gers were herded to other forms of transportation.

Romero would be busy for hours sorting out the details of Silas Lawson's last moments, so Lydia walked slowly out of the station and down the stairs alone. The gray sky had the heavy look of snow, and the temperature was plummeting toward an-other record-breaking freeze. As Lydia headed home, she worried that someone without his own home to go to would be sleeping out in the cold that night.

NYPDAUGHTER
by Triss Stein

Joe had a plan for his children's lives and it didn't include following him into the police force. They were going to take their hard-earned college degrees and get jobs that were safer. And better paid. And cleaner.

The plan for his argumentative daughter Ellie was law school. Now she had just told him she'd be taking her degree in sociology straight to the police academy.

His wife said, "Somewhere up there, your parents are laughing."

"It's not the same." He said it loudly. "It is not at all the same."

"It's exactly the same. Your mother used to call me up crying every time a cop was hurt. She thought I could persuade you to give it up."

It was true, he admitted to himself. The NYPD had never been his parents' plan for him either. He was supposed to take *his* hard-earned diploma and get a job where he wore a tie every day

"Yes, but that was me," Joe said to his wife. "I could handle it. I was a big, tough guy, even if Mom couldn't see it. Street smart. It was different. She's five-foot practically nothing. I wish they would have kept the old height requirement."

"It's not different. Ellie isn't your baby, any more than you were your mother's. She can press two hundred pounds and she's got a mouth on her that'll rip off skin. She'll do fine."

"What if ...what if she gets involved with another cop? You

don't know what scum some of those guys are. Most of those guys."

That's when she started laughing at him. "You know, that's exactly what my brother said when you wanted to ask me out. 'I don't care if he's my partner, I don't want you dating a cop.'" She patted his shoulder. "Remember? It worked out okay, didn't it?"

"But…"

"And now, " she said, putting down her dish towel, "I'm leaving before I start screaming at you."

He admitted to himself at last that there was not a damn thing in the world he could do to stop this. He couldn't keep his daughter from chasing some scumbag across a roof or mouthing off to a punk who'd take offense with violence. He couldn't protect her from the temptations or the despair that sometimes hit good cops. And he couldn't stop thinking he was supposed to.

All he could do was use his many connections to watch out for her. And he could never let her know.

That was the best he could do, being a father.

Actually, my old man wasn't as good at keeping his watchfulness a secret from me as he thought. I caught on when he knew I was being transferred before I did. Then I blew my stack to my mother. I might have used the word "spying." I certainly used the word "respect," combined with "lack of."

My mom told me all about how my father felt and said I had to try and understand. So I tried. Sometimes I succeeded, and sometimes I just yelled at him.

One day, when I'd been on the job about a year, working in Prospect Heights, Brooklyn, I walked into Rivera Ace Superette, a little grocery on my beat. I was through with work, not in uniform, and I just wanted a cold soda. To tell the truth, Dad was right about just one thing: I *was* five-foot nothing, and I didn't look like a cop in my jeans and sandals and baseball cap. I looked like any kid on the street.

So there I was, rummaging around in the cooler while Mr. Rivera talked to a white guy in a sharp suit. His voice was very low, but I caught the words. "I just don't have it today. It's summer, my customers go away, and it's been a bad week. Please. I just can't." The guy never even looked my way, but Rivera was begging me with his eyes though I didn't know what he was begging for. Go away? Stay and help? Keep quiet?

I was thinking, "What the hell is this?"

The guy in the suit wasn't considering me at all. He was all business, removing his sunglasses, looking into Mr. Rivera's eyes, and tapping his rolled up newspaper on the counter. It took me a little while before I realized the paper had a metal pipe inside. Rivera kept darting his eyes down at it.

Finally the man said, "Day after tomorrow. That's it. End of story." He slammed the countertop with the newspaper, and the hidden pipe clanged against the tile. When I heard the door close, I came out from behind the shelves and said, "Mr. Rivera, what is this? Are you in some trouble?"

"Who, me? Naa. What could be wrong?"

His hands shook and his smile was as fake as the ten dollar "gold" watches people peddle on the street.

I shook my head. "I know when something isn't right. It's my job, isn't it? Should I take out my badge to remind you?"

"No, no, no. You think I don't recognize you in your street clothes?" He winked, doing a weak imitation of his usual self. "Cops sure have gotten cuter over the years. Here, honey, you take the soda, a gift from me, and I'll throw in a whole flavor pack of chips. All different kinds. A meatball sub to take home for supper, too." As he talked, he hustled me toward the door, loading me up with random extra snacks on the way.

You didn't have to be a cop to guess the problem was over some kind of payoff. Protection money? Loan sharking? I knew real banks wouldn't always lend money around here, so people in need had to get it somewhere else. Gambling? Mr. Rivera didn't seem like the Atlantic City type, but really, how could I know if he had a bad betting habit combined with worse luck?

I wanted to help. I was outraged that a thug had invaded this neighborhood I'd been assigned to protect. Besides, Mr. Rivera was a nice old man. Everyone liked him, from the cops who stopped in on patrol, to the mouthy underage kids trying to buy beer, to the old ladies who wanted a bar of soap and a half hour of conversation. That's probably why he'd managed to stay in business all these years.

The neighborhood has gone up and down a few times, I've been told, slowly dying with drugs and gangs, reviving as some of the century-old row houses were bought by stable immigrant families and then by young professionals. The area was Arab on the edges, West Indian at the core, sprinkled with Dominicans, and yuppifying on some blocks. The gangs were on their way out, but they weren't gone from everywhere.

Mr. Rivera just hung in there, adding ginger beer and hot pepper sauce and grape leaves, and lately balsamic vinegar and organic granola, to the corn flakes, Budweiser, and baby food, and he'd survived all these decades.

I made up my mind to find a kid named Omar. I'd picked him up once for minor mischief, and when I let him go with just a warning to choose his associates more carefully, he'd been grateful. Now he worked part-time for Rivera. I told my partner Jimmy what was up, and he hung back to let me talk to my own source.

I caught up with Omar a block from his school. "Let's take a walk," I said.

"Am I in some kind of trouble? 'Cause I'll tell you right now, I didn't do nothing."

"See that you keep it that way. Today, I'm only looking for some information."

"I don't rat on my friends." Tough words in a shaky voice.

"Do some of your friends need ratting on?" Omar looked shocked. "No, no, just kidding. It's Mr. Rivera I want to know about."

"Good man. Never does nothing wrong. Won't even sell

smokes without you have an ID."

"Just what I figured, but I also figure he's in some kind of trouble and he won't tell me what it is."

Omar went completely silent and looked around nervously.

"What do you know?" I asked.

"Not much. Mr. Rivera, he don't tell me nothing."

"That doesn't mean you don't see plenty. You're a smart guy. Come on, just give it up and don't waste my time."

He swallowed hard. "Okay, a couple of times, I was there stocking shelves and this kind of snaky dude comes in. White guy, silk suit, flashy rings."

"Big sunglasses? Dark hair?"

"You know him? And him and the boss have words, you know? And Mr. Rivera, I know he was scared."

"Excellent information. Thank you. Anything else?"

"I never seen him again, just those times."

I stopped right there on the street, looked him straight in the eyes as tough as I could, and said, "I'm counting on you to tell me if anything else happens, if he comes back. Anything. Are you hearing me? "

He nodded solemnly. "Mr. Rivera, he's been good to me. You want me to keep looking out for him, I'm down with it. I come to you if there's anything up?"

"Sounds like a plan."

We were almost at the playground, crowded with teens playing basketball.

"Okay, scram. You don't have to walk past your friends with me."

The day the man said he would come back, I was already there, doing a prolonged examination of the different brands of crackers in the store, purposely hanging around after my shift. The shelving kept me mostly out of sight but allowed me to see right up to the front. I was in the perfect undercover outfit, street clothes, disguised as a regular citizen.

Mr. Rivera had turned white when I walked in, but I didn't

say a word. I just picked up a plastic shopping basket and stepped to the back of the store. When the mystery man arrived, Rivera handed him an envelope. I didn't just imagine his shaking hands.

The man in the suit wrote in his little book, slammed his fist on the counter, said "Next time I won't be Mr. Nice Guy," and walked out. Because I had positioned myself where I could see him leave and get into a double-parked black car, I made it to the front of the store just in time to write down the license plate.

Mr. Rivera put his hand over mine and moaned. "No, no, no. You mustn't do that. You don't understand."

"Tell me about it." I patted his trembling hand. "I want to help. I *can* help."

He shook his head. "No, honey, you can't. And I'm not getting you involved in this. I got to lie in the bed I made."

I said, "I understand," and left. Of course that was a lie. I did *not* understand, but I was going to.

After that I decided to stop by the store more often, and Jimmy and I stayed on the lookout for that guy or that car all the time. I was alone when I did finally spot the car. I felt a petty satisfaction in writing him a parking ticket, but he caught me at it, grabbed my hand, crushed my fingers into the pen, and said, "Let it go."

I looked him straight in the dark glasses and said, "Can't do that. If you don't know it's illegal to park at a hydrant, I'd be happy to send you back to driving school, but I'm sure you do know better." I handed him the ticket.

"*You* should know better. I don't pay tickets. I don't even *get* tickets." He ripped it to confetti, threw the tiny pieces into the gutter, and gripped my arm tight enough to bruise. "Don't make this mistake again." He was in his car and peeling down the street in an instant.

Then I cursed myself for not responding faster. Preferably with violence. I knew he meant to intimidate me, but I wasn't intimidated. I was furious.

I didn't know what to do about it though. I could imagine my sergeant's face if went to him saying some jerk was being mean to me on the street. And I couldn't look up the guy's plate number on my own. It had to be part of an investigation. And there wouldn't be one, unless Rivera made a complaint or I caught the jerk at something.

I needed advice. I thought about calling the best cop I knew, but though I kept opening my cellphone, I couldn't bring myself to punch any of the numbers labeled "Dad." A call on purpose would be too much of a concession. Instead, I would cadge dinner and free laundry at the folks and kind of slip my concerns into the conversation.

There was the usual discussion about how my car was running, then the usual attempts to find out about my love life. I fended them off, also as usual. When I did bring up the Rivera situation as casually as possible over Mom's peach cobbler, Dad looked startled. He made a fast recovery, but I knew I had seen it.

"Rivera's place?" he said. "It's still there? I remember him from way back when Sandy and I were assigned to the neighborhood, a couple lifetimes ago. There was one time…" He was starting a yarn. I knew he was blowing a smoke screen. I just didn't know why.

I cut in. "Obviously it still is there. I just can't figure out what my next step should be."

Dad looked away, as if he couldn't look me in the eyes, and said, "Your next step should be stepping away."

"You're kidding."

"No, I'm not. Ellie, listen to reason for once in your hothead life. You're still new at this. You have no idea what you might be getting into. Chest deep. Scum running this kind of racket, these bullies, you have no idea what they can do." His tone rose at every word. I forgot, for a while, that his voice had started with a tremor.

"I'm not new anymore." I could feel myself turning red. "And

I'm not a hothead, either. I sure didn't battle expressway traffic all the way out here to be insulted like this." Where was Mom when I needed her? Down in the basement with my laundry, I'd bet.

"Honey, I'm just looking after you. Hand it over to the big boys. This is quicksand…"

"Dammit, Dad, I'm a cop. Get it? COP. I can put a six foot drunk in cuffs!" I stood up ready to stalk out. "If you won't help me, I'll handle it myself!" Then I did stalk out, so angry I left my laundry behind.

I would go talk to the man I used to call Uncle Sandy. He wasn't my uncle, but my Dad's old friend, one of the guys in the photo on Dad's dresser, clowning for the camera the day they'd graduated from the academy. My first shift on the job Sandy'd called to kid me about how long a Barbie doll from the neat, green suburbs would last here on the mean streets of Brooklyn. "Just watch me" was all I answered.

When I phoned him, he said "Advice? I'd be flattered. Sure, honey, meet me when you get off today. Bridge Inn on Flatbush. You know it? Couple blocks from the Brooklyn Bridge approach? We can grab a beer before we head home."

Why did everyone call me "honey"? I wondered. I bet they wouldn't if I was five ten and had big biceps.

The bar was dark and cool and almost empty in the late afternoon. Sandy looked older than I remembered but he still had that full head of gray hair my bald father envied.

Sandy nodded as I described the situation, and he said, "You did right. Something sounds dirty there. You got the plate number? Good girl! Give it here and I'll follow up. He didn't look like a gang banger, right? More mature guy? We both know what it sounds like, but a hunch ain't evidence. I'll look around in the neighborhood myself, ask a few questions, talk to my friends in Organized Crime." He could see me hesitate. "What's wrong?"

"I feel kind of like I found this, so I want to see it through. You know?"

"Sure I know. But you can't investigate. You don't have the

rank, you're in uniform, you're going to attract too much attention."

He put up a hand to stop my protest.

"All kinds of people will get messed up if you step into deep waters you don't understand. Good people too. Even the best people." He gave me a hard look. "Get me? Forget this now."

Then he smiled. "You're a real officer in the making, but you'd be in over your head on this. I'm just looking out for you. I've got to do that, you know. The first time I met you was a Christmas party. You were just a tiny thing in a red dress with a candy cane in your hand."

Something I did learn from my dad—if you want to get someone to talk, shut up yourself. The silence makes people nervous and they rush in to fill it up. My brother and I spilled a few guilty secrets before we caught on to that one.

He returned my blank gaze, then suddenly laughed out loud and patted my hand again. "Honey, you've got the look down perfect, but you should know you can't kid a kidder, not one who's been on the job longer than you've been alive. I'm not falling into that pit, so just trust me, and stay off it. No more parking tickets."

By then we were out in front, ready to go our separate ways. He chucked me under the chin, kissed me on the cheek, and said, "You're a good girl. You'll be a good cop too."

All the way home, I was thinking hard. I didn't remember the Christmas party, but I did remember him at barbecues on our deck, frankfurters on the grill, beer bottles in a tub of ice. I would be running in and out of the sprinkler with the other little kids, or sneaking beers behind the garage when we were older. None of those kids were his, and if he was "uncle" Sandy, I didn't remember an "aunt" Sandy to go with him. Maybe a few different women on his arm over the years, all with bright red lipstick.

Walking down Memory Lane was certainly very sweet, but I had to wonder how a middle-aged white guy in a suit, asking questions, could be less noticeable than me, in this mostly immigrant, mostly dark-skinned neighborhood. I could pass for one of the students who shared the cheap apartments, but who wouldn't make him for a cop, no matter how plain clothes he was? And all those warnings? I couldn't get rid of the hunch he was gaming me somehow, but I couldn't figure out why. I even wondered if he had talked to Dad about protecting me. I wouldn't put it past either of them.

I started to call Dad and confront him on that, but I knew my interrogation skills were not yet up to breaking him down. Oh, right, and I wasn't speaking to him anyway.

The next morning, on my way in, I stopped to get an iced tea and Mr. Rivera could barely get a paper cup off the stack. All the fingers on his right hand were bandaged and splinted.

"What happened?"

He looked wary and then smiled sheepishly. "I was moving a case of beer and I dropped it. Broke some fingers." He shrugged. "I know, I know, my wife says I'm too old for this kind of thing, but what can I do? I got to run the store."

"Geez, that must have hurt! "

"I'm taking a lot of aspirin." He winced. "It's not working as good as last time, though." He seemed to hear his own words and closed his mouth abruptly.

"Last time ? You've done this before?"

He shook his head. "Yeah, I drop things sometimes. This is hard work, this place. Sometimes I fall, I get hurt."

He shoved the tea at me, and muttered, "Got to get back to shelving."

A little chill ran down my back. I'd been taught that accident-prone is how women who are being abused describe themselves. "I ran into a door." "I fell down the stairs."

I slammed my fist on the counter. "Damn it, I know what's going on! And I talked to a family friend who's a detective and he's looking into it. We can help, you know!"

The old man had tears in his eyes. "You don't know nothing about what's going on. Now get out. I've got work to do." He went to the door, turned the sign over to say "closed," and held the door open. It was way more than a hint that I should go away.

I did, but I was going to look for Omar today. He found me first, though, before I even reported to work.

"That badass guy we talked about? He was in one more time, with someone else. And the someone else has been there a couple of times too. Just didn't notice him before." A sudden stop and a long silence, as if he was having second thoughts about his information.

"Come on, buddy. I don't have all day."

A big swallow. A look all around. A whisper. "He seemed like he could be a cop, only in regular clothes."

"What did he look like?"

"You know. A cop."

"I'm a cop, Omar. Did he look like me?"

"Hell no."

"Give, damn it."

"He was a white guy, old but not real old. Big."

"And? What else? You must have noticed something."

Omar shot me a look of disbelief. "Now why would I notice anything else? He's just some old white guy in boring clothes." He put himself to the trouble of explaining. "I noticed the other white guy cause of his flashy suit and rings."

I gave him a hostile look. He conceded.

"Oh yeah, this one was wearing a jacket. Ugly nylon hoodie kind of thing."

I thought, a jacket on a hot summer day? To hide a gun? Omar could be right about him being a cop.

Silence .

"Come on, spit it out."

"I don't really know anything else, but seemed like Mr. Rivera was more scared after."

So, the nasty guy in the big black car never paid tickets, someone had hurt Rivera, a possible cop had visited, and Rivera seemed more scared afterward. What the hell had I gotten into here?

Omar took off, and then came back for just a second. "Forgot something."

"Tell."

"He had a friend with him, one of those times, waiting out in the car. I mean the maybe cop guy."

"Yeah?"

"Well, you said you wanted to know everything so I'm telling you. " He shrugged. "I didn't get a real good look, but he was a white guy too, and maybe bald? And the car was different too. Still a boring cop car, like they always drive Fords? Ya know? No style. But this one had like three shields on it." He made a sketching gesture with his hand. "Dark red." He ran off again.

Dark red. Three shields was a Buick. I knew that right away, because it sounded like my mom's own car. The description sounded like her car, and it felt like a stomach punch, because it also meant I knew a bald cop who drives a similar one when his own is in the shop.

My dad? Involved in this, whatever it was? Officer Do It By The Book? How could that be? And I remembered the look Sandy had given me when he said good people could be messed up by my questions. What did he know?

I couldn't swallow. I couldn't seem to breathe. Jimmy joined me then, and asked what was wrong, but I couldn't, and wouldn't, tell him. I couldn't tell anyone. It was probably way past time to talk to someone above me about Mr. Rivera, but now I couldn't, not if my dad was in some kind of trouble. Even if it was a trouble he chose.

Maybe if I hadn't been so distracted, I would have wondered why Rivera's store was already closed in the early evening. Normally, he did a brisk business in late-night desperation for cigarettes, a six-pack, diapers, condoms, and lottery tickets. It wasn't until much later, when Jimmy and I were on patrol in the dead of night, that the uneasiness finally hit me.

We went back, peered into the store windows, tried the door, checked the window security gates. There was nothing, until we finally saw a thin line of light coming from the metal hatch that covered the sidewalk chute down to the basement. No window in the front, so we slipped silently around to the back.

Guns out, holding our breaths, bent low, we crept up to the ground-level basement window and lay right down on the pavement to see in. Sure enough, there was Mr. Rivera, tied in a chair, bleeding, and two men. One was the menacing man I'd seen in the store, still in dark glasses.

The other was Sandy.

I cursed under my breath, shook my head, and put my finger to my lips when Jimmy turned to me with a question on his face. He moved away from the window to call it in. Rivera shouted, "Go on an' hit me again. I don't care. I got no more. You bled me dry, you mother..." They cracked him across the jaw before he finished. Jimmy and I looked at each other and knew we had to go in right now, hoping our back-up was on the way. Jimmy kicked in the flimsy back door.

What came after was massive confusion, shouting, running, a gun being fired. More cops came in behind us. A window broke. Someone untied Rivera. Then someone hit me in the face.

Next thing I knew, I lay on the floor and a light was shining in my eyes. I heard sirens and cursing, and someone shouting that it was a mistake, didn't they know who he was? People in EMS uniforms were lifting a stretcher.

And my father was there.

"Dad?"

"Come on, kiddo." He helped me up. "I'm going run you over to the hospital. Ambulance has the other guy. They said I can take you."

"I don't need a hospital." I touched my cheek and winced. "I just need some ice."

"Yeah, well, I know you're tough but your mother would never forgive me if I didn't get you checked for a concussion."

As we drove through the empty early morning streets, I was just able to mutter, "What did I miss?"

"Not so much. Two men arrested."

My head was starting to hurt as much as my cheek, but I had to know. "Rivera?"

"Ambulance. He was hurt pretty bad but conscious. Jimmy's okay."

"What was it? Did Rivera finally say?"

"He couldn't talk much, but from the little we got, looks like some kind of protection racket. We'll be looking for more and I'm damn sure we'll find it." Then he said, "Nice work, baby girl," but he sounded grim.

My brain had finally started to work. I struggled to sit up straight. "Dad! What were you doing there? And you were there before too, weren't you? The bald man in the car like Mom's? The other guy—was that Sandy?" I felt like a dope for not guessing sooner.

During the long silence that followed, I dreaded hearing his answer, and I dreaded hearing any lies he might tell. I wished I hadn't even asked.

"You knew about that that day? I had no idea what Sandy was up to. He said he was stopping in for a candy bar." Another long silence. "I've been keeping an eye on him lately. That's why I was there tonight. I followed him because I was worried about you." Dad finally muttered, "I thought you were dating him."

Then I really sat up, astonishment overcoming pain. "What are you talking about? Have you completely lost your mind? "

"Yeah, that's what your mother said too, but just listen. Honey, he's a player. Always has been, and the older he gets, the younger the girls are. Who knows what they see in him? Besides," he said, "someone saw you." He flinched at my indignant gasp. "Outside Bridge Tavern, looking affectionate."

"You *spy* on me? Is that what you are saying?"

"No, no, it's a cop bar. Someone saw you. Spying? What do you think I am?"

I didn't have the energy to take him up on that one then and there. I would, though, sometime down the road.

"Hey, here we are." Since he'd called it in, hospital workers rushed up to the car, opened the door, eased me out into a wheelchair. "No more talk now." His relief would have been comical if I'd been in any condition to appreciate it.

We continued later, as we waited in an emergency room cubicle.

"I was only asking his advice about Rivera. And he warned me off. That lying phony. And then I didn't want you to know, when I started wondering about him. I thought you might be… that you'd be hurt." I swallowed the next words. My dad would never know I'd been wondering about him too.

We'd been protecting each other.

"That time when I told you about all this? Why did you seem so surprised?" I still had to know.

"We broke up something like this, years ago, right there, me and Sandy. " He shook his head.

"He was a great guy, Sandy, all those years, except for the women. A great cop. Who the hell did he turn into? If he needed the dough, dammit, I wish he would have come to me." My father stopped, looked away so I couldn't see his face.

Then they came to take me for x-rays. After, I slept, and they woke me up every two hours to look at my eyes and ask me my name and age. Every time, there was my dad, dozing in a dark corner of the room.

I woke up the next afternoon with a fierce headache and bruised face, and they said I could leave. Now Mom was there too, with clean clothes, make-up for the bruises, and Chinese food—and they took me home.

In the end, it was pretty much what it had seemed, a small-time punk trying to become a bigger one; a cop who was willing to help out for a piece of the action; and the small store owners, many of them immigrants, many not too sure that this wasn't the normal American way of doing business, many convinced by an officer's involvement that they had nowhere to turn. Small potatoes as crime rings go. Small, unless you were one of the victims.

Once word got out that Sandy had been arrested, a whole neighborhood of business owners came forward, ready to make statements. My partner and I couldn't buy our own hot dogs or soda or coffee on the street. We were invited to a Jamaican barbecue and a Palestinian wedding and were guaranteed a lifetime of manicures at the Korean nail salon.

Mrs. Rivera and Omar kept the little grocery going until Mr. Rivera was out of the hospital.

And I finally introduced my parents to my boyfriend. He isn't a cop but the real estate agent who found me my apartment. He wears a tie to work every day and is sure I will get my detective shield in record time.

The House at Lake Place
by Dorothy Mortman

She was very old, and her skin very wrinkled, with the look of well-worn leather. I wondered about her age, and she, peering at me through thick eyeglasses, must have read my mind. "One hundred and two come this October. Born in this house, lived in this house all my life, through eighty years of marriage."

I was doing my graduate thesis on Lady Deborah Moody, a feisty lady who'd arrived in New Amsterdam in 1643, wheedled a charter from Governor Willem Kieft for a small tract of land, and founded Gravesend Village.

Village Road, Lake Road, Gravesend Neck Road, streets laid out to her master plan remained, tucked into the Gravesend section of Brooklyn, and in the midst, the cemetery, and a few houses, even now standing, after more than three hundred fifty years.

Mrs. Hannah Hicks Platt was the local historian, still active with the Gravesend Historical Society, her memory sharp despite physical infirmities.

She stood up, slowly reaching for her cane. "Would you like some tea?

"Letita," she called, not waiting for my answer, "make us a pot of tea and some scones." She turned to me. "How can I help you?"

"I need background about the area. If you have any information on what it was like in Lady Moody's time."

"I can tell you what it was like when I was young, not too much changed from the original. The changes came after the war."

"The Korean War or Vietnam?" I questioned.

"The Second World War, honey. This was all farmland," she continued, "the streets as you see them, set out in a square, are from the original time, even the cemetery. Those buildings—" She pointed to the apartment buildings bordering Gravesend Bay. "Co-operatives, I hear. They all came after the war. And Norton's Point had a lighthouse keeper, not an automated flashing light."

I tried to get back to my point of interest. "That large house on the corner of Lake Place and Van Sicklin, is that really Lady Moody's house, and was there a Hessian soldier buried there?"

She looked straight at me, her small eyes boring into me, her mouth pursed in a thin line. I was taken aback. Was that topic forbidden territory? I sat still, not knowing how to salvage the situation. Fortunately, Letita came in with the tea and scones, setting them down on the table. As Mrs. Platt busied herself serving us the tea, she relaxed, and finally she spoke.

"That's only a rumor. No one is quite sure which of the houses was Lady Moody's, and as to the Hessian soldier..." She paused. "Well, you know Lord Howe and General Cornwallis, along with thousands of Hessian soldiers, marched through this area in the Revolutionary War. Story is Stephen Voorhies shot one stealing his cow and buried him in the cemetery, but if he's there no one has found his grave. Of course Stephan is buried in the cemetery.

"The cemetery? Is it used now?"

"Oh no, hasn't been used that I can remember. All the graves are from Colonial times.

I ventured back to dangerous waters. "And the house on Lake Place?"

For a moment she was silent. "There was a murder there, a horrible murder, but not in Colonial times, although the house dates from Colonial times."

The teacup rattled as her hand shook, and she set the cup down. She sat quietly, deep in reverie, and I dared not intrude on her memories.

I heard the grandfather clock chime, and automatically I

counted the hours. Two o'clock. She stirred then, and looked at me. "It's not from the time you are researching, but you might be interested."

She reached under the small end table to her left and pulled out a large album. Carved with great care on its wood cover was the inscription *Daril and Hannah Hicks Pratt*. Carefully, she turned the pages covered with photographs until she reached what she was looking for. "This was me at eighteen."

Centered among three very pretty girls was the young Hannah Hicks, blond hair tumbling down to her shoulders. The eyes, clear in the photograph, a bright blue. It gave me a pang to realize how beauty could be destroyed by age.

"This was Annabel," she said, as she pointed to the one on the right, "and this one"—she paused—"on the left is Lolita."

Lolita was clearly the most beautiful of the three, although tact forbade me from saying so. Beautiful raven hair offset her alabaster white skin. She reminded me of a very young Ava Gardner.

Not quite sure what to say, I reached for the insignificant. "This must have been hand painted. I don't think there was colored film that long ago."

A pigeon landed on the window sill, and Mrs. Platt rapped on the glass pane to shoo it away. I looked across to the cemetery. "Ever bother you to be so close to a cemetery?"

"At my age? I know I'll be in one soon enough."

"Never thought you might see one of those Revolutionary War soldiers rising from his grave?"

"They're as quiet as mice. Best neighbors you could have."

"Lolita? Sounds Spanish," I ventured, trying to get her back to her story.

"Italian, I think, but poor Lolita was an orphan being raised by an aunt, a cold and unfriendly woman. No wonder Lolita fell under the spell of Raymond Lansing."

"You didn't like him?"

"We didn't trust him. Actually I didn't trust him. Most of the other women were enthralled by him. Oh, he was a handsome devil all right." Was it my imagination, or did I see her blush?

The pigeon returned with a friend, or maybe its lover, but this time my hostess paid them no mind, too engrossed in her memories.

"Almost eighty years ago, seems like yesterday. He was twenty years older than Lolita, and with a great deal of money. Inherited, he said. The plans for their wedding excited the whole community. Florists, caterers, dressmakers were in a stew to prepare for the event, and to attend to the three hundred invited guests. Oh, he paid for the whole thing, of course.

"Tappan's Hotel, on Emmons Avenue, a magnificent establishment with crystal chandeliers in the grand ballroom and windows that overlooked and opened onto Sheepshead Bay. Burned down some years back, and they never rebuilt it. I was pregnant with my first, Janet, but still in the small months so I was able to fit into my ball gown."

"Was he of the neighborhood?" I interrupted.

"A distant cousin of Jane Stillwell. He stayed with her while he renovated the Van Sicklen House on Lake Place, a Georgian that was always out of step with the area. He spared no expense. Italian marble replaced the stone on the fireplace mantel. Parquet flooring in the entrance foyer, instead of plain wood."

She paused, remembering. "But the wedding," she continued, "was like a coronation of royalty. They were a magnificent couple. His looks enhanced by his full-dress evening wear, no mere tuxedo for him, and she in white brocade designed in Paris. We danced and danced, until sunrise, and then we were regaled with an elaborate breakfast."

She moved forward and banged on the window in anger, or was it pain? The startled pigeons flew off. This time I didn't imagine the tear that rolled down her cheek. Emotional wounds take a long time healing, some forever.

"That October..." She shuddered. "It was as if an evil spell descended on this place. It all began that Halloween. The desecration of the cemetery, old tombstones thrown over. We blamed that on the children, although all swore on the Bible they were innocent. It didn't help when Sam Whitehead insisted he saw a Hessian soldier come up out of a grave. Poor Sam, usually drunk—he could see a lot of things not there. And then the robberies, or is it thefts?—I never do get the words right—began. Money and jewels seemed to be the thief's penchant."

This time the pigeon, back alone, just rested for a moment on the sill and then flew off quickly. He knew he wasn't welcome here.

"In all the robberies, we never saw anybody about—but Sam, usually drunk, kept insisting he saw the soldier in the cemetery a few other times, which of course made no sense. No Hessian soldier was buried in the cemetery that we were aware of, and the stolen objects were very real, not much value to a ghost. Thankfully nobody was ever hurt. Most thefts occurred when the houses were empty."

Letita stood at the door. "Would you like fish for dinner?"

My hostess nodded in agreement and turned to me. "Would you care to stay for dinner?"

"Sorry, another time perhaps. I don't like to leave my husband to fend for himself on short notice."

I didn't wish to offend her, and fortunately, she didn't seem to be put off.

"The night before," she continued. "Lolita knocked at my door after dinner. She was clearly distraught. I barely recognized her, she was so changed. She was so thin and pale. All her beauty was drained from her."

This time Mrs. Platt cried openly, huge drops glistening on her face. "I don't know what else I could have done. I made her tea. I listened to her. 'Raymond goes out a lot,' she claimed, 'and he can be cold and cruel, like Aunt Mary.' My heart tore at her words, but I didn't know what to do.

"'Should you leave him?' I begged her, but she only shook her head and went away.

"I couldn't sleep all that night, and as soon as Daril left for work, I walked to her house. I was in my seventh month and carrying big. Walking was hard for me.

"I rang her bell but no one came to the door. Fortunately, we rarely closed our front doors in those days, and even though the robberies made us a little more cautious, her door wasn't locked. I walked in over the carefully polished floor and saw her, a bundled mass at the front of that imported staircase. I bent down and tried to lift her and saw the bulge of her eyes, the discoloration at her neck. In one last gasp, she whispered 'Hessian soldier' and died in my arms. I screamed with all my might and tore at my hair and then must have fainted.

"I awoke in my own bed, Daril, the doctor and Leona James standing over me. I could hear the rumble of voices in the living room. Poor Leona, Lolita's cleaning lady, had found us both when she arrived. Raymond was nowhere to be seen.

"Evidence pointed to Raymond being Lolita's killer, though no one could make any sense of her reference to a Hessian soldier. That night the police put out an alert for his capture, and I gave birth to Janet prematurely."

I heard the clock chime three.

"Did they catch him!" I couldn't wait for her to continue.

"No, he was never seen again."

She was composed now, the anguish released. "I have the key if you'd like to see the house."

"How come you have the key? Who owns it these days?"

"Raymond actually owed more money than he had. The house was auctioned off after Lolita was buried, and Vitagraph Studios bought it. They made some movies here and figured they might use this house as a prop for one of their films. They lost interest and tried to sell it or at least rent it, but while there were a few renters, those didn't stay long. The last one insisted the house was haunted, but considering they moved out in the middle of the night owing the butcher and the baker, and God knows who else, who can say?"

"And now?"

"They gave it to the historical society. Good way to get rid of it."

I glanced at my watch. Three-thirty. Since this was October, the sun wouldn't set before six. I'd have plenty of time to have a good look. "I'll take the key."

It was a short walk down Van Sicklen, past Village Road South and Avenue V, a total of ten minutes. Since the house was a modified Georgian, the front stoop was only three steps up to the mahogany doors. I expected to have trouble opening the doors, but they swung open easily. I guessed the society was giving the home some care. But I was only half right. The inside was covered with dust. Then I shuffled the dust at my feet enough to see the parquet flooring.

I glanced at the curved staircase ahead and paused. Mrs. Platt's voice echoed in my head, "I saw her, a huddled mass in front of the imported staircase." It was imported, all right, Italian maybe, beautiful wood banisters covered in the white of dust. Carefully, I stepped to the side, almost as if I were avoiding a body, and began to climb. A wide veranda surrounded the second floor, and brushing aside some of the dust, I could see the rich wood of the hand railing underneath.

The master bedroom faced the Atlantic Ocean, its view from the floor to ceiling windows now compromised by the apartment buildings in the distance. A large fireplace stood centered on one wall. I ran my hand over a marble mantle carved in oval fashion. The outline above it indicated that a large mirror or picture once hung there.

Through a side door was a large bathroom, fully equipped with an enclosed walk-in shower to the side of the tub. Even the handles on the doors were intricate works of beauty. Whatever else you could say about the mysterious and elusive Raymond, he had good taste.

Three other bedrooms occupied the floor, each with its own bathroom, and each only slightly smaller than the master bedroom. No wonder the movie studio saw value in this house.

I descended to the main floor and entered a large living room. Here, the fireplace encompassed almost the entire side wall with built-in bookcases on either side. The ten-foot ceiling, with windows the same height, increased the sense of space. There must have been a lake opposite the windows once, but now they faced Gravesend Neck Road to the front and Gravesend Cemetery to the side. I turned to go, but as I stood in the doorway, a ray of setting sun shot across the side of the fireplace bouncing off something that shot the ray back in my direction.

I retraced my steps and examined the side of the fireplace, but I saw nothing. Then I carefully slid my hand down the side, and my finger caught a tiny lever, no bigger than the loop on a key ring. I pressed, but nothing happened, and then I put my thumb against it and pushed hard. Noiselessly, without so much as a hum, the fireplace swung open. Beyond it loomed a black abyss.

Reaching into my purse, I grabbed the emergency searchlight I carried. The size of my thumb, it gave off a steady but narrow beam. Playing it against the bottom of the fireplace, I could see two steps with the promise of more. Logic dictated I stop right there and get help before I descended those stairs, but curiosity dulled my senses. I did one sensible thing. I used my cellphone to dial Mrs. Hicks Pratt. Letita answered. I spoke rapidly because my phone was flashing weak battery. "Tell Mrs. Pratt I'm going down a staircase behind the fireplace in the library."

"What?" she questioned. "What are you saying?" and then the phone went dead. I cursed myself for having forgotten to charge the battery last night, but pretty sure my flashlight wouldn't fail me, I proceeded slowly downward, reaching tentatively with my toe for the next step and counting as I went. Twenty steps and I was down in what looked like a wine cellar. Slowly, I played the beam of light against the brick walls. Something glistened in a corner. I edged closer and bent down. A necklace with a large stone. Might be a ruby, but it might be paste. I poked with my hand, finding more: rings, earrings, and another necklace or two, wrapped in a huge metal chain net—like medieval armor—fastened to the wall. I moved my searchlight and jumped back. Entangled in the side of the net, the arm bones half in and half out of the iron link, was a skeleton. I moved forward again, covering it fully with the light. It appeared to be wearing some form of uniform, partially shredded with age, but even to my untrained eye, not three hundred years worth.

I recoiled in horror as I realized that death had come to this poor soul slowly and unbidden. Trapped and unable to free himself, he, and I assumed it to be a he, could only hope that someone would find him and save him, but no help had come.

It was then I became aware of my own predicament. Making my way up the uneven steps, hidden in darkness, would be much more of a challenge than going down. I decided to hold the flashlight in my mouth and crawl up on my hands and knees, but I couldn't seem to gauge the next step up as I had going down. Now I did feel fear. Would I die here, starving and without water, as I waited desperately for help?

It was then, while I sobbed mutely, that I became aware of a draft coming from the far wall. Could there be another way out? Crawling over on my hands and knees, I played the searchlight toward the draft of air and voila—an opening! A tunnel! The opening wasn't very big, but big enough to get a full-sized man through, and I was a small woman. Carefully, I inched my way ahead, on hands and knees, searchlight in my mouth.

After a while, my mouth ached from the uncomfortable position, my hands were scraped raw from the rough flooring, and my claustrophobia was on the rise. I was fast approaching hysteria. Only the desperation to get out kept me moving, and then—bang, I was up against a wall. Trapped! I was terrified, and then I saw the light, a small gleam coming from above. Desperately, I reached upward and pushed. The ceiling moved slightly but held firm. This time I partially stood, using both my hands and my head to push. The wooden panel above slid away, just enough for me to work my way out.

Exhausted, I fell out onto the ground. Night had come, but

I was so glad to see the stars that I sat and cried, not realizing I was sitting on a gravestone. It took awhile to sink in that I was in the midst of the Gravesend Cemetery, that I had come up out of a grave. Well, I guess old drunken Sam hadn't been so wrong after all.

Now calm, I walked toward the front gate. Padlocked. Now what? I was never going to be able to climb over that gate. Not a soul was on the sidewalk outside. I looked across to Mrs. Pratt's house. Had Letita given her my message? Only a small lamp was lit in the front room. "Help! Help! Help, anyone," I screamed. Finally, I became more inventive. "I'm trapped. I'm dying, someone help me."

A man in the house to my right opened his window. "What's all the commotion?"

"Help me, " I wailed. "I'm trapped inside the cemetery."

By then, an anxious Letita had come out the front door and crossed the street. "Mrs. Arlen, we've been worried sick about you. Whatever are you doing in the cemetery? We've got the police out at the Lake House looking for you. You look awful. Whatever happened?"

"I think I know where Raymond Lansing is," I announced.

"Who?" she asked.

"It's okay, Mrs. Platt will know." It was as I suspected. Although it couldn't be proved by any forensic evidence, the skeleton was assumed to be that of Raymond Lansing, and the uniform, cleaned up and examined, a Hessian soldier's. Dressed as a Hessian soldier and using the cemetery as his starting base, Raymond's robberies had been easy. Anyone seeing him come up out of a grave wasn't likely to mention it, except for Sam, that is.

That was what poor Lolita meant by "Hessian soldier." She must have found out the truth and threatened to expose him, and he killed her to protect himself. It seemed like poetic justice that he'd been entrapped by his own device, or greed, if you will.

Engineers examining the tunnel, a remarkably constructed affair, they claimed, dated it to the sixteen hundreds, the date of the house. Speculation was that being near the ocean, it was used for contraband, or perhaps even runaways from the law. It might even have been used in some way during the Revolutionary War.

I had tea with Mrs. Hicks Platt a week after all the facts were known. "I'm not a vicious person," she confided in me, "but Raymond's death was well deserved. He killed a sweet trusting girl to cover his evil."

QUEENS

Murder in the Aladdin's Cave
by Lina Zeldovich

Eve entered the semidarkness of the Aladdin's Cave pulling a small, wheeled suitcase with her costume and props. Middle Eastern music set the mood, and people danced between tables and chairs, their hips rising and dropping to the beat. The dress of the diverse Astoria crowd ranged from grunge to extravagant, the women wearing everything from jeans to gowns while men wore T-shirts or jackets and ties.

"The diva is here," Roy Robson greeted her from behind the bar. He slid a martini toward his customer and, no doubt hoping for a kiss, leaned over toward Eve. Eve smiled politely and offered him her cheek.

"See that table full of loud Turks?" He pointed at the largest table in the house. "The guy's celebrating his fiftieth birthday, and they're spending money like water. Already asked me for, like, fifty singles. Make sure you shimmy around them long enough to get it all."

Ali, the second bartender, greeted Eve with a respectful head bow. As usual, he was dressed elegantly, tonight in a camel cashmere sweater.

"It's a pleasure to have you with us again, Miss Gülnar," he said in slightly accented English without stopping his mixing and shaking. A Muslim, he had never tasted alcohol, but that didn't prevent him from pouring drinks with amazing speed and precision. "Would you be dancing the Candlelight Dance tonight, and if yes, would you like me to light the *shamadan*?"

The *shamadan* was a special candelabrum for belly dancers to wear on their heads. The Candlelight Dance was Eve's specialty.

"Yes, please, and thank you," she answered.

Ali gave her another courteous bow, his kind brown eyes glowing in Aladdin's dim lights. Roy leaned over the bar again, and Eve drew back. It wasn't even ten yet, and he already smelled of beer. The rules of bartending weren't meant for Roy. In fact, no rules were meant for Roy. That was probably why women liked him so much, ignoring that he was always drunk and broke.

"Old Vasilakos is loaded with cash today," he teased with a raised eyebrow. "He asked about you, so make sure to bring it by his table too. Oh yeah, Mehmet says you're on first."

Eve barely had twenty minutes to change. She tried to push across the restaurant to the Sultan's Tent from where the dancers made their entrance, but wheeling her bag through the dancing crowd wasn't easy. Aladdin's Cave was just as cramped as most other New York restaurants. There was no real stage. The dancers shimmied in the center aisle along the tables, teasing customers by throwing veils around them and pulling them up to dance. The tight quarters helped to create the Aladdin's intimacy and charm. After two hours in the Cave, people felt they knew each other.

Avoiding a bunch of young jumping girls, Eve made a sharp turn and bumped headfirst into Alfonso.

"Hi chica," he said giving her a sultry grin as he balanced a tray full of dirty dishes. His slippery eyes ran up and down her body, and his black mustache stuck out like porcupine needles. Bumping into her probably made his day.

"Hi," Eve said dryly, dodging him. Keeping her head down, she brushed past Boris Rublev's table, avoiding his bodyguard's eyes. Rumors had Boris in the Russian mafia, and everyone walked on eggshells around him. Luckily, he liked full-figured women. Eve was happy she wasn't his type. She rushed into the tent, pushed on the door, and burst into the dressing room. A woman in harem pants and a white lace bra too small for her voluptuous breasts gasped and wrapped her arms around herself.

"Oh, Eve, you scared me!" she breathed out with relief.

"Leila! I didn't know you were in here. Why didn't you lock the door?"

"Because a screw fell out, and the stupid bolt doesn't hold. Mehmet said he'd send someone to fix it." Leila adjusted her bra and opened her arms for a hug. "I haven't seen you for ages."

Eve gave her a hug and a kiss. "I'm glad you're dancing again. I guess you're over it? I mean, over him?"

"Oh no," Leila smiled. "We're back together. We're getting married!"

"Married?" Eve was stunned. She vividly remembered Leila's hysterical crying when she found out her secret boyfriend had a bride. "Didn't he get engaged?"

"It's over," Leila declared happily. "They broke up."

"No kidding."

"He never loved her," Leila snapped. "He had to marry her for money."

"I thought you said his family wanted him to marry her."

"Yes, because she was rich. But he never loved her. He loves me! He told me so."

"So he broke the engagement?"

"No," Leila said with a catty smile. "I did. I called her and met with her and told her he had been seeing me for a while. She was so mad she broke the engagement."

"I can't believe you did that."

"Allah, what else could I do? It was my only chance. Who'd ever marry me now when I'm not a virgin? My parents would kill me if they found out. They'll be mad at me for not marrying my own kind, but it's better than never getting married at all."

Eve shook her head in sympathy, but she knew many Muslim families still had an old-fashioned view of marriage. You married your own kind and virginity was vital. Eve's parents were unique in giving her a Western upbringing. Others were not as lucky, including Ali, who resisted an arranged marriage until he was forty. Finally, he gave in to the family pressure.

"*İnşallah*—God willing—my wedding will be soon," Leila sighed. "All these years of dancing will pay off."

"So can you finally tell me who he is?" Eve asked, but Leila shook her head, choosing to remain secretive about her boyfriend. Eve suspected he was somebody who worked for the restaurant. Sometimes she thought it was Mehmet, but Mehmet couldn't have a bride. He was already married, and men didn't marry multiple wives in the States.

"He bought me an engagement gift," Leila said proudly. She took a veil out of her bag and spread it out. Two golden dancing peacocks were embroidered on the red silk. Leila did a butterfly veil flip, stretched it behind her waist and snaked her corpulent hips against the shimmering fabric in figure-eight-like moves.

"Like it?"

"It's beautiful," Eve said. "But isn't it too heavy to dance with? All those beads?"

"They're very light," Leila assured her and did a thrilling *maya* —a downward single hip sway, also in a form of a figure eight. "And what are you gonna wear tonight?"

Eve took out her costume. Just a long black skirt and a top with jingling coins, no match for Leila's extravagant golden peacocks. Eve had only one show-off item, a hand-made hip scarf with beads, coins, and Arabic embroidery that read *Salaam Alaikum*—"May peace be upon you."

"How will you find yourself a husband dressing up like that?" Leila rolled her eyes. "Have you looked in the mirror? You need kohl. You need more lipstick."

As an ancient tradition, kohl was used to darken the eye area for a more dramatic look. Although it no longer contained lead and mercury, Eve stayed away from it.

"I don't like wearing too much lipstick," she said, taking off her jeans and shirt. Mother Nature had given her shiny black hair, dazzling eyes, and silky white skin. Too much gloss or make-up made her look like a slut.

Leila rolled her eyes again. "Get ready, then. You're on first."

It was considered more honorable to dance second, but dancing after Leila was a waste of time. Her voluptuous form swept through the Cave driving men out of their minds. Eve had seen Leila stretch her gorgeous body crosswise from one table to another, her hip touching one tablecloth and her breasts quivering over the other. Eve could do a running shimmy for ten minutes without working up a sweat, but she simply didn't have Leila's flesh.

Swinging her veil, Leila warmed up by practicing rib-cage slides and chest thrusts. Suddenly, the door pushed open, and Alfonso barged in. Leila's breasts, barely covered by white lace, rooted him to the floor, eye-squared and dumbstruck. Leila screeched, threw the veil over herself, and caught the veil on the back of the chair, pulling the delicate silk.

"What the hell are you doing here?" Eve, still in her underwear, screamed.

"Mehmet say bring a screw," Alfonso mumbled, his eyes darting back and forth between the dancers' bodies. He didn't even try to avoid looking.

"Give it to me," Eve yanked the screw from his hand. "Did you bring a screwdriver?"

"Mehmet no say screwdriver." Alfonso grinned, not in any hurry to leave. "I coming back."

"Get out of here." Eve pushed him out the door. "Asshole!"

She pulled a hair clip out of her hair and used the metal part as a screwdriver. "That'll do for now."

Leila examined her veil inch by inch. "Did any beads come off? It was so expensive!"

Eve dressed in her costume and tied the scarf around her hips. She watched Leila sit in front of the mirror, take a bite of her favorite Turkish delight, and start painting her cheeks.

"I'm not dancing *Raks al Assaya* tonight," Leila said wearily.

"I'm too old for that. It's so hard to jump with all these pounds I put on thanks to my break-up."

She held out the box of Turkish delight. "You want a sugar fix?"

"No, thanks." Eve was only two years younger than Leila, but half her size. She intended to stay that way. "You gotta lose weight. You're only thirty-eight. How will you ever again dance *Raks al Assaya*?"

"*İnşallah*, I won't have to dance at all," Leila laughed. "I'll be a married woman soon. I'll stay home and wait for my husband. It'll be wonderful."

"Lock the door when I leave before some idiot barges in again." Eve covered herself with her veil and stepped out into the velvet tent. She heard the bolt click behind her. The lighted *shamadan* Ali had prepared for her stood on a tray. Eve carefully placed it on her head, framed it with her arms in a Pharaoh-like fashion and closed her eyes to summon the spirit of the dance. But, instead of the usual thrill, she had a strange feeling that somebody was watching her from behind.

"Ladies and gentlemen," she heard Mehmet announce into the mike. "The Aladdin's Cave is proud to present to you its most beautiful pearl!"

Balancing the *shamadan* on her head, Eve tried to look back, but saw only the thick black folds of the tent. The band started a *taksim*—the slow beginning of a dance without the drums, played only with violin, flute, and oude, a distant relative of a lute. Eve had no time to look around for what she sensed. She had to dance. Maybe it was just her imagination.

"Ladies and gentlemen," Mehmet shouted to the cheering crowd again. "Please put your hands together for the gorgeous and glorious Eve Gülnar!"

Eve stepped out of the tent with an elegant Persian walk. The *shamadan* candles glowed in the darkness, casting shadows on the many faces. Eve glided along oblivious to the crowd, her wrists drawing graceful circles in the air, her body swaying from side to side, carried by the music. For her, the dance wasn't an instrument of seduction, but a mystical trance.

The music changed to the old Egyptian, country-style beat. Following the rhythm, Eve started a hip-lifting walk. She reached the center of the floor and switched to the ribcage circles and undulations while slowly descending onto her knees. Her entire body snaked under the *shamadan* as if she were born without bones. Mesmerized, the crowd drank in her every move with the thirst of desert Bedouins.

Eve tilted backward slowly until her shoulders almost touched the floor. Arms spread out, she nearly lay on the parquet, but her head still held the *shamadan* upright. The crowd moaned in awe. The back dip was the culmination of the Candlelight Dance. Her body rising and falling like ocean waves, Eve returned to an upright position and slowly rose to her feet. With a toss of her head, she flipped off the *shamadan* and caught it in the air. Like a genie from a bottle, Ali emerged next to her to take the *shamadan* into his helping hands.

The band started playing the *Karshilama*, a quick, cabaret-styled Turkish favorite. Eve whirled around the floor, her veil flying after her like a golden flame. The crowd cheered, screamed, and whistled. Vasilakos tossed a bunch of singles at her, and she swept her veil over him as a thank you. She danced around the Turkish table, pausing at every chair to impress them with her hip drops and snaps, her figure eights and mayas, her snaking rib circles and taunting chest thrusts. The Turks cheered and clapped. When she wrapped her veil over the birthday boy's neck and pulled him out to dance, his friends joined him, tossing singles, fives, and tens in the air. A few Turks chased Eve, trying to tuck twenties into her hip scarf. She wanted to send a flying kiss to Roy for tipping her off about the partying Turks, but didn't see him at the bar. Holding hands, the Turks formed a circle and danced around Eve. After a few minutes, everyone in the Cave jumped and swayed, even those who had never before danced to a Middle Eastern beat.

Finally, the oude and violin broke in, and Eve hopped up on her toes, sweeping around the Cave in an extreme running shimmy. Her hips vibrated so fast the twenties the Turks had tucked into her hip scarf blew away, flying through the air. The beads and coins jiggled and quivered around her hips as if gravity no longer held them. Eve circled the floor one last time, sent good-bye kisses to the crowd, threw an obligatory smile to Boris Rublev —and disappeared into the velvet tent.

Covered head to toe by her gorgeous veil, Leila lay back in her chair. She was still dressed in her harem pants and a white bra.

"Leila!" Eve called, surprised. "You're on! Wake up! Get moving!"

Leila didn't respond. Through the transparent silk, her face appeared calm and peaceful as if she were asleep. But the delicate peacock embroidery of the scarf was ripped, and the twisted red marks on her throat didn't look like smudges of lipstick. Shocked by a sudden realization, Eve gasped, holding her hands to her throat. Her strong legs had carried her through the long dance, but now they felt soft and rubbery.

Through the thin red fabric, Eve held her henna-painted palm to Leila's neck—to feel the woman's pulse.

There was none.

"She was strangled with her own veil," Eve spoke to the officer. "The beads scratched her neck. They were all over the floor."

"Forensics will determine cause of death," he replied, securing the entrance to the dressing room with yellow crime-scene tape. No one was allowed in or out of the restaurant until the detectives and forensics finished their work.

"You're saying no one could've sneaked in?" he asked again, skeptically.

"To get to the tent you must walk through the dance floor,"

Eve explained one more time. "I would've noticed."

"And you said someone was in the tent?"

"I'm not sure," Eve shook her head. "It was just a feeling. But he couldn't leave the tent without passing by me on the floor."

"Well, he certainly didn't climb out the window, 'cause there is none." The officer shrugged. "And if you heard her lock the door behind you, she had to open it for him willingly. She must've known him. Do you know if she had any enemies?"

"She had a lot of fans in this place." Eve sighed. "But enemies... Not that I know of."

"Hey, Nick." The second officer stuck his head into the tent and gave Eve an up-and-down look. "If you're done, they've got good coffee here. Turkish coffee!"

Nick left and Eve breathed out with relief. His penetrating stares made her uncomfortable. She was cold, too, but her clothes were inside the dressing room, which was now a crime scene. The situation felt unreal. Eve wrapped herself into her veil, sat down on one of the tent pillows, and started thinking.

Enemies. Somehow Eve felt Leila's death was connected to her crazy marriage plan. Grabbing a husband the way Leila had was kind of weird. What if she'd pissed him off by ruining his wedding? What if he wanted to restore the arrangement and get rid of Leila? Poor, stupid Leila thought she finally had a husband lined up, but the man had killed her.

Eve's theory seemed to make sense. The only man a near-naked Leila would open the door for was her fiancé. So Eve's long-time suspicion that Leila's mysterious lover worked in the Cave must be true. That's why Leila had been so secretive about it. But who could he be?

Absentmindedly, Eve began fiddling with the beads and coins of her *Salaam Alaikum* scarf. Her grandmother used to twist the rosary even when she wasn't praying. She said it gave her wisdom.

"Could it be Mehmet?" Eve asked the beads. Mehmet was married, but Eve had heard rumors of him hitting on young belly dancers. Maybe Leila was ashamed of having an affair with a married man and made up the bride story. Little lies didn't bother her. Maybe she was hoping Mehmet would divorce Faisel. Maybe she'd threatened to tell Faisel, and Mehmet had killed her. Maybe she'd even told Faisel. It was just like Leila, trying to get married at any price, even "not her own kind."

Damn! Eve flung the beads away. Here was the biggest flaw in her logic. Mehmet was Turkish and therefore Muslim. He was exactly "Leila's own kind." Eve could see Leila turning a wife into an unwanted bride, but Leila wouldn't say her boyfriend wasn't her own kind if he was.

If the boyfriend wasn't Turkish and Muslim, who was he? Vasilakos, the Greek? He had propositioned women at the Cave. But he was old and without a wife or a bride. He admired Leila, but who didn't? Every time she danced, the men went wild. Eve started fiddling with the beads again. No, Vasilakos was too ridiculous a thought. It had to be somebody younger.

Alfonso? He sure drooled over Leila. Just look how he'd acted earlier when he'd burst into the dressing room. Maybe he'd promised to marry her to get her into bed. Eve found Alfonso repulsive, but Leila was so obsessed with marriage that looks might not have mattered to her. She saw marriage as the ultimate success, the highest conceivable point of her life with no possible ambition beyond. What Eve deemed a death sentence, Leila viewed as paradise. Still, Eve couldn't believe Leila would give herself to Alfonso over all her other offers.

Eve continued to play with the beads and think. People often overlooked unlikely suspects to find out later that the butler did it. Maybe Alfonso the busboy had killed Leila. Maybe he wasn't her boyfriend. Maybe he'd just wanted to try his chances. He hid behind the tent after she threw him out of the dressing room and waited. Why hadn't Eve thought of that before?

Eve jumped to her feet and ran out of the tent. She looked around the Cave, inside the kitchen, and even the men's restroom, but couldn't find Alfonso.

"Ayshe..." She stopped a young waitress carrying cups of Turkish coffee to the customers who still wanted their dinners and deserts even in the midst of the police investigation. "Have you seen Alfonso?"

"Sh-sh," Ayshe held her finger to her lips. "Don't say his name. Mehmet hid him in the cellar."

"Mehmet—what?"

"Don't ask me." Ayshe raised her palm defensively. "I don't own the place. You want coffee? This one's no sugar."

"Why is he hiding Al? He thinks Al did it?"

"Speak to Mehmet." Ayshe darted away. "I don't make the rules here."

Eve saw Mehmet at the bar pouring himself a drink. Apparently, alcohol was not a sin tonight.

"Allah, what an unfortunate girl!" Mehmet whined to Eve. "Why did she have to die in my restaurant? Didn't she dance in other places too?"

"Mehmet, why did you hide Al in the cellar?"

"Sh-sh!" Mehmet brought his voice down. "What else could I do? He doesn't have a green card. They find him, I'm in trouble. And he gets deported."

"He might've killed Leila! He broke into the dressing room and…"

"He told me," Mehmet cut her off, his eyes darting around. "He was so scared when the police came, he wet his pants. He's an idiot, but no killer. Besides, I sent him to the cellar to find a bottle of 1995 Greek Amethystos right before I announced your number. He spent half an hour searching for it."

Eve looked Mehmet in the eye. "And where were you when I danced?"

Mehmet twitched, spilling wine on the counter. "What do you mean? Are you saying I…"

"I'm just asking where you were," Eve said. "You stood at the mike when I started dancing, but later you disappeared."

"Allah the merciful." Mehmet covered his face with his hand, squishing his puffy cheeks with his fingers. "Now people are gonna start asking questions."

"What questions?"

"I don't know. People always ask questions. You're asking questions."

"I have an important question. Do you know who Leila's boyfriend was?"

Mehmet downed his wine. "How do I know? Maybe she had a dozen of them."

"Don't say that!"

"She got around," Mehmet grunted. "That's why she couldn't find a husband. No one would marry her. Her only chance was to find somebody American. They don't care about that sort of thing."

"American," Eve echoed. And then it hit her. Roy! Roy Robson, the ladies man, the playboy. Why hadn't Eve thought of him before. Leila could easily have fallen for his Irish sweetness and bad-boy charm. Compared to Leila's own kind, Roy was romantic, athletic, and charismatic. He probably bought flowers, kissed her hand, and treated her like an equal. He might've even promised to marry her. He didn't realize how much of a problem Leila's virginity loss was for her. He was used to American women. While he would never have a bride chosen by his family, he always talked about marrying rich. A drinker and a gambler, he owed money to everybody. Maybe Roy'd found a rich girlfriend and then dumped Leila. Maybe Leila went to talk to the woman and screwed up his plans. Maybe Roy needed to shut her up. But how did he get to the tent without Eve noticing?

Eve twisted her thinking beads again. Roy was at the bar when she started the *Karshilama*, but he was gone when she danced with the Turks. Yet, she hadn't seen him pass her on the floor. Could he have slipped by while the Turks danced around her? That was it! The floor was packed, everyone was dancing and he…

"Excuse me, miss," a harsh voice interrupted her thoughts. She looked up and saw officers Nick Donahue and Paul Carella standing next to her. Mehmet was gone.

"Yes, Officer?"

"Did you say Leila Farsakoðlu was still alive when you left the room?"

"Yes."

"So you were the last person to see her alive?"

"Yes."

"Which means you could've killed her, gone out, performed, returned to the dressing room, and claimed you found her dead."

Eve's eyes rounded in shock.

"Is that true, Ms. Gülnar?"

"No," Eve whispered, shaking her head. "I found her dead when I came back."

"We're not at all sure that's true."

The absurdity of the situation left Eve speechless.

"In any case, Ms. Gülnar," said Paul Carella, "We're going to escort you back to the tent and you're to remain there until the detectives arrive."

In the tent, Eve threw herself on a pillow and wrapped her hands around her head. She couldn't believe this was happening to her. She was being accused of Leila's murder. How would she prove anything if she was stuck inside the tent and couldn't even walk around asking questions?

Ayshe poked her head in.

"You look like you danced with a demon," Ayshe said. "You want some coffee? Mehmet said we can use *Petakzade* tonight. It's the best."

"Coffee," Eve uttered staring in the distance with unseeing eyes. "Yeah."

Ayshe disappeared. Mehmet came in.

"Is that true—they think you killed her?" He plopped on the pillow next to Eve. "What are they, idiots? You're half her size!"

"Mehmet, where's Roy?"

"I'm sure he's around. The cops aren't letting anybody out."

"Where were you when I danced?" she asked again. "You never answered me."

"Allah, why do you think I killed the poor girl?" Mehmet raised his eyes to the ceiling. "I don't think you killed her, but you think I did. Where's the justice?"

"I just want to know if you saw anyone come in or out of the tent."

Mehmet sighed. "I don't know. I wasn't even on the floor. I went to the cellar because Alfonso couldn't find that Amethystos bottle. I looked everywhere and couldn't find it either. I called Roy at the bar and told him to ask the customer if he'd be satisfied with a 2000 Amethystos. He said 'no' and Roy came down to help us look for the cursed bottle, but we still couldn't find it. I'm out of it."

"So Roy was in the cellar with you?"

"Yes. Why are you asking? You think Roy did it?"

"Somebody did it. Somebody Leila knew. She opened the door for him."

Mehmet took a deep breath and threw a quick look around.

"I'll tell you who did it."

"You know?" Eve was stunned.

"Of course! Isn't it obvious? Who do you think is capable of murder here? Who do you think I pray to never have in my restaurant?"

Eve was perplexed. "Who?"

"The Russian." Mehmet shook his fists in the air. "Boris. The mafioso. I pray to Allah to keep him away from me, but he always comes."

"Why would he kill her?"

"Does the mafia need a reason? Maybe she threatened to tell his wife they had an affair. Not a smart move with a Russian mafioso. They're even brutal to their own people. And now it's me who's in trouble!"

"Does he have a wife?"

"He had a few of them…I heard."

Eve twisted the beads. Boris. He was neither Turkish nor Muslim. Why hadn't she thought of him? He was capable of murder. He'd been at his table when she began dancing with the *shamadan*. He was at his table when she ran back into the tent. But was he there all the time in-between?

"We have to tell the police."

"Are you nuts?" Mehmet hissed. "Even if they arrest him, the lawyers will bail him out, and my restaurant will get blown up. Or worse, I'll get shot."

"What if the cops arrest me?"

"*Inşallah*, they won't."

Eve buried her face into her hands, ready to cry. Mehmet patted her on her shoulder in a soothing gesture. Just at that moment, Ayshe and Ali walked in carrying a tray of Turkish coffees.

"Have some." Ayshe lowered herself onto a pillow and handed Eve a cup. "Are you crying?"

"They think I killed Leila," Eve sobbed.

"Unbelievable," Ali whispered.

Roy burst into the tent.

"Are these fucking pigs harassing you? They have no right! Don't talk to them without a lawyer. I know a good one. He'll get you off the hook. He reduced my charges of gambling to a misdemeanor."

"We can't let them arrest Eve," Ayshe cried. "Eve, you have family in Turkey?"

Eve tried to sip her coffee, but tears welled up in her eyes. "Yes…but…"

Ayshe turned to Mehmet. "We have to do something!"

"Tsk, tsk," Mehmet clicked his tongue and put his hand around Eve's shoulder in a fatherly gesture. "I have an uncle in Istanbul. He owns a shop in *Kapali Çarsi*—the Grand Bazaar. He does well. We'll put you on the plane tomorrow morning.

You'll work in his shop for a few months till this settles, then you come back."

"She hasn't done anything wrong," Roy fumed. "She's innocent. Why does she have to run away? Innocent people don't run away in this country."

"This country, that country." Mehmet waved his hand dismissively. "Cops don't care who's innocent. They just need to point a finger at somebody and say case closed."

Roy blew up. "You don't believe in justice?"

Mehmet shrugged. "I believe in justice, cops believe in justice. I believe in God, you believe in God. But our gods are different. You wanna trust your life to whichever God is stronger?" He raised his eyes to the ceiling. "Allah, I don't recommend."

Eve began to tremble so badly she couldn't control it. The cup fell out of her hand, and the coffee spilled on the floor.

"She's freezing, poor thing." Roy plopped down next to Eve and hugged her. "Ali, give her your sweater."

"I didn't kill anybody," Eve cried out. "I don't want to run away. I was born here. This is my home. But I'm so scared."

"Sometimes you have to go away to find your home," Mehmet assured her. Ali took off his camel wool sweater and handed it to Eve. She pulled it on and buried her face into the warm cashmere.

"Thank you," she sniffed. "Ayshe, I spilled your coffee, I'm sorry…"

"Don't worry," Ayshe comforted her. "Mehmet hid Al and he'll hide you too."

"Try this one, Ms. Gülnar," Ali picked another cup from the tray. "I made it. It's different."

Eve held the cup with shaking hands and took a sip. It tasted of cardamom, which Turks didn't put in their coffee. Ali made it his way, from an Arabic recipe. Eve didn't like cardamom, but appreciated the care. So much like Ali.

Thanks to the sweater and coffee, her shivering eased up, and she started thinking again. She wasn't running away. She was innocent. She took another sip of coffee, wincing at the cardamom taste. She was going to find out who did it. Even if it seemed she had exhausted all possibilities. Wait a second. How could she have missed it. The thought was so startling, she broke into a sweat. Ali! She'd completely excluded him from her suspect list because he was Muslim. But he wasn't Turkish. He didn't fit Leila's parents' strict definition of "her own kind." God, what a cardamom taste could do.

But what if she was wrong? Mehmet, Roy, Alfonso—she'd accused enough men today. Ali, of all people? Ali, so courteous, polite, caring, and friendly?

Beads of sweat started trickling down her face. She wiped them off with her puffy sleeve and the soft sweater scratched her. Surprised, Eve looked at the sleeve and frowned. Hidden between the thick threads of camel hair was something small and twinkly. Eve fingered it out from the threads and looked at it closely. It was a little golden bead from Leila's veil.

"Oh, my God," she cried out, knowing she was right this time. "You did it. You killed Leila."

She faced shocked stares.

"It makes perfect sense." Eve glared at Ali. "It all comes together. Didn't you finally agree to marry the bride your family chose for you? Didn't you have an engagement a few months back? That's exactly when Leila had her nervous breakdown and stopped dancing. And then she went and talked to your bride, didn't she?"

A nervous quiver passed through Ali's face. "I don't know what you're talking about, Ms. Gülnar."

"My god, what an embarrassment it must've been for you and your family," Eve went on. "I'm sure the only way to restore the arrangement was to get rid of Leila. So you promised Leila you'd marry her to shut her up and then you killed her. You strangled her with your 'engagement gift'—the peacock veil. That's why this bead is on your sweater. I'm sure there's more than one because the veil was totally destroyed."

"You're distraught, Ms. Gülnar, and you're worried about your safety," Ali announced with sudden arrogance. "It's understandable for you to be illogical."

"I'm damn logical." Eve slammed her cup down so hard the coffee sloshed out. "I just never thought of it till I smelled cardamom!"

"I'm out of here." Ali got up, the picture of frustration. "But I'd like to have my sweater back, please."

"Your sweater is full of evidence." Eve screamed. "Roy, don't let him go."

Roy placed his big heavy arm on Ali's shoulder and forced him back on the pillows. "Sit down, pal. Let her finish."

"How do you suggest I did it, Ms. Gülnar?" Ali hissed. "You saw me when you danced."

"Oh, I know how you did it," Eve yelled. "You brought the *shamadan* into the tent and hid behind the fabrics. Then you knocked on the door when I left and Leila opened. Of course, she opened it for you. You were her fiancé."

"I was not her fiancé," Ali shouted finally losing his cool. "You're talking nonsense. If you remember, I took the *shamadan* from you when…"

"Exactly," Eve cried out, pointing her finger at him. "That's how you made your exit. Very clever, Ali, very clever! You slipped out of the tent to take the *shamadan* precisely when I finished. That way it looked like you were around. Hey, Roy, was Ali with you at the bar when I did the Candlelight Dance?"

Roy shook his head. "No. In fact he wasn't at the bar ever since he left to light the damn thing."

Eve jumped on her feet. "He was hiding behind the tent."

"You, witch," Ali shouted, no longer able to control himself. "What do you know? That stupid whore screwed up the arrangement my family made years ago. They would've disowned me if I didn't restore it. But this stupid broad didn't want to listen to any rationale."

He made a beeline for the tent's exit, but both Roy and Mehmet grabbed him and pulled him down.

"You're going to tell all this to the cops, aren't you pal?" Roy growled. "And if you won't, I'll call a coupla friends of mine and once they talk to you, speaking to the cops would feel like a pleasure."

Nick Donahue and Paul Carella walked into the tent with a plainclothes cop.

"Detective Dave Higgins, NYPD," he introduced himself up holding his badge.

"Right on time, pal," Roy said with scorn. "The murder of the Aladdin's Cave has just been solved."

The detective looked around, his eyes pausing on the jiggling coins of Eve's hip scarf.

"Solved by who?" he inquired.

"By our Hipscarved Sleuth." Roy gave Mehmet a wink and extended his hand toward Eve as if introducing her to the audience. "Ladies and gentlemen, put your hands together for the gorgeous and glorious, Eve Gülnar!"

THE LIE
by Anita Page

When my father said, "Becka, we have to talk," I thought I was going to hear yet another installment of the Last Will and Testament. It was the day after Christmas, 1989, and we were sitting in what he called his Florida room, sipping beers and listening to the whirr of the sprinkler system on the golf course outside his West Palm condo.

I fought off impatience. At eighty-four he was entitled to his obsessive concern about leaving his affairs in order. But he didn't want to discuss codicils. Instead, in the restrained and slightly ironic tone he always used when talking over matters that deeply moved him, he told me about the guilt he'd been living with for forty years, ever since that summer night in Queens in 1949.

I was surprised. We'd never before spoken of that night except obliquely. And in my mind, he bore no guilt for what had happened. I reminded him that he'd tried to talk Lou Labowski into not taking his gun.

"Did I?" my father asked. He didn't remember standing up to Lou. Knowing he'd done that helped a little, he said. "Lou was a dirty cop, a thug. There's nothing worse." Then my father looked at me, confused. "But you were just a kid. I'm surprised you remember any of it."

I remember every minute of that night, I wanted to say. All the details, all the shadows.

On the last day of school, Tommy Labowski and I, both nine years old, celebrated summer by going into the woods behind our street to collect bottle caps. We were scrabbling through dry leaves when we heard the crack of a branch and looked up to see a man in a brown jacket watching us. We got to our feet, surprised but not scared. This was Queens, USA, and our fathers and uncles were home from the war. We thought our world was safe.

Tommy looked at me significantly and made a slight gesture with his head. I saw then that the man's fly was open and he was exposing himself. "He was playing with his thing," was how Tommy later put it to his father.

As the man started talking, asking our names and how old we were, Tommy yanked my arm, saying we had to go home because our father was a cop and he was waiting. There were some lies in the statement and some truth. For one thing, we weren't brother and sister. And while his father *was* a cop, he wasn't waiting for us. My father was an accountant, and I realized that the man in the woods wouldn't have been scared at the thought of an accountant in a suit coming after him.

When Mr. Labowski finally got home and heard from Tommy's mother what had happened, he, my father, and Kathleen's father from down the street went to search the neighborhood. Later, I heard my father say to my mother, "Thank God we didn't find him. I don't know what the hell Lou"—Mr. Labowski—"was going to do if he got his hands on him."

A picture came into my mind then that made me sick: Mr. Labowski clobbering the guy with his nightstick. The man had been pale and wore strange clothes for a hot June afternoon in the woods—a brown suit jacket, dark blue pants, and a white shirt buttoned to his neck—but he hadn't hurt us. So he'd been playing with his thing. I didn't see what the big deal was.

After the fathers got back, Mr. Labowski laid down the law to the whole gang of us: me and Tommy, Freddie from across the street, Kathleen, and Joey Boy—who was always hanging around the edge of the group. The woods were off-limits.

"You've got a whole street to play on, including your own backyards." Mr. Labowski made a sweeping motion with his meaty hand to show us just how big the street was. His sleeves were rolled up and we could see the anchor tattooed on his arm. "Plus, those woods are private property. You kids don't even belong there."

Before the war, our part of eastern Queens—Cambria Heights, where we lived, and Queens Village and Laurelton—had been farmland, potato farms according to my parents. The farms had disappeared after the war, replaced by streets, each having a particular style house. On our long, wide street the houses were small brick bungalows with patches of lawn at the front and narrow driveways on the side.

Ours was the last street in the development. Behind it were the woods, old houses that had been there before the war, and the dark grocery store where our mothers sent us for bread and milk that was sometimes sour and had to be returned. We didn't know anyone who lived back there, except for Mrs. Giacomelli who always wore black and eyed us with distrust when we stepped into her store.

Mr. Labowski was right about one thing. We had a whole block where we could play ball, ride bikes, and roller skate. By the next summer our mothers would let us ride our bikes down to the storefront library on Linden Boulevard and the playground at P.S. 147. But that summer the block was still our world, and we felt as if we owned it. No one minded that we played in the middle of the road because hardly any traffic came that way. Our street dead-ended at the service road to the Cross Island Parkway. On the other side of the parkway was Nassau County, a foreign country, not part of Queens or even New York City.

We missed the shady mystery of the woods. Some of the fathers, including mine and Tommy's, had planted trees on the narrow strip of grass between the curb and the sidewalk, but only years later did those trees cast shadows big enough to count as shade. The woods were where we found bottle caps that we used for treasure in our games and the dead branches we needed to build Flash Gordon's spaceship.

A week or two after the off-limits law was invoked, a group of us were poking around behind Mr. Labowski's tool shed. Maybe we hoped to find something we could use for the spaceship, or maybe we were just feeling restless. The woods had never seemed so desirable, now that we weren't allowed to go back there. When I saw Freddie whispering to Tommy, I knew they were cooking something up. I guessed that next they'd get rid of Kathleen and Joey Boy, who always told their mothers everything.

As soon as Joey Boy saw they were hatching a plan, he started whining, "No secrets, no secrets."

But Tommy ignored him and announced that everyone had to go home. Kathleen, who never seemed to catch on, just shrugged and dragged her heels down the driveway to the street. But Joey Boy sat down in the middle of Tommy's yard and announced that he was staying right there.

"PRIVATE PROPERTY, runt. Beat it!" Freddie shouted in his face.

Joey Boy left, then stopped at the bottom of the driveway and yelled back, "I'm telling my mother what you said."

Freddie jumped up and down, waved his arms, and yelled, "Oooh, oooh, I'm scaaared."

Tommy and Freddie and I made a big show of going home too, but ten minutes later we met on the grassy verge that separated the parkway from the service road, where Freddie announced his big idea.

"We're going to the woods," he said to me, wiping his nose on his arm. He was tall and already muscular.

I knew he hoped I wouldn't come and he'd have Tommy to himself. I remember looking at Tommy, trying to send him a silent warning. It was his father who'd said the woods were off-limits, and he was the one who'd get the strap if his father found out.

When Tommy shrugged, I knew he was acting tough for Freddie. "He said we couldn't play there, but we're not playing. We'll just get some branches and take them down to Freddie's yard. We'll build the spaceship there."

"You don't have to come if you don't want to." Freddie gave me his coolest stare. He was the kid who climbed the fence by the haunted house, chased balls onto the parkway, and stole gum from Mrs. Giacomelli's store. His parents both worked and his grandmother was in charge of him and his brother. I'd heard my mother say that the old lady let those boys get away with murder.

Tommy, on the other hand, never got away with anything. I knew that because my bedroom was right across the driveway from his. Whenever I heard his father yell, "How many times do I have to tell you…?" I knew Tommy was going to get a beating and I put my pillow over my head so I wouldn't hear him cry. But I guessed Tommy was more afraid of Freddie thinking he was a baby than of his father's strap.

"I'm coming too," I said.

The patch of woods butted up against the backyards of the last three houses on our street. We thought of it as a deep, dark forest, but it was more like an overgrown wooded lot. As soon as we walked down the short path to the clearing where we'd collect dead branches, we heard the black dog bark. The dog belonged to the old man who lived in the house just behind mine. Sometimes I watched him, half hidden by the shrubs my mother had planted against our back fence, working in his garden, pulling weeds, or watering his tomatoes. His garden ended just where the woods began.

I wondered whether the woods belonged to the old man. Whenever we went back there, the black dog would bark and the old man would yell, "*Tacere*. Shaddup you." But he never came out and scolded us kids.

I remember walking around the clearing, kicking dead leaves and picking up branches even if they were too short for the spaceship. The worst that would happen to me if we were caught was a lecture, but I knew exactly what Tommy would get. I told myself that we were safe at that time of day, with the fathers at work and the mothers glad to have us out of their hair. But still I wanted to get out of there. "Let's just go," I urged Tommy.

Freddie wasn't in any hurry, though. One of the trees, with thick low branches, was good for climbing, so he shimmied up, straddled a branch, and started making monkey noises.

Then we heard a sound behind us, and Tommy and I spun around. I felt my heart pound and hoped it was the man in the brown jacket, not Mr. Labowski.

But it was Joey Boy who jumped out from behind a tree, his face wild with triumph, yelling, "I'm going to tell!"

In a second I planted myself in front of him, fists on my hips. "Number one, if you tell, you can never play Flash Gordon again for the rest of your life. Number two, everyone knows you're a liar anyway, so no one will believe you."

Just then Freddie yelled from his tree branch, "He's coming after us!" He pointed in the direction of the old man's garden. "And his THING is OUT!"

Even before Freddie hit the ground laughing, Joey screamed and started running but didn't get far. He tripped over a tree root, flying forward. As he fell, his head hit a large rock just off the path.

We started to laugh at the sight of him lurching forward, but then froze when we heard the clunk of his head against the rock. We stood silently, waiting for him to get up. When he didn't, I walked over and knelt down next to him, willing him to get up or at least move, but he didn't move an inch.

I looked over at the boys and said, "I don't know if he's breathing." I felt myself tremble, afraid to say the word *dead.*

Of the three of us, it was Freddie who panicked and wanted to run. Years later, when we were in high school, Tommy told me that Freddie had an uncle who'd done time on Rikers Island. Whenever he was bad his father would yell, "You're gonna end up just like Frankie." Maybe the sight of Joey on the ground, head bloody, convinced Freddie that Mr. Labowski was going to cuff him and ship him off to Rikers with his uncle.

I grabbed Tommy's arm. "What if he's not dead yet?" I demanded. "What if he dies because we leave him here?"

Freddie was bawling by then and I told him to shut up so I could think. I knew we couldn't just leave Joey, and I also knew we had to come up with a story that would keep Tommy out of trouble. I remember that moment in the woods, with the light filtering through the trees and the black dog barking in the garden. That was when I figured out what we would tell our parents.

We saw Joey going into the woods, I told the boys. We followed him to tell him he wasn't allowed. While we were talking to him, the man in the brown jacket came back. Then we all started to run away, but Joey tripped and fell and hit his head.

"What happened to the man?" Tommy's face was red like his father's and he was sweating.

"He ran away when he saw Joey fall. He probably got scared. Okay?"

Okay. They agreed. It was a good story.

The worst part was telling Joey's mother, who we hated. She was like Joey, skinny and small. Her eyebrows made her look surprised and her black hair was always in rollers on top of her head. Every time Joey ran home telling on us for some insult or slight, she'd come down the street after us, yelling, "You lousy kids, picking on him because he's smaller than you."

I was sure she'd yell at us when we told her what had happened to Joey, but she didn't. She ordered me to take her to where he was and, as we ran down her walk, shouted back to Tommy, "Go tell your mother to call an ambulance."

When Mr. Labowski got home, he sat us down on the front stoop and started asking questions. He asked about the man and not about going into the woods, but I made sure to say that we hadn't gone there to play but just to get Joey out. I'd never told a lie before, not to an adult and not on purpose. I was surprised at how easy it was.

Mr. Labowski twisted his mouth and said to Tommy, "You got yourself a lawyer, huh?"

When he asked if we were sure it was the same man we'd seen the other time, I said quickly that Tommy and I hadn't actually seen him. Only Freddie had seen him from up in the tree. Since Freddie said he'd been wearing a brown jacket, it probably was the same guy. I thought I was being clever, making the lie as close to the truth as possible, but as soon as I said "up in the tree," I knew I'd made a mistake.

"Oh yeah, up in the tree?" Mr. Labowski said, in a voice that told us he knew we'd been playing there after all and would deal with us later. Then he started asking Freddie questions about the man.

Freddie sounded so nervous that I didn't think Mr. Labowski would buy a word of our story, but he did.

It was still light out when my father and Mr. Labowski and Kathleen's father went searching for the man. Before they got into Mr. Labowski's car, I heard my father say, "Why don't you leave that home, Lou." He was looking at the gun Mr. Labowski had in his holster.

Mr. Labowski laughed and slapped my father on the back. "Don't worry, Harry. It never hurts to have it." Then, talking out of the side of his mouth, he said, "This is the second time we're going out looking for the sonofabitch. Believe me, if we find him, there won't be a third time even if I have to shoot it off him." Then they got into the car and drove away, toward the parkway.

Our mothers sat out on Tommy's porch waiting for the men to come back, and also to find out if Joey was going to die. Tommy's mother had tried calling Mary Immaculate Hospital, but, she said, just try getting anything out of those damn nuns. Then she apologized to Kathleen's mother, who was Catholic like she was, but who actually went to church.

We kids waited over on my stoop. Patrick Reilly, who lived

in the house on the other side of Tommy's, sat with us even though he was twenty and in college. He had pale blue eyes and straight brown hair that always fell over his forehead. The whole street knew that Patrick Reilly was going to be a priest when he finished college because he had a calling. I was intrigued by the word and at night I imagined Patrick, two houses away, having conversations with God.

While we waited, I kept thinking about Mr. Labowski shooting "it" off. I'd figured out what "it" was, but worried that if Mr. Labowski did that, the guy would die. Then I reminded myself that we'd made the whole story up. The man hadn't been in the woods, so the fathers wouldn't find him and I didn't have to worry about him getting shot.

Then the dark blue Oldsmobile that belonged to Joey Boy's father came down the street and stopped in front of Tommy's house. When Tommy's mother rushed down from the porch, we started to go too, but Patrick Reilly said, "Let's just stay here."

Tommy's mother walked over to the car and leaned down to talk to Joey Boy's father. Then we heard her say, "Oh thank God. Thank God for that." As the car pulled away, she walked back to the porch announcing, "A mild concussion. They're keeping him overnight, but the doctor said that he'll be fine."

I remember feeling dizzy with relief. Freddie gave a whoop and jumped from the third step down to the sidewalk, bumping into Tommy. Then the two of them started jumping around, pretending to box. I made a face at how silly the boys were acting, and Patrick Reilly winked at me.

Just then we heard an explosion of sound coming from the parkway, brakes screeching, metal crashing into metal. Suddenly, people were coming out of their houses, everyone racing in the direction of the noise.

When we got onto the grass verge, Tommy and Freddie and I squeezed between the grownups to get up front so we could see. All the cars on both sides of the parkway were stopped. One car had smashed into the side of another and a third car, with its front smashed in, had spun around and faced the wrong way. I saw my father leaning against Mr. Labowski's car, which was up on the grass. He had an expression on his face that almost made him look like a stranger. Mr. Labowski was giving orders, yelling to a neighbor to call for an ambulance and to call the 105th Precinct.

Then Tommy jabbed my arm and pointed to Kathleen's father, who knelt beside something in the road. At first it looked like a bundle of old clothes. I remember thinking someone had thrown old clothes out a car window and that's why the cars had crashed. But then I saw a head covered with blood and a brown jacket with an arm extending out of the sleeve, and I knew who it was.

People moved aside to make a path for the old man, the owner of the black dog, who was charging across the grass toward the body in the road. When he saw the body he made a noise that I'd never heard a person make before. It sounded like an animal's howl. He dropped to his knees and threw himself onto the body, crying, "Giorgio, *mi figlio, mi figlio.*"

Mr. Labowski was running his hand through his hair, saying, "Jesus H. Christ," again and again. Then he reached down to touch the old man's shoulder. The old man struggled to his feet and looked wildly around, at Mr. Labowski, at the people standing outside their cars, and at everyone crowded onto the grass. For a second I know he looked at me. He shook his fists at the sky and in a hoarse voice bellowed, "*Assassino! Assassino!* Who killed my Giorgio?"

Mr. Labowski, his hand still on the old man's shoulder, spotted us and called to Patrick Reilly to get us the hell away from there. As Patrick led us across the service road, an ambulance and two police cars came screaming down the street. People moved out of the way so the cars could get up on the grass.

We followed Patrick back to my stoop.

It was starting to get dark by then and the street felt deserted. I thought we must be the only ones who weren't down by the parkway. I listened while Patrick tried to answer the boys' questions, explaining what he thought had happened. He said it looked like Giorgio, the man in the brown jacket, had run into the middle of the parkway and a car hit him. Then the other cars smashed into each other when they tried to stop.

"It was an accident," he said. "A terrible accident."

"But why did he run into the road?" Freddie asked. "The guy must have been nuts."

Patrick met Freddie's words with silence. Then he said, "From what I heard, Tommy's dad wanted to talk to him. He got scared and ran away."

"Jesus H. Christ," Tommy said. "He just wanted to talk to him. He wasn't going to hurt him. The guy didn't have to run away."

"I guess he didn't understand that," Patrick said.

"Is he the old man's son?" I asked, even though I'd already figured out that he was.

Yes, Giorgio was the old man's son, Patrick told us. He'd been away for a long time, first in the army and then in a hospital. He'd just come back that summer to live with his father.

"Did you know him?" I asked.

"I talked to him once," Patrick said. "I didn't really know him."

I felt myself try to push against time, almost like pedaling backward on my bike. What if Giorgio hadn't come back? What if Joey Boy hadn't followed us into the woods? What if Freddie hadn't scared Joey Boy? What if—and now I was back in the woods, with Joey Boy lying on the path and the dog barking in the garden—what if I hadn't been so smart and thought up the lie to tell Mr. Labowski?

I felt Patrick rest his hand on my head, and he said, "It was an accident, a very sad accident. It wasn't anyone's fault." But I knew that wasn't true. The car hitting Giorgio was an accident, but the lie that had been so easy to tell was not.

I remember the way the concrete stoop felt on my bare legs and the chill that suddenly took over my body. I hugged myself to keep from shivering and listened to Patrick Reilly's voice, quiet and calm, talking to the boys. Suddenly I knew what I would do. Kathleen had once explained confession to me: You tell the priest your sins and he tells you to say some prayers and then God forgives you. Kathleen was positive that you didn't have to be Catholic. God forgave everyone as long as they confessed.

That's what I would do, I decided. I would confess, tell Patrick Reilly about my lie that had sent the fathers looking for Giorgio, chasing him onto the parkway, into the traffic. If I confessed, God would forgive me. But I would have to wait until Patrick Reilly became a priest.

My father died two months after that Christmas visit. I didn't tell him the part I'd played in Giorgio's death. I like to think I kept it from him for his sake, and not my own.

After the funeral I flew back to New York and drove through the old neighborhood. In the early sixties, realtors had swarmed like locusts through that part of Queens. They'd knocked on doors, warning families to sell or they'd be the last white people on the block. By the late sixties, my family and most of those who'd settled the street twenty years earlier had moved to Nassau County.

When I took my ride through the neighborhood in early 1990, Linden Boulevard was shabby and run down, lined with empty storefronts. But the residential streets were quiet and neat, with well-tended homes and mature shade trees. The woods and the old man's house were gone. The whole pre-war neighborhood behind our development had been replaced by small frame houses with picture windows and narrow front lawns.

I parked across the street from my old house, wondering about the people who lived there now. Someone had taken down my father's cherry tree and added on a front porch. Tommy's house had changed as well—dormers had been added to the attic—but Patrick Reilly's house looked the same.

Years before, a neighbor with whom my parents kept in touch reported that the priest at a niece's christening turned out to be, of all people, Patrick Reilly. When my mother passed the news along, the promise I'd made to myself that night, sitting and shivering on the stoop, came flooding back. I could actually do it now, I thought. I could track down Patrick Reilly and tell him what I'd never told anyone else. But what was the point? I'd long ago stopped believing in redemption.

A DAY AT A TIME
by Fran Bannigan Cox

Peggy juggled hope and fear like jello in her pudgy palms on the day her father, Jackie Vincent, was released from Coney Island Hospital's detox unit with warnings about the condition of his liver. He'd been dried out more times than she cared to remember.

Peggy thought back to the morning she couldn't get him off the bathroom floor. In desperation she had called 911. They came while her mother, Eileen, with the logic of senility, wrestled with the vacuum hose, insisting she could help if Peggy would just be a good girl and open the bathroom door. Shineese, her mother's caregiver, couldn't get the nozzle out of Eileen's hands until Peggy came out and talked her mother into having a "nice cup of tea" in the kitchen. "Nothing for *you*, dear," her mother had said, chuckling, as they guided her to a chair. "Too much baby fat on ya."

With her mother settled at the kitchen table, Peggy watched with relief as the EMS workers took her father off her hands.

The day he was discharged, she had to dig out of a pile of dirty February snow the sanitation department had dumped on her Toyota. She had no trouble locating the detox unit. It was right next to the psych unit she remembered wasting time in a year ago trying to convince the interns her weight problems were just from being a "nervous eater."

Peggy signed her dad out on the strength of his promise to remain sober. As he repeated it, she repressed the derisive snort that rose to protect her from the rage and despair she felt for all his broken promises.

Pleased with himself, he regaled her with the jokes he'd told to the other "inmates," as he was tickled to call the guys on the ward. Everyone told her what a funny man her father was. She felt guilty that she had to force herself to laugh at his jokes. He had made a lot of jokes the day she'd graduated from St. Stephen's High, but most of the punch lines had been slurred. Her mother'd taken him out of the auditorium before Peggy got her diploma because he wouldn't stop making fun of the valedictorian.

Now, as they drove east in rush-hour traffic on the Belt Parkway, she told him this was his final chance. "Three strikes and you're out, Pop," she said, wondering if she could really make it stick.

He reached across the space of the front seat to pat her thigh hidden under the voluminous folds of her poncho, calling her by his pet name for her—the one she hated.

"Crisco," he said. "Remember? Fat in the can?" He chuckled as he always did at his little joke. "Don't worry. This time I'm gonna hit the sonofabitch outta the ballpark."

She flinched at his touch and reached for the last chocolate Krispy Kreme doughnut she'd left resting on the dashboard. As they passed Floyd Bennett Air Field, once the launching pad for fighter pilots in World War II, her dad repeated his claim to be the mechanic who had run the place and won the war. She had heard it all before and tuned out on his historical fantasy.

Her cellphone rang against the hum of the metal grid road bed of the Marine Park Bridge. When she reassured her mother that they would be home in fifteen minutes, her father interrupted to say he needed to stop at St. Stephen's Church in Breezy Point for an AA meeting. As proof, he held out the cardboard schedule of meetings given him by the hospital staff. It looked just like the one they had given her for something called codependent meetings.

She waved it away, resolved not to be his keeper.

She replaced the phone next to the gear shift and put on her blinker for a right turn off the bridge, following the signs to Breezy Point and the beaches known as the Irish Riviera. She and her last boyfriend used to drink in a bar down there while they waited for the ferry to Sheepshead Bay. Twenty years ago? Probably.

Her cellphone rang again. She knew it was her mother who had forgotten she had called three times already. Peggy didn't pick it up. She turned off the phone so she wouldn't hear the flood of calls that would follow.

"How's she doing?" her father asked, surprising her. He hadn't pretended interest in his wife even before Alzheimer's had sunk its hooks into her.

When Peggy answered him he began fiddling with the radio dials. She cursed herself for getting sucked in again. She really had to stop hoping.

"It's broken," she said.

She parked in front of the church.

"Don't worry. One of the guys'll drop me off, later," Jackie said, leaning into the car window to kiss her cheek with the smoke from his cigarette.

She watched him walk up the wet concrete path to the rectory. Smoothing the sleek black pompadour he was so proud of, he looked jaunty in the decrepit camel hair coat he insisted on wearing. Without turning around he lifted his hand in the air to wave before he disappeared around a bank of soggy rhododendron.

She made a U-turn and headed for the one-bedroom apartment she shared with her parents in Neponsit, a mile away. Even though it wasn't a good idea to leave her mother alone for any length of time, she decided to stop at the 7-Eleven for supplies anyway. Peggy reassured herself she had locked the pet gates to the kitchen and the bathroom, locked the windows, and left newspaper on the floor. Her mother wouldn't remember Peggy's absence or the reason for it.

No point in worrying. She just hoped her father wouldn't insult Shineese's successor if she could get one.

Three weeks later, as the sun disappeared behind the metal lattice of the Marine Park Bridge, Peggy turned her father's car into the parking lot for Field 10 at Riis Park, New York City's public beach on the Atlantic Ocean in Rockaway. It was only one exit away from Neponsit. A fog horn sounded behind her in Jamaica Bay.

She drove her father's car past the empty toll booths and the "Lot Closed" signs to park next to a clump of beach plum bushes and scrub pine, out of sight of the road. The lot was deserted except for two seagulls that waddled over to inspect the car. Most of the lights surrounding the lot flickered ineffectually. Only three lights at the far end of the field had come on. Their pale halos of mist promised the arrival of more fog as soon as the sun made its disappearance complete.

Her father stirred in the back seat, babbling and dribbling nonsense onto the vinyl seat cover. The car stank of the vomit Peggy had hoped would choke him. It was the remains of lobster fra diavolo, his favorite, the dish he ate with his cronies to feel like a Mafia kingpin at Bramante's in Sheepshead Bay. She wondered if she was the only one who saw through him.

It seemed like a lifetime since Jimmie O'Connor, the bartender of Smiley's, the dive on the corner of Coney Island Avenue and Avenue M had loaded her father into the backseat because she had flashed a Jackson at him. Two women from her job at Zilka's Fine Jewelry pretended not to notice her as they walked to the elevated subway entrance on the other side of the street, but she saw the smirks that decorated their red lips when they passed. So what, she thought. She'd still take her cruise to Paradise Island tomorrow come hell or high water. She had three years of earned vacation time waiting to be spent. She patted the nonrefundable ticket in her blouse pocket, reassured.

She wondered if they would tell her boss. She had managed to keep him in the dark that afternoon by bribing her father to leave the store. He had used the money to get plastered. What had she expected?

Only an hour had passed since she had collected Jackie. All the windows in the car were open and she began to shiver despite the hat, gloves, and scarf she wore over her poncho. The sleek French twist with side curls the hairdresser had promised her would stand up to the strongest wind was beginning to unravel.

"Goin' somewhere, sweetheart?" the hairdresser had asked, suggesting Peggy get her nails sculpted in the new design of diamonds on a field of black. Peggy was so unused to the long nails that when her cellphone rang, she could hardly work the keypad.

"Yes, Ma, I know. No, there aren't any wild dogs in the kitchen. I'll be right there," she said, over her mother's continuous stream of incoherent paranoia. "Don't cry. Ma, listen. If you're a good girl I'll bring you pistachio ice cream."

She put the phone down on the passenger seat, leaving it on so her mother would be reassured that someone was listening to her continued rambling. An occasional grunt would keep her engaged for hours, and Peggy had purchased unlimited family minutes. She was pleased with herself.

As she sat watching the gulls wheeling in the gray sky, she thought about what she had learned at the Overeaters Anonymous meeting she'd let a friend drag her to a week ago. The girl next to her had shared about her mother. "I won't let her eat up my life anymore," the woman had said.

"Bingo," Peggy agreed out loud, smacking her palm against the wheel. It was time to take her first steps: only half a box of Krispy Kremes today and kill her father.

She hauled her six foot, two hundred fifty-pound frame out of the car and returned the seat to its close setting for Jackie's short body. The parking lot was empty except for the gulls waddling along the lines of grass that insisted on struggling to live between the cracks in the pavement. The birds raised their throats to the dark sky squawking their ownership of the lot.

A fine mist rolling in from the sea added to the bite of the cold air that smelled of salt, seaweed, and damp boardwalk. Peggy took several deep breaths and listened to the low rumble of waves crashing against the beach. She could hear the thin whine of her mother's voice, but the words were unintelligible. She yelled in the direction of the phone. "I hear you, goddamit."

She put two Ziploc bags of Krispy Kremes in one jacket pocket and her bottled water in the other. She picked the phone up off the front seat and said, "Coming, Ma." Then she shut down the phone and stuffed it in with the doughnuts. Opening the back door, she dragged her father out onto the concrete. That move broke the nail on her right forefinger.

Jackie mumbled a bit but stayed put against the wheel of the car.

Peggy took off his shoes and put them on over her flats. She got the wheeled grocery basket out of the trunk. Although he complained feebly, she worked his legs into the cart. As she raised the cart, his legs bent a little against the wire, allowing a portion of his backside to rest against the top rung. Another sculpted nail, half daisy, half diamonds, on her pinky broke. That was the last straw. With new energy Peggy pushed the cart forward. He hardly weighed anything. His body had stopped accepting food, preferring the ready availability of sugar from alcohol instead. Might as well be dead, she thought, as she had so often before. She took his weight against her and pushed the cart forward with a bark of laughter that sounded almost exactly like the rasping cry of the gulls. She wondered where he had lost his coat.

It was a short walk from the parking lot to the showers, past the red, turreted bathhouse built by Jacob Riis, a nineteenth-century philanthropist who had risen to great wealth from the slums of the Lower East Side. Peggy wished she'd had a father like that.

Dousing him in the bath house shower before she brought him home seemed like a good idea. Leaving him to freeze was a better one. He wouldn't feel a thing most likely. He'd be gone in an hour. But she found the showers had been turned off for the winter.

She resented the waste, but she emptied her entire two liter bottle of Evian water over his custom-made shirt. At least, he was clean. He flailed his arms but fell against her quickly as she wheeled him back to the men's room and down the long corridor past twenty-five toilet stalls to the last cubicle. It was impossible to get him onto the seat, so she left him on the stone floor, tucking his legs around the base of the "terlit," as he called it. She put his shoes near his feet.

A little bubble of fear rose in her throat that he might survive and tell on her.

He vomited again and began to gag on it.

It's not decent, she thought, trying to steel herself to turn him on his side. She went "Brooklyn" on him, the way her mother used to, the way the counter men did when he stiffed them—reeling off a string of neighborhood insults to rouse him until she was hoarse. It was getting too complicated. Keep it simple, she told herself. She closed her eyes and patted the tickets resting over her heart. "Not again, not again," she murmured over and over.

Then, she remembered her insulin kit. It was the work of a moment to dig it out of an inner pocket and fill the syringe with air. She injected it into his tongue. "Good night," she told him.

She felt for the phone in her pocket. When her mother picked up, she said, into the silence on the line, "Everything's okay, Ma. I'm getting the ice cream, now," waiting for any sound on the other end of the phone that might mean she wasn't alone. She pushed "END."

"I must be crazy," she said, out loud, watching her father's face turn blue. Her voice bounced off the cold tile walls but she heard no other sound in the icy stillness. She watched his chest for a long time. It didn't move.

Peggy stepped out onto the deserted boardwalk and down two concrete steps to the sand. It was so dark she could hardly see the ocean. She tucked the empty cart under her arm and walked a mile to Neponsit in the wet sand along the edge of the water where her deep footprints were swallowed by the incoming tide. Each wave that swept in brought with it the phosphorescent remains of tiny sea creatures, impossibly small points of light like glowing embers, like the places in her body beginning to feel alive again.

"I'm coming, Ma," she said into the cell.

STATEN ISLAND

FAMILY MATTERS
by Peggy Ehrhart

"It's Mutt," my dad's voice said. "You busy?"

I had a surveillance job for an insurance case on my calendar, but he sounded so worried, I said, "Nothing I can't postpone."

"Will you come out here?" I could hear his stereo blasting out bebop.

"What's up?"

"You know Eric? The bass player? Cops think he killed his ex-wife. He's in jail."

"Where do I come in?" I asked. It was a gorgeous fall day after a week of rain, and a ride to Staten Island on the ferry would feel like playing hooky.

"He's innocent. I told him my daughter would get him out."

"He can't make bail?"

"He's a musician, Davis."

Visions of the PATH train replaced visions of the ferry. If I was going to talk to Eric, I'd have to go to Brooklyn. Staten Island doesn't have a jail.

I put on the radio while I dressed, and Eric's ex-wife was the big local story. She had turned up along Richmond Terrace that morning with her head bashed in.

I hardly recognized the dejected man sitting on the other side of the Plexiglas screen. The last time I'd seen Eric Nelson, he and my dad were gigging at the Zinc Bar with a saxophone player. Eric had seemed monumental: six feet tall, with ruddy skin and unruly gray hair. The three of them were grooving like it was still the fifties, and Miles Davis—yes, I was named for him—was the invisible fourth member of their combo.

Now he had shrunk. "Thanks for coming," he mumbled, looking not at me but at the grimy surface of the counter that supported the Plexiglas.

"My dad says you're innocent."

"Of course." He raised his eyes. They were pale blue. "I would never lay a hand on her."

"So how come they arrested you?"

"I don't have an alibi," he said, and he lowered his eyes again. "It happened last night, around midnight."

"What do you mean you don't have an alibi? You must have been *somewhere*."

"I wasn't," he said.

"Did the cops go over your car? Whoever killed her had to get her to Richmond Terrace."

"They don't know where my car is."

"Do you?"

He bit his lips like he was trying to lock his mouth.

I got my ferry ride as the sun set behind the Statue of Liberty.

It was Sunday, so some of my fellow passengers were daytrippers, out for the ride. Others claimed their cars from the commuter lot or caught busses heading for the tidy enclaves that make up most of Staten Island. But I just walked up the hill to my dad's. He rents two rooms of a ramshackle stucco house carved into apartments, on a street where kids in baggy jeans and knee-length T-shirts loiter.

I could hear the drums before I could see the house, tucked as it is between two apartment buildings.

"Hey, Mutt," I said, hugging him at the door. He said something, but I couldn't hear it over the music blasting from the stereo. Ernest, the Dalmatian that Mutt had rescued when a neighbor moved, sniffed my crotch.

"I've been jamming along with those sessions I did with Miles in '59," Mutt said after he turned down the stereo. "Man, I was hot."

He headed toward the stove, a few steps to the left of the drum kit that dominated the room. My dad looks like an energetic wizard, tall and skinny, with piercing eyes and wispy white hair. "Tea?"

"Sure."

"Sit down. Eat something." He gestured toward the table that doubles as his desk and reached me a box of wheat-germ cookies. "You saw Eric?" he asked after he got the flame going under the kettle.

"He doesn't have an alibi, and he won't say where his car is." Ernest laid his bulky head on my thigh and gazed at the cookies.

"He didn't do it," my dad said. "He still loved her."

The kettle whistled and Mutt set a pair of mismatched cups on the table, lowered tea bags into them, and filled them with boiling water.

"Cops are lazy." He perched on the stool he uses at his drum kit. "They won't look any further. But you can."

"Well," I said. "The logical question is whether she hooked up with anybody after she threw Eric out."

"And she did," my dad said, slapping the table. "I knew you'd have an idea."

"Who's the guy?"

Mutt ran into the other room, where newspapers were scattered around a Barcalounger that he'd rescued from the trash. "This guy," he said, hurrying back and pointing to a half-page ad for Island Pre-Owned Cars. "Tony Ferrara. Linda was engaged to him. It tore Eric up because he always thought the two of them would get back together."

The next day I returned to Staten Island in my car, a ten-year-old gray Honda. It's the perfect car for a PI—completely nondescript.

The trip from my place in Hoboken took me down the turnpike, across the Goethals Bridge, and past the spot where Linda Nelson's body had been found. Richmond Terrace outlines the top of Staten Island, from the dusty wasteland of the Howland Hook Marine Terminal to the bustling grunge of the St. George area. Along the way, Richmond Terrace skirts a few miles of woodsy scrubland, a nature preserve littered with junk despite the "No Dumping" signs.

I was poking along behind a bus, taking in the view of Bayonne across the Kill van Kull, when I saw the crime-scene tape. A solitary cop lounged behind the steering wheel of a patrol car parked half on the shoulder of Richmond Terrace and half on rutted dirt that gave way to scruffy grass.

I pulled up opposite him.

Before I had a chance to turn off the ignition, he was striding toward me. I rolled down my window.

"Oh, Officer," I said. "I hope you can help me." My usual cool-weather outfit is jeans, cowboy boots, and a leather jacket, but today I had substituted a slender skirt and cleavage-revealing sweater from the thrift store, both pale pink.

"This is a crime scene, ma'am," he said gruffly. He was a young guy, baby-faced. The gruffness came across like an act he'd picked up from TV.

"People dump things here," I said. He nodded. "My students are looking for dump sites to photograph."

He backed up and scrutinized my license plates. "Jersey doesn't have trash?"

"We want to document the whole tri-state area." I put my hand to my mouth like horrified people do in comic strips. "This isn't where that poor woman was killed?" I let my eyes go wide.

I'd learned to be a detective while I was living in Hollywood, trying to make it in the movies. My acting jobs weren't bringing in enough to live on, so I went to work for a very cool PI named Joe Dogherty.

"She wasn't killed here, ma'am," the officer said. "This is where the body was dumped."

"I see you've got the tape up—and we wouldn't be doing the project for awhile. But would you mind if I get out and look closer."

He shrugged. "Okay by me. The crime scenes unit is done."

Gazing into the brush punctuated by stunted trees with scanty leaves just starting to turn yellow, I could see tires, a toaster and microwave oven, a computer monitor, a muddy suit jacket, all kinds of miscellaneous junk, and a pair of women's shoes—purple, with gold stiletto heels. One was perched on top of the computer monitor, and the other lay near a decaying branch. Most of the stuff looked like it had been sitting there through last week's rain, but the shoes looked new.

"Those shoes seem new," I said. "They're not her shoes?"

"She was wearing shoes."

As Hylan Boulevard curved out of the Grasmere neighborhood, I could see Island Pre-Owned Cars in the distance. I knew that's what it was because of the metallic banners fluttering in the breeze.

A guy about my age greeted me when I entered the office, a 1950's-style layout with floor-to-ceiling windows. Two desks were arranged against the only windowless wall, and the wall was covered with plaques and framed photographs.

"Is Tony here?" I asked.

"He's not in right now," the guy told me. He had the self-confident air of a grown-up high-school jock and was wearing a slacks and sports jacket outfit that looked like it came as a set.

My eyes scanned the photos on the wall. One of them showed an older guy shaking hands with Hillary Clinton.

"Is that him?" I said. "He looks like you. Is he your dad?"

The guy put out his hand. "I'm Frank Ferrara," he said. He had blue eyes and a salesman's smile.

"Maybe you can help me," I said. "I just moved here and I need a car." I continued to study the pictures. "Don't mind me," I added. "I'm kind of nosy."

"You're living on the Island?"

"Yeah." Near the Hillary Clinton picture was one that featured Tony, another guy, and a woman, maybe in her mid-thirties.

"Who's the woman?" I asked. "She looks like you, too."

"That's my sister Dianne." I was pointing at the picture, and I noticed his eyes lingering on my naked ring finger. "You moved out here all by yourself?" he asked.

"I'm a big girl."

"What's a single woman want to live on Staten Island for?"

"Manhattan's expensive and Brooklyn is crowded and Queens is dirty and the Bronx is scary. This is just fine."

He laughed. "You sound like Goldilocks and the Three Bears."

"Who's the other man in the picture?"

"That's my Uncle Mike."

"Where do your sister and your uncle sit? I only see two desks."

"Uncle Mike's dead now." Frank touched his chest. "Heart attack."

"How about your sister?"

"She doesn't work here." He stepped toward the door that led to the cars.

"What does she do?"

"She manages a beauty school."

"On the Island?"

He turned back to look at me. "You're awfully curious."

"I told you I was nosy. Does the beauty school have a name?"

"What is this?" He laughed. "Do you want to look at cars or not?"

"Okay," I said, giving him a flirtatious smile. "Let's look at cars."

Forty-five minutes later, I sat in a coffee shop browsing through the Yellow Pages and copying down the names, addresses, and phone numbers of all the beauty schools on Staten Island. Then I got in my car, took out my cellphone, and worked my way through the list, asking for Dianne Ferrara. I got lucky on the fifth call, but I didn't wait for Dianne to pick up her extension. I just flicked off the phone with my thumb and headed for the Parisian Beauty Academy.

It wasn't much to look at—a stucco box streaked with rusty stains and plopped down in a gravel parking lot. But the sign on the door said "Deluxe Salon Services at Discount Prices—Walk-Ins Welcome." I crunched over the gravel and walked in.

Nobody was at the reception desk.

In the next room, heads were lined up on a counter, women's heads, with poreless rubber skin and lustrous hair that seemed to grow out of tiny holes in their rubber scalps. One of the heads, a brunette whose high brows gave her face a surprised look, was having her hair set by a young woman with vivid orange curls. Other young women were working on the rest of the heads.

"Somebody'll help you in a second," the young woman with the orange curls said. "Have a seat."

I settled into a chair covered in cracked naugahyde and grabbed a magazine. The cover showed a gorgeous model in narrow-legged jeans, a filmy top that flared to her hipbones, and stiletto-heeled shoes.

The next thing I knew, Dianne Ferrara was striding toward me. From the neck down, she looked like the model on the magazine cover, complete with impractical shoes and fashion forward outfit. From the neck up, she looked like her brother, except she'd plucked her brows into graceful curves, darkened her lashes, and emphasized the shape of her mouth with wine-colored gloss.

"Here's a customer for you," she said to the young woman with the orange curls as she studied my hair. "Shampoo, trim, and blow dry?" I was tempted to resist the trim, but it occurred to me that between the gush of the water and the roar of the dryer, there'd be no opportunity for a chat.

I complimented my stylist, Cherry, on her orange curls and her shampooing technique, so by the time she had my hair toweled off and combed out, she was putty in my hands.

"How are jobs for hair stylists now?" I asked. I opened the magazine absentmindedly. It was clear that Dianne Ferrara got her fashion ideas from the publications in her reception room.

"Oh, good. Really, really good." She had a sweet, high-pitched voice and pale eyes that blinked a little too often. "I want to work in Manhattan." She giggled. "That's my dream."

"When do you finish here?"

"I'll be done by Christmas. It'll be sort of my present, you know?" Another giggle.

Meanwhile one hand lifted bits of my hair and the other snipped the ends with a pair of surgical-looking scissors. "Not too much off," I said. "If it's too short, it won't dry right." I still had the magazine open, and a small clump of hair fell onto an image of a gorgeous model in uncomfortable-looking shoes.

"This seems like a pretty nice school." I glanced around the room. Dianne was standing in the doorway.

"Oh, it is. It really, really is." Cherry leaned down and whispered, "I'd say that even if the manager wasn't listening." She punctuated the statement with another giggle. "She's such a wonderful person. Too bad she's leaving."

"Where's she going?"

"Florida." Cherry had worked her way around to my bangs. "Close your eyes," she murmured. I could feel tiny clumps of wet hair skim my eyelids and my cheeks. "She's leaving in a year or so. That's what I heard anyway." A soft brush dusted my face.

"Why Florida?" I said.

"It's warm all the time, and it's pretty. Wouldn't you want to live there?" She ran the brush over my face again. "You can open your eyes." She reached for the hair dryer.

When she was done, I gave her a ten-dollar tip.

Out in the reception room, I fished out another ten-dollar bill and handed it to Dianne Ferrara. My hair looked pretty good, and the price was right.

"I hope you'll come back," she said.

While I tucked my wallet away, a burly guy in biker's garb entered.

"Is that the restroom?" I asked, spying a door with the outline of a woman on it. "I'll just pop in for a second."

"Did you find them?" I heard Dianne ask as I closed the door behind me.

The building was fairly new and cheaply built—I'd noticed that from outside. The restroom door was one of those hollow jobs. I held my breath and stuck my ear against the flimsy wood panel that made up the inner surface.

A male voice said something I couldn't make out, then Dianne said, "One thing at a time. I give him a year. Tops."

I drove to my dad's, and we walked up the hill to Eric's place, an apartment in a nondescript brick building. We knew he wouldn't be there, but that was the point. A couple of black kids loitered on the sidewalk, grooving to whatever they were listening to on their iPods. I reached for my lock-pick kit.

"Whatcha got there?" My dad eyed the plastic case.

"We have to get in," I said. I studied the lock and selected a pick.

He pulled a set of keys from his pocket. "You can save yourself the effort," he told me. "Eric liked me to keep an eye on the place when he had road gigs."

Once we were inside, he headed for a stairwell at the back of the tiny lobby. "I don't trust the elevator," he called over his shoulder.

The stairwell was amazingly dirty, and it smelled like Mc-Donald's takeout.

Being in somebody's house when they don't know I'm there always gives me a creepy feeling. I wonder what they'd have gotten rid of if they'd known somebody was going to be snooping.

At first glance it was pretty much what I expected—music gear in the living room, dirty dishes in the kitchen, and an unmade bed in the bedroom.

In the bathroom, a couple of none-too-clean towels hung from the towel rack. I wasn't convinced that Eric was innocent, so I shoved back the shower curtain and checked the tub for signs of blood or dirt. But I found nothing except the grime that accumulates in tubs that aren't scrubbed very often.

Back in the bedroom, I twisted the knob on what I assumed was the closet door. That's when things got interesting.

The door was locked.

"Hey, Mutt," I called. He was in the living room thumping on one of Eric's basses.

"Find something?" he yelled back.

"Have you got a key for this closet?"

He came in jingling the keys. "There's three on here," he said, "the downstairs door and the upstairs one, but I think the little one is for the mailbox."

I tried the closet door once more, then got to work.

"What do you think is in there?" my dad said, stooping to watch as I inserted the pick and listened for the click that would tell me I'd nudged a pin out of the way.

"Something he wants to keep private," I said. I held up a finger. A click, and then another click, told me I was getting close. A few more clicks and I twisted the pick. Then I turned the knob. The door swung open to reveal women's clothes. Lots of them.

"That looks like Linda's stuff," my dad said. He shook his head. "The poor guy. It's like a shrine." He fixed me with mournful eyes. "He couldn't be the one that killed her."

"Fancy stuff." I reached for a black and pink taffeta number with a full skirt and a scoop neck outlined in sequins and held it to my shoulders.

"Wait a minute," my dad said, a look of horrified puzzlement on his face.

"Not my style?" I laughed.

"That can't be Linda's."

"Better taste?"

"No, it's not that." He smiled sadly. "Linda was tiny."

Still holding the dress to my shoulders, I looked down. The waist hung three inches below my waist, and the skirt, even though the proportions of the dress suggested that it was meant to skim the calves, reached my ankles.

"This is huge."

My dad nodded. "Huge."

"Something that might fit Eric."

He nodded again. "Something that might fit Eric."

I pawed through the dresses—silks, satins, some trimmed in lace, one with marabou waving gently around the neckline. And arranged in neat pairs below were shoes, high-heeled shoes, in colors that matched the dresses. I turned toward my dad.

"He never said anything to you?"

"No," my dad said. "He didn't."

"Did Linda know?"

He shrugged. I reached for one of the most striking dresses and fingered the fabric, purple shantung with flecks of gold.

I remembered the shoes on Richmond Terrace. Purple, with gold stiletto heels. The criminal leaves something at the crime scene and takes something away. Everybody knows that now because they watch *CSI*.

So let's say somebody drags a body through the mud. He gets mud on his nice purple shoes and he says to himself, mud will get in the car, and the cops will find the mud and pin the crime on me when they check my shoes. Better to jettison the shoes along with the body.

I couldn't imagine what else I might find to rival this discovery, but for the sake of thoroughness I headed for the kitchen.

"Is Eric's grandmother still alive?" I wanted to know as soon as I looked around.

"How could she be?" he asked. "Eric's my age."

"What do you think this means?" I pointed to a calendar. The square for October 20th, the previous Saturday, had been filled in with the notation "Grandmas—8 sharp."

"Don't have a clue," my dad said.

The next morning, the yellow tape and the cop car were gone from the dump site, together with the purple shoes. But checking on the shoes wasn't the main reason for my visit.

I paced along the road, scanning the strip of dirt between the asphalt and the grass that edged the scruffy woods. I was looking for tire tracks. Asphalt wouldn't retain much, nor would grass—dirt would.

Cop cars and the crime scene guys had come and gone over the past couple of days, and any tracks near the road had been pretty well obliterated. But leading right into the trash pile, there was a bare patch of earth where cars backing up with stuff to dump had worn away the grass.

I studied it, looking for patterned grooves. I noticed several sets, and it was obvious that a few brands of tires had left marks in last week's fresh mud. But one seemed most recent, overlapping and obliterating parts of the others.

Back at my car, I pulled my casting kit, a plastic zipper bag, and a bottle of water out of the trunk and set to work making an impression of the tracks.

When I got to my dad's place, he was still asleep. I made a cup of herbal tea—I was longing for coffee, but he doesn't keep it around—and sat at the table in the kitchen while he and Ernest snored in the next room. Several copies of the *Village Voice* were lying on the kitchen counter. I was idly paging through one when something caught my eye—that week's band lineup for the Coven Club.

I picked up another copy of the *Voice*, an older one, and checked the ad for the Coven Club. Same deal. Forgetting my tea, which was pretty forgettable anyway, I rummaged through the whole pile of papers, getting more excited by the minute.

I left a note for my dad, slipped out the front door, and took the ferry to Manhattan. There, I went strolling down Second Avenue, past the curious assortment of storefronts that make up the East Village—tattoo parlor side by side with Ukrainian bakery, thrift shop neighbor to upscale restaurant.

The Coven Club turned out to be a storefront with the windows painted black and a wood-plank door like something from a medieval castle. The bartender was a blond guy with a stud in his lower lip. He was leaning on the bar and absentmindedly humming along to a song that featured a tormented vocal against a synthesized rhythm backup.

It was early, and only a few people were drinking, spread out along the rough wood bar so nobody was right next to anybody else. Before I sat down, I scanned the wall opposite the bar. Posters from the bands that played there were tacked up, some simple black and white, done crudely on purpose to look homemade, others full-color professional jobs.

The one I was looking for made me giggle when I found it. It was a poster for a band called "The Grandmas." The lead singer was posed like a diva with an armful of flowers, while another band member was knitting. A third sipped from a china tea cup, his pinkie in the air.

Yes, *his* pinkie. They were all guys in drag, and Eric, number four, wore the taffeta dress with the sequins around the neck.

I climbed onto a bar stool a few stools away from the nearest person, a young woman in leggings and an oversized gray turtleneck.

"Music tonight?" I asked when the bartender set a draft in front of me. I raised it to my lips and tilted it back till I tasted beer instead of foam.

"Only weekends."

"When will the Grandmas be back?"

"Not sure," he said. "They're havin' some problems."

"Did they play Saturday?"

"Nope."

"Were they having problems then?"

"Nope." He shook his head. His blond hair was shaped into stiff points that didn't move when his head moved. "Private party."

"Do you know where?"

He looked at the young woman in the turtleneck. "Did Jason say where the Grandmas were playing last Saturday night?"

"Uptown somewhere. Some big deal thing in the East Sixties."

I took the Number 6 train up to 68th, then cut over to Fifth and zigzagged south. It was pretty much one consulate after another, grand brownstones with flags in front and Department of Transportation signs restricting parking to cars with diplomat plates. At the corner of Fifth and 64th, a tow truck was hauling somebody's BMW away.

I pulled out my cellphone.

My dad's machine picked up the call, and his recorded voice told me he was hip to my jive and he'd catch me later. I prayed he was just feeling lazy, not out walking Ernest or drumming so loud he hadn't heard the phone.

"Mutt?" I said to his machine. "This is important. Please pick up."

In a second I heard his real voice. "What's happening?"

"What kind of car does Eric drive?"

"I don't know…a van or something, maybe one of those Econoline things."

"Color?"

"White?" He took a bite of something. "By the way, he's out."

"What?"

"Out on bail. His son sprang him."

The tow pound is on the Hudson at 38th Street. I'd been hoping to see a lot with all the towed cars looking kind of like the lot at Island Pre-Owned, something where I could browse along till I found Eric's van.

But wherever the cars were, they weren't visible from the street, so I walked up a narrow ramp that led to the office.

The tow pound lady's head nearly filled the frame of her grime-streaked window. There were five other windows just like it, and a row of twenty beat-up plastic seats bisected the large room. I was the only customer.

"Registration and license?" She was a pleasant-looking black lady in a chartreuse sweater and hoop earrings.

"I don't have them," I said. "I lost my wallet."

She raised her hands to where I could see them through the window and made a palms-up gesture. "Nothin' I can do for you then." She smiled like this was good news. One of her front teeth was outlined in gold.

"Is there some way I could make sure it's here," I said. "Make sure it was towed and not stolen. I've been having a lot of bad luck…"

"I got hundreds of cars here—"

"Where are they?"

"Out back." She tilted her head toward a doorway at the far corner of the room.

Before she could say anything else, I scuttled past the other five windows and launched myself through the doorway.

Rows and rows of cars. Then a cop blocked my way and nodded back toward the office.

Back at the window, I begged. "*Please* tell me if it's here," I said. "*Please.* It's gonna take me a lot of effort to come up with one hundred eighty five dollars—"

"Plus twenty a day for storage," she said. "And whatever the ticket was for."

I let my lip quiver like I was about to cry, then I hid my face in my hands. "Oh, no," I murmured in my most piteous voice. I let my hands fall away. "It's a van," I said. "An Econoline. White. Maybe the officer…" I glanced toward the doorway. He was standing inside now, and I gave him a mournful smile.

She sighed. "Okay," she said. "Tell him I said it was okay. But you stay inside."

It took fifteen minutes, but he confirmed that, yes, a white Econoline van had been towed the previous Saturday night. "Sorry it took me so long," he said. "There's a lotta cars out there. After a while you forget what you're lookin' for."

So Eric must have come home on the ferry.

Rows and rows of cars, I said to myself as I headed east on 38th. Just like the lot at Island Pre-Owned. So many cars the cop hardly knew what he was looking for. A person could hide a car in a lot like that.

It was dinner time when I got back to my dad's. I hadn't even eaten lunch, so I took him for Chinese food on the crowded shopping street down the hill from his place. On the way, I bought us some beer.

"How long has Eric been out?" I asked after I'd opened two beers and waved away the glass he offered.

"Since Sunday afternoon." He smiled sadly. "Plenty of time for him to retrieve his fancy shoes." I had told my dad about my early-morning visit to the dump site.

"Don't worry, Mutt," I said. "Those weren't his shoes. He didn't do it." I took a long swallow of beer. "I'm glad he's out."

"He didn't even call his kids," my dad said. "They heard about it on the radio."

"Why wasn't he home when we went to his place?"

"He's staying with his daughter."

Then my dad told me about Eric's kids, the college-professor son and the daughter with the law degree and the top-level government job.

"Still no alibi though?"

My dad shook his head. "No alibi."

I told him about the Grandmas, then said, "I guess he'd rather have his kids believe he killed their mother than let on that he likes to wear women's clothes."

"I don't know," my dad said. "I asked him that. I told him we found his dresses in the closet." He picked at the label on his beer. "I think there's more to it than the dressing up thing, but I don't know what it is."

We ate our stir-fry, then I drove out to Island Pre-Owned Cars.

The lot wasn't as dark as I would have liked. Floodlights on tall poles made the cars gleam like it was noon. And that stretch of Hylan Boulevard is wide and bustling, even at night, with a McDonald's on one corner and a gas station on another.

I took a deep breath, pulled out my lock-pick kit, and tried to fake the pose of a passerby interested in the cars. Meanwhile, my fingers maneuvered the pick into the padlock that secured the gate.

As I worked, a bus wheezed up and some people climbed off. I could hear them talking, and I felt my busy hands grow clammy and a pulse start ticking in my throat.

The rush of the bus's departure muffled the clicks I was listening for, so I turned around casually, leaning against the fence to hide the lock from anybody who might wonder what I'd been doing there.

A man headed in my direction.

"Hey," he shouted. My throat tightened in alarm, and I slipped the pick into my pocket.

He sped up. In a minute he stood next to me. He was an older guy, dressed in dark pants and a tailored jacket that looked like part of a uniform.

"Been standing here long?" he said.

"No," I gulped. "Not really."

"Notice the number on the bus that just left?"

The tightness in my throat dissolved. "No," I said. "Sorry."

"Which one are you waiting for?"

"Umm…none of them. I was on my way to get a burger when I stopped to look at the cars."

"In the market for a car?"

"Not really." I looked at my watch. "Better get going." I took a few steps.

"You're on foot?" he said. "Do you live around here?"

"No…I mean yes." The light turned green and I sprinted for the corner.

From the vantage point of McDonald's, I watched until another bus lumbered up and the chatty guy vanished.

Five minutes later, I was back at the fence, hearing the satisfying click that told me I'd edged the last pin into position. I twisted the pick and the padlock sprang open with a louder click.

Then I headed for the back of the lot. If I wanted to hide a car, even if I was hiding it by putting it in a lot full of cars, I'd put it where it wasn't visible from the street.

Tucked into a shopping bag, I'd brought the cast of the tire tracks from the dump site. I'd Googled one of those websites that lets you attach tire makers to tread patterns, and I knew I was looking for a set of Goodyear Wranglers.

A row of cars, mostly Japanese, were lined up against the

stretch of chain link fence that divided Island Pre-Owned from a lot covered with scrubby brown grass. Even back here the lights were bright; in fact when I looked toward the street, the flood-lights made me feel like I was onstage. So I crouched down and crept from car to car like a frog, knees bent and hands braced against the asphalt.

Lots of cars had Goodyear Wranglers, and I checked each set, looking for a pattern that matched the cast: the result of the tread the tire started out with and its subsequent adventures.

Half an hour later, my calves ached from the strain of my constant crouch, and my fingers throbbed from the cold and the roughness of the asphalt. A chilly wind had sprung up.

I'd worked my way through the cars behind the office and was now at the other side of the lot, trying to stay low enough that the cars between me and the street shielded me from sight.

I was checking the back left tire of a Toyota SUV with Good-year Wranglers when I noticed something that made my heart beat double-time. The steady zigzag of the tread was interrupted by gravel wedged into the rubber grooves.

I rocked back into a sitting position, stretched my cramped legs, and pulled out the cast. In effect I had used the prints at the dump site as a mold to make a replica of the tire that created them. The cast I now studied in the beam of my flashlight featured zig-zag grooves interrupted by lumps, as if something had wedged in the treads of the tire that had made the original print.

Something like gravel.

Something like the gravel in the parking lot of the Parisian Beauty Academy.

I'd found the car I was looking for, but I wasn't done yet. I set to work on the tailgate lock.

It was a tough one, and my hands were so cold and scraped that I could hardly feel them. To make matters worse, since the Toyota was backed up against the chain link fence that marked off the side of the lot, there was no way I could do what I had to do and not be visible from Hylan Boulevard.

My ear was so close to the lock that my icy fingers fluttered against my cheek as I worked. I listened for the clicks that would tell me the lock was ready to open. My eyes were closed in concentration. When I heard the final click, I opened them.

Out on Hylan Boulevard, a cop car slowed.

I dropped to the ground and willed myself to become invisible. I waited what seemed a very long time but was in reality probably about two minutes. No car doors, no voices, no footsteps, so I raised my head and looked toward Hylan. A stream of headlights flowed by as the cop car inched along the curb.

I watched as he glided past. When I couldn't see him anymore, I rose to my knees and gave the pick a final twist. The tailgate popped up. I picked up my flashlight and leaned into the back of the SUV.

It was lined with a dark, furry material that had seen better days. The nap was worn off in spots, matted down in others. I shone the flashlight on one of the matted spots. Since the furry stuff was dark, I couldn't tell whether what had matted it had also stained it. Not wanting to confuse things by leaving a sample of my own DNA, I resisted the urge to spit on a tissue and rub the spot to see what came off.

Instead I scraped at it with the tip of the lock pick till some powdery bits came loose, then I covered my fingers with a tissue and pinched the bits up. When I added a bit of saliva, I came up with a blotch that looked like a bloodstain.

As I tucked the tissue away, I heard voices.

"False alarm the other night," one of them said. "I thought you had a break-in, but it was only your sister and her friend. They said they were picking up papers for your dad."

The tailgate was still open. I lowered it as quietly as possible, but I couldn't risk the noise latching it would make. Then I crawled under the car, inching forward on my elbows, the smell of dirt and motor oil in my nostrils.

The other man spoke. It was Frank Ferrara. "Thanks, officer," he was saying. "I appreciate you keeping an eye on the place."

"All in a night's work." The cop laughed.

"Back here by the fence, you said?"

"Messing around with this Toyota."

I could see their feet, standing near the driver's-side door. My chest was pressed against the asphalt and my heart beat so hard I was sure they must feel it through the soles of their shoes.

Their feet now moved toward the back of the car.

"The tailgate's unlatched," the cop said. I heard a squeak, and the car shuddered as the tailgate popped up.

"Anything in there?" Frank asked.

"Lemme grab my flash."

A circle of light appeared near the cop's feet. It vanished for a minute—I guess he was checking inside the car—then began to dance around the back tire. It danced along the side of the car, checked the front tire, and then it was shining in my face.

"Somebody's under here," the cop said. I heard a click as a holster unsnapped and a swish as a gun was unholstered. "Come on out," he said. He sounded bored, like he'd said the same thing a million times.

"I have to back out," I said. "That's how I got in." My heart pounded even harder now.

"Make it quick."

A few minutes later, I'd pulled myself to my feet and was inspecting the condition of my hands, trying to brush off the bits of asphalt that hadn't worked their way into my skin.

The cop still held the gun on me. He was a bulky guy with a red face and little close-set eyes. Frank Ferrara stared at me and frowned like a guy who'd just discovered somebody put something over on him.

"What are you up to?" he asked.

At the same instant, the cop said, "Got an explanation?"

I took a deep breath. "Actually, I do." With shaking hands, I handed him my PI license.

He looked at it skeptically, stared back and forth from the picture to me. Finally he grunted and shoved his gun back into his holster, but he didn't snap the holster closed. "What are you doing here?"

"This car was used to drop Linda Nelson's body at that Richmond Terrace dump. There's dried blood in the back."

He started to say something but didn't get a chance to finish because Frank Ferrara snatched the cop's gun.

I pushed my jacket aside and pulled out the five-shot snubby that Joe Dogherty had left me in his will. Frank's eyes went wide and his jaw dropped, and the cop grabbed the muzzle of the gun Frank was holding. He twisted it toward the ground then delivered a karate chop to Frank's wrist. In a few seconds the cop had his gun back and Frank was wearing handcuffs.

"He and his sister killed Linda," I said. "With a little help from his sister's boyfriend."

"Not sure I can see why they'd do that," the cop said, panting a little.

"Linda was engaged to their father," I told him. "They didn't want her to inherit his money. Dianne got mud on her purple stilettos while they were dumping the body, so she dumped those too. Then she sent her boyfriend to retrieve them."

"Tony's not old," the cop said. "He could hang on for twenty-five more years or longer."

"Maybe," I said. "But his brother died of a heart attack last year, and Tony's only a couple years younger. Dianne was already planning what she was going to do with her share of the inheritance."

The new arrests in the Linda Nelson case weren't the only sensational news in the next morning's Staten Island *Advance*. The main headline read, "New York Pols in Gay Sex Scandal."

The article described lavish orgies at taxpayer expense, complete with kinky musical entertainment, in an Upper East Side penthouse.

"This guy," Eric said, pointing to the photo that accompanied the article. "My daughter—Suzie—works for him. It's all out in the open now, but before…? If I told the cops where I was Saturday night, it woulda gotten in the tabloids…some headline like 'Drag Queen Alibi, ' and lots of other stuff too, like who threw the party and who else was there. What would've happened to Suzie's career if her boss got outed on the front page of the *Daily News* all because of her dad?"

WESTCHESTER

NONE OF THE ABOVE
by Deirdre Verne

"So who took it?" Donna plunked herself down on her diva chair and popped open a can of soda. A speck of carbonation shot out and landed on the red velvet upholstery.

"Shit, I keep doing that." A well-manicured fingernail quickly scooped up the splotch. I know Donna loves her new chaise. It's one of those Hollywood-style divan couches most often used by starlets with the vapors. I watched Donna stretch out her five-foot-two frame, toss off her stiletto heels, and rest her soda can on her ample bosom. Ten red toes gleamed back at me. I might have to spoil the fantasy and tell Donna there is no attractive way to get on and off the vapor couch. Especially, if you're packing an extra ten pounds into a pair of skin-tight black leggings.

Donna took a slurp and motioned for me to sit down.

"Kick back, Prof, and gimme some scoop."

I settled into the non-coordinating black leather recliner and curled my legs under me, then glanced around the room and took in Donna's décor. Imagine if Maurice Villency and Victoria's Secret had a one-night stand and spawned a line of furnishings destined for a Poconos honeymoon suite. Yes, I know. It hurts to think about.

I looked away from the leopard print ottoman, and I focused my attention back to Donna.

"I have no idea who took it."

"I'm telling you, it was Horse Girl."

"I don't think so."

"Okay, how about Miguel the Mower?"

"No."

"Fine, then it was Hot Paolo Pizza Boy."

"Donna, drop the stereotypes. It's getting offensive."

"You started it, missy.

She had a point there.

The suspects in question were my students—good kids representing the wide demographic make-up of Westchester County, NY. My classroom was a mix of the traditional landscape—Italian and Jewish families who had migrated north from the Bronx; wealthy, landed families from northern Katonah; and a smattering of African-American kids from neighborhoods in and around our biggest city, White Plains. Add to that a huge influx of Hispanic families climbing their way up through quasi-industrial areas like Port Chester and a sprinkle of Asian families who all but owned smaller villages like Hartsdale. Then throw people like Donna into the mix, and you got a boatload of Brooklyn from just over the bridge.

I wasn't stereotyping. I was being efficient. Each semester I had more than a hundred students across four courses. It took me two months to get their names down, so colorful descriptions filled the gap. Donna added the flourishes.

"How 'bout that hot Italian kid you were telling me about?" Donna had asked earlier.

"I never said he was hot. I just said he was Italian and his parents owned a pizza place on Arthur Avenue in the Bronx. And his name is Anthony."

"Right, him—Hot Paolo Pizza Boy. Tell me again what he looks like."

Could I help it if her monikers stuck?

I chose to forgo a full body description of Hot Paolo and opted for the issue at hand. A stolen test. As I explained to Donna, I had passed out thirty-two sequentially numbered test booklets and thirty-two answer sheets. At the end of the test, I'd had thirty-one test booklets and thirty-two answer sheets. Someone had walked out with the test. Of course as Donna'd so logically pointed out, I could have asked the students to put their names on everything, but I didn't. Hey, I'm new at this teaching thing.

Two years ago I left my high-paying job as an advertising exec in Manhattan for the greener pastures of Mommyhood. Nine months into a seemingly endless pile of laundry, I realized my brain had shrunk. The opportunity for adult conversation was limited. My globe-trotting husband averaged more miles in a month than Phileas Fogg had logged in 180 days. I was deliriously happy caring for my newborn son, Randy, but I couldn't spell my own name—Zoe Johnstone. Or rather now, Professor Zoe Johnstone. An esteemed, fulltime member of the Business Department at Hudson College located thirty minutes north of the city in Westchester County, NY. Ta daa!

The magical balancing act had begun. Half a day exercising my brain and the other half exercising my heart. Donna was the key to the act. My babysitter, my best friend, and now my sister in crime.

I took a quick peek at my watch—three p.m. If I let Donna suck me into a few hours of super sleuthing, I wouldn't get a chance to squeeze in some grading tonight. I started to rise from the recliner and beg off but was quickly sideswiped by the immutable force of an investigative Donna.

"Come on, sweetie. Pop a squat and let's figure out which one of your co-eds swiped the test." She grabbed the baby monitor and held it to her ear. "The kids are asleep so we've got a good hour to pin the crime on Horse Girl. I got my eye on her." Donna jabbed a threatening nail tip at me.

In the world outside of Donna's head, Horse Girl responded to the name Naomi Stone. Tall, rich, beautiful, and unbelievably spoiled, Naomi hailed from Bedford Estates, a never-ending hamlet of horse trails and gated homes. From the minute I'd handed Naomi the syllabus, I could tell the line had been drawn. In her eyes, I was the help. Naomi had pushed her hand toward me and politely asked me to email her the syllabus. The strange thing is

I actually considered it. The request was made with an air of authority and detachment that only comes with inherited wealth. I put her copy of the syllabus on my desk, turned my back, and said no. Gotcha Horse Girl! Later Donna put me in my place.

"That's it? All you said was *No*? What are you nuts?" Donna was enraged at my benign reaction. "You gotta set that girl straight. You remind the Bedford beauty that it's a privilege to sit in your classroom. That's right, dammit. A privilege. She works for you this semester and not the other way around. Got it?"

I had to admit Donna was pretty good when you got her going. I considered her offer to stay and nail Horse Girl's head to wall. I mentally reworked my afternoon schedule and ignored the fact that Donna had put the kids down for a nap at three p.m. Randy would be up until at least ten p.m. tonight, ruining any chance for me to grade papers. Truth be told, I was no match for Donna. She had me every time. Including the day we met.

When I'd landed the teaching job, I'd realized I needed someone to watch Randy for about twenty hours a week. I decided to do my course prep work at home and spend as few hours out of the house as possible. Initially, I had no idea how the nanny thing worked, but I quickly learned that twenty hours a week did not constitute a job.

Turns out, suburban Westchester nannies are looking for big-time money and big-time hours. I interviewed a stream of Jamaican, Hispanic, and Eastern European candidates asking at least six hundred dollars a week. In exchange, the winning nanny would show up at seven a.m. and stay twelve straight hours. My child would be fed, bathed, walked, and read to. My house would be clean, laundry folded, and meals prepared. Randy could even learn Spanish or Polish or at the least adopt a Caribbean accent. Imagine that. I could hire someone to live my life and do it better than me. I'd opted for Donna.

"Here's the deal." Donna had leaned forward, grabbed both my hands, and delivered an impassioned speech. "I don't need the money, and I don't like babysitting. I got two kids of my own.

Why would I want Randy too? The sad thing is I've been bored out of my mind since we moved up here from Long Island. I hate this McMansion my husband bought, and I hate my neighbors. Not that they'd dare to lower themselves and say hello to me."

Donna had glared through her Palladian front window and motioned her head across the street. "I swear my loser neighbor has a supersonic garage door opener. He opens the door a half mile away, zips in, and shuts it just to avoid conversation. What I need is someone to talk to once in a while and maybe a play-mate for my kids. So what do you say? You and me. Three kids between us. The college is a stone's throw away from my house. You drop Randy off on your way, chat me up, and pick him up in the afternoon."

I remember looking at Donna at that particular moment. She was like no one I had ever met. Brazen, ballsy, loud. But underneath that halo of thick, dark hair and teeny-bopper attire, I sensed a pure, genuine soul. And, she was the only one who would take the twenty hours. We could have shaken on it, but Donna'd already had a tight grip on my hands.

"See. You're in. Thata girl!" Donna offered me a sip of her soda and listened again for the kids.

"Sure. Why not?" I settled back down into the leather recliner and accepted my fate.

"Gimme a recap"

"Right. Well, the test was this past Monday. After the test I collected the materials and headed back to my office. I counted only thirty-one. I ran back to the classroom but no loose test. Then I ransacked my office. No test."

Donna nodded solemnly and motioned for me to continue.

"The class met again today. Wednesday. I walked in and the students could see I was pissed off. I told them what happened." I sank back into the chair and relived the enormity of my next move and the students' subsequent reaction.

"Okay, guys. Bring it down a notch." I'd dropped my books on the podium using the thunk to silence the class. Then I crossed my arms over my chest and assumed a fed-up pose. I started right in. No pleasantries.

"Someone stole the test. I don't know if it was on purpose or not, but a test is missing. You may not be aware, but I put a number on the back of each test. I passed out thirty-two exams and thirty-one were returned."

The room was quiet. A number of jaws dropped. "I'm going back to my office. I'll return in an hour. The test better be on this desk or in my mailbox on the fourth floor. If the test isn't returned in the next hour, I'm failing the entire class." I walked out.

On my way down the hall, I noticed the classroom next to mine was open. And empty. I darted in and pressed my ear against the wall. This type of maneuver ranks right up there with reading your teenager's diary. And just like a hidden diary I got an earful of crap I would have rather not known.

I listened in as Rodney Purcell, the star of the football team, pulled the trigger first. Eddie Sanchez was his victim.

"You stupid fuckin' spic. Put it on the desk."

"I didn't take no test, homeboy. My guess is that the football team needed a little something to study from. Last I heard, you guys are back out on drug alley unless the team grade-point average goes up past zero."

"Why the fuck would I risk my football scholarship on a lameass scheme like this?"

"What's the good of scholarship if you ain't got no team." Hey, good point, Eddie. I see the debate club in your future.

"If you ask me," Eddie continued, "I'm putting my pesos on Lady Naomi."

"Surprise, surprise," Naomi purred. "You know my name."

Oh, my God, what a royal bitch. Naomi's tone dripped with self-importance and condescension. In her sphere of existence, Eddie was just an anonymous face relegated to the service entrance.

Naomi issued a bored sigh. "Why in God's name would I take the test?"

"Because, Naomi, rules don't exist for you." Right on, Eddie. You are one insightful guy.

"Then I guess I'm free to go." I heard Naomi's chair drag across the institutional linoleum.

And then a door slammed at a deafening level.

"Zoe!"

"Shit!" I popped off the wall like a rubber ball and rebounded into an overhead projector. "Geez, Bob. You scared the daylights out of me. Why did you slam the door?" Bob, my best school buddy, stood leaning against the classroom door smiling at me.

"What the hell are you doing, Zoe?"

"Shhh. I'm eavesdropping on my students. Quick, come here." I made some room for Bob and filled him in on the stolen test. We caught the end of Anthony tearing apart Donald, the computer geek, when Bob suggested we do something more professional like get a cup of coffee.

We headed over to the cafeteria, while I checked my watch and reminded Bob I had to scurry back in a half hour to see if the test materialized. We grabbed our coffees and took a seat away from the crowd.

"So you told them you were going to fail the whole class?"

I shrugged innocently and sipped my coffee.

"That's harsh, Zo."

"I didn't really think about the consequences."

"That works well if your last name is Machiavelli." Bob started to crack up.

"Thanks for your support and encouragement in my time of need."

"Okay, okay. What are you going to do?"

"Well, if the test is returned, then I do nothing but thank the class for their honesty."

"And if it's not?"

"That would be Plan B, right?" I asked Bob. "Yeah, well I don't have one of those."

I left Bob in the cafeteria and headed back to the classroom.

Guess what? No test in the room and no test in my mailbox.

I recapped all of this for Donna, including my conversation with Bob.

"I like Bob. He's good people," Donna offered.

"Yeah. You definitely need at least one confidant at work. I can tell Bob stupid shit like this and not feel bad about it." I confirmed Donna's assessment of Bob.

In fact, Bob Carlin and I had started at Hudson on the same day, both of us newbies straight out of the business world. Bob, an attorney, had given up the faintest hope of ever making partner. The two of us had spent the last couple of years in complete cahoots laughing about students, administrators, and the other profs around the campus. Bob had even crossed the great work divide and joined Donna and me for pizza night with the kids.

"Who does Bob think took the test?" Donna asked me.

"Funny—he didn't say. He actually has a lot of the same students in his business law class so he knows the crowd. I think lawyers are used to protecting their clients. He does think I need to come clean, however."

"What do you mean?'

"Well, he knows I can't really fail the whole class. But he's afraid my poor judgment will get back to the administration and I'll be penalized for making a rash statement to the class."

"Why?"

"Well, this falls under the banner of Classroom Management. An experienced teacher isn't supposed to create a negative learning environment."

"Whoa. I feel a load of crap coming my way." Donna started to chuckle.

"Stop laughing. This is for real. A good teacher is supposed to defuse situations like this. Not instigate them. I'm telling you it was like a WWF pro-wrestling match in that classroom after I left."

"So Miguel the Mower held his own, huh?"

"Yeh, Eddie is a good kid, but there is certainly some friction between the racial groups on campus."

"Wake up, honey. That's old news in Westchester these days."

"True." I pondered the students' reactions. I have to admit I was amazed at how quickly the accusations took on an ethnic slant. Bob was right. This could get out of control, and my head would be the one on the chopping block. Bob had suggested I go right to the dean and tell him what'd happened before the circumstances went any further. He said I should play up my inexperience, take the blame, and then promise that the situation would be remedied in a few days. Bob's plan had some merits, I thought. Typically, a disgruntled student will head straight to the dean. And when a teacher *really* screws up, it is not unusual for a herd of students to pack the dean's office to file a formal complaint. When I'd first started teaching, an unassuming professor had inadvertently used the wrong answer key to grade an exam. True was False and False was True, and so on and so forth. Well, you would have thought the students were protesting the Vietnam War.

According to Bob, it's always better to apologize before you actually get caught. However, if the whole thing simply blew over, my reputation would remain unscathed. In the world of academia, reputation is everything and medieval-style rewards and punishments often surface. The teacher with the wrong answer key had ended up in a basement office. I recounted to Donna all the ways I could get screwed at work.

"So in addition to getting a verbal lashing, I'll probably get a hideous schedule next semester. I'll be assigned an eight a.m. class with a four-hour gap before the next one meets. Then I'll be assigned rooms with zero acoustics and no air circulation. But the real threat is tenure. I could be asked to leave."

"Zoe, come on. That isn't going to happen. You're a great teacher."

"It could happen. But even if I get tenure, I'll definitely be passed over for a promotion."

Donna and I went back and forth trying to figure out which student had a motive to steal the test. In a while, however, a crackling from the baby monitor signaled that our time was up. I tossed a sleepy Randy into the car and headed home. Five o'clock. Not bad. Enough time to bathe Randy and throw some dinner together.

I lugged Randy through the front door and rolled him onto the couch. Then I flicked on the TV and surfed to the Cartoon Network. Maybe Sponge Bob could revive Randy from his late afternoon slumber. As I whizzed past the news channels, an image of Hudson College caught my eye. I whizzed back and caught the end of a local report. A male student at Hudson had been jumped late in the day just off campus. The unidentified student was in serious condition at White Plains Hospital.

I looked over at my answer machine. The light was blinking furiously. *Oh, God, please tell me this didn't involve Eddie.* But the message from the dean's secretary told me otherwise.

I ran into the kitchen, grabbed a handful of animal crackers, and crammed them in a Ziploc baggie. Swooping up an utterly confused Randy and packing him back into the car, I headed straight for the hospital. So much for this whole thing blowing over.

I artfully talked my way past hospital security, using Randy's stroller as a bulldozer. The crazy mother routine comes in handy at times. I worked through the hospital labyrinth and ran straight into Dean White shifting his lanky six-foot frame uncomfortably outside Room 309.

I cringed. Dean White was a decent man. When I'd interviewed for the position, he was one of my biggest supporters despite my lack of prior teaching experience. The closer I got to him, the more I felt the connection between us erode .

"It is Eddie?" I asked.

"Yes, it is." Dean White responded flatly. "Eddie actually asked for you."

"Oh."

"He said to tell you he didn't take the test." Dean White's little forehead vein had reached full pumping potential.

"And?"

"And then he passed out."

"Can we talk?"

"I think it would be better if we scheduled a meeting together tomorrow. I have to deal with the family now." And with that, he turned and entered Eddie's room.

I chugged the stroller back down the hall, took out my cell, and punched in Bob's home number. A nasty nurse started to come after me pointing animatedly at the no cellphone sign. For God's sake, wasn't a cellphone for emergencies? I gave her the finger and shoved the stroller into a stairwell.

"Bob?"

"Hey Zo, what's up?"

"I'm in White Plains Hospital."

"Crap!" I could feel Bob sit straight up, through the phone. "Is it Randy?"

"No, no. He's fine." I looked down at Randy resting comfortably in his stroller. "It's Eddie Sanchez. Someone jumped him. It's about the test."

"You're kidding."

"No, I'm not. It's serious. He got the shit beat out of him. God, it was probably Rodney or maybe Anthony. Who knows?"

"Zoe, you are screwed."

"I know. I know. Any suggestions?" I thought hard, with no result.

"Well, first thing tomorrow, you need to call the teachers' union. If the school administration takes action, then the union will give you legal representation."

"Geez, Bob. You're giving me legal advice. I was just looking for a pep talk."

"No pep talk. Your job is in jeopardy. Call me after you talk to the union rep."

I closed my cellphone and sat down in the dirty stairwell.

Randy handed me an animal cracker and patted me on the head. One impulsive move, and my life blows up. Go figure.

The next morning, I dropped off Randy at Donna's house an hour earlier than usual. I already had a headache and my stomach was upset.

"Hey, sweetie! Did you come early for breakfast?" Donna passed me a gooey donut and fired up the coffee maker. I put down the donut and gave Donna the once over. She was still wearing her pajamas, if you could call them that. I tried not to stare, but the yards of lace, satin, and ribbon were a sight to behold. Quite a step up from my old T-shirts and sweat pants.

I let out a heavy sigh and caught Donna's attention. "Eddie's in the hospital," I said.

Donna quickly sashayed over and led my paralyzed body to a kitchen chair. I started to blubber. The blubbering soon enough gave way to sobbing. Randy kept trying to shove the donut in my face. Funny, I thought. I guess every time he cried, I gave him a cookie to cheer him up. I took the donut just to get rid of him.

"First off, the real problem is not the test." Donna dragged a chair up next to mine and leaned into me. "The problem is the kids. The white kids resent the Asian kids because the Asians are taking all their scholarships. Both the whites and the Asians resent the black kids, and all three groups hate the Hispanics. The test just set off those tensions."

"I know, but people will only remember the test."

"Well, then we need to figure out who took the test and shift the blame to them. We'll let the cops deal with whoever attacked Eddie."

"Okay." I sat up and sniffled back some sugary snot. "Thanks. I guess I'll call you from work and let you know what happens after I talk to the union." I kissed Randy goodbye and set off to face the music.

I drove the two miles to school at a snail's pace, taking a detour through Kensico Cemetery just to cheer myself up. At least I wasn't dead, I figured. The cemetery covered fifteen lush acres and had housed a myriad of Westchester families over the last century. The view was stunning, steep on a hill overlooking the great Kensico dam, a major reservoir serving Manhattan. I looked at the names on the older headstones from the car. Burns, Richardson, Mitchell, Goldfarb, Pagnelli. The landscape had clearly changed over the years. I wondered if Mr. Burns would mind when Mr. Vasquez moved into the next plot for eternity.

I pulled into teachers' parking with a good forty-five minutes to kill before my class. With plans to head straight to the teachers' union offices, I tossed my bags in my office . Anthony caught me just as I was locking my door.

"Hey, Prof!"

"Hi, Anthony."

"So, Prof, you heard about Eddie?"

"I did, Anthony. I called the hospital this morning and the floor nurse said he was resting comfortably."

"Cool. You know I didn't take the test."

"I'm not sure it matters who took the test anymore."

"I know where I can get a copy of it," he added coyly.

"What?"

"I said I know where I can get a copy of it."

I unlocked my office door and invited Anthony in. "Okay. What the fuck is going on? Are you here to blackmail me?"

"What? No way." Anthony was sincerely offended. "I'm trying to tell you that whoever took the test sold it to one of those online sites that sells term papers, tests, whatever. You know what I'm talking about."

I had in fact heard about these sites. Over the past few years an electronic black market had not only surfaced but had flourished. Students could search for pre-written term papers on topics ranging from opera to operations software. Stolen midterms and final exams sorted by school and course code were an easy click away. The site was a death sentence for teachers. Developing a good test is hard. There are just so many multiple choice questions in the world. A publicly available test bank kind of takes the mystery out of earning a grade.

"What's the test selling for?" I asked.

"Fifty bucks."

"Fifty bucks? Great. My career is on the line for fifty bucks. Can I find out who sold it to the website?" I spun my chair around and looked out the window. How the hell had this happened to me? I swung back and faced Anthony.

"Actually, it's on the line for two hundred dollars. The website pays the seller a flat fee of two hundred dollars and then the site resells it at fifty dollars a copy. Anyway, it's totally confidential, and no way in hell will they talk to a teacher."

"That makes sense." I looked at Anthony. I knew that face. Randy had the same one. It was the *I really want to tell you something* face. Like I spilled a gallon of milk on the living room rug. I could usually break Randy in less than sixty seconds. Anthony might take little longer.

"So?" I nudged.

"Yeah, well." Anthony squirmed a little. I could see he wanted to talk, but I'd have to let him stew awhile. Out of the corner of my eye I could see the little blue Microsoft Outlook box in the lower corner of my computer screen blinking new email messages at me. All from Donna. I counted at least three. With Donna there is always a fine line between nagging and genuine concern. I turned my attention back to Anthony.

"Come on, Anthony. You must be here for a reason. Help me out."

Anthony stretched his legs and got comfortable with his confession.

"I couldn't actually get them to reveal the seller, but the site lets you ask questions about the test. You know, like on eBay how you can email the seller questions?"

"Go on."

"So I asked the seller a bunch of questions. How old is the test? What textbook did the class use? Does the test include essays? A bunch of shit like that."

"Right. And?"

"The seller is no dummy. Whoever stole it is an A student."

"Why do you say that?"

"Because it wasn't like reading a MySpace page. It was like chatting with an honor student." Anthony twisted his face in disgust. "Like Donald, the computer freak."

"Geek," I corrected.

"Huh?" Anthony shrugged. Whoops! I'd forgotten who I was talking to.

I waved my hand impatiently. "Maybe the seller wanted to appear professional so buyers wouldn't question the price."

"No, this dude was just way smart."

I rose from my desk and shook Anthony's hand. "I'm really, really sorry this happened. Thanks for coming to me."

"No prob, Prof."

I was already dialing Donna before Anthony left my office. She picked up on the first ring.

"Hey, Donna, it's me."

"Hey, me. You got dirt?"

I told Donna about my meeting with Anthony, and we went back through my class list and reevaluated the students, given this new bit of information. If the thief was a top-notch student then that narrowed the class by about two-thirds. Rodney was out of the running. He really couldn't risk his football scholarship, and he wasn't all that bright. Naomi might have taken it and not even realized it. No malice intended, and no motivation to sell it online. Anthony was in the clear, while poor Eddie was an absolute victim in this mess.

"What can a kid get for two hundred dollars these days? I don't think money is the motivator," Donna said.

"That's a good point."

"Whoever stole the test wanted to embarrass you or maybe

take away some of your power," Donna continued with her line of thought.

"Okay, so I'm looking for a student who maybe I embarrassed in class. A smart student I took down a notch."

"Exactly."

"You know, Donna, that's really perceptive. Sometimes the bright kids try to challenge you. If a teacher gets defensive, she may shoot back at the student even harder. In the end, the student usually loses."

"Is it that easy to crush them?" Donna asked.

"Well, when you've taught the same lesson a hundred times, it's not hard to outwit even a savvy student."

"The problem is," I continued, "I can't remember doing that this semester. It does happen, but so far this semester it's been smooth sailing. I don't really have any aggressive students this term."

"Maybe the slight wasn't obvious to you, but the student took it hard."

"Could be, but that doesn't help me now."

I hung up the phone and looked at my watch. Time for class. Too late to beg the union for help.

Walking to class was like walking the Green Mile. By this time every student on campus had heard about Eddie and THE TEST. I'm sure the gossip was taking on mythic proportions. A reality show was probably in the works. I slithered down the hall feeling like the rat I was. I rounded the corner and forced myself over the threshold only to be met by Dean White, already holding court in front of my class.

"Good morning, Professor Johnstone." The dean reflexively stuck out his hand. We shook. Professional but cold.

The dean launched into a lecture on ethics, humanity, academic freedom, religion, and good ole American ingenuity. I had no idea how he connected the themes, but the end result was spectacular. He made each student feel individually responsible, yet empowered the group to fix the problem. He laid blame on me but helped the students appreciate and empathize with the plight of an authority figure. And finally, he praised Hudson College for embracing differences head on even if it was hard to navigate the new social structure. His speech was the greatest public relations address ever! Of course it had nothing to do with me or Eddie or the test. It was a highly orchestrated attempt at saving the reputation of the college. And if that wasn't enough, the dean dismissed the class after his twenty-minute oratory. How could the students not love him? Go Hudson!

The dean gave me a perfunctory nod and asked me to see him later.

Some of the students came up and shook my hand. A few students made plans to visit Eddie. Anthony winked at me and tilted his head toward Donald the Computer Freak/Geek. I said my goodbyes and walked back to my office with my chin held high.

So high in fact that I missed a three-foot, two-year-old running head first into my shins.

"Randy?" I kneeled down and gave my son a great bear hug. "What are you doing here?"

"Hey, honey." Donna brought up the rear dragging her two kids and Bob behind.

"Donna, this is not good. You can't show up with the kids. I'm already persona non grata around here."

"I know, sweetie. We were headed to the park, but the kids really had to pee. Bob took Randy to the bathroom, and we hung out in his office for a bit."

"All right. Can we just move the party to my office before the dean sees us?"

"Sure thing," Donna said and waved goodbye to Bob.

"Glad I could help." Bob gave us the thumbs up and scooted off.

Donna grabbed my upper arm with a kung fu grip and spit

in my ear. "Your office now!"

We hustled down the hall while I rubbed my arm. Shit, she was strong. We had barely moved the crew into my cramped office when Donna whipped out a Wiggles cassette and popped it into the VCR. She put the volume on low and passed out a bag of M&Ms to each of the three children. Randy's eyes lit up.

"Park it," she ordered me. "I need to ask you some questions."

"Shoot."

"On the day of the test, did you stop anywhere between the classroom and your office?"

"No. I mean yes." I stammered. "I went to the ladies room."

"How many stalls?"

"It's just a single bathroom, and the door locks."

"Okay, then you went back to your office?"

"No, I stopped by the teachers' lounge and picked up my mail."

"Do the students have access to the lounge?"

"Yeh, it's an open room. Students come in and out all the time to drop overdue papers and homework in our mailboxes."

"Besides the random student, who else was in the lounge?"

"Oh God, Donna, I don't remember. I think some of the secretaries were having a cup of coffee. I had a quick conversation with an English adjunct and a math professor." I tried to stretch my memory, but those nine months staying home with Randy had killed one too many brain cells. "I think Bob was goofing on me about my coffee addiction. The usual stuff."

"So you fixed yourself a cup of coffee. And you left the stack of tests where?"

"Near my mail slot." I said the words very slowly. "Out—of—my—sight."

"Zoe, why did Bob tell you to come clean and approach the dean before it got out of hand?"

"I told you already. He thought it would help me save face."

I could feel the anger welling up in my chest. "Donna, don't even go there."

"Exactly how many law firms did Bob work at before he came here?"

"Donna, stop now."

"Nine, Zoe. He worked at nine different firms and never made partner." Donna shot her hand out at me. "Don't argue. I called the American Law Association this morning and checked."

Then she asked, "Who is your competition for tenure and promotion?"

I refused to speak.

"Say it, Zoe. Your competition is all the people who started the same year as you."

I spun my chair toward the wall. Real mature, but I didn't want Donna to see me lose it. If she was right, and I prayed she wasn't, then I was a complete fool. Losing the test and endangering one of my students had already killed my credibility on campus. Getting backstabbed by a friend, and a good friend at that was like rubbing salt in a deep wound. I turned back toward Donna ready to face the music.

"Honey, Bob set you up." I could see Donna was trying to soften the blow. "Unfortunately, he probably didn't know it would explode like this. My guess is he was just going to post the test on that website and put a wrench in your reputation." I watched as Donna leaned down to take something out of her bag. She put my test on the desk.

"I wasn't headed to the park," she said. "I never take the kids to the park. I was looking for a way to get into Bob's office. Randy really did have to pee though. Bob offered to take him while we waited in his office. The test was right in his top drawer."

Donna and I sat quietly for some time. It was tough. I watched the Wiggles perform one of their inane dances and tried to control my breathing. I wasn't sure if it was the pounding of my heart or Donna's voice that broke the silence.

"Zoe, it's time. Go see the dean and tell Bob he needs to go to the union."

"I can't go to the dean. I have no evidence," I blurted out. "I can't just plunk down the test and tell him my babysitter finagled her way into Bob's office and took the liberty of searching through his drawers."

"Hmm," Donna pondered.

"Yeh, hmm," I pondered back. I rubbed my face and stood up abruptly. Then I sat back down and repeated the routine two more times. On the third round, I picked up the phone and dialed Bob's office. I put my finger over my lips and whispered *shhhh* to Donna.

"Oh, Bob, I'm so glad you're there. Look, it's all coming down and I really need you."

Donna eyed me curiously.

"Yeh," I continued. "The dean just called. He's on his way here. He wants to meet with me, but the union rep is up in Albany for a conference. I need you to stand in. Can we meet in your office? I've still got Donna and the kids here." I winked at Donna. "Great. See you in ten."

I hung up and dialed the dean. His secretary patched me right through. Sometimes it pays to be a pariah.

The dean came on the line, and I tried to channel my old self—that aggressive, fast-talking, quick-thinking advertising exec who could pull together an impressive presentation in the snap of a finger. Yes, that was me. I was that savvy woman in a tight skirt maneuvering a multimillion-dollar client into a record-setting deal. I still had it. I worked my mojo on the dean and he agreed to traipse across campus and meet me on my own turf. I was back, baby.

I turned on my computer. Last part of the plan. One catch. Bob needed to be logged off from his office computer for this house of cards to remain standing. A crucial fact I should have checked minutes ago. My blue computer screen asked me for Bob's school password. I typed in "Buster," the name of Bob's cat, remembering back when we were friends. This was the kind of stuff we knew about each other. Bingo. He was off. I was logged in as Professor Bob Carlin. I logged onto Word and frantically scanned Bob's documents. If Bob was in fact selling my test, he'd need an electronic copy. Shit, there were hundreds of documents here. I glanced at my watch. No way I'd have time to search through the haystack. Instead, I typed in the web address for TestSwap.com, my exam's new home. I found the tab for morons who forgot their password and turned toward a mystified Donna.

"Okay, here's where you come in." Donna suddenly snapped to attention.

"Bob isn't on his computer so I was able to log on as him. I thought I'd find my test, but I'd need a week to weed through these files, and the dean is already on his way over. Instead, we have to show that Bob has an active account at TestSwap." Donna nodded skeptically. "If Bob is in fact the seller then he must have an active account with TestSwap. Right?" I pointed to the computer screen.

"Look, I need you to fill out the 'Forgot Your Password' form." I jotted down some notes for her. Like Bob's mother's maiden name being Marsh. Again, from back when he and I were friends.

"Here's the most important part. You need to log off as quickly as possible." I stood up and glanced at the kids curled up on my ancient office couch and headed out.

I met Dean White in the hall fresh from his hike across campus. I stuck my hand out with confidence and led him to Bob's office.

"If it's okay, Dean, I feel better having a friend with me." The dean nodded and we all sat down.

"Bob, do me a favor." I smiled calmly. "Will you go to Test-Swap.com?"

Bob shot me a curious look. "I'm not sure that is advisable, Zoe." Ah, ever the lawyer. Amazing he had never made partner.

"No, no. I think it's important to show the dean how this

whole thing works."

I turned to the dean and in my most innocent and self-deprecating voice, gave him the full-court press.

"First, I'm so embarrassed I was careless enough to let a test go missing. The fact that my knee-jerk reaction in class caused physical harm to a student is something I'll have to live with for a very long time. You may not be aware but the test has since ended up on one of these black market sites. Clearly, this is mortifying. But I think it's important to see how insidious and damaging these sites are to our profession. I'm not the only victim."

"You've piqued my interest, Professor Johnstone," the dean said. "Go ahead and turn on your computer, Professor Carlin."

The minute the dean gave the command I could see a slight quiver in Bob's hands on the keyboard. I watched as his fingers labored over the word "Buster." Then with even more hesitation Bob typed in "TestSwap.com." TestSwap's homepage opened with a **Welcome Back**! posting. I crossed my fingers, hoping the dean would see where this was going.

"My, my, it looks just like eBay," the dean remarked. "And they're welcoming you back, Bob. I guess you've been here before. Have you got a password?"

Bob faltered. On some level he must have known I was on to him, but he clearly couldn't figure it out. He cleared his throat and addressed the computer screen.

"A password? No, I think that is only if you are buying or selling, just like on eBay." Bob tilted his shoulders slightly toward the dean with his eyes still focused on the screen. "Out of curiosity, I have checked out the site, but anyone can do that without a password." Bob's twisted body language screamed guilty. I turned toward the dean. The dean looked at Bob and Bob looked at the computer. We held our Bermuda Triangle formation for an entire minute until it happened.

"Professor?" the dean whispered.

Bob grunted.

"Your password." The dean pointed to the flashing blue Outlook box in the bottom right-hand corner of the screen. Then the dean stood up and came around the desk still pointing at the glowing Outlook box hovering on the screen.

"Right there. You just received a reminder email from Test-Swap with your password."

The dean addressed me in a fatherly tone. "Zoe, would you mind stepping out and giving Bob and me a chance to chat?"

I rose to leave as Bob's eyes swayed my way.

I smiled politely at him as I passed and silently mouthed the name "Donna." He deserved an explanation as well as a swift kick in the butt.

WHAT ABOUT HENRY?
by Pearl Wolf

"I want a divorce, Gertrude." Henry Kaye hated his wife. He hated her cheeriness in the morning. He hated her perpetual calmness, a trait he had loved her for once because his mother had been a screamer. But that wasn't why he wanted a divorce.

Gertrude lifted Henry's head and turned the pillow. "Why?" she asked.

"Because I'm in love with a man."

She squinted at him with faded blue eyes that betrayed nothing. "Would you like some tea?" She wiped his brow with a cool cloth.

"Didn't you hear me? I said I want a divorce because I'm seeing a man."

"Yes, dear. I heard you. Don't raise your voice. Remember, you're not well, Henry. I'll make you some tea, dear. Be back in a jif." She patted his hand and turned to leave.

Henry watched his wife waddle out of their bedroom. She'd become heavyset through the years, the weight unfortunately distributed below her waist, endowing her with an extraordinarily broad rear end, which rested on elephantine legs. Her blonde hair had turned to straw, the result of endless bleaching.

How he disliked her! He shook his head slowly, weariness weighing on his frail shoulders. He'd recently lost fifteen pounds as a result of double pneumonia. At fifty-five, he was no longer the handsome man he had once been. For one thing, he was bald. For another, he'd become round-shouldered.

Henry had lived a secret life for years, wandering in and out of gay bars and frequenting public bathrooms in Manhattan well known to homosexuals. Such encounters had led to shame and guilt, but that was all in the past. That was before he'd met Trevor Wilson. It was a wonder to Henry that he could attract such a handsome young man. Henry loved Trevor with all his heart.

And Henry could no longer bear the sight of his wife. He ached to be rid of her, the sooner the better. When he'd married her thirty-five years ago, he hadn't let on that he was gay. He'd hoped the passion he felt for men would somehow disappear with the joys of marriage to his slim, quiet, pretty, blonde, blue-eyed, eighteen-year-old wife. He hadn't needed long to discover that, for him, married life held no joys. His wife was as placid and contented as a cow in a grassy field.

Why then, had he married? Through the years, he had often asked himself that question. He'd certainly never loved Gertrude. Had he married, then, to please his parents? Perhaps, but they were dead now. Had he married to conform to society's norms? Perhaps that, too. Now it no longer mattered.

All that mattered to Henry was his darling boy, twenty-three-year-old, blond Trevor, whose laughing green eyes sparkled, whose sculpted cheekbones brought to mind Michelangelo's David.

Henry didn't care that his darling boy was a drifter. He viewed the avarice in the boy's heart as a mere trifle. In fact, Henry enjoyed lavishing attention on Trevor. He enjoyed buying him clothing. He enjoyed holding his hand in a movie theatre. He enjoyed taking him to fine restaurants, taking care that the eateries catered only to gays, so no one who knew Henry in his other life would discover his relationship. He and Trevor spent a lot of time in gay restaurants and bars on the East Side in the 50s. There, Henry would coddle his darling as though he were a fragile egg.

Over the years, Henry Kaye had become a wealthy man, not so much because of his clever business sense, but because he had produced a product someone else desired, and the timing had been right. He'd taken his small vitamin firm public years ago when IPOs were the darlings of Wall Street. Two years later, a large pharmaceutical giant had bought out his growing company for millions.

Henry smiled to himself at the recollection. His wife had no clue, thank heaven. He retained twenty percent in Class A, dividend-paying shares in the pharmaceutical company and invested the millions he received in safe securities.

Thanks to Henry's clever lawyer, Bill Brandon, the firm had agreed to retain Henry as a consultant and provided him with a fancy office in Manhattan. Every day, he took the train from his and Gertrude's modest home in Yonkers into Grand Central Station, but neither his presence nor his advice were ever required, so he was free to roam the city at will.

He kept to himself the fact that he'd purchased a studio apartment in New York on the Upper East Side where he changed into expensive clothing and stayed over as often as he could. Trevor lived there now, which made Henry all the more eager to recover from pneumonia and resume his exciting life in the city.

Gertrude knew nothing of his life outside their home, and Henry made sure to keep her in the dark. With that in mind, he never bothered to take her to the lavish company Christmas parties or other special celebrations. Henry gave his wife a modest weekly allowance and a credit card for emergency expenses, which she rarely used.

Gertrude Kaye was secretly proud that she could manage their household so efficiently on the money her husband provided. She spent her days keeping their home neat, doing the wash, ironing Henry's shirts, shopping, cooking, caring for their small garden, and attending garage sales when they didn't interfere with her favorite daytime soaps. She took an occasional extension course in gardening or cooking at the local community college in Yonkers, to keep up, you know, she told her husband. And she never complained about Henry's occasional absences overnight, or the missed dinners she'd prepared for him. Nor did she ever question him about his life away from her.

Instead, she found solace in performing her wifely duties in their cozy little house in a modest, middle-class neighborhood. She kept an unvarying cleaning schedule on little note cards where she recorded special household tasks in addition to her daily chores. She cleaned the oven once a month, washed the curtains twice a month, turned the mattress every week, scrubbed the bathroom tiles by hand once every two months, and so on. It gave her pleasure to check off the chores and write down the date the task was performed. Those little checks gave purpose and a sense of accomplishment to her life.

In the early years, she had hoped for children, but when they went to a fertility specialist, they discovered that Henry had a low sperm count. The specialist suggested in-vitro fertilization, which they tried, but it didn't work. Eventually, when the specialist suggested it, Henry balked at using another man's sperm. Nor would he agree to adopt. He couldn't love a child who wasn't his issue, he protested. Gertrude gave in as she always did to Henry's wishes, and so they remained childless.

When Henry lost interest in sex, she didn't complain. She would have continued, for she grew to look forward to it as the years went by. And Gertrude supposed he was embarrassed when he became too old to perform his spousal obligations.

She'd left him an article about Viagra on his night stand not long ago, but it only served to make him angry. She dreaded the times when he showed his anger by not talking to her to, not even answering simple questions such as, "What would you like for dinner, dear?" Or "What time will you be home tonight?"

Now, Gertrude pursed her lips and stared at the leaf she'd retrieved from the jar of dried leaves she'd hidden on the top shelf of the kitchen cabinet. She'd discovered its uses as a result of one of the extension courses on gardening. As was her habit, she'd taken copious notes in class. The botanist who'd taught the gardening course said this particular leaf was harmful if ingested.

Gertrude fretted over the leaf, trying to decide how much of it she ought to use. Would one be enough, she wondered. No matter, she thought. She could always use more another time, if necessary. She hummed to herself as she pounded half the leaf in the brass mortar and pestle she'd purchased for a dollar at a yard sale.

"I've brought you some tea and biscuits, dear."

"Don't ignore me, Gertrude. We need to talk about the divorce. I plan to be very generous. You can keep this house and I'll continue your allowance. I'll call our lawyer as soon as I'm better. You probably should get a lawyer too. I'll pay for that as well," he added, thinking his offer a magnanimous one.

"Drink your tea, Henry."

"Don't you have anything else to say?"

"Why, no. Nothing at all. Why do you ask?"

"You don't behave as if you've heard a word I've said."

"Of course I have. You're dating a man, and you want a divorce. Do I have that right?"

"You might at least have the decency to admit that you're angry with me."

Gertrude's eyes widened in surprise. "But I'm not angry, dear. I'm perfectly willing to grant you a divorce if that is what you wish. I love you and I want you to be happy."

Her calmness irritated him no end, and his disappointment in her lack of reaction came as a surprise. In his mind he'd expected a river of tears and a blast of recriminations. He'd fancied that she'd plead with him to stay. He'd envisioned a stormy scene meant to arouse his guilt. He'd had a vision of his wife hurling objects at him, beating his chest with her fists, begging him not to do this to her. That she seemed not to care rather hurt his pride. Foolish thought, but there it was.

He tried to focus on Trevor, to regain the peace he'd just lost, to no avail.

"I'll have some more tea," he growled, not bothering to mask his disgruntlement.

"G…g…rt…ude," he gurgled, yet no sound came. Henry tried, but he couldn't raise his right arm. He lay there for what seemed like hours, his mind frantic over his own helplessness.

"Have you had a nice nap, dear? The doctor said that rest is important for your recovery. He'll be here any moment, you know. I want you to look your best," she prattled as she fussed over him, taking no notice of his terrified, rolling eyes, taking no notice of his inability to speak as she wiped his face with a cool cloth, puffed the pillow under his head and straightened his sheets. "Your lips are dry, dear. I'll just fetch some cold water. Be right back."

"I'm afraid your husband has had a severe stroke, Mrs. Kaye. Can't understand it. He was well on the way to recovery, which is why I sent him home from the hospital." The doctor shook his head in puzzlement. "I'll have to readmit him for tests. We need to know the extent of the damage to his heart. Shall I call for an ambulance?"

"Of course, doctor." Gertrude wiped a tear. "Will…will he die?"

"Not if we move quickly. Nowadays stroke patients recover with the right treatment."

"That's a relief. And please. Do whatever is necessary to make him well again. We've been married for thirty-five years. He's such a wonderful man. I…I can't imagine life without my Henry."

Soon after her Henry was hospitalized as a result of his unfortunate stroke, Gertrude Kaye dressed in her only suit—navy blue—and a white blouse buttoned to the neck. She met with their family lawyer, their estate planner, and their accountant at their lawyer William Brandon's New York office. She displayed no surprise at hearing the extent of their wealth, behaving as if she'd known of it all along.

"You will all continue to advise me as before?" She asked the question in an anxious tone.

"Of course," murmured Brandon.

"And I'll continue to keep your books and send you a monthly report, Mrs. Kaye," said the accountant.

The estate planner, a jovial man older than the other two added, "And I intend to keep these guys honest." After the obligatory chuckle from the other two, he added, "Do you have any plans of your own, Mrs. Kaye?"

"Oh yes, I do. I most certainly do."

With the help and the approval of her retainers, Gertrude sold the house in Yonkers while Henry was still in hospital. She purchased a huge mansion in the most prestigious section of Scarsdale and hired a well-known New York architectural firm to redesign it to her specifications, paying particular attention to the needs of her severely handicapped husband. She spared no expense, so that by the time Henry was released from the hospital, the work was completed.

Within six months Gertrude lost sixty pounds. Her faded blue eyes disappeared under intense blue contact lenses, and the best plastic surgeon in New York removed all facial and body wrinkles. She installed two gyms in the new house, one for Henry's physical therapy and one for herself, where she worked with a professional trainer and a masseuse every day.

Gertrude's one aim in life was still to be the perfect wife. Whether Henry appreciated her or not, she felt driven to carry out her role.

Gertrude hired a personal chef who prepared all their meals according to the guidelines designed by their expert nutritionist.

The well-known, expensive salon she frequented in the city corrected years of abuse to her hair and her skin, so that Gertrude Kaye became a stunning looking woman who appeared to be twenty years younger than her fifty-three years.

"Henry? I have a surprise for you. Trevor's come to live with us to take care of you. He's going to take you for a walk. It's a lovely day." Gertrude patted Henry's hand and smiled at Trevor.

She'd discovered Trevor through the enormous credit card bills he had racked up. He'd been living in Henry's little hide-away studio apartment and having a high old time, not caring a whit about Henry's disappearance from his life. Gertrude offered the young man a choice when she found him out. He could come to live and work in Scarsdale as Henry's companion and she would agree to pay his bills and close the credit card accounts, or she would have him jailed for embezzlement. Since jail didn't appeal to him, having had a taste of it a few years before for a similar crime, and since he had no other means of supporting himself, he had no choice but to agree to her terms.

Henry had become a hostage in his own body. He watched helplessly as Gertrude took charge. He watched helplessly as she changed her appearance. He watched helplessly as she installed Trevor to care for him. He watched, appalled, when Trevor sucked up to Gertrude, when he fawned over her. Henry became paranoid, but he had no way of showing his feelings, locked as it were, in the prison of his mind.

He hated his wife. And now he hated his former lover, whom he'd previously adored. He sat in his wheelchair day in and day out, willing his eyes to send an appropriate message of hate to both of them, to no avail.

"You look awesome in that blue suit, Mrs. Kaye. It lights up your eyes, you know. You should wear that color more often. Where are you off to today?"

"I have several appointments in the city so I'll stay at the apartment tonight. I need a new gown, make-up, jewelry, and I'm thinking of buying a new fur coat. Nothing fancy. Just a short jacket, actually. Sable, perhaps. I'm hosting my first charity dinner and ball next month at the Pierre Hotel."

"You'll want to look your best, then." Trevor beamed approval at her. Neither paid attention to Henry's pathetic attempt at a scowl.

She bent to kiss her husband's cheek. "Bye, darling. Have a nice outing with Trevor. The fresh air will do you worlds of good. I'll see you tomorrow. Love you." And, in her own way, she did.

"Oh, oh, oh," she moaned. "Touch me there, my love. And there and…there." The pleasures of multiple orgasms were relatively new to Gertrude, and she treasured every one of them. Bill Brandon, her lawyer as well as her lover, was six feet tall, muscular as a result of regular workouts, dark-haired, brown-eyed, and utterly sexy. Gertrude had known when she'd first met him that he would become her lover. The fact that he was married, far from irritating her, pleased her no end. It meant he wouldn't make jealous demands on her. It added to her sense of well-being. After all, everyone knew she already had a husband. Everyone knew how devoted she was to Henry.

Whenever she spent the night in the city, Gertrude's lover spent it with her. He lived in Greenwich, but his office was on Park Avenue in Manhattan. His wife and he had a clear understanding, since neither of them wanted a divorce, which would surely hurt their three adorable children. His wife didn't interfere with his affairs so long as he didn't interfere with hers.

Gertrude's first sexual adventure outside of marriage introduced her to the delights of passion, delights she had never known with Henry. Bill certainly understood how to pleasure a woman in bed. He'd had lots of practice with lots of women.

"Want to hear something amusing? Trevor's been coming on to me. He's a looker, I'll give him that, but he doesn't turn me on. Not like you, my sweet."

"I live only to please you, duchess," Bill answered in his sleepy, sexy voice, a voice that thrilled her.

"Order a new tuxedo and charge it to me, darling, for my charity ball. I want you to look magnificent. I want you to turn every woman's eyes green with envy when they see my gorgeous escort."

He raised an eyebrow. "Your escort? Is that all I mean to you?"

She laughed. "No, of course not my precious. Our arrangement is perfect, don't you think? Everyone knows you're my attorney, and the fact that you're married makes it safe to be seen with poor lonely me whose husband is ailing. Besides, I've invited half the big honchos from Henry's pharmaceutical company because they have such deep pockets. Of course, we're neither of us in a position to let it be known that we're lovers. Even so, I want you to know that you've brought more happiness into my life than anyone has ever done."

"Come here, my blue-eyed beauty," he growled playfully. "I can't get enough of you. Climb on top this time."

"Ooh! How naughty! You know I can't resist when you lure me with those sleepy, sexy eyes." Gertrude's swollen lips kissed, her hands aroused and guided, her body undulated, back arched in sheer pleasure, her sensuous moans filled the studio apartment.

In the heat of their lovemaking, neither heard the key in the door, but the flashbulbs caught their attention at once. A startled Gertrude snapped her head around to face the door. The photographer, before he fled, clicked several shots in rapid succession of a nude, startled woman on top of a scowling man.

"You positively eat the camera, you know. Very sexy, Mrs. Kaye. Very photogenic," said Trevor, a satisfied smirk on his face. He handed her the incriminating pictures. "I would never have guessed you enjoyed sex so much. Henry told me you weren't sexy, but he was wrong, wasn't he?" He smirked again, clearly in control. "We could try that position together. I'm bisexual, you know."

Gertrude smiled sweetly, innocently, as she examined the photos.

"Don't think these are my only copies, by the way. I've hidden the negatives along with instructions to be released to the police should you do anything rash. Might hurt your lawyer, too."

"How much money do you want for these, Trevor dear?"

"Oh, I want more than money. I want it all. I want you. I want this house. I want the studio apartment in New York. I want this life. Everything."

She thought a moment. "What about Henry?"

"What do you mean?"

"I mean what will you do with him? If you want it all, including me, we'd have to marry. But you can't marry me as long as poor Henry's alive, can you?"

Trevor didn't seem to be very swift. A lifetime of relying solely on his good looks had perhaps left little room for intellectual development. "I hadn't thought about that."

Gertrude examined the photos once again, secretly pleased at how sensuous she looked. "I'm fond of you, Trevor. And frankly, I'm tired of leading a double life."

"And your point is?"

She grasped her chin and tapped one finger on her cheek. "We have two options, as I see it. We can become lovers and I'll give you a generous allowance, but as long as poor Henry is alive, our relationship must be kept under wraps. No dinners at fancy restaurants. No theater trips. No travel together."

"What's the other option, Mrs. Kaye?"

"Call me Gertrude, Trevor dearest. Think about it. You're so clever. I'm sure you'll come up with something suitable." With Trevor to care for if Henry passed on, Gertrude felt assured she wouldn't be alone.

She meant her dazzling smile and her flattery to intoxicate him, along with the thought of becoming the husband of the enormously wealthy Mrs. Kaye.

Gertrude made sure of that Henry could hear the passionate moans and groans of his wife and his former lover. She always left the door between their bedrooms open. Their sweet talk undoubtedly sickened him, and she knew that Henry hated them both. No doubt he wished that he were dead. No doubt he wished that they were dead.

She understood that Trevor, underneath it all, was unsure of himself. He demanded she tell him over and over again how good the sex was. He'd been accustomed to being any man's boy toy for too many years. He must find it hard to get used to pleasing a woman sexually. He must find it even harder to say no to anything Gertrude wanted him to do, for she believed he fancied himself in love with her.

Yet Gertrude missed Bill. She could no longer go to the city to see her lawyer. Trevor made sure of that. She phoned him in secret when she was certain Trevor was out of earshot, but it wasn't enough for her.

"Can you arrange it for me, darling? Find a reliable firm to install the equipment? They can do it in the afternoon, when Trevor takes Henry out for his daily walk. But they must be discreet. I'm going to tell the servants that the men are installing a medical warning system designed for Mr. Kaye."

Gertrude listened intently to Bill repeating his complaints about not seeing her. "Patience, darling. Patience. Just remember that I love you," she whispered before she hung up.

"No. Don't tell me what you're going to do to Henry, Trevor dear. I can't bear to hear the details. Just tell me what day it will be, so I can be out shopping or something. Think about us, our future together, and do it."

Trevor Wilson didn't disappoint. He pushed Henry in his wheelchair to the edge of the stairs and appeared to trip, sending them both hurtling down. He suffered some bruises, but it was well worth it.

The coroner ruled Henry Kaye's demise an accidental death. Gertrude felt that everything was working out.

Gertrude had Henry cremated, his ashes placed in an urn in an expensive crypt at the Scarsdale Presbyterian Church cemetery's burial grounds. She let it be known that such an arrangement was her dear departed husband's wish. At the memorial service, everyone said Mrs. Kaye made a touching widow. She wept copious tears for her loss. Probably only Trevor wasn't fooled, though her acting ability must have amazed him, since her grief seemed so real. And, indeed, Gertrude did feel sad. She'd been married to Henry for so very long.

Henry's pharmaceutical company sent a huge flower display with a banner that read, "Rest in Peace." At the direction of the minister, friends, colleagues, and neighbors made donations to poor Henry's favorite charity, TSVS, better known as "The Stroke Victims Society." Gertrude Kaye was on the board of directors there.

"How long must we wait?" Trevor whined a few weeks after the memorial service.

"For what, dear?"

"Why, to marry, of course."

"I've no intention of marrying you, Trevor darling."

"Wh…what on earth do you mean? I still have those pictures!"

"Of course, Trevor. But I have something, too. Perhaps we can trade."

He eyed her warily. "You're bluffing."

"I never bluff, dear."

"What are you driving at?"

"You need to see this, darling." She handed him a padded envelope the size of a small book.

"What is it?"

"It's a video of you pushing my poor Henry down the stairs."

"But how…?"

"Those men who installed the medical warning system? There's no such thing. It was really a hidden video camera. Shall I put the tape on for you?"

Trevor watched the video with growing horror. It dawned on him that the evidence was clearly incriminating. He could get life for killing Henry.

"You…bitch!"

"Shall we trade, dear? This tape for your negatives."

Trevor Wilson turned beet red. He let loose a string of bitter curses and dire phrases meant to show this woman who was boss. She listened to him rant without saying a word.

"Don't excite yourself so, Trevor. You're still recovering from those nasty bruises. It's a wonder to me that you didn't break any bones. Clever of you to fall down along with Henry. And brave, too."

"I'll make you pay for this, Gertrude. I have my ways, you know."

"Don't threaten, dear. It spoils your looks. Your adorable face turns blotchy when you're angry. Where are the negatives?"

He grumbled in defeat. "In the safe in my room."

"The combination, my sweet?" Trevor hesitated. "Don't be difficult, dear."

Gertrude wrote the combination down as he spoke. "Turn right three times and stop on six. Left twice and stop on seven. Right four times and stop on ten. When you hear the click, you can open the safe."

With her customary efficiency, Gertrude placed the negatives and the videotape into the fireplace. Together, she and Trevor watched the sensuous flames consume the evidence incriminating them both.

"Well, that's that." She fluffed Trevor's pillow and wiped his brow with a cool cloth. "There. Does that feel better?"

"What am I going to do, Gertrude? I have no money and no place to live."

"Oh, don't worry. I'll take care of you. We'll talk about it just as soon as you're well enough. Here, drink this. It will help you sleep."

"What is it?"

"Just some soothing tea to calm your nerves."

FRIENDLY WITNESS
by Erica Harth

"Surely you can't be serious," said Karel Anton as the slow, forward thrust of a knife backed him up against a tree. He sounded to himself like a character from one of his Grade B movies. After a split second in which he saw his assailant grin crookedly, the knife plunged directly into his heart.

Just to make sure, the killer thrust the weapon into the body a few more times.

That afternoon thirteen-year-old Chris Gooding and her best friend Rosie Lescinkas were sprawled on the white chenille-covered twin beds in Rosie's room. Rosie's violin, secure in its case, was sitting on her desk. All the windows were open to a balmy spring breeze.

"What's Hew-ack?" Rosie asked.

Chris sat up, shaking out her thick, black pony tail. "Rosie, why don't you forget about your violin once in a while? This is 1952, for Pete's sake. You don't know what HUAC is? Haven't you ever heard of the Hollywood Ten? Don't your parents ever talk to you?"

"Yes, that's all they've been blabbering about all day, Hew-ack. I figured it was political so I didn't listen. Politics is too *boring*."

"So you bug me instead. Rosie, this is a big deal. This guy, Karel Anton, who's going before the House Un-American Activities Committee, the Red-hunting one, he's going to get a lot of people around here into trouble. Like maybe my mother."

"It's like McCarthy?"

"Yeah, except McCarthy's in the Senate."

"I don't see what Anton can do."

"He can do a lot, believe me. If he tells the committee you're a Commie, they haul you to Washington and *you* have to testify. And if you won't admit you're a Red or you won't rat on your friends, then they throw you in jail, for maybe six months, a year, who knows? And even if you don't go to jail, you can lose your job, and your life will be ruined."

Rosie was quiet, her face crunched up in a frown. "So you think they could get our parents?" she finally asked.

"Search me. Even if our parents aren't Communists, they live here on Red Hill, and they have a lot of friends. And even if you're just friends with Communists you're in hot water."

"Well, if Mr. Anton is such a big, famous director," said Rosie, "he can't care all that much about Croton."

Chris straightened up importantly. "Look, Mr. Anton likes it here. My mother says that Croton reminds him of Hungary, where he comes from. He's been a summer person here forever. He knows everyone in the Croton Players, too, and he always goes to rehearsals when he's in town. Besides which, he can get from here to Broadway in an hour."

"Yes," said Rosie, "but he's a long way from Hollywood. And why's he so interested in the Croton Players?"

Holding a clip to refasten her ponytail, Chris shook her head pityingly. "Because—oh, Rosie, use your head. He's always looking for new talent. Don't you remember Ginger Polk who used to live here and ended up in one of his movies? Anyhow, he's staying around Croton for a while this year. My mother says he's going to direct a Broadway musical." She stood up and stretched. "C'mon. Let's go get a Coke."

The four parents were sipping cocktails on the Lescinkases' diminutive patio just off the dining room. Mt. Airy Road's leafy treetops trembled in a sudden gust that fleetingly chilled the assembled group.

The girls brought their Coke-filled tumblers to the glass-topped outdoor table, crowded with bottles and a large platter of hors d'oeuvres.

Chris restrained a childish urge to ask her father for the olive in his martini glass. Sandor Lescinkas looked slightly potted, she thought. His eyes were glazed over. Maybe it wasn't his first drink of the afternoon.

Chris's father, Gil Gooding, chuckled bitterly. "Well, Anton can say what he likes about me. There's not much they can do to me now." Her father had already lost his syndicated comic strip, which was considered dangerously close to subversive by the mainstream press.

"And besides which, you're the village manager now—an upright citizen," said his wife, Maya, reaching out to pat his hand and nearly overturning his glass in the process. Was her usually calm mother a little nervous? wondered Chris.

Sandor Lescinkas, a broodingly dark, stocky man, clenched his right fist.

Rosie's willowy blonde mother, Lili Lescinkas, was like the sunlight to her husband's shade. She gestured toward Maya. "What about your wife?"

Chris's mother laughed. She smoothed out her Indian print skirt. "Me? I'm strictly small fry. Just because I got to know Hallie Flanagan in Russia?"

Mr. Lescinkas twisted both his hands together. "Aw, Maya, it isn't as if she were just any old friend. After all, she got you in with that crowd of New Dealers in the Federal Theater Project."

Chris watched her mother set down her glass on the table. "Anton's got nothing on me."

Her father attempted a grin, which came out more like a grimace. "Well, be nice to him at the rehearsal tonight."

Chris picked up a slice of cheese. "Oh, is he coming to the dress rehearsal?"

"What time is dinner?" Rosie asked.

Rosie's mother brushed back a lock of her glistening hair from her face. "He certainly won't name *me*. What do they care if I was once in the French Communist Youth?"

But now she's the famous artist Liliane Carrière, thought Chris. *And look at all the famous people they go after.*

Mr. Lescinkas started to say something, then changed his mind.

"Who knows?" shrugged Chris's father, in reply to Mrs. Lescinkas. "You're an American citizen now, so your past counts. Living in Croton-on-Hudson doesn't help you, either. And you can't trust any of these friendly witnesses." As he leaned back for a swallow of his martini, he nearly dislodged the chewed up pencil that habitually perched on an ear.

A silence fell over the group, and Sandor Lescinkas dropped his hands to his sides.

Chris decided that she preferred the stuffed mushrooms. "What's a friendly witness?"

Rosie's mother turned to her. "They inform. They tell the investigators what they want to hear about the supposed Communists they know."

"Oh, so they're rats," said Chris. "They don't sound very friendly to me."

Mrs. Lescinkas smiled. "They're friendly to the committee."

Gil managed a wink at his daughter. "But luckily we don't have many friendly witnesses here in Croton—especially not on Mt. Airy."

No one had to tell the girls that woodsy Mt. Airy Road, known to locals as "Red Hill," was home to all kinds of leftist artists, actors, writers, and assorted "Bohemians."

Rosie yawned. "Mama," she asked, "when are we having dinner?"

"We'll have dinner early, won't we?" Chris said. "Before my mother goes to the dress rehearsal."

Mrs. Lescinkas stood up. "Oh, yes, you're absolutely right. Come, Rosie, help me set the table. We have to get Mrs. Gooding to the dress rehearsal on time so that Mr. Anton can discover her for his next movie."

But Karel Anton never made it to the rehearsal.

With much effort Chris was able to worm the story out of her mother. It seemed that Anton had been entertaining some distinguished guests from Manhattan: a couple of potential backers and his choices as leads, Charles Treadwell, the internationally celebrated singer and actor, and Anna Maria Calderón, the opera star.

The housekeeper told the police that the only unusual event of the day was a phone call to the director from an unidentified person who presumably asked to meet with Anton right before the rehearsal. Anton had announced to his guests that he needed to leave a little earlier than he had planned, and he left at seven-fifteen for the scheduled eight o'clock rehearsal.

"So when did they find out what happened?" Chris asked.

Her mother's face was lined with uncharacteristic worry. "I don't know, dear. But I assume that when he didn't come home on time someone called the police."

The police found Anton's body beneath a clump of trees near the parking lot at the rear of the high school, where the Croton Players both rehearsed and performed. The autopsy, performed quickly because of the victim's celebrity status, apparently had revealed no indication of a struggle, no sign of resistance on the part of the sixty-eight-year-old Anton. The first stab of the knife must have been fatal, and yet the killer hadn't stopped there. "Someone wanted to make very sure Anton was dead," Chris's mother told her father later on that night.

Out of respect for Anton, the Croton Players deferred opening their play until a week after the funeral. Then, before the curtain rose on the first act, the director, Leland Lennard, stepped out onto the stage to deliver a brief eulogy for Anton. Almost no one in the audience had known Karel Anton personally.

Lennard's delivery was dry. "I remember when he became naturalized. He threw a big party to celebrate becoming an American citizen."

"Yeah, he was two hundred percent American," Chris heard Mr. Lescinkas whisper to her father. "Lennard hated the guy—he was sure that Anton would name him."

Judging by the cheers and hearty applause, the audience loved the play, *Skyward*, billed as "light summer fare." It was the perfect antidote to the fear that had shadowed the village since the day of the murder. Lennard reappeared in front of the curtain at the end to take a bow with his cast, and there were numerous curtain calls. The audience clamored for the playwright, Crotonite Wayne Geller, who, flushed with excitement, also bowed in acknowledgement. This was his first performed stage play. A few years ago he had sold a script to the Lux Radio Theater, but it was never produced.

Maya proved herself a first-rate comedienne in her role as a young, wayward wife who is so obsessed by her newfound passion for air travel that she pesters a handsome neighbor, a commercial pilot, to help her enter training as a stewardess. Her husband, adamantly opposed to her plans, finally foils her by pretending to be having an affair with the pilot's wife, who goes along with the game. Maya completely won over the audience with her wide-eyed portrayal of the wife's utterly naïve ultimate surrender when she "finds out" about the phony romance.

After some discussion, the Players had decided to go ahead with their traditional opening-night cast party. "If we're old enough to stay home alone at night, we're old enough for the cast party," Chris had successfully argued, so for the first time Chris and Rosie were allowed to attend. Everyone was going, from Rosie's artist mother who had, as usual, worked on the sets, and Rosie's father, who hadn't done anything, to the stagehands and the playwright, went to the party.

It wasn't at all as exciting as Chris had anticipated. For one thing, the Lennards' house on Mountain Trail, to which she had never been, was kind of rundown. Window screens were either splintered, with poorly patched holes, or else missing altogether. The light bulb in the fixture over the front door was out, so everyone had to dash madly after the Lennards in a sudden thunderstorm in order to get into the house safely. For another thing, the actors were just standing around rehashing the performance. Then Rosie went off into a corner to chat with Caleb, the Lennards' older son, who attended the private school where Chris's mother taught drama. Chris felt distinctly like a third wheel.

Leland Lennard's wife, Honey, had prepared mounds of delicious pastry, though. Clutching a petit four and hoping to escape her parents' notice, Chris quickly grabbed a glass of champagne and stole into a room off the first-floor hallway.

It looked to be a library or a study, probably Lennard's. In a corner by the window stood a big armchair covered in faded chintz and a footstool that didn't match. All available wall space was filled with sagging bookshelves. Smack in the middle of the room was a scratched-up wooden desk piled helter-skelter with books and papers. A rickety wooden desk chair was pushed up against a slightly open drawer. Chris switched on the floor lamp next to the armchair and began inspecting the books on the shelves. Stanislavski—she had heard of him. He had something to do with the "method acting" her mother was always talking about. A complete set of Shakespeare. Lillian Hellman, Tennessee Williams. Lennard certainly had "catholic taste," an expression, as Chris had just learned, that didn't mean a penchant for crucifixes.

She downed at least a third of her glass in one gulp, anticipating with pleasure the mild champagne high she had once before experienced. Leland Lennard, she remembered her mother saying, had come back to New York from Hollywood, where after a brief, luminous career he was pretty much "washed up." He had hopes of returning to the legitimate theater. But one off-Broadway flop caused him to give up his relatively expensive apartment on the Upper West Side and rent a house year-round in Croton.

A booming thunderclap startled Chris into action. As a fork of lightning flashed outside the dusty window, she moved over to the desk, pushing aside a large envelope that rested precariously on the open drawer. Wow! The return address was for the New York City offices of Cohen and White, the celebrated composer-writer musical comedy team. Chris had seen many of their musicals. She automatically pushed at the drawer to close it, but it seemed stuck. She tried pulling it all the way open and nearly fell backward off the chair as the drawer, along with its contents, spilled onto the pine-planked floor.

Sitting down cross-legged in front of the mess, she sifted through it. Here was a medal for some honor that Mr. Lennard had won in 1942. Had he been in the army? A photo of a much younger Lennard with an actress who looked famous, but Chris didn't know who she was. A bunch of paper clips, some rusty. A menu from Sardi's. A card from the singer Lotte Lenya thanking him for the roses. Carbon copies of typewritten letters. An empty key ring with a charm of the Empire State Building. Chris picked up the drawer and tried to replace it, but it still stuck in the same place. She slowly pulled it out again, set it on a space she cleared on the desk's surface, and began to put back the scattered contents.

As she gathered up the pile of carbon copies, she noticed a familiar name. Sandor! Could that be Rosie's father? How many people were named Sandor? Chris slapped the pile on top of the desk, tried to settle herself into the desk chair (it sat unevenly on the floor), and began to read.

The letter was dated December 1951.

Dear Sandor,

I have not forgotten your wonderful support in the dark days of the Spanish Civil War. I personally really benefited from your efforts. Now I'm back here in Manhattan pretty much disillusioned with Hollywood. One of those bastard Friendlies will name me any day now. Thought I'd do better in New York than in the movies, but I may have been wrong.

Rents are pretty steep here in the city, and I've decided to move the family to Croton. Maybe you can help me find a house to rent. At the rate job offers are coming in, the move won't affect me professionally at all. I need something big enough for the four of us (two separate bedrooms for the two boys), but nothing lavish. I trust that you...

The Spanish Civil War? Chris had heard a lot about it from the grown-ups around her. The three years of bloody battles came to an end the year both she and Rosie were born—1939—when the good guys, the Loyalists who wanted to save the republic, lost to the Fascists. It was a tragic, heroic story that had always appealed to Chris, and she loved listening to the record of Spanish Civil War songs in her parents' collection.

But Mr. Lescinkas? What did he have to do with that war? She didn't think that he had gone to fight with the Abraham Lincoln Brigade, the American unit of international volunteers for the Loyalist side, because he often talked about the "poor devils" who had signed up. As she understood it, the international brigades were filled with Communists and also anarchists—whatever *they* were. She had been told that Mr. Lescinkas was in Europe at that time, but he was supposed to have been studying architecture. That was when he had met Rosie's mother, in 1938, and had rescued her from the Nazis and brought her back with him to the United States. Could he have fought in Spain too?

Hm-m-m. Dropping the letter to Mr. Lescinkas onto her lap, Chris reached for the large envelope from Cohen and White, which was only loosely sealed at the top. Carefully she pried it open and drew out the contents. Her eye lit on the cover letter, stamped "Confidential" in large red letters. She separated it from the other papers, which she returned to the envelope.

Another fork of lightning flashed savagely, snuffing out the lights in the house—but not before Chris heard a tentative twist of the doorknob and felt more than heard a footfall approaching her from behind.

"You're a bit young for spying, aren't you?" someone hissed in a suppressed voice that was difficult to recognize. The person—whether male or female Chris wasn't able to tell in the sudden darkness—placed a rough hand on her neck. She sensed a sting on her upper right arm. "Now just get out of here." The presence retreated, and the door closed almost soundlessly.

Her heart pounding, Chris felt her way cautiously to the armchair and stuffed the letter to Mr. Lennard, together with the one from Cohen and White, underneath the large seat cushion. She fumbled back toward the door and stepped out into more darkness. From the living room she heard muffled laughter, the clink of glasses, and a bustle of activity. The man who played the husband was saying, "Maybe Anton is roaring his disapproval of our performance from up above."

In the uncomfortable pause another man added, "Or from down below."

Lit candles began to sprout, and Chris made her way into the living room.

"Well, I think he would have *liked* our performance," Maya said, just as her daughter approached.

"Christabel!" she cried. "What on earth has happened to you?" Following her mother's eyes, Chris realized that blood was slowly dripping down her right arm.

She felt a twinge of guilt. "I, uh,…don't know."

"Here, let me look at that," said Henry Carroll, whose wife, Iona, played the pilot's wife. He was a physician. Maya, who was dabbing at Chris's arm with her handkerchief, stepped back, and Carroll peered at it closely.

"Looks like quite a nasty cut to me. Now young lady, were

you playing with a knife, or perhaps a letter opener? Let's get her an antiseptic and a bandage."

Chris's father had appeared, and the trio stared intently at her.

"No, of course not," she said, regaining her composure. "I must have bumped into something in the dark."

"Did you say a *knife*?" Agnes Beckwith piped up. She had been hilarious as the wife's mother.

A shocked silence stilled the guests.

Chris became aware that her arm was throbbing.

"I think," Dr. Carroll said to Chris, "that you and I will take a little ride to my office."

Someone pulled out a flashlight, and Chris was obliged to go along with her mother and Dr. Carroll to the doctor's office. The doctor called the town medical examiner, who came right over. Head down, Chris mumbled through the gist of her story, omitting the detail of her discovery. If the injury was caused by a knife, the two men agreed, it undoubtedly wasn't the same one that had killed Anton. The murder weapon hadn't yet been found, but it was unlikely that the killer was walking around with it, ready to use it again. The instrument that had injured Chris could have been another, less lethal knife, or possibly a letter opener. The fact that this type of weapon was used again, though, was suspicious.

By the next day, Chris was impatient to see the letters that she had squirreled away in Mr. Lennard's study. Her parents hadn't exactly grounded her, but since yesterday they were tracking her every move.

"Is Mr. Lescinkas a Communist?" she couldn't resist asking her mother.

The head of lettuce that Maya was about to shred fell into the kitchen sink. "Why do you ask?"

"Well, I heard someone say something about him and the

Spanish Civil War at the cast party," Chris lied. "And he and Rosie's mother are always talking politics." She had thought up her answer in advance.

Her mother retrieved the lettuce. "So what? Your father and I discuss politics a lot, and we aren't Communists."

"Yeah, but what about the Spanish Civil War?"

"Mr. Lescinkas didn't fight in the Spanish Civil War. He was in France and Switzerland studying architecture during those years. Besides, not everyone who fought in Spain was a Communist."

Suddenly Willie, the family's Airedale, who had been snoozing under the kitchen table, scrambled to his feet with a yelp, as three men appeared at the door leading from the kitchen to the back yard.

One of them came forward, doffing his hat and shaking forsythia petals from his light tan jacket. "Excuse me, Ma'am. We knocked at your front door, but got no answer, so we thought we'd try the back."

Maya glanced back at the partially shredded lettuce in the colander. "Come in, gentlemen."

The man in the tan jacket introduced himself as Tom Bonetti, district attorney of Westchester County, and presented the two others, FBI officers.

Maya ushered them into the living room, and when they were seated, offered them iced tea, which they refused.

Willie excitedly pushed open the kitchen door and made a dash for the smaller of the two G-men, knocking over the fedora he had placed primly on his knees. The little man, who had been introduced as Alfred Pike, recoiled in fear. "Mrs. Gooding, can you do something about your dog, please? Maybe he would like to go out and play with a bone?"

"Fred doesn't like dogs," said the other FBI officer, unnecessarily. He was much taller than the agent Willie had pounced on, Chris noticed. The two men were like Mutt and Jeff.

Chris got up. "I'll take him out."

"Thanks, darling," said her mother. "And then maybe you better go upstairs."

The district attorney raised a hand. "Please. We'll need her here. We want her report of the assault at Mr. Lennard's house." After getting permission, he lit up a Chesterfield, took a few puffs, and then laid it down to smolder in a large ceramic ashtray provided by Maya.

"Mrs. Gooding," he began, "you were at the dress rehearsal."

It was more a statement than a question, but Maya assented.

"Had you been expecting Mr. Anton to attend?"

"I hadn't been expecting anything. Frankly, I didn't think about it. Sometimes he came and sometimes he didn't."

"But since he was going to testify before HUAC in a very short time, wouldn't you have been thinking about him?"

"Not any more than usual. His testimony wouldn't have anything to do with me."

It was kind of like a tennis game. Chris had to keep swinging her head from her mother to Mr. Bonetti and back.

But then "Jeff"—Mr. Pike, that was—broke in. "Mrs. Gooding, you want us to believe that you weren't nervous about the hearing? What about your work for the WPA, and Hallie Flannigan, and so forth?"

Her mother's voice was even. "It's well known that I worked for the Federal Theater Project and that I knew Hallie."

"Yeah," put in Mutt, "but how well known is it that you also worked for that front organization in New York, the North American Committee to Save Spanish Democracy? Isn't that where you first met Sandor Lescinkas?"

Chris looked inquiringly at her mother. She'd never heard of the committee. Obviously it had something to do with the Spanish Civil War. That war again!

Her mother went on responding, as if Chris weren't even in the room. "I met Mr. Lescinkas through my husband. They were friends from college."

"Yeah, from City College," Jeff said, twirling his fedora over his knees. "Where all the Commie kids went."

Bonetti stubbed out his cigarette. "All right, Pike, let's get back to business. What time did the rehearsal end, Mrs. Gooding?"

Chris had stopped listening. It seemed that there was a lot her parents had never told her, and she was trying to digest what she had just heard.

Dr. Carroll was right; Chris's wound was nasty. The cut healed very slowly, causing her pain for several days. But what was bothering her wasn't her arm. She couldn't get the adventure in Leland Lennard's study out of her mind. She was convinced that whoever had warned her off with a knife (or a letter opener?) had killed Karel Anton, and that what her assailant didn't want her to find would lead her to the killer.

"Rosie," she said to her friend on one of their walks home from school. "I have to get back into Mr. Lennard's study. How can we do it?"

Rosie's quills shot up. "What do you mean, *we*? Listen, you're not going to drag me into one of your crazy plots. We could get ourselves killed. And you better stay out of it, too."

"Oh, Rosie, you're such a scaredy-cat. Nothing's going to happen to us—we'll plan it very carefully."

Rosie's slight frame stiffened. "You mean *you* will, Miss Nancy Drew."

Chris was about to reveal that the case was much closer to their lives than Rosie could imagine, but she held her tongue. As far as Rosie knew, Mr. Lescinkas was a just a plain old liberal, like Adlai Stevenson. Even the possibility that he might be a Red would drive her nuts. Rosie had been rattled enough when she found out that her mother had been in the French Communist Youth. And practically every night she had nightmares about the Soviet Union dropping atom bombs on New York City.

As it turned out, events answered Chris's wishes. Later that week, a private reading of one of the plays that the Croton Players were considering for the fall season was about to be cancelled, because Agnes Beckwith, the hostess, was called out of town on a family emergency. Lennard stepped into the breach to offer his house. Someone else could read the role assigned to Agnes.

Chris got to work that night over the after-dinner dishwashing. Chris always dried. "Mom, I want to come with you to the reading."

"Why in heaven's name?" asked Maya. "I thought that our readings bored you."

"Yeah, but I heard that *You Can't Take It With You* is a really funny play—please can I go? I promise I'll be quiet and not bother anyone."

Chris had nothing definite in mind. She had only the vaguest idea of the layout of the Lennards' house. The bedrooms had to be upstairs. There was a bathroom on the first floor, across the hall from the study. She might just be able to swing it.

The night was unseasonably warm, and the Lennards had a fan going in the living room. So much the better, thought Chris.

Honey Lennard was stirring a giant pitcher of lemonade that she had set down on a large, rectangular knotty pine coffee table. "Now we're in for it," Chris heard her say. "Anton might have named any one of us. You don't have to be a big fish to fry in Joe McCarthy's country."

"So," said the woman who had proposed *You Can't Take it With You*, "we can postpone worrying about losing our jobs and going to jail and worry instead about being murder suspects?"

The man who'd played the pilot in *Skyward* cupped his hands around his mouth, megaphone style. "Hey, everyone, we're talking about *us*. You don't think that anyone who killed Anton would be sitting here now, do you?"

Leland Lennard rapped a pen against the pitcher of lemonade. "Kids, can we get on with what we're here for?" He clapped his hands together. "Let's go, everyone, Act One."

In fact the play was very funny, and Chris found herself getting so caught up in it that she momentarily forgot about her mission. The readers took a break after each act, and there would be a discussion following the final act. Chris bided her time.

At the conclusion of the reading, people got up, stretched, visited the bathroom, and took drinking water from the kitchen. Honey Lennard brought in several plates of cookies and more lemonade. Once everyone had resettled for the discussion, Chris headed for the hallway, figuring that people would think she was going to the bathroom. She shut the bathroom door noisily and waited. She could hear talking, punctuated by laughter, coming from the living room. As quietly as possible, she let herself out of the bathroom and into the study.

It was in some disarray following the investigation that was still ongoing. Maybe they'd taken the evidence, Chris worried. She looked in vain for the pile of letters from which she had plucked Lennard's to Rosie's father. The sticky drawer had been closed, but it wouldn't open easily, and she was afraid to force it. The large envelope from Cohen and White was still on top of the desk, but it was emptied of its contents. She approached the armchair softly.

Suddenly a crinkly sound distracted her. She whirled around to see a piece of paper sliding under the door. She grabbed it and read, in large, crude letters, "If you know what's good for you, don't touch anything here and get out!" She tiptoed rapidly to the door and listened. Footsteps retreated down the hallway. If she didn't want to be discovered, neither did her pursuer. But maybe he'd come back for her. She had to act quickly.

Clumsily, she picked up the seat cushion. The two letters were still there! After a moment's hesitation, she folded them together and tossed them out of the unscreened open window, which was propped up with a stick. As she had intended, the letters fell behind the shrub below, effectively concealing them from the view of anyone facing the house. *But what if he comes back in here and looks out the window?* she wondered, as she closed the study door behind her.

In the living room all was as before. Her mother sat on the floor, her back against the couch. Mrs. Carroll, looking very languid, lounged in an oversized armchair.

"Well, it'll be a challenge," Iona said.

Lennard was standing. "It's a great play. We should take it on."

"We've had to double up to do the reading," someone else said, "isn't the cast a bit large for us?"

Mrs. Lescinkas' feet were resting on the coffee table. "I'd love to get my hands on the sets. But the props will be a killer."

As if a director had suddenly motioned for quiet, no one said a word.

"I mean," she amended, "many of the props will be hard to find." Her husband, who had insisted on coming along, squeezed her hand.

"Who'll be our Grandpa Vanderhof?" someone asked.

The husband in *Skyward* raised a hand.

"Who are you kidding? Even good make-up won't make people believe you're an old man. I'd go for Ed, if I were you," said Iona.

No one made a move to leave the room. If the killer got up now, he would be very conspicuous. Chris was itching to retrieve the letters. But she had run out of plausible excuses to leave the room. If she headed toward the bathroom again, her mother would surely come after her, thinking something was the matter.

"It's clear that we all love the play," said Wayne Geller. "That's not the problem."

Maya stood up and stretched. "Look, it's getting late. To-morrow's a work day for me. Can we please try to come to a decision?"

Chris could have hugged her mother.

They agreed to put the play tentatively last on the schedule and then meet again soon to make their decision.

The usual parting chatter would come next, Chris knew, as

it always did at the grown-ups' affairs. But her mother was eager to get home. *Now or never*, Chris told herself, as she moved discreetly toward the front door. If her mother couldn't find her after she finished saying her goodbyes, it wouldn't matter. She wouldn't leave without her daughter.

The small foyer opened directly onto the living room. To the rear of the living room, in a wing added to the original structure, were the hallway that led to the bathroom, the study, and one more room. On the right of the living room, a door led into the dining and kitchen area.

The light bulb over the front door was still out, so the curving pathway leading from the front door to the road was completely dark, to Chris's relief. But the moonless night that gave her cover also slowed her down. No lights were on in the wing of the house she was aiming for, so she couldn't immediately locate the study window. As her eyes became accustomed to the darkness, she was able to inch toward what she figured must be the window she wanted.

She wedged herself between the shrubbery that encircled the house and the exterior wall. Nuts! The bushes were all prickly! She would be covered in scratches. But the letters were there, on the ground only a foot or two in front of her.

A crunch broke her concentration. She straightened up, on the alert.

"Don't touch those papers!" the raspy voice hissed from behind her left ear. The rough hand was at her neck.

"Mom!" shouted Chris. "Mom, I'm out here!"

The front door opened, sending a shaft of light onto the walkway, but leaving Chris and her pursuer in relative darkness.

"Mom!" Chris shouted again. "I'm stuck!"

The knot of people at the door didn't include her mother, but it broke up immediately as the adults scattered in search of the girl.

"Don't move," the voice whispered in her ear, the hand still on her neck. "Just hand me those papers."

She bent down to pick them up, the strange hand sweaty on her neck. The letters were caught in a web of brambles.

Suddenly the whole area was illuminated. Someone was turning on all the first-floor lights.

The pursuer took off quickly and noiselessly across the lawn, his back to Chris and the other guests. Chris had just a second to confirm that the culprit was a man. The papers were still in the shrub.

In the general hubbub over finding Chris safe and sound, no one noticed the man who'd fled or Chris slipping some papers into the back seat of the Goodings' car. She forced herself to wait until her parents were in their bedroom before she returned to the car for her booty.

In her own room, she unfolded Cohen & White's confidential letter to Mr. Lennard, which was dated the day of the murder.

Dear Leland,

As you may have heard, we are preparing production with Karel Anton of "Down to Earth," a synopsis of which is enclosed. We have received communication from one Wayne Geller alleging that the musical, commissioned of us by Mr. Anton, is an unacknowledged adaptation of Geller's own play, "Skyward," the current Croton Players production of which was directed by you. Since both Mr. Geller and Mr. Anton are interested parties in the outcome of this allegation, Stanley and I thought we would submit the synopsis to you for an independent evaluation. Mr. Geller has sent us a copy of his play, but we prefer to reserve judgment until we have heard from you. If for any reason you prefer to decline our request, would you kindly return the synopsis to us?

With our thanks, I remain yours sincerely..."

The handwritten signature was "Eli," under which was typed "Elijah White." On the lower left-hand corner of the letter was the notation "cc Wayne Geller."

Chris wasn't sure that she had grasped the full meaning of the letter, so she reread it carefully. Finally she understood that Anton had supposedly fed Geller's ideas to Cohen and White. Wasn't that called plagiarism? Geller had clearly found out about Anton's musical somehow or other. All those theater people seemed to know one another. They feed on gossip, her mother said. Anyhow, Cohen and White always produced hits, so they—and Anton—stood to make a lot of money. Wayne Geller would get nothing, not even credit. But how dumb of Anton if it was true! Wouldn't he get found out one day? Unless…unless maybe Mr. Geller could bargain with him… She was about to run and ask her mother, but the bedroom door was closed, which signified "Do not disturb." She slipped the letter under her parents' door.

About twenty minutes later, Maya came marching into Chris's room. She waved the sheet of paper at her. "Christabel. Just what does this mean?"

As Chris sheepishly revealed to her mother the gist of her private investigation, her mother gazed at her with increasing astonishment.

"So Wayne…" Maya muttered, more to herself than to her daughter, "Wayne must have been furious at Anton. Maybe he wanted to reach an agreement with him the night of the dress rehearsal. Or maybe…maybe he was just plain furious…" She shuddered. "And you took the letter! No wonder he went after you!"

She got up suddenly and ran downstairs, Chris following at her heels.

"Mom, what…?"

Her mother was on the telephone.

"Croton police? Let me speak to Chief Inspector Mangone, please."

Two days after final exams it still wasn't quite warm enough to go swimming. The girls were once again relaxing in Rosie's room, Chris lying on one of the twin beds, Rosie sitting on the white shag rug between the two.

"I know you're a big hero," Rosie said, "but you could really have gotten killed. Mr. Geller was ready to get you the way he got Mr. Anton. Won't that letter from Cohen and White put him in jail?"

"You should thank me, Rosie. I saved our parents a lot of bother."

"What do you mean?"

"Well, they had already questioned my mother, and your father was probably next."

"My father? What for?"

Chris explained to Rosie as best as she could what she had learned from her mother. Both Rosie's father and Chris's mother had for a brief time in 1938 and 1939 been members of the Communist Party, long enough to do their part for the Loyalists in Spain from afar through the North American Committee to Save Spanish Democracy. But with the signing of the Nazi-Soviet pact in 1939, both had definitively left the Party.

"So Mr. Geller killed him just because Mr. Anton was going to turn his play into a musical?" Rosie asked her friend.

"Yeah, but that's serious. They were stealing his ideas, and they were going to get rich from them. Probably Mr. Geller wanted to force Mr. Anton into a bargain. Like maybe to list him as one of the writers of *Down to Earth*—you know, the musical—and to pay him. Or maybe just to pay him off on the sly. Who knows what he wanted? But whatever it was, he didn't get it, and he was mad as anything."

"He wasn't worried about Hew-ack?" asked Rosie.

"Of course not, Rosie. He's not a Communist. He's just a murderer."

THE OUTER REACHES

CASINO GAMBLE
by Nan Higginson

We arrived at the Native casino incognito, as Meg had insisted. Nothing labeled us as high-school teachers or as killer sleuths. We were merely two women of medium height, medium weight, medium age with unremarkable hair caught in half-hearted ponytails, wearing frayed baseball caps, faded tee's, scrub pants, and sandals. In the glittering casino we didn't deserve a second look, except out of pity.

We'd been feeding nickels into Native machines for three hours when Meg seized my arm and dropped to her knees.

"Hide me! Quick, Em!" She crouched low, face to the coin drop.

"What the hell?" I scanned the crowded casino but caught sight of no invading forces. One diamond-encrusted blonde rushed past, looking as if she'd swallowed a live squid. Her entourage of beefy males scurried to clear a path to the bathroom. A stray accountant-type, briefcase clutched to his chest, raced to keep up. Other than that, the casino crowd looked normal.

Meg kept her face hidden. "Shhh! She just came in. Big hair over by the big wheel."

"Who?"

"Irene Mayfield. President of the PTA!"

"Oh, for cripes sake!" I pulled Meg's arm, trying to unlock her fetal position.

She beat on me with her backpack. "If Irene sees me, I'll be fired."

I caught her pack as it ricocheted off my knee. "Get a grip. This isn't illegal. Teachers are allowed to gamble."

"Maybe down on Long Island, teachers can gamble, but upstate? With Queen Mayfield as head of the PTA? Nuh-uh! She's on a witch hunt for any sign of lax morality. I *need* my job. She had a conniption fit last summer with all that news coverage on our catching the teacher killer. Wanted to know what I was doing, hanging out with the killer's sister-in-law. I almost lost my job then, and here I am, still hanging with the likes of you."

For a smart woman, Meg can be fairly dense. "Your PTA Queen is *here*. Don't you get it? You could blackmail *her*." I went back to dropping nickels in the slot. I was down ten whole bucks and had no intention of leaving until I got back every nickel. Meg dithered. Poor girl. Born with a paucity of defiant genes. I tried to infuse her with some of my excess attitude whenever possible, but I didn't have much hope. Passive aggressive is more her style.

"Meg, cool your pits. The wicked witch is playing poker. Her back's to the world. She's busy pretending she's not here, either."

"That's it. I'm done. Time to go." Meg tugged her backpack onto her shoulder and headed for the exit. Unfortunately, she was my ride.

I stood my ground as best I could. "How about some pizza? My treat. I'll meet you at the snack bar. In a minute."

Meg pretended to be deaf. She picked up her pace toward the door. Passive aggressive, duly noted.

I surrendered my well-primed slot machine to the next lucky player and chased after Meg. We negotiated our way toward the exit, against the flow of energy. Halfway down the marble corridor I spotted a small crowd being held at bay. A velvet rope separated them from the snack bar. My antennae twitched. My stomach grumbled.

A burly brute pushed past me, headed for the clutch of hungry gamblers.

"What's going on?" I asked, speeding up to his gait. Lunch was on the line.

"Somebody's been shot. Maybe dead." He muscled through the crowd.

A shooting in a casino? And me, a journalism teacher right there when it had happened? I elbowed my way along, behind the big lug, towing Meg by her wrist, feeling like a star reporter. A gaggle of red-hatted women complained as I pushed through. Meg apologized all the way.

My linebacker stopped at the velvet rope, with me alongside. A phalanx of beefy men in shiny suits stood by the counter. A uniformed Nation Patrol officer herded workers into the back. Meg shouted, "Ginger! Is everything okay?"

No response, except from beneath the heat lamps, where plump pizzas called my name.

The linebacker leaned over the rope and whistled, "Hey! Kelso! What's up? You need help?" He reached to unlatch the rope from its stanchion, forcing Kelso to come to us.

"Don't need help. We got enough men."

"I could help block the highway."

Meg gasped.

"Done."

Meg grabbed my arm. I jumped.

Kelso glanced at me. "She with you?"

The linebacker frowned my way. "Nope."

"Then escort her out. Her and them others. You can do that for us."

And that was that. Despite my pleas for one orphaned slice of pizza, our linebacker led us away and out the door. Meg rushed toward her car. I slogged along, commiserating with my forlorn tummy, feeling rejected deep in my reporter's soul.

Meg jumped into her Jeep, gunned the motor, and jerked us into drive before my door closed.

"Whoa there, sparky. What's the rush?"

"You heard them. There's been a shooting in the casino. We've got to get to Millie's house before they block her in. We have to stop the bloodbath before it gets started."

"What?"

Meg's knuckles turned white as she spun the steering wheel. Her face tightened.

"Take a deep breath," I used my calm voice. I'd seen her like this before. Last year, hunting down the teacher killer. Meg's repressed superhero tendencies erupted back then. When Meg the Mouse morphs into MegaWoman, you'd better buckle up. But this whole bloodbath thing was over the top, even for her.

We passed a swath of official vehicles gathering at the crossroads and turned off the beaten track. Meg hit the gas.

A rusting Caddy stuffed with men rocketed past. Rifles and shotguns nosed from open windows. Was I in Baghdad? "What the hell is going on?"

Meg ground her teeth. "You might *think* it's all nice and rustic around here, but there's an ongoing feud within the tribe over the casino. Lots of bad blood. Lots of spilled blood over the years. You ought to know—the Shinnecocks down on Long Island are splitting over building a casino. Same problem as here. Traditionals fight to stay true to their cultural roots. They see the casinos as destructive, greed-based institutions. Casino Natives want to make their nation a huge economic force so they can shape their own future. No longer victims. No more broken treaties."

"Let me guess. Hotheads on both sides. The shooting at the casino means escalation time. Both sides are checking their ammo right now. Target practice zooms. One accidental gunshot later, and it all goes to hell."

Meg nodded. "With nationwide ramifications. Friends of friends show up to support each side. Drive-by shootings happen. The feds and troopers show up and it's war."

"War?"

"The Natives' greatest fear is the invasion of their sovereignty—meaning state troopers and FBI, most specifically. So, if anything goes wrong, we're on our own. Keep your eyes open and your mouth shut."

Meg braked against a sharp turn. The shoulder strap tightened against my neck. Hot air blasted through the unreliable vents. I felt like a kidnap victim.

"If one of the Traditionals is involved in the shooting at the casino—or if the casino police *think* one is—it's explosive. Since we got boosted from the casino, our only chance is Millie. She's the lynchpin of the Traditionals. She'll have more information than anyone else, outside the casino."

"Whose side are you on?"

Meg shot a fierce look my way. "I'm a teacher. A trained conciliator. I've got friends on both sides. Kids from both sides in my classroom. That's why I've got to get to Millie's."

But I was allergic to stray bullets. "Shouldn't we go back and check in with your husband and the kids? Make sure they're safe and sound?"

"Gotta check with Millie before her place gets blockaded. She's probably under surveillance by casino troops already, but we should be okay. Consider us a fact-finding crew. Neutral. Remember that."

"If the road's closed, is the casino closed, too?"

"Nope. Can't block the profits. Casino customers have instant access. No troopers or anti-casino Natives get inside, though. The place is under selective lockdown and the customers don't even know it."

Meg turned onto a dirt road so fast that my seatbelt locked up. The Jeep bucked, snapping my neck.

"The big guy who walked us out the door? He's one of the peacekeepers who stays on the reservation. I get information and pass it to him and vice versa."

"Sounds as if you're doing that sleuthing thing again. You promised Ted you were done with this. He'll blame me, for sure," I complained.

Meg scowled. The Jeep flew over a hillock. Meg banked hard.

"Don't let Millie's poverty fool you. It's typical for Traditionals living in Native territory. Casino money changes everything. Millie's a prime matriarch opposed to the casino, so she's cut off from casino funds. A little army's protecting her. They'll be testy, but we'll be safe if you follow my lead."

We pulled up at a rickety trailer about the size of a modest master bedroom. Cars, mostly wrecks, formed a protective circle around the trailer. Three men with automatic rifles stood by the door.

Meg stopped me from jumping out. "Wait to be invited. Take off your cap. Let them see your face," she said as she shook her hair free of its ponytail. "These guys were Marines. Fought in the Persian Gulf War. They know what they're doing. Just don't make any fast moves."

"I thought we were in a hurry." My cap came off. I tried to smile.

"We are, but you don't get inside without an invite. And don't say anything unless asked directly. Just shut up and listen. Like a fly on the wall."

Meg nodded at the stern-faced guard headed toward us, rifle cradled in his arm. He signaled her to lower her window.

"Mrs. Woods, is that you?"

Sometimes being a well-loved teacher can be a good thing.

"Yes, Lionel. How's your son? Having a fun summer vacation, I hope?"

Millie waved us in from her doorway. Since Meg was a familiar, I was granted entry as an extension of their trust. When I stepped into the smoky interior, someone mentioned seeing a blue light. I wasn't sure what that meant, but others grunted in agreement and made space for me at the end of a bench, so I guessed a blue light was a positive.

Well-armed Natives—men and women of all ages and body types—filled the trailer. Humidity mixed with sweat and thick tobacco smoke. No one noticed me melting in the corner, listening intently. Meg kept her silence, too. Millie stayed busy in the eye of the storm, making powdered tea without ice. Her refrigerator, like every other item in the trailer, had seen better days. So had Millie. She wore a lifetime of battles on her face. Her wrinkles had wrinkles, but her strength was obvious. One good sign: no alcohol in sight.

The folks at Millie's interacted like members of an extended family, with Millie at the heart. The group included hotheads and grouches, the hopeful and the brittle. Cellphones sang out for attention. Their owners stepped outside, then returned to speak in private or aloud. Some spoke in their own tongue, others blended their language with English.

Millie's phone rang. Conversation stopped abruptly. It rang again. The bulky yellow phone was hardwired to her kitchen wall, its spiral cord sagging to the floor. Millie wiped her hands on a towel before touching the phone. We listened in silence, hearing her end of the conversation, interpreting her monotone as best we could.

Millie replaced the phone and spoke to the group. "Neh. The casino-visiting man—Samperson—dead. Pistol. Close range, neh. Five or eight of ours being held by casino security, along with others, neh."

Millie's husband, known as "Pop," and a couple of the Native kids were nowhere to be found.

Meg shifted in her seat and hitched her chin toward the door. I waited for her to stand before I did.

We excused ourselves. Meg shook hands with Millie, leaving a couple twenties in her palm. Lionel, our escort in, drove alongside us until we were safely on the U.S. highway, in very New York State territory.

While Meg drove, I jotted notes. Writing gives me a sense of control, a sense of not being in way over my head. I checked with Meg to keep my notes accurate.

As Millie had said, Mel Samperson, a Donald Trump wannabe, was dead. Meg had read about his arrival in the papers. She filled in the gaps. He was a city slicker visiting the casino with his trophy wife, Liz, and their lawyer, David Costa. The lawyer looked like a weasel married to his black leather satchel. Quite a threesome. While across the state, developers were busy building racinos—casinos connected with horse racing—Samperson wanted to be one up from the pack. He was learning how to invest in Native casinos and profit from the tax exemption.

I read more notes. "He was shot with a handgun, close range. They didn't find the gun. But he was killed in a storage room, pants down."

Meg chuckled and caught herself up short. "Sorry. It's not funny, but it's…"

"…a real visual, that's for sure."

Meg tapped the steering wheel. "I just wish James and the two kids weren't missing."

"James? Millie's husband?"

"Yeah, and the two kids—not theirs. Tina Keene. A good kid with a bad rep. Angry teen. Likes notoriety. Kids in school say she's loose—sleeps around—but I don't buy it. Locals are hard on the Native kids, unless the kid's a star athlete."

"And Eddie Nolan's her boyfriend?"

"Yeppers. Tina and Eddie." She frowned. "Did you catch anything more on them?"

"The two gals next to me said Tina's been working at the casino, against her mother's wishes."

"I didn't know that. Her mom works the snack bar. She's the one I called to before. Ginger. Always wears a smile. Makes a mean milkshake."

Sure, rub it in. No pizza. No milkshake. Being a caped crusader's best friend isn't always fun and games.

Houses began showing up here and there. Back to familiar ground. The houses multiplied. A sidewalk showed up and ran for a quarter of a mile, serving a dozen sedate old homes, then ending at a church yard. That was my old hometown of West Otter. The casino incident, and our time with the Natives made Sleepy Hollow look good. Another half mile and we turned into a cul de sac named Supreme Court, where Meg lived. The boonies. For real.

I looked through my notes. "Eddie went to the casino to get Tina after work, just before the guy—Samperson—got shot. Right? So Eddie and Tina were probably there when the shooting happened. Then Millie's husband took off for the casino. Must have crossed our path. Not a suspect. But nobody's heard from any of them since the murder."

"They could be held by casino security or the Nation Patrol, or they could be in hiding. Did you see that one guy at Millie's? Pounding his fist, saying something about Tina getting big tips from Samperson. As if she was getting paid for work above and beyond the call."

"Sounds nasty."

"Hate to admit it, but Tina just might trade oral sex for some liberating bucks. Heck, if white chicks don't think it's sex, why would a kid from the reservation disagree?"

"Any chance her boyfriend caught them in the act and killed Samperson?"

"Don't think he owns a gun, let alone would shoot anybody. He's a little slow, you know? Follows Tina around like a puppy. "

We pulled into Meg's driveway. Ted waved from the open garage where he was refinishing yet another piece of furniture.

"Hi, hon," Meg called. He'd probably been too busy in his workshop to hear about the murder. I followed Meg's lead and kept mum about it. She said our shopping trip had been disappointing. We'd be going out again tomorrow, to the mall. Then she invited him to come along, clever girl. Ted would prefer slicing his fingers to the bone to going clothes shopping. We were golden for another day of sleuthing.

I headed for my summer campground hideaway. This was as far from the Big Apple as I ever wanted to be.

Meg's call woke me the next day at the crack of ten. She

showed up fifteen minutes later, and we were back in the casino within the half hour, dressed like bums once again.

We found ringside seats at the snack bar counter, settled in, and felt the air turn cold. Kelso, the goon who'd ordered our eviction yesterday, showed up with a cheesy smile.

"Well, look who's back. Twice in a week? A little out of the ordinary, isn't it, Mrs. Woods?"

Meg sat perfectly still, as if ignoring him would make him go away. The man was a twit in wolf's clothing. I stood to full height, pretended I didn't look like a bag lady, and stared until he turned to face me.

"Excuse me, Mr. Kelso. Did you come by to offer us a comp meal? For the one we missed out on yesterday?"

He tightened when I pinned the name on the donkey. He worked his jaw, but had no answer.

"You seem to know Mrs. Woods. Since you mentioned that today's trip is 'out of the ordinary' for her, I guess you've looked through your videotapes and checked your records. Did you find the killer, or just clips of my friend depositing money in your machines?"

Kelso had no intention of mentioning anything connected with casino security.

"You planning to comp us a meal, or planning to apologize for treating us like unwanted guests?"

Our waitress stayed by the coffee machine, pretending that nothing unusual was going on. Kelso turned and caught her eye. He gave her a gesture that included both of us in a meal comp, executed an about-face, and stormed off.

Meg smiled as the waitress brought the coffee pot. "Hey, Ginger." Meg's voice held the slightest hint of relief. "Glad to see you. Come, meet my friend."

Ginger filled our cups in wary silence. She vanished and returned with two lunch-plate specials. She hesitated before leaning over, then planted her elbows on the counter, and whispered, "I don't think Tina's being held here. I don't know where she is. Gotta hope she's safe." She leaned closer. "Security's keeping me here, but it's okay. Any news from Millie?"

House arrest? Was that possible? "What? Are you under arrest?"

Meg kicked me under the counter and whispered, "She's a Native. U.S. laws don't stand here. The casino police are in charge. Just shut up and listen."

Ginger shook her head. "Guess I'm a suspect. They'll let me go once they know I didn't kill anybody. Don't know who did." She looked bone tired. "If you come across anything about Tina, let me know."

"Not to worry," Meg said. "My daughter and her friends on the outside have been busy all night text messaging back and forth, full of plans to search for Tina and Eddie today." She patted Ginger's red knuckles. "They'll show up, wondering what the fuss is about. Couple kids, goofy in love, don't you think?"

Was she talking about the same girl who gave it up to Sam-person in the storage closet? Or, maybe took it from him? Surely Meg hadn't forgotten.

Ginger had another pair of customers at the corner booth. She refilled our cups and dropped extra creamers, then left. Meg took a couple tentative bites of her free meal. I wolfed down my share and eyeballed Meg's seeded roll.

"Think we can get a couple free muffins as dessert?" I asked. The answer came over my left shoulder. The man's voice made me jump.

"I'll snag a couple for you. Whatcha up for? Blueberry? You look like a blueberry kinda gal."

I snapped around and gave a quick glance at yesterday's line-backer who'd led us to the velvet rope, then escorted us to the door. "Wrong-o. I'm a chocolate chip type."

The galoot reached his long arm over the counter to the goody case, glommed three of the best cholesterol pumpers, and delivered them to us, en route to the stool next to me.

Meg kept her eye on Ginger, but gave an official introduction.

"Rick, Em. Em, Rick. He's the peacekeeper from yesterday."

Rick stood, shoulders back, chest out, like a kid presenting himself for inspection. He watched for his impact. My cheeks turned traitor, surrendering to the urge to blush like a school girl. What was this?

I sank my teeth into the gooey muffin and couldn't resist a smile. I like spunk, and the guy had a clean edge to his manner. He was certainly dressed better than we were. Meg gave me a shake of her head, then bit into her muffin.

Rick frowned. "I heard about you. Last summer. Caught the killer. Any chance you're still packing that six shooter?"

Okay, that creeped me out.

Meg smacked his arm. "That's it. You can leave now. Thanks for the muffins."

"But…"

Meg grabbed him by his bolo tie and pulled his face to hers. "Listen, friend, we're not looking for trouble."

"Just looking for a killer? Again?" His eyes twinkled with the accusation.

"Just looking for some information. Got any news to share?"

Rick tried to straighten up, but Meg held him fast. "Nothing to report at present, ma'am."

"Are the two kids safe? Millie's husband?"

"Don't know where they are. Not here."

"Got any leads as to the killer?"

Three women chatted their way toward us, interrupting our privacy. Meg released her grip. Rick smoothed his lapels. "Catch you gals later," he said.

Rick dropped a business card on the counter next to me, along with ten dollars for the muffins and a tip. He headed for the gaming room.

I flipped his card with my fork. "Rick Holland," I read aloud, "Problem Solver."

"Private phone number?" Meg teased.

"And an email addy. Both preprinted, I might add. Not something special. Nothing like a valentine. Don't get so ooey-gooey."

"I saw you light up like a cheap date. Admit it, Em. He's your type."

She knew me too well. "Any male that walks upright looks good to me, lately," I confessed.

I finished off the muffin slowly, giving Ginger time to come back with more coffee, but she had lost any desire to chat. So far, we had nada.

Law enforcement still was all over the place. Hosts in the gaming room steered clear of conversation. Nobody lingered in the back. I found myself looking for Rick, hoping to maybe get some crumb of a lead.

We didn't have the heart to gamble. I said I'd rather drop another twenty into Millie's palm, even if it meant sitting in a hot trailer in a land not my own. Meg nixed that idea. Too risky at this point. Millie was in lockdown mode. But I was hooked on the search. We needed to find a way back into the action.

I grabbed a newspaper when we stopped for milk and eggs and bacon on the way home. Bacon was a key ingredient in Meg's marriage. Whenever things got dicey, she made Ted a slab. He went into a food rapture and Meg was golden girl again. Did I mention he was a bit too overprotective? Thought I was the troublemaker? Still, he was the hottest guy I knew. Too bad Meg had snagged him before I set eyes on him. And too bad he was a sucker for home-cooked meals. Far as I was concerned, that made him a high-maintenance stud.

We traipsed back to the Jeep, my nose in the paper.

From what I could tell, Mrs. Samperson and David Costa, the lawyer, had been photographed at a quick press conference run by the casino.

"Will you look at this! Says here she's 'the grieving widow.'

Doesn't appear too grieving to me. Must be hard to look pitiful when your face is full of Botox." I kept ranting. "What widow shows up at a photo op baring her cleavage for all to see?"

"Probably didn't expect to be wearing widow's weeds while up here. Give her a break."

Why? Dishing was an art form, but Meg didn't have the flair for put downs. "And this lawyer looks like a cartoon, holding his satchel up as if it's a bulletproof shield." I held the photo toward Meg. "He's so short his nose would poke right into her cleavage if they faced each other."

Meg nearly off-roaded, trying to catch a glimpse of the photo.

"No mention of any suspects being held for questioning by the troopers. No mention of casino muscle, either. Wonder if the Nation Police have any of their own casino-backers in the hot seat."

"Other than Ginger?"

"You think she might have killed Samperson?"

A burst of music announced an incoming call, then I listened to the one-sided conversation between Meg and her daughter, Laurel. Suddenly we were speeding down the highway. "Laurel wants a ride over to Sally's house. Wants to sleep over. Says they're planning a movie marathon. It's a cover. Something's up. She's not close to Sally."

"Sally's a pusher? She's got drugs?"

Meg laughed. "No. I think Sally found out something about the murder and the girls all want in on the action."

"You going to let Laurel go?"

"Watch."

We dropped Laurel and her overnight pack at Sally's door, as Laurel insisted. Adios. La-de-dah. We parked beyond visual range and returned on foot. I circled around to the back door, while Meg knocked at the front. The kids ran for the kitchen exit. I blocked it, as promised, and we corralled the girls around the large kitchen table. Sally's folks owned a big new house, which marked them as newcomers to the area. Locals couldn't afford a huge kitchen with granite counters.

The gaggle of young teens looked like mini-Jessica Simpsons, with a dash of Britney, but their braces gave them away. Laurel was beyond pissed at her mother's intrusion. She went into silent rage mode, shutting off all access, which was just what Meg had hoped for. With her own daughter silenced, Meg turned to the girl beside her.

"What's the news on Tina?"

"Tina who?"

"Nice try. We're not leaving until we know what you know."

And the standoff was officially sealed. Meg had blown it. The girls turned silent, an impossible feat under most circumstances. They chewed cuticles, examined hair for split ends, blew bubbles despite their braces. I poked around for something to break the silence and came up with popcorn. Although no one seemed interested, the aroma was tough to ignore. I pulled out the first bag's worth and popped in another. I passed the bowl. Some started munching. Others treated it like poison. Sodas circulated. Time passed. I looked around.

"Where's your mom, Sally? Upstairs?" I asked, as if I knew which one was Sally.

"Gone for Chinese. She'll be right back."

"Chinese?" My heart skipped. "There's a Chinese place around here?"

Meg tssked. "La Choy Special. Chinese in a can. Don't get your hopes up." She glanced at her watch. The grocery store wasn't far. Sally's mom would be back soon, and we'd lose our prime time with the girls.

I refilled the popcorn bowl and casually released an innocent comment. "I'm so glad to hear that Tina's safe!"

"Me, too!" The girl beside me nearly choked trying to take back her own words. All eyes turned toward her. Meg made a shushing sound and started working the crowd. Although she had flubbed the kickoff, she was back in full glory. She stepped out of the mom role and went into the partnership approach. Her "we're all on the same side" speech worked wonders. It worked because Meg was honest, and she loved kids. The kids knew that. Once the pump got primed, the news began to flow.

The instant messages had arrived in spurts over the past twenty-four hours or so. Laurel, with Meg's sleuthing genes, had saved all the messages to a file, which she refused to give us. She held the cards. It was information we wanted. Third-hand information would never hold up in court, but it could help cool the feuding Natives. The text was cryptic. Luckily, the kids helped us translate into real English.

It turned out that Tina was busy silently text messaging while Millie's hubby wasn't watching. She and Eddie were in hiding with James. She didn't know where. They were in a basement, which meant they were probably off the reservation.

Tina's communiques included messages from her mother. According to Ginger, Samperson's wife was pregnant. But, Samperson wasn't the likely father, Tina insisted. He kept asking Native girls to strip for him in private. When Tina finally had, he'd only watched. His manly tool never rose to the occasion, no matter how much he tried to get it to happen. Tina was glad to take his money.

Laurel looked up from her file. "That's what you call 'beating dead meat,' isn't it?"

I grabbed Meg before she fainted dead away. Laurel owed us one for that cheap shot. "We've got to find out where Tina's hiding," I said, "or get her to tell the troopers what she knows."

"No way." Laurel stood, defiant. The other girls stood beside her. "Tina won't talk until her mother comes home from the casino. Said she'll run if we squeal. And we're keeping our promise. Blood oath. Tina's safe. We want her mother safe, too. Period. End of discussion." She sat down with a thump. The girls nodded agreement, all around.

And that was that.

By the time Sally's mom arrived home with the Chinese food, we were back in Meg's Jeep, heading for dinner at Meg's house. The bacon was in the pan before the Jeep's engine cooled. Ted wouldn't know what hit him. But Meg was still sputtering over her daughter's casual chat about sex, so I tried to keep her focused.

"You're missing the point. We got good news. We've been assuming this murderer's an Indian—I mean Native. Got so tangled up on what might happen that we lost track of looking across the board for the killer."

"But this murder is tied to the casino. That's what this is all about." Meg sliced into a tomato. Its juice oozed onto her cutting board.

"Maybe not. Maybe it's about adultery and greed."

Meg scowled and tossed a stray piece of lettuce into the garbage.

"Let's do this like last time," I suggested. "Most likely suspects? First, the Natives: Tina, Eddie, Ginger."

"Ginger?" Meg stopped mid-slice.

"If some old guy tried to use your daughter as a sex partner, wouldn't you want to finish him off?"

Meg contemplated her knife. Held it up to the light and watched the tomato's juice drip down, onto her hand. "Maybe."

"Okay, I'm calling in the reserves." I pulled Rick's phone number from my purse and tapped it onto Meg's phone. He'd been busy putting out fires all day long, he said. Within ten minutes I had a dinner date for Friday night and a gist-of-the-story from Rick.

I reported to Meg. "His money's on James having the kids hidden, as Laurel said. Under wraps until the killer is found. Nobody from the casino wanted Samperson dead. Matter of fact, his death on their land has them applying the screws to get confessions. So far they don't have any great leads. The bullet came from a fancy little gun, not the typical Native gun. Makes them suspect there's a mastermind behind the murder. Maybe somebody trying to close down the Native casino so they can open one of those racinos and keep the money in white pockets."

Meg tended the bacon. She put me to work slathering mayo on white bread.

"I asked about Widow Samperson, so he's doing a background check on her and the lawyer. He was surprised to hear of her pregnancy, but didn't make much of it. The lawyer's the brains of the operation. The widow's being wined and dined by the casino boys even as we speak. Her hubby's dead, but his money's still available. The Natives seem to be putting together an investment package that will line their pockets with Samperson's estate."

Meg stopped all progress on our dinner. I had her full attention. "Okay, let's just run this out for fun," I suggested.

I snagged a piece of stray bacon and worked at blending the kids' scuttlebutt with Rick's commentary. "The kids say Samperson was impotent. Wife Liz wasn't. Lawyer Costa was Samperson's key business ally. Lawyer consoles the horny wife. She gets unlucky. If hubby finds out, it's 'bye, bye, Mr. Moneybags.' If Samperson dies, Liz hits the jackpot, and so does the lawyer, who knows how to invest her inheritance."

After a moment I added, "What better place to get away with murder than in a casino where the first concern is the uninterrupted flow of cash?"

"Whatever happens in Vegas, stays in Vegas?" commented Meg. "Are we agreed on Liz Samperson and Lawyer Costa as the prime suspects?"

I nodded. "But we need the smoking gun, or an eye witness, or access to security tapes. They gotta have security cameras all over the casino."

"You'll never get near them. Neither will anyone else." Meg grabbed her phone and called Dawn, her next door neighbor, for an update. Dawn's husband, Jake, was a state trooper, and the troopers' wives were gossiping like the school girls. The women were betting on the wife as the most likely suspect because the husband had been caught with his pants down, and they didn't even know about her pregnancy or Samperson's weak member.

And according to Dawn, as long as Liz stayed on casino property, she was safe from arrest.

Liz and her lawyer had done their duty by the state police, volunteering their statements. Each was the other's alibi. The pair would probably leave as soon as the autopsy was complete, unless the troopers could build a case. Dawn was worried about the hot-headed warriors, too. Until the killer was found, warriors on both sides would remain on high alert, adding to their stockpiles, preparing for more killings on Native ground.

While Meg finished her work on the dinner, we cackled for the duration and baited our hook.

We arrived at the casino after lunch the next day, this time outrageously incognito with ersatz eyelashes and high heels. Sales tags from our designer outfits were tucked safely out of sight, with our ensembles ready for return once our caper was completed. We came armed with phony half-off coupons that I'd concocted, supposedly for the new high-end boutique located just off reservation property. Thanks to years of finessing the school newspaper layout, I can create some pretty authentic looking documents. I wouldn't call it forgery, but it wasn't kosher, either.

We played the slots near the bathroom waiting for our pigeons to appear. I was down fifteen bucks when Liz and Costa swung past, surrounded by suits.

We followed the group. Before they settled into chairs at a Texas Hold-Em table, Meg had Liz focused on the phony sale coupon. Liz was an easy mark. She'd spent too many days away from a half-price sale, and widows have to watch their purses.

Once settled in, Costa kept Liz supplied with crackers from his open satchel to soothe her pregnant tummy. Liz was off to a bad start with her cards. Costa kept doling out the crackers and fresh money. Meg whispered with Liz as if they were best friends. I leaned over, between Liz and Costa, trying to seem interested in joining the game. When the two weren't looking, my reckless foot kicked over the lawyer's satchel.

We made a mass grab for the satchel. They didn't stand a chance. Crackers spilled onto the floor, the laptop slid half out of the case, and I lost my footing. Anyway, that's my story and I'm sticking to it. I knocked the lawyer against the table. Apologizing profusely, I used my sturdy derriere to block all view. I scooped the crackers and laptop back into place, and at that moment I spotted the fancy little gun at the bottom of the attaché case, just where I hoped it would be.

My face burned red hot. I righted the satchel. The gun remained hidden. Suits surrounded me. Meg pretended not to know me as I was ushered away from the gaming tables.

Meg found me waiting for her outside the door and beamed triumphantly. She had slipped our phony coupon to Liz, urging her to mind the limited hours. The sale was only good from three to five today, and the best stuff would probably be gone by three-thirty.

We hid behind some potted palms as Liz rushed by into the bathroom. When she emerged, freshly lipsticked and less green, the entourage conferred over her prize coupon. The men shrugged. Liz headed for the hotel elevator, taking charge of her own destiny. The lawyer, satchel to chest, trotted behind. The goons rocked on their heels for a heartbeat or two, then sauntered off in pairs.

Meg gave a thumbs up. My stomach tried to unknot. We hustled out of the casino and headed for the safety of official U.S. territory, where feuding Natives couldn't interfere with our plan.

Meg called Dawn on speaker phone to say the scam was working. Dawn was to bring her trooper hubby, Jake—and his weapon—to the boutique by three-thirty, using whatever means necessary. Jake would swoop in and make an off-duty arrest.

"On what grounds?" Dawn asked.

Meg looked sick to her stomach. "Ahhh. We didn't figure that out yet. Just get him here. On time."

The clerks at the boutique studied us suspiciously. We pretended to be rich bitches, wearing clothes we'd bought there and put on charge cards that morning.

Liz Samperson and David Costa arrived unescorted, off Native land, on U.S. territory at a quarter of three. I hid behind lavish curtains that lined the dressing room. Costa glommed a cushy chair, pulled out his laptop, and settled his satchel onto the floor beside him. Meg gave Liz a big hello, as if they were old buddies.

The boutique clerks buzzed about, thrilled at the prospect of selling their full-priced duds to Ms. Rocks-A-Plenty. Meg squashed all comments about the half-price sale, lest the clerks overhear. Liz darted in and out of the dressing room with one designer outfit after another, checking with Costa, flirting for attention. He reacted in a nerdy way, but they were clearly a couple. She was certainly no grieving widow.

We waited for Dawn and Jake to arrive, growing more nervous by the minute. Liz plowed through the frocks at an ever-slowing rate. The power of a half-price designer clothing sale can only last just so long when you're pregnant. I put in an urgent SOS to peacemaker Rick. Not that he had any authority, but it felt right. He didn't answer though, and my message went on his voice mail.

Liz changed back into her street clothes. She rummaged through her purse for the half-price coupon that I had snatched during her first show-off session with Costa. Liz turned to Meg.

"I can't find my half-price coupon! Must have left it on the bed back at the hotel when I switched purses. You've got yours, though, right? I'll buy it from you, okay?"

The sales clerks spoke up from the other side of the curtains. "What half-price coupon?"

I stepped out of hiding, and Liz, who undoubtedly recognized me from the gaming table upset, screeched. Costa shouted for

Liz. The clerks swept aside the curtain. Meg and I stood there, in the suddenly-open space, feeling naked.

Costa rushed in, grabbed Liz, and headed for the door. The clerks blocked us in the dressing room. Costa stopped to scoop his laptop back into the satchel. The satchel fell over. The gun clattered out. The clerks screamed.

Costa grabbed the gun and swung it toward us. "Stop screaming. We're leaving." He pointed the gun at me and said, "You. Stay put or..." He waggled the gun.

I got the message.

Costa's free hand was on the door when Jake and Dawn pulled in, with Rick on his motorcycle, right behind. One clerk shouted, "Look out! He's got a gun!"

Jake pushed Dawn out of harm's way, grabbed his gun from his ankle holster and shouted, "State trooper. Drop the gun." Rick put a restraining arm around Liz.

And that was that. Costa and Liz claimed their innocence, but the grand jury didn't buy it. In the end, the murder had nothing to do with the Natives and everything to do with lust and greed. Millie's husband James came out of hiding along with Tina and Eddie. Ginger went home. The threat of war between the Traditionals and the pro-casinos took one step back from the brink. Disaster averted. We thanked Jake and Dawn for saving our hides.

Since then, Meg's been busy making mouth-watering appeasements for Ted, and Rick's working on turning me into a biker chick. Not bad for a summer vacation, all things considered. Life is a gamble. What really counts is how you play the game.

MURDER IN THE MILL
by M.E. Kemp

Big Bill Haywood focused his one good eye on the body re-
clining upon the mill floor. She might have been asleep, this
young woman in the white shirtwaist. Her knees were bent beneath her long black skirt, and one lace-cuffed hand rested by
her dark hair. But the young lady wasn't asleep—she was dead.
Bill couldn't take his eye from the girl's face with its bulging, red-
streaked eyes and cold, blue-tinged skin.

"Christ, I thought it was Elizabeth!" His big voice boomed
and bounced off the office walls. Everything about Big Bill was
outsized: his rotund frame, his hands like cured hams, his bound-
less energy, his talent for organizing labor. With all the other
IWW organizers in jail or run out of town, they'd called in the
big gun.

Big Bill Haywood came out of the West, one-eyed, larger than
life, weapons ablaze. One ham fist waved his IWW card; the other
clutched the *Little Red Songbook*, the bible of the International
Workers of the World. The IWW had twenty-five thousand fac-
tory workers out on strike in the silk mills of Paterson: weavers,
dyers, and child-workers in solidarity for an eight-hour day and
decent pay. Right now, there was trouble in Silk City. On top of
the mill owners refusing to negotiate with the foreign immigrants
who slaved in their silk mills, one of the good citizens of Paterson, New Jersey, had crossed the line to murder.

"Elizabeth is speaking in Haledon today."
The reminder came from a tall, ungainly woman with a nar-

row face and pronounced dark brows. Lotti O'Reilly was an outspoken member of the strike steering committee. Bill admired her intelligence and her capability, just as he respected the ability of his young IWW colleague, Elizabeth Gurley Flynn. The fiery Elizabeth was a favorite with the massive crowds of strikers at the Sunday meetings held in the nearby town of Haledon. IWW Meetings were outlawed in Paterson. *Foreign agitators* and *dangerous revolutionaries* were a couple of the milder terms used by the mayor, the police, the press, and the church

"Who is she?" Bill gestured at the body, his bulldog face unusually solemn.

"Her name's Anna Rubinski. She's a broadloom weaver and a member of the steering committee. Show him the note, Timmy." Lotti nodded at a lanky fellow with ginger hair and a thick ginger mustache.

The man in a collarless striped shirt, his wide suspenders holding up brown trousers, scowled under his ginger brows.

"Timmy." Lotti repeated the name with quiet authority.

Tim O'Reilly took a grudging step forward. He held out a folded paper.

Bill accepted the paper. He noted the ginger man's strong fingers, the heavily freckled hand. No dirt or dye beneath the fingernails; Timmy wasn't a worker. Management or police, Bill suspected.

"My brother-in-law, Officer Tim O'Reilly." Lotti introduced her relative with an awkward motion.

Bill opened the sheet of paper to read a message hand printed in black letters. *Anna—Meet me in the office at 10:00 tonight. Together we can stop this madness.* The note was signed with two capital letters, *E H.*

"She was lured here with this note," Lotti said. "E H—that's Evan Hawkins. He's the manager of this mill and the one who found the body. He's the nephew of the owner."

A flush crept up Big Bill's thick neck. "Those fat cats…they'll do anything to stop the strike, even murder a young woman. It's a new low for the scum. But what can you expect from men who feed their dogs the best steak while their workers starve?"

"Well, the killer wasn't Mr. Hawkins. He was at a banquet and ball last night." Ginger-haired Tim spoke in a defensive tone. "The mill owners and their wives were all there. So were the photographers. He and his fiancée had their picture taken—it's in the morning paper. The photographer said it was taken around ten o'clock last night. Hawkins says he didn't write the note, either." Tim folded his arms across his shirt and thrust out his chin, daring Big Bill to contradict him.

"The ball didn't end 'til six a.m.," Tim continued after a sharp nudge from his sister-in- law. "He came straight here to check on the mill—he does that every morning. He walked into the office and found the body. He was still in fancy dress when I got here. Poor guy, he was white as a sheet—looked like he was going to faint. One minute he's at a ball with his fiancée, the next he's here with a corpse. He was really upset."

"Anna had a fiancé, too. She was going to be married in July." Lotti spoke in a voice of careful control. "The young man is also a member of the strike committee."

"A bride? The cowards killed a young bride? As if murder isn't enough for the poor family to handle, she leaves a young man to mourn for her." Bill's face turned fiery red. "Our people have been beaten, thrown in jail and run out of town, and we've kept our hands in our pockets. Do they think the workers will stand for murder? We'll arm and defend ourselves if we must." He balled a huge fist in a threatening move.

Lotti touched Bill's sleeve. "That's just what they want, Bill," she said quietly. "It would give them an excuse to call in the militia—the bayonets. Even the police chief understands that would mean violence he wouldn't be able to control. That's why he agreed to let us help find the killer. That's why Tim's here. Chief Bimson agreed to let Tim handle the case. We need your cooperation."

Big Bill Haywood glowered at the ginger-haired man, who to his credit glowered right back.

"Find the bastard that did this. That's all I care about."

Haywood strode over to a long table, plucked a cloth from a neatly stacked pile and shook it out over the body. The silk cloth, billowing light as down, floated out and settled over the corpse. "Poor girl." Big Bill shook his head. "Poor girl." He stood in contemplation for a moment.

"Hadn't you better get over to Haledon?" Lotti asked, breaking the silence. "You'll need to keep the crowds in line when word gets out about this. Everyone liked Anna."

Bill gave a brief nod and strode from the room.

"It's a good thing you're my brother's widow, Lotti. You know that, don't you?" Tim O'Reilly stood as stiff as his voice. "You've got me pals with the boss of the outside agitators. Bill Haywood's a dangerous man, Lotti. He's been on trial for murder himself. How do you know *he* didn't kill the girl? Maybe he *wants* to bring in the militia. You heard him threaten to arm the strikers. I don't know, Lotti, I just don't know." O'Reilly wiped the back of his sleeve across his forehead.

"If it weren't for Big Bill keeping a lid on things, we would have had riots a long time ago." Lotti said. Her knees made a cracking sound as she knelt beside the body. She pulled back the pale blue cloth from the victim's face. "Someone's trying to make it look as if management's involved. I'll bet the mill owner put pressure on Chief Bimson to let us handle this. He gave in too easily when I asked if we could take a look at the body. A young woman found murdered in Mister Hawkin's office—that wouldn't look good in the newspapers. He couldn't hush that up. Come on, Tim. Get this thing off her neck. It wouldn't do for her family to see her like this. Terrible way to die, strangulation."

Lotti O'Reilly had seen death in many forms: sometimes in the mills, sometimes on the streets, sometimes in the home. She'd laid out her own husband after he'd been crushed trying to stop a runaway carriage. Michael had been a Paterson policeman. In those days, at the turn of the century, the police were considered the protectors of the community. Now, in 1913, they were the enemy.

Lotti smoothed back a lock of Anna Rubinski's dark hair. "She was a good woman, Tim. She was smart and lively, and she made good wages on the loom. She didn't have to support the strike, but she saw that others weren't as fortunate as she was."

"You're determined to find the killer. Is that it, Lotti?" Tim's ginger mustache twitched. "You're going to interfere whether I like it or not." The latter statement was made with a hint of defeat.

"Well, the workers won't talk to you, Tim. You've arrested too many of them. But yes, we are going to find the killer, you and I. It's what Michael would do."
Tim O'Reilly folded his arms over his suspenders. "I'm not Michael, Lotti. He was the best on the force."

"It took Michael years to be the best. You'll learn, Tim. You'll learn just like he did."

Lotti rose from beside the body, her knees making another crack. "Get that thing off her neck, Tim. Let's have a look at it."

Lotti caught a glint of silver knife as Tim bent over the body. He straightened, holding up a thin black cord in one hand.

Lotti tried her best to keep her eyes from the ugly red line cutting into Anna Rubinski's white neck. "Cover her face, please."

Tim bent once again, his sure fingers sliding the flap of soft fabric over the distorted features.

Lotti accepted the black cord from Tim's hand. She held it by one end, letting it dangle before her eyes. "Silk," she said. "From a braid of silk. You wouldn't think silk would be so strong, but it is. Stronger than steel when it's wound like this."

"Great. There are only three hundred silk mills in Paterson. It could've come from any of them, but she was killed in this one, the one where she worked. Why was she here, in a closed mill, meeting the manager late at night?" Tim's mouth pursed in disapproval.

Lotti sighed. "I can't believe there was anything between them,

Tim. Anna would have come if she thought they could find a way to settle the strike. You go talk to the owners—better yet, talk to the servants. See what they have to say about this man, Hawkins. I want to talk to the women she worked with. May I tell the parents they can come get her now? Is that all right with you?"

O'Reilly nodded. "I'll tell the man on duty."

Lotti gave the cloth-covered body one last look. She crossed herself. The dead woman had been Jewish but it seemed the right thing to do.

Lotti turned to leave, but she paused by the door to the office. "Oh, can I have a piece of that cord? I want to show it to someone."

O'Reilly nodded. He slashed the cord at one end and handed the piece to her. "I don't think Bums Bimson cares what we do. He wants to wash his hands of the whole thing," he observed. "I pray to Jesus the owners aren't involved in this or there'll be blood on the streets."

Lotti wrapped the piece of cord in a white handkerchief. "The chief's afraid of the owners. If he can pin this murder on the strikers, you can bet he'll do it. We have to find the killer before both sides turn violent." Lotti stuck the handkerchief in a ragged pocket and took her leave.

The tenements where Anna had lived were almost empty of sounds except for the clack of Lotti's heels on the rickety wooden staircase. Thousands of the strikers were at the Haledon meeting. Word of Anna's murder would spread as fast as the waters over the Paterson Falls. Big Bill would have to keep the anger of the masses in check.

The aroma of boiled chicken and onions told Lotti that at least some of the women were home preparing dinner for their menfolk. While these tenements were as crowded and ramshackle as most, the broadloom weavers living here made better wages. They could afford meat once a week. Lotti knocked on the door where the smells came strongest.

"Hannah! Hannah Goldman!" she bawled out, announcing herself. "It's Lotti!"

If Lotti thought she was the bearer of bad news, she was behind the times. Three other doors opened and four women in long skirts and white shirtwaists slipped out to sit on the top steps and pry the latest details of the murder from her. At first the women excoriated Evan Hawkins, the young boss: "I heard he tried to seduce...very friendly at the company picnic...wouldn't give me the time of day..."

Then came the commiseration for the young and handsome fiancé and reminiscences of Anna's other beau: "Poor Sam...a good catch...a better catch...should have married him when she had the chance..."

Lotti's ears were burning when she left the tenement in the Jewish section of town for her old family neighborhood five blocks away.

Her long stride carried her to a shabby gray, two-story tenement, its shutters painted a once bright, now faded, shade of blue. She walked around to the back and climbed three steps onto a vine-encrusted porch. There, she knocked upon a post to alert the old man to her presence. Her uncle sat slumped in a wooden rocker, head thrown back, mouth open, eyes closed. "*Zio,*" she called out.

At the sound the old man jerked upright. Lotti ignored the seconds of confusion that clouded his features until the blue eyes focused on her. She strode forward to greet him.

"How are you, *Zio*?"

"Who is it?" The old man's tone was testy, but his eyes sparkled. "Is it my brother's daughter, the one who forgets her old uncle?"

"It's me, *Zio*—your own Carlotta. I could never forget you. How could anyone forget the handsomest man to come out of Palermo?" She bent and kissed a wrinkled cheek.

"Why you never come see me no more?" He scowled with

silver brows. "Two, three Sundays now, you no come eat with the family. Come eat with your own, not them Micks you married."

Lotti patted her uncle's leathery hand. "It's the strike, *Zio*, and your two sons can't make it to Sunday dinner either. We have to meet in Haledon."

"The strike…the strike…" The old man mumbled something under his breath.

"Yes, and you'd be out there with us if *Zia* would let you. I came for your help, *Zio*. Let's see if you still have your wits about you." Lotti suppressed a smile at the old man's scowl. She dangled the piece of black cord before his face. "Where did this come from?"

The old man snatched the cord, holding it up and squinting at it, one eye closed. He twirled it around in gentle spirals. His fingers were stained mahogany from years of working with dyes. His knuckles were pitted, while his nails were eaten away and blue-purple from the acids used in the process. "Not ours," he said. He dropped the cord into her outstretched hand.

"Whose?" she asked, her voice challenging him.

"The Jews." He spoke with the utmost indifference.

"Names?" Lotti persisted.

"Names…names? I'm an old man," he said. "What do you want from me?" The whine in his voice was offset by the glint in his blue eyes.

"You know every dyer from here to Pennsylvania." Lotti shook a thin finger at him. "You took one look and knew it was a Jewish dye. How did you know that?"

"That black…if you weren't so blind, girl, you'd see there's red in it. That shade comes from a bush in Russia. The Jews come from that place where the bush grows."

"You dyers, you all have your secrets. What else can you tell me, *Zio*?" Lotti tried with little success to keep her voice calm. One name and the murder of Anna Rubinski might well be solved. Justice for the parents and a boost for Tim with Chief Bimson.

The old man tilted his head, eyes narrowed, as he looked up at her. "And if I told you, they wouldn't be secrets, would they? You want secrets, you go talk to the Jews." He clamped shut his mouth. The pink skin of his lips was mottled with white flakes.

Lotti knew she wouldn't get any more from him. She bent and kissed the top of his head, bidding him farewell with a promise to return.

Lotti could hear the sobs and moans through the Mendlesons' wooden door as she made several rapid knocks. Sam Mendleson must be taking the loss of his fiancée with terrible grief.

Several minutes went by before the door opened a crack. Two beady eyes peered out of the dark.

"May I speak to Sam Mendleson, please? I want to express my regrets…"

The door opened wide enough to let Lotti into a room that smelled of cabbage. Immediately, her arm was grabbed up by a thin claw, and a tear-stained face was thrust up to hers. "He didn't do it! He didn't do it! Please, lady, don't let them take my Sammy away!"

Lotti, at a loss for words, patted the thin arm in consolation. It was so dark she could barely see the slender man who crossed the room and gently removed the woman's hand from her arm.

"Mama…the policeman just wanted to talk to me. It was his duty. That's what he does."

"You're a good boy, Sammy, a good boy…"

Lotti watched the young man lead his mother to a shabby stuffed chair and help her down into it. The man straightened and then turned to the visitor.

"I don't mean to intrude…" Lotti began, "but I'm Lotti Reilly from the strike committee. We're all so very sorry for your loss, and we intend to see that justice is done."

"Justice…" the old woman moaned. "Justice from those Cossacks…"

Sam Mendleson held one finger to his lips to quiet his mother, and the old woman mumbled, then lowered her head. He thanked Lotti for coming with a quiet dignity that impressed her.

"I take it the police have been here," she said.

"Yes, but they didn't arrest me," he answered, black brows raised in surprise. "I was here with my mother—last night was the Sabbath. A policeman came about an hour ago and asked me where I was last night. They said someone murdered my Anna, but I knew that because Anna's brother came and told me this morning. That's all the policeman asked me, but my mother is afraid… The police with the strikers…" He did not have to go on. Thousands of strikers had felt the officers' brutality firsthand.

Lotti thought it would only get worse for Sam; the police would naturally suspect him, with his fiancée meeting another man late at night.

"Mr. Mendleson, what was your job?" Lotti asked. She fingered the handkerchief in her pocket and the lump of chord that formed in its center. Should she pull it out? What would the expression on his face tell her then?

"I oil the machines in the Doherty mills. If I were Christian and born in this country, I would be fixing the looms." The note of bitterness in his voice was unmistakable. They both knew the rate of pay was much higher for the man who repaired the looms, but that was reserved for the native-born craftsmen—and those men hadn't gone out on strike with the rest.

"Do you know anything about the dye process?" she asked. Lotti felt herself take a short breath and hold it. She was so close to her answer.

Sam Mendleson shook his head. "I don't know about the dyes. That's closed, too, but at least us Jews are allowed to be dyers."

"Can you give me the name of a Jewish dyer? I need to talk to a dyer."

"I don't really work with the dyers," Sam said.

"Old Rebbe," the old woman called out from her chair across the room.

Sam Mendleson gave his head a tiny shake of agreement.

"Old Rebbe—he knows everybody. I forgot about him. Old Rebbe Riffenburg, that's who he is, and he lives around the corner." Sam added explicit directions as he apologized to Lotti. "Sorry, I'm not much help to you. I can't think straight. Who would harm my Anna?"

At the name, the old woman in the chair began to wail.

Lotti let herself out the door, leaving the young man to comfort his mother.

Old Rebbe Riffenburg turned out to be more shriveled and desiccated than Lotti's own uncle. She moved closer to his chair at his motioning with mittened hands.

"Come closer, girlie, I won't bite. Hee-hee! I know who you are, girlie. I know your uncle, Salvatore, too. He sent you to me?" Old Rebbe spoke with a thick accent.

At Lotti's denial, he chortled. "Wouldn't tell you, would he? Hee-hee! He's right, too. It's one of ours who's dead." He peered up at her with lively eyes.

Lotti took out the piece of cord and held it before the bright, sparrow eyes. He tilted a head tufted with gray wisps of hair and examined the black string. The narrow lips pursed together like those of a baby bird waiting to be fed. The frail body rocked slightly side to side. Finally he nodded.

"The dyer is Abie Bachman, the *macher*. I'd know that color anywhere. I worked in the dye house with his father. Now there was a *mensch*, I tell you. Abie ain't fit to lick his father's boots." The bright eyes clouded over with reminiscences. Old Rebbe began to speak in more Yiddish than Lotti was able to understand.

She kissed the old man's withered cheek in farewell and took a quick leave from a cheerful granddaughter. How much like *Zio* the Rebbe was. Between the women's gossip, her own uncle, and Old Rebbe, she now had an answer for Tim to investigate.

The thousands of strikers who lined the roadway of the funeral cortege shook Tim O'Reilly. Men, women, and children threw red carnations on the casket as it passed on its journey to the cemetery. Tim and Lotti watched at a discreet distance as black-clad men lowered the flower-strewn casket of Anna Rubinski into the ground. A red shower rained down. Red carnations lined the grave, red carnations tumbled from the lid of the coffin, red carnations buried the pine box from view.

Big Bill Haywood's voice with its words of consolation carried over the cemetery grounds. The father of the murdered girl stood beside him, stiff, dry-eyed, and grim-faced. The mother's sobs were audible from beneath her full black veil. The two brothers of the dead girl looked on with lowered heads, black derbies in hand.

Tim O'Reilly shifted his freshly polished boots. The strikers were in a foul mood, and he couldn't blame them. What a low trick it was to lure a young girl to her death! The killer had played a game of hide-and-go-seek, but Lotti assured him the man would have to be at the funeral or appear conspicuous by his absence. Tim would have to grab him before the mob did.

As if echoing his fears, Bill Haywood boomed out a warning to the crowd. "Your power is in your folded arms. Any other violence you may commit is less than this, and it will only react upon yourselves."

Tim felt a grudging admiration for the big man. He wished the security guards hired by the mill owners would act in as restrained a manner as the strikers. The Paterson police might have bashed a few heads, but they mostly had made arrests—thousands of arrests. And the newspapers called for the blood of the workers. Well, they'd got it now, and the only thing standing between Paterson and anarchy in the streets was this one man.

Ragged voices broke into a hymn as Big Bill stepped back.
Arise ye prisoners of starvation!
Arise ye wretched of the earth…
Tim shivered as the voices swelled around him. These people

were pretty much the wretched of the earth, but they had their pride. They sang like that in jail, too. Lotti stood beside him, her angular figure covered by a black dress that hung in uneven folds to her calves. Black didn't flatter Lotti's thin face, he thought, but she was a smart woman. She'd been a good wife to his brother and a good friend to him.

The crowd drifted past the open grave. People threw more red carnations down into the pit until the hole was covered in red velvet. Tim couldn't help a glance into the scarlet pit as he stepped past it, his sister-in-law upon his arm.

Big Bill was in a rumpled brown suit, wearing a big, battered hat—a cross between a proper homburg and a cowboy sombrero. He'd turned away from the grave as a crowd of mourners filed by it. Now he stood in the background, playfully swatting off children who clung to his legs like leeches. One boy hung on his back, two thin arms tight around Bill's neck. The children were as dedicated to the strike as the adults. They worked in the mills, too.

Lotti tugged twice on his coat sleeve before Bill noticed her. "Tim's ready to make the arrest," she said, her voice quiet but clear.

Bill nodded, pried a few more tykes off his trouser legs, un-hooked the thin arms that strangled him, and gently slid the boy off his back. "Go to your mothers," he told the children. "I'll see you all at supper tonight." The children scampered off.

Big Bill sauntered over to the family group still poised by the grave. Lotti and Tim O'Reilly followed him. Bill nodded to the father, walked past him, and caught the arm of a lean, dark-bearded man dressed in a black suit.

"Say, ain't you Abie Bachman from the Anarchist Union?" Heads turned at the sound of Big Bill's booming voice.

The bearded man looked pleased to be recognized. "Why, yes, I am," he said.

Bill turned to O'Reilly. "This is your man." His one good eye glinted.

When Tim O'Reilly stepped forward to make the arrest,

Bachman's struggles to escape were feeble, caught as he was in the bear grip of Big Bill Haywood.

Bill watched O'Reilly lead off the anarchist. "Good man, for a bull," he said. He looked down at the woman in the ungainly black dress. "How'd you know who did it, Lotti?"

Lotti O'Reilly didn't answer at first, her eyes fixed upon the departing murderer. Her thin dark brows were drawn together in a frown. She gave her head a slight shake and glanced up at the big man. "It was the cord around her neck, poor girl…" She fell silent, her gaze dropping to the gravesite and its masses of scarlet.

"Lotti?" Bill prompted.

"I've been in silk my whole working life, Bill," she said in her matter-of-fact voice. "I know that dyers have their secret mixes. I may not know which dye comes from which dyer, but I know people who do. They brought my uncle over from the Old Country because he's an expert in dyes. He took one look at the black dye of the cord that was used to strangle Anna Rubinski and he told me it came from Russia, the same area the Jews come from. The dye—it's made from a certain plant that grows in that region. Abie Bachman came from that region in Russia." She thought of the fragile old man who'd fixed his snapping blue eyes upon her as he refused to give her the dyer's name.

"Why'd Abie do it, then?" Bill asked. "He's from the Anarchist Union. Was he trying to start a war between the workers and the mill owners?" Big Bill had to keep different factions in solidarity with the strike.

"No, Bill, it was the old story of jealousy…nothing but jealousy." Lotti cleared her throat as if to dispel a bitter taste. "Abie Bachman courted Anna before she chose Sam Mendleson. He convinced Anna's mother that he was the better choice; he had a better job than Sam, made more money than Sam, and he even owned his own house. It was Anna who insisted on marrying Sam. She loved him." Lotti thought of the sad-eyed young man. She knew the pain he would go through, losing the person you most love in this world. She looked up at the big man beside her.

"Last summer at the mill picnic, Bachman noticed that the manager of the mill singled Anna out for his attention. They were walking and laughing together. The girls at the mill gossiped that Mr. Hawkins was always stopping to talk to her, to praise her work, to hang about her loom... A rich man, nephew of the mill owner, from a good American family—how could Abie Bachman compete with that? He was so angry that he went to the father and claimed the mill manager tried to seduce his daughter."

Lotti's voice dropped off as the Rubinski family prepared to leave the cemetery. The father supported his wife with his arm around her waist. She leaned heavily against him. The two grown sons followed behind, black-coated figures of sad dignity. Lotti and Bill watched until the group was out of sight.

"The old man should've suspected Abie Bachman," Bill growled.

"How was the father to know?" Lotti asked. "They came from the same village in Russia, Bill. Immigrant families stick together—they live together, in the same part of town. It was like that when my father came, when my uncle came over. It's like that now for the Jews." You stick together, Lotti thought to herself. *Zio* was still unhappy with her for marrying an Irishman.

"Well, I hope the Rubinskis find some peace in the knowledge that her killer's caught. I hope they hang the bastard," Bill growled. Big Bill was a plainspoken man. "Although he was probably right about the manager's intentions..." he added.

Lotti shook her head in disagreement. "Mr. Hawkins had nothing but good to say about Anna. He told Tim she was always the lady, that she never encouraged any attentions beyond her work, and that he respected her. Anna was his best worker—he held her up as an example to the other broadloom weavers. Bachman was so jealous of Hawkins, he planned it so that the mill manager would get the blame for Anna's murder."

"Well, the body was found in his office. The owners don't hesitate to use violence against the workers. *I* thought it was

Hawkins," Bill said. He paused for a second. "I tell the strikers that their power lies in keeping their hands in their pockets, but I was ready to grab a pipe and knock the head of the first mill owner I met. Some example I set."

"Bachman planned it, Bill. It wasn't a lover's quarrel—he didn't kill her in the heat of passion. That's what makes me so angry. He sent that note. He lured her into the mill. He planned to kill her and to blame it on Hawkins. I can't forgive him for what he did."

"It was a really nasty piece of work." Bill nodded his big head in agreement. "We might have retaliated and the newspapers would've believed it was all our fault. They would've called for our blood." Big Bill regarded the woman in the plain black dress standing so stiff and straight. "You know what you did, Lotti O'Reilly, you and that young bull of yours—you saved this city from being torn apart. The streets of Paterson would've been soaked in red, and most of it woulda' been our blood." He placed a rumpled arm across her thin shoulders and gave her a playful shake, one that would have felled an oak, but Lotti stayed upright. Her face was so sad—Bill didn't like to see anyone sad. "You kept the peace, Lotti, that's what you did. You can be proud of that."

Lotti exhaled. "I hope the family does find peace. When you lose a loved one, sorrow becomes a heavy burden."

"Well, young lady, you've certainly lifted a heavy weight from my shoulders." Bill gave her another comradely shake.

Lotti grasped the rumpled coat sleeve around her shoulder and lifted it an inch in the air. "And you'll lift a heavy weight from me if you just remove your arm, Bill Haywood."

Bill gave a great guffaw. "Come on, Lotti. Let's go scold the anarchists for breaking solidarity. That'll cheer you up." He offered his elbow to escort her and she slid her arm through, accepting his offer. They strolled toward the one horse and buggy left in the cemetery.

The Authors and Their Stories

• **Cynthia Baxter** writes the *Reigning Cats & Dogs Mystery Series* for Bantam Books and is about to launch a second series that Bantam will publish concurrently. Under her real name, Cynthia Blair, she wrote 42 contemporary women's fiction and young adult novels published by Ballantine Books, Fawcett Books, and HarperCollins.

• **Meredith S. Cole**, a graduate of Smith College, has directed theatrical features, including *Achilles' Love* (a romantic comedy distributed by Castle Hill) and *Floating* (a drama about five friends growing up and apart). Cole teaches directing at the School of Visual Arts, writes and produces ads, and freelances for Food Network, USA, Lifetime, and TLC. Before starting to write mystery stories, she wrote screenplays .

• **Fran Bannigan Cox**, a visual artist with numerous gallery shows to her credit, was director of the Soho Meditation Center in NYC from 1983 to 1989. Cox has a Master's degree from Hunter College and is a certified yoga teacher. She is the co-author with her husband of *A Conscious Life*, a self-help book published by Conari Press, Berkley.

• **Peggy Ehrhart** holds a doctorate in medieval literature. She has studied African drumming in Ghana, worked with Habitat for Humanity in India, and practices jazz guitar at the Jazzmobile in Harlem. Her publications include an award-winning academic book and award-winning short mystery stories. Ehrhart's full-length blues mystery, *Sweet Man Is Gone*, will be published by Five Star in 2008.

• **Erica Harth, Ph.D.**, professor emerita at Brandeis University, has published books on early modern France, as well as essays and articles on a wide range of subjects. She recently edited a collection of original essays entitled *Last Witnesses: Reflections on the Wartime Internment of Japanese Americans* (Palgrave/St. Martins, 2001, 2003).

• **Marianna Heusler**, a teacher and school librarian, has more than fifty short stories and four novels in print. *The Night the Penningtons Vanished* was nominated for an Edgar, while *Buried in the Townhouse* was nominated for the Franklin Award. Her *Murder at St. Polcarp* will be released by Hilliard & Harris in the fall of 2007.

• **Nan Higginson**, winner of the Phyllis Whitney Creative Writing Award, edited and contributed to several anthologies published by the Middle Country Public Library. As a journalist, she freelanced for *Newsday* and local publications. Higginson taught literary arts (including journalism) and social studies for 24 years.

• **Randy Kandel Ph.D., J.D.**, is an anthropologist, a practicing attorney, a professor at John Jay College of Criminal Justice, and an administrative law judge. Although a newcomer to mystery writing, she has a book in print on family law. Her story, "Shoreline," won first prize in an online competition. She is president-elect of the Sisters in Crime New York/Tri State chapter.

• **M. E. Kemp** wrote both textbooks and articles on government before choosing mystery. Her new book just out, *Death of a Dutch Uncle*, features fraud, corruption, and murder in Colonial Albany.

• **Ronnie Klaskin** has an MFA in fiction writing from Vermont College and has attended Bread Loaf Writers' Conference many times. Her short stories have appeared in *Ellery Queen Mystery Magazine* and in the anthologies *A Hot And Sultry Night for Crime* edited by Jeffrey Deaver and *Murder in Vegas* edited by Michael Connelly.

• **Chelle Martin,** a New Jersey native with a degree in business and marketing, has short mystery stories in numerous anthologies, such as the recently released *Gone Coastal* from a West Coast local chapter of Sisters in Crime.

• **Margaret Mendel** has two Master's degrees—one in counseling and one in fine arts. She has published short stories in *Global City Review* and *Reflections Edge.com*. She won two awards from the Bronx Council on the Arts, and read a story of hers in a World Trade Center Memorial TV presentation.

• **Terrie Farley Moran** has a B.A. in political science and served as an administrative manager in New York City government until her recent retirement. She was born and brought up in the Bronx and turned fifteen a few weeks before Roger Maris broke Babe Ruth's home run record in 1961.

• **Dorothy Mortman** is a retired New York State tax auditor who spends her time traveling and writing. She published "Curiosity Almost Killed the Cat" in *The Raconteur* magazine and "The Guide" in *Whispering Willow Mysteries*. Several of her stories have been honored in competitions. Mortman is currently at work on a novel.

• **Anita Page** has had short stories published in the Ball State University *Forum, Heresies, Jewish Horizon*, and *Mouth Full of Bullets*. She's currently seeking an agent for her first novel, a dark cozy mystery set in the Catskills.

• **R. M. Peluso** is an interfaith minister as likely to pen wedding ceremonies as mysteries. In her earlier career as a bilingual speech pathologist, she worked in New York's Latin communities and has long been a Latin music aficionado. Reverend Peluso's first Belinda Torres story won the 2002 McAleer West 35th Street award for best original story featuring a private eye, co-sponsored by Private Eye Writers of America and *Crimestalker Casebook*.

• **Triss Stein**, a longtime librarian and dedicated Brooklynite, is the author of two mystery novels, *Murder at the Class Reunion* and *Digging Up Death* (both from Walker). She is hard at work on the first book of a new series set in Brooklyn neighborhoods.

• **Deirdre Verne** is the curriculum chair of marketing at Westchester Community College, where she has been teaching for the past seven years. Prior to joining the faculty, Verne worked in new product development and marketing for Time Inc., representing magazine titles such as *Fortune, Money,* and *Parenting*. She holds a BA in economics from Georgetown University and an MBA from Hofstra.

• **Pearl Wolf**, now retired, was director of retiree programs for the United Federation of Teachers. A school librarian and an educator who taught on every level from elementary school to universities, Wolf is the author of three children's books and two adult novels, *Song of Miriam* (2003) and *Dying to Teach* (2005). Her current work in progress, *Too Hot for a Duke*, is a collaboration.

• **Lina Zeldovich**, a bilingual writer and poet, grew up on the classics of Russian literature and started writing at age five. She is the author of three mystery novels (*The Dissident's Daughter, Painstalker, I-Predators*), short stories, and a published poetry chapbook. Belly dancing is her second passion.

• **Elizabeth Zelvin**, a Licensed Clinical Social Worker with a Master's degree in social work, is a long-time New York City psychotherapist who has directed alcohol treatment programs. Zelvin's *Death Will Get You Sober*, the first of a series featuring Bruce and his friends, will be published by St. Martin's in 2008.

Sketches done by:

• **Kat** is a freelance artist who studied fine art for five years in Queens, NY, and in St. Petersburg, Russia, after graduating from Queens College with a psychology degree. She works in several mediums and has displayed her work in numerous Manhattan and Brooklyn galleries. Preferring an eclectic clientele, Kat is currently working on album art for a heavy metal band as well as artwork for a high-end clothing line. To contact Kat via email: splendid.kats@gmail.com.

Cover Art done by:

• **Rebecca A. Kandel,** a native of New York, is a photographer and designer with an MFA from the California Institute of the Arts and a BA from Hampshire College. Her photography and design work have been in exhibitions throughout the United States, Europe and Central America as well as in journals, books and periodicals in both English and Spanish. Kandel lives in Los Angeles where she runs her own photography and design company, teaches and lives with her husband, Doug and their daughter Naomi.